TO KILL A PRINCESS
The Diana Plot

a novel of conspiracy, fact and fiction

By TIMOTHY B. BENFORD
author of The Royal Family Quiz & Fact Book

AMERICAN BOOK PUBLISHERS
a subsidiary of Culhane Book Distributors
954 Stuyvesant Avenue, Union, New Jersey 07083
emai: AmericanBP@aol.com

ALSO BY TIMOTHY B. BENFORD

NONFICTION

The Royal Family Quiz & Fact Book

The Ultimate World War II Quiz Book

World War II Flashback

The World War II Quiz & Fact Book, Vol. I

The World War II Quiz & Fact Book, Vol. II

Pearl Harbor Amazing Facts!
(also available as an eBook)

The Space Program Quiz & Fact Book

TRUE CRIME

Righteous Carnage
The List family murders in Westfield, NJ
(also available as an eBook)

NOVELS

Hitler's Daughter
Wants to occupy The White House

The Ardennes Tapes
Pray that somebody listens

For Marilyn, yet again

ACKNOWLEDGEMENTS

For various reasons, I am unable to publicly thank certain people who contributed unselfishly to this book with their time, knowledge of the subject matter, specific incidents, personal experiences, talents, good advice, or other areas of expertise in the non-fiction information I've used. To do otherwise would betray trusted confidences.

However, the contributions of the following individuals were also enormously helpful as well, and they can be named. To them I express my deepest appreciation and gratitude: Carole Bentley; Elizabeth Conrad Benford; Thomas A. Benford; Susan Benford Jung; Sandy Hayes; Karen Jackson; Karen Johnsen; Jan Purcell, Lorelei A. W. Valverde; and last, but not least, my wife, Marilyn, always the first reader of my work.

COVER PHOTO by the Earl of Snowdon, courtesy of British Information Services

FIRST EDITION: July, 2006
PDF eBook EDITION: June, 2006

Library of Congress Cataloging in Publication Data
Benford, Timothy B.
   TO KILL A PRINCESS, The Diana Plot

ISBN: **0-9710560-3-X**

PROLOGUE

Saturday, August 30, 1997
Paris, France

Something was bothering Archie Blair. He had been in Britain's Secret Intelligence Service, MI-6, for nearly a decade and had shadowed Princess Diana a number of times. Yet he couldn't shake the feeling this assignment was different.

The MI-6 operative was part of a six-member team assigned to covertly observe Princess Diana's movements in the City of Light since her arrival earlier in the day. Diana and her latest love interest, Dodi al Fayed, had flown here at the conclusion of a Mediterranean holiday spent aboard his father's yacht, *Jonikal*.

Archie's hands were locked behind his back as he slowly walked through the lobby and corridors of The Ritz Hotel, in deep thought, rehashing the events of the last few hours.

A half hour earlier, Archie received a phone call from Sir Warren Wormsley suggesting he shut down the operation and return with his team to London this very night. It struck Blair as odd, since, as a *retired* deputy director of SIS, such a call was not even Sir Warren's to make. Furthermore, Archie could not recall any surveillance of Princess Diana ever having been terminated. It just didn't happen. She had been under absolute scrutiny for years.

Sir Warren was the *de facto* head of a powerful and influential group of loyal monarchists, known as 'The Committee,' which Archie and other agents believed operated with the advice and consent of the Palace. Though retired, Sir Warren was still known to have considerable influence on matters involving the Royal Family.

During their conversation Sir Warren told Archie about a confidential report suggesting the divorced Princess of Wales was pregnant. Could it have unnerved Sir Warren, and the Palace, so much that they were truly befuddled and didn't know what to do next?

But pulling the surveillance off Princess Diana so Archie could return to London and huddle with The Committee the following morning to discuss the situation didn't even *sound* logical. Without an official confirmation from his superiors in SIS, Archie Blair was unable to comply with Sir Warren's request. Unless he was ordered to terminate the assignment, Blair would remain at The Ritz Hotel and carry on.

Archie paused in front of the Vendome Bar and glanced inside the richly wood paneled room. A pianist was playing soft mood music while a nearby harp was idle and unattended.

He entered and slowly strolled through the room, past the pianist, and paused again when he came to the open double doors leading out to a garden terrace replete with statuary, lush plantings and cozy glass-topped wrought iron tables with matching chairs. The terrace was nearly empty with only three tables occupied out of ten times that many.

Experience told Archie that Sir Warren always had a backup or contingency plan. The loyal monarchist had beaten the drum so often and loudly about the consequences of a bastard pregnancy that for him NOT to have an alternative ready to kick in was totally out of character.

Archie shook his head and was about to turn and leave when his attention was drawn to a female figure wearing long black clothing hardly ten feet away facing in the opposite direction. When she made a half turn and reached into a large satchel next to her chair he realized she was a Muslim, replete with a face veil.

With all that garb on why would anyone choose to boil out there in the heat when they could be in the air-conditioned inside? he wondered. Archie hardly finished the thought when he got the answer.

The woman retrieved a large phone from the satchel and put it to her ear. Archie recognized the phone immediately. It was a prototype developed for SIS some years ago but rejected for some now obscure reason. He was certain there was not another one like it in the world. And he knew the agent who 'inherited' it and still used it. What was she doing in Paris, in disguise? She wasn't part of the SIS surveillance team.

He fought the impulse to rush over and confront Megan Price, but instead he went into the garden and quietly slipped into a chair at the table closest to and behind her.

Archie waited until she returned the phone to the satchel and rose to leave. He quickly caught up and purposely strode in step beside her, inching up just enough so she could recognize him. But he didn't say a word. They walked together side by side through the Vendome Bar and into the corridor. She never tried to drop back or forge ahead. Finally, she slowed as they approached a housekeeping storage room. She looked from left to right before opening the door and going in. Megan closed the door once Archie was through it and flicked the wall light switch. She had been in the room before.

She undid the button and the veil dropped revealing her face. Her look was somber.

"Was it the phone?" she said casually.

"Yes, that monster phone. Big mistake keeping it all these years, it's a dinosaur," he replied. Then added,

"How long have you been here, Megan?"

"That doesn't matter. We both have our jobs to do. . . but you and the rest of the MI-6 team are supposed to be on your way back to London now, so we wouldn't trip over each other tonight."

"Is that what Sir Warren told you? That he was getting the regular surveillance team out of the way so you could go about your dirty business?"

"Well, to tell you the truth, the old man seems to be losing it. He didn't remember, or didn't know, that the agent in residence would be in charge of you and your London crew. Yes, that was Sir Warren telling me your team would still be in Paris tonight, and I should take care not to bump into you."

"Who's here with you, Megan? I'd like to know who's been laughing behind my back all this time?"

"No one from the service. I'm working with foreigners . . . rogue agents. In truth, it's their show, I'm just an observer and adviser."

"What are you talking about? foreign 'rogues'? I don't believe MI-6 would turn over the Diana problem to foreigners. Unless. . . you're not officially here for the service."

"Very good, Archie. I'm *not* here for the service. It's one of those nasty little 'Committee' missions Sir Warren and Smythe-Pembrooke come up with every so often. And, by the way, nobody has been laughing at you. This is top secret special ops. Diana is not involved. . .or I should say she is not the target."

Megan stepped from where they were standing to a low stack of boxes she could sit on and moved a hefty plumber's wrench from atop the boxes. Archie leaned against the wall across from her.

"I'm missing something here," Archie said. "Diana and her boyfriend arrived in Paris today. Sir Warren tries to disband my team because he doesn't want us bumping into you, or vice versa? And you're telling me Diana isn't involved? Do I look like I was born yesterday?"

"I didn't say that. I said she wasn't *the target*. She's involved. These rogues are from the Middle East and they have a score to settle with Mohamed Fayed. Diana happens to be the 'Judas Goat' leading Dodi here to slaughter."

"Why would Sir Warren and The Committee want to get involved in somebody else's war?"

"Oh, Archie, come on. I know you received the pregnancy report, Sir Warren told me. Now think about it: A car accident in which Diana's lover is killed and she injured enough to terminate her pregnancy. And if that doesn't do it, Sir Warren has people at the hospital to make sure Diana isn't pregnant when she leaves. Actually she will never be able to become pregnant again."

"I've given it thought, and I'm *not* convinced the report is genuine!" Archie blurted out. "It's too convenient. I think it's bogus, a sham. But why? To justify your mission with these killers?"

"Bogus? That's ridiculous. But even if it is a fake, so what? After the accident and Diana's trip to the hospital we'll never have to worry again about her becoming pregnant."

"Do you hear yourself?" Archie asked in amazement. "You're saying the end justifies the means. What have we become, judge, jury, and God himself in making such decisions? MI-6, The Committee, Sir Warren, me, you, all of us . . .now deciding who will die, who will never be born because these lives don't fit into a neat, organized tradition and structure to preserve the monarchy?"

"Powerful and quite moral. I applaud you," Megan snapped. "But I don't recall your having such bouts of conscience in the field when I snapped a few IRA necks to save your ass. . ."

"How can you be sure Fayed will be killed but Diana will survive?" Archie interrupted.

"Oh, she'll probably be cut up and bruised, maybe even get a broken arm or leg. Just enough to guarantee an ambulance ride. It's been well thought out and under control. . ."

Her cell phone's strong vibration interrupted their conversation. Archie waited as she removed it from the satchel. She expected it to be Ali. Instead it was the German watching the video monitor back in the room.

"Yes?" Megan said as she rose to her feet.

"Hello," the German replied, "I just got some news that may be of interest and thought I should pass it on." He was going out of his way to show his value for future missions.

"Go on, and make it quick. I'm in the middle of something." She looked at Archie and shrugged as she nonchalantly picked up the wrench, flipping and catching it the way jugglers toss bowling pins.

"I just got off the phone with Rolf, he was drunk and told me both back seat belts had been filed down."

"What???" She immediately stopped toying with the wrench. "Bloody hell, that mucks up everything! Only the rear seat belt buckle behind the driver was to be filed down. The side where Fayed *always* sits."

"Yes, that's what Rolf said at the time. But tonight he told me the big Englishman called and said they now wanted *both* belts filed down. He wired Rolf an extra $5,000 not to say anything to anyone, including me or you. Rolf offered to share the money with me."

"Why did he tell you now?"

"I think he realized I'd find out when the shit hit the fan, and he knew I'd kill him," the German replied

In her mind Megan quickly replayed what she had just been

told and came to a stunning conclusion.

"Those dirty conniving bastards in London. They're setting me up to take the fall!" Megan realized.

"Screw London, just tell the towel heads here that the mission is aborted," he said.

"Stay in the room. Don't leave till I get back." She ended the call and slipped the phone into her pocket.

"What's that all about?" Archie asked.

"There's been a new development. Our friends and mentors in London have their own agenda." Her mind was racing. Sir Warren and Smythe-Pembrooke had deceived her. It wasn't just the K Team trying to kill Dodi. That was just the convenient cover. All along this whole thing had actually been *a plot to murder Diana*!

"They always intended for Diana to be killed in the car as well." She looked at Archie. "It appears I've been played for a fool, Archie. . . But I can still stop it."

"Wait a minute," he grabbed her by the shoulders. "Stop what? A car accident?"

"Yes. Get out of my way, I've got to get to the shop across the street." She tried to break free of his grip but he stepped sideways blocking her.

"If you're telling me the truth, let me go with you. I can help."

"Are you crazy? These are the foreign rogues. They're Middle East murderers, they'll kill you as soon as they see you. They won't ask questions."

"Then let me get some of my team. It'll only take a few minutes to group up."

"I'm sorry, Archie. That's not going to happen."

All he saw was a blur as Megan smashed the heavy wrench against his right temple. One well-placed shot made him crumble to the floor unconscious. Had she wanted to, Megan could have killed him with it. She dropped the wrench to the floor and picked up her satchel from against the boxes she had been sitting on.

How had it come to this? How could it all have gone so terribly wrong?

CHAPTER ONE

Island of Nevis, West Indies
Four years and eight months earlier, December, 1992

The corners of Princess Diana's mouth curved upward ever so slightly as she took the proffered hand of the Scotland Yard protection service detective and stepped out of the vehicle into the lush entrance courtyard at Montpelier Plantation Inn on the small West Indian island of Nevis.

The princess' signature blond coiffure had been set aflame by the tropical sunlight and appeared more lustrous than usual. Her hardly audible "Thank you" was genuine and intended to be personal, specific to the detective assisting her.

During the 18th century, Montpelier Estate was a working sugar plantation and site of the 1787 marriage of future Admiral Lord Horatio Nelson to a wealthy local widow, Fanny Nisbet. The tree under which the couple was married is a short walk down the road from the inn's entrance. Most of the sugar fields of the original 30 acre estate have given way to indigenous vegetation, though a small portion of land is still farmed for sugar used in the kitchens of the Montpelier Plantation Inn.

The Governor General of Nevis had met Diana and her two sons upon their arrival on the island hardly 45 minutes earlier and now formally introduced Montpelier's owners, James and Celia Gaskell and their children, to the princess. Close by, but at a respectful distance, two of the five Scotland Yard Special Branch Detectives assigned as the royal protection detail appeared to be casually taking in the surroundings. Smiling and not shifting her gaze from the proprietors, Diana's eyes suddenly darted from right to left looking in vain for her two boys, 10-year-old Prince William of Wales and 8-year-old Prince Henry of Wales, known the world over as Prince Harry. The 'heir and the spare,' as the British tabloids were wont to call them, were not beside her. They had exited the opposite side of the vehicle. But Diana was satisfied the other three detectives who were not in sight were most likely with the boys.

The Royalty and Diplomatic Protection Department (RDPD) is a branch of the London Metropolitan Police, commonly known the world over as Scotland Yard. The RDPD detectives provide security for the Sovereign of the United Kingdom and members of the British Royal Family in the same way that the Secret Service protects U.S. Presidents and their families.

Replete in freshly cleaned and starched attire, the inn's small staff stood nearby observing the royal arrival and mentally burning personal memories of the historic visit forever into their minds. Once some brief niceties were exchanged, the Gaskells, in turn, introduced the staff to Diana. As the obligatory task was completed, a young voice interrupted the uncomfortable pause.

"Mummy! Look at this strange old tree!" Prince Harry's surprised voice carried from the other side of the car as he moved into her line of sight. He and Prince William were in awe of the large Benjamin Ficus Weeping Fig that dominated the courtyard and gave its surroundings the appearance of a tropical garden.

At just under 50 feet when fully grown, this particular tree appeared close to that height. Large and imposing, with its twisting maze of visible invasive roots, arching and drooping stems, it had a wide girth that belied its size. Its leathery, glossy dark green leaves and thickly vegetated branches provided a protective umbrella from the sun or rain when guests traveled between the main building's public room lounge, directly behind the tree, and the inn's registration desk and business office off to the left of the main wrought iron gate.

"Oh, my goodness. It's magnificent" the princess said in response, as she walked the few steps around the car to where her sons were. The two princes were quickly joined by the two Gaskell children, who were close in age to the two princes. As she had correctly assumed, the detectives were where William and Harry were. The Gaskells, the Governor General, and others followed.

"It must be a very old tree, don't you think?" Diana queried, nodding at her sons.

"Actually, your Highness, James planted it in the 1960s. Its Latin name is <u>Ficus Benjamina</u>," Celia Gaskell proudly pointed out.

"1966, to be precise," James proffered softly, adding, "That would make it all of 26 years old!" he said as they caught up to their royal visitors.

"Fooled me!" Diana said with a surprised grin.

The Gaskells, the Governor General, and the staff all politely smiled.

James and Celia Gaskell owned and operated Montpelier and, this Royal visit notwithstanding, were quite proud of the historic property and the refinements and restoration they had lovingly done to it. As recently as the 1940's, Montpelier was in ruin and overgrown by vegetation. Set 750 feet above sea level on one of the islands undulating hills, the once working sugar plantation, greathouse and the dozen guest cottages, spaced apart amid a profusion of shade trees, shrubs and plants, offered a proper amount of seclusion and privacy. Though the tone was predominantly British, as was the inn's guest list, Montpelier had earned, and deserved, its reputation for impeccable service and privacy among discriminating guests worldwide.

Las Vegas, Nevada, touts the slogan *'What happens in Vegas, stays in Vegas.'* On Nevis, what happened at Montpelier truly always did stay at Montpelier…in perpetuity. This tradition of protected privacy had been one of the features which attracted Diana there.

Earlier this month the magazine *"Woman"* voted Diana as the "Most Beautiful Woman" in Britain. A few days later the world learned that Diana and Charles had officially separated after almost ten and a half years of a publicly perceived 'fairytale' marriage.

In truth, it had been anything but. And much care had been taken to ensure that this holiday trip to Nevis would insulate Diana and her sons from the intrusive, peering eyes of cameras and the gawking stares of royal watchers, that international cadre of people who wanted to know every last detail about their private lives.

By marrying the Prince of Wales and heir-apparent to the English throne in 1981, Lady Diana received the title Princess of Wales and should most properly have been spoken or written of as "Her Royal Highness." Yet, she was commonly called Princess

Diana or, more frequently, Princess Di. Both of the latter were incorrect. But to a worldwide following of admirers, such informal references to her suggested a longed for intimacy.

Even before the honeymoon was over there were hints the marriage was not the fairy-tale story spoon-fed to the world by the palace spin doctors.

As the years wore on, what the public became aware of as small tears in the marital fabric quickly became large, ugly rips. Though they remained a publicly visible couple at functions, Diana and Charles had effectively separated by the late 1980s, he living in the country at Highgrove, she in London at Kensington Palace.

The Queen blamed Diana for the problems she was causing for 'The Firm,' as the royal family was wont to refer to themselves in private or with those with whom they were close. Other critics of The Princess of Wales agreed. They charged that Diana was unstable and temperamental and pointed out how she had all of the Prince of Wales' longstanding staff members discharged.

Her behavior had also estranged her from several close friends and family members including her father, mother, brother, her sister-in-law Fergie, The Duchess of York, entertainer Elton John, and even several members of her own staff, who quit after unpleasant confrontations.

When the couple formally separated, the media took sides in what was being called "The War of the Wales." The trip to Nevis with her sons was Diana's first foreign outing since the separation.

"Are there a lot of trees like this on the island?" young Prince Harry asked, pointing to it.

Before either of the Gaskells could answer, his brother's voice rang out.

"Harry! I found the swimming pool!" William, who with one of the Gaskell children had wandered away from the courtyard, was a few yards distant at the top of the stairs on the stone path from which Montpelier's pool was visible. He was quickly joined by the three other children and the ever-present protection detectives.

"Well, your Highness, I intended to give you our grand arrival tour of the property, starting with the main building," James Gaskell smiled, indicating the massive stone building behind the Benjamin Ficus. "But it appears the princes have set the pace and discovered Montpelier's most popular area already. Why don't we just follow their lead and join them?"

"I think that's a proper suggestion, Mr. Gaskell," Diana replied. "Please lead the way."

"Please call me James, your Highness," he offered politely while probably thinking *anything but Jim*. No one called him 'Jim.' The formal James Gaskell was uncomfortable with the diminutive.

"We'll have the driver take your luggage to the cottage," Celia added as the group began walking, "and it should be there after the pool visit and our little tour."

The Gaskells had painstakingly planned precise welcome arrangements and a brief, but thorough, property tour for their royal guests. However, the unplanned diversion to Montpelier's pool was something of a distraction. And James Gaskell was an organized, punctual individual who earnestly worked at keeping things on schedule.

****

In London, only days before Diana and her sons' trip to Nevis, and shortly after Prime Minister John Major read the Buckingham Palace announcement to Parliament that their Royal Highnesses, the Prince and Princess of Wales, had commenced a formal separation, another organized, punctual individual, but totally unlike the courteous, mild mannered James Gaskell, was in a furious rage.

"Damn shameless fornicators! The Prince and the Princess, both! A disgrace to the Crown," Sir Warren Wormsley ranted to small gathering of like-minded, wealthy and influential colleagues. The group was gathered around the massive and highly polished Teakwood table on the seventh floor in the private board room of Sir Warren's large office. Among them were three former government ministers and two members of what could be called the extended Royal Family: one, a cousin on the Queen Mother's side; and the other with blood ties, thrice removed, to Prince Philip and the late

Lord Louis Mountbatten.

At different times over the years, Sir Warren himself had been a deputy director of the United Kingdom's external security agency the Secret Intelligence Service (SIS), commonly known as MI-6, and its counterpart, MI-5, which was responsible internal security. Though now retired, many in the cloak and dagger community still considered Sir Warren to be among the most knowledgeable 'spooks' in the country.

The nine powerful men Wormsley was addressing represented a select who's-who list from Britain's private business sector and government. They were devoted and obsessed with preserving the monarchy and protecting *'The Firm.'*

In one form or another, and comprised of various numbers of members over the decades, the present gathering were the zealot inheritors of a sacred cause, which came into being after Oliver Cromwell and his Roundheads defeated the royalists and Charles I fled to Scotland in 1653. Though their identifying name had changed several times in the passing centuries, the current members privately spoke of themselves informally as The Committee. Such wealthy loyalists were often referred to as the "British Establishment." In fact, this particular group saw themselves as the monarchy's *Praetorian Guard.*

Their privileged and entrusted positions, fueled and reinforced by their own self-importance, made them privy to much of what happened inside the royal family before such stories were gossiped about or revealed by the media. When that happened, The Committee frequently mounted organized campaigns to discredit the credibility of the source.

Information that didn't come to them through normal channels was clandestinely acquired by other means, including illegal telephone taps and parabolic eavesdropping devices covertly obtained from MI-5 and MI-6, the intelligence agencies which had been monitoring Charles, Diana, and other royals for several years.

Besides Sir Warren, various others on The Committee had direct and valued connections with some of the agents conducting such surveillances. Consequently, very little that happened behind closed royal doors escaped The Committee. They truly believed that what they were doing protected The Firm's public image, and the monarchy itself. When necessary, they did whatever was needed to maintain the historic *quid pro quo* including the most final solution of all: terminating nuisance or dangerously bothersome threats with 'extreme prejudice,' a gentlemanly sounding euphemism for murder.

"An *utter* disgrace to the Crown!" Sir Warren concluded with emphasis as he paced feverishly from one end of the room to the other as his trusted audience sat and craned their necks to visually follow his movement. He appreciatively took in the several nods of approval from the gathering, then drew silent. He turned to face the floor to ceiling window which dominated the room and took in the magnificent view of St. James Park, nearly 80 feet below, and the dome of St. Paul's Cathedral stabbing the sky some distance away.

The meeting was the third in as many weeks to reflect and comment on what progress was being made to discredit author Andrew Morton's book *Diana: Her True Story*. The tome had been published a few months earlier, and while popular with the masses it was met by a chorus of abuse and outrage from the British Establishment. Much of the furor had been instigated and executed with the able assistance of The Committee.

This particular gathering was one of several pro-monarchist groups, each with its own agenda for dealing with royal problems in general, and the Morton book specifically. But the men in this room were by far the most powerful, influential, secretive, and most dangerous of the lot.

"They'll be the ruination of all we've protected these many years," a near equally agitated attendee at the table suggested. The sentiment, too, was followed by unison nods, including Sir Warren, still gazing out the window.

"Such public and deplorable sexual shenanigans are weakening the monarchy," Miles Blair proffered. "God forbid Charles ever actually ascends to the throne. Something must be done before Diana *and Charles* turn Buckingham Palace into a brothel! It seems every week some newspaper or magazine is pooling the people about all this royal misbehaving. More and more, they're clamoring for Prince William to move up, ahead of Charles in line for the throne . . . and, if the truth be known, I personally don't think that's such a bad idea."

"Be realistic, God Save The Queen…but Elizabeth won't live forever," another chimed in. "Charles is the rightful heir and even if he is old and gray when she leaves us, he will be king, our king!"

Sir Warren spun around from the window.

"Yes, he'll be king, if they haven't crippled or destroyed the monarchy so badly the people reject it in disgust. But after Charles what?" Sir Warren asked, then immediately answered his own question. "Prince William becomes king. I fear that if his parents go through with a divorce and the prince is raised by his mother, hopefully, by then, the 'defrocked' Princess of Wales, who can say what kind of libertine upbringing the lad gets? Good Lord, she's had lovers smuggled onto the grounds in car trunks! Once divorced what kind of shameful conduct will we see?" Sir Warren looked at each of his listeners but didn't see any indication his words or meaning generated passion. So he went on. "Suppose she kills herself? Suppose in her own demented way she decides to take her two sons with her in a death wish as well? You've all heard the tapes."

Yes, they had all heard the secret SIS tapes which Sir Warren had managed to obtain. When Diana was pregnant with Prince William in 1982, she overheard a phone conversation in which Charles openly professed his love to Camilla Parker-Bowles. The distraught princess attempted suicide, and killing the baby in her womb, by throwing herself down a flight of stairs. This was the first of several attempts she made before the birth of William. In another incident, she pierced a knife into her chest, wrist and thighs. In still another, she deliberately crashed her head and upper body onto a large glass cabinet.

The Palace intervened, and Diana then discreetly underwent psychiatric treatment for a few months. The royal marriage, which had captivated the world with its fairy-tale romance and great fanfare hardly 11 years earlier, was privately in shambles.

"Sir Warren, you always tend to paint a 'worse case' scenario," Committee member Leslie Wilford chided. "Suicide and murder of the two princes? Don't you think that's a bit dramatic? Divorce, yes, quite possible, I'll admit. But The Firm can recover from that." His tone was smug.

"Oh, surely, Charles will have a hand in rearing both princes," Miles Blair, pointed out, to several affirmative nods. "It would be utterly inconceivable to believe Charles would remove his influence and let his son, the next heir-apparent to the throne, just be raised by the boy's mother. My wife says some in her Bridge group are calling Diana *an adulterous whore*," the father of MI-6 agent Archie Blair concluded. An almost unison round of agreeable nodding frustrated Sir Warren, and he began pacing and talking again.

"Listen to me. Based on what we've heard on the tapes, we all know that this separation is a precursor to divorce. Ugly and messy as that is, we can't ignore it," Sir Warren said with conviction, adding, "They've *both* carried on with other lovers and, thanks to the tabloids, quite publicly, despite their woefully inept efforts to the contrary. Remember, Charles isn't shameless in this mess.

"Once the divorce happens, Diana and Charles will no doubt have some sort of joint-custody arrangement. Both will influence the way William and Harry turn out," Sir Warren was reaching his stride. He had brought the conversation to a boiling point and now it was time to see how far he could push it. He continued.

"But suppose Diana decides to re-marry?" He paused to let the thought sink in. "Or worse, just keeps on having one wanton fling after another and eventually becomes pregnant, or contracts AIDS or some other social disease? Lord knows, she has slept around enough, by my count with at least a half a dozen men. What kind of impression will this have on William? What will be his choices: The carefree, unstructured libertine lifestyle his mother practices or the historically structured and proper rearing of a future king?

"Then there is William's father, our future king, carrying on with that married Parker-Bowles woman. Suppose *she* becomes pregnant? Young William may well come to the conclusion that both his parents sexual antics are the way things are and, God forbid, William *himself* begets a bastard pretender to the throne! Why should William bother with the stuffy, anachronistic pomp and circumstance of being king? Will he even want, or deserve, to be king with the kind of example his parents have given him?" He looked around the table, but the expected nods were in the minority.

"When it's time for him to become king, William could well abdicate in favor of some sexually active commoner he'd taken up with." Sir Warren paused briefly and looked around at his audience. "That's happened before, as we all know," He continued shifting his attention from one person to another. The reference to the abdication of Edward VIII in 1936 to marry the American divorcee, Wallis Simpson, made a few at the table inwardly grimace.

"However, it could even be worse. 'King William' could be so disillusioned by events in his life and his upbringing he might even attempt to dissolve the monarchy altogether!" Sir Warren's comment brought an audible sigh from several in the group.

"Rubbish!" Leslie Wilford interrupted again. A few others tapped their water glasses on the highly polished table surface showing support with a chorus of "Hear, hear!" The diminutive, scholarly looking Wilford had never been one of Sir Warren's most loyal supporters. But in recent memory both men found themselves at odds more often than not. Sir Warren's eyes were aflame as he briefly locked them on Wilford.

"You disagree. . . all of you?" Now Sir Warren studied the group. "What if William does choose to marry someone not worthy to be queen consort, say another Wallis Simpson, to be specific, or worse? Perhaps the public will throw up their hands in disgust and say they've had enough, *insist* that Parliament dissolves the monarchy. It would be Cromwell and the Roundheads all over again. . . but this time permanently.

"Gentlemen, I tell you, as God is my witness, we're on very thin ice here. If things remain on their present course such events could indeed unfold. They're dangerously possible. We could see the demise of the monarchy in our lifetime, one way or the other." There was conspicuously mild nodding from the group. In an instant Sir Warren wondered if perhaps he'd gone too far too soon?

"I say this, and hear me well: We, as a group, must use our resources and increase our surveillance on Diana. Everywhere, all the time. Beyond what is already being done. She is quite unstable. I don't want to get a call one day that she's gone off the deep end and done the unthinkable and done in the two princes along with herself! As for Charles' philandering, I'll make certain a few well placed words reach Prince Philip's ear. Charles may be The Prince of Wales, but he still does what daddy says."

The argumentative Leslie Wilford spoke again, "I think we can all agree this separation, and *perhaps* even an eventual divorce, could be a serious crisis," he said in a mock patronizing tone. "But the Crown will survive. It lived through Edward's abdication for that bloody American harlot, and our history is a litany of one unfaithful monarch after another. The people understand royal *male* infidelity and perhaps even expect the king—in this case the Prince of Wales—to have a mistress or two hidden behind some cupboard. . ." he glanced around the table but, as was true for Sir Warren, Wilford didn't detect widespread support for his comments.

". . .and as for Diana's mental state," Wilford continued, "I say much of it is rubbish, including the so-called suicide attempts. *Three* unsuccessful tries? Please! They were not sincere attempts. She was trumpeting clarions for attention and acceptance, attention from Charles and acceptance from the Queen. Real acceptance in The Firm, not just lip service! We all know that anyone who truly wants to end their own life does it right the first time, period."

"You're missing the critical point, Leslie!" Sir Warren interrupted. He didn't want the topic being sidetracked. "It's not Charles' dalliances with Parker-Bowles, or that Diana is using that to end the marriage, which we have to fear. If that's all there was to it, and if Diana had the fortitude to simply accept what was, be discreet in her own affairs, and not have encouraged this separation, then I agree we could all live through this.

"But it's HER and her mental state, whether you believe she is daft or not, and the long reckless parade of lovers that have changed the situation and mucked things up royally. This is going way beyond the scandal of Edward VIII's abdication. In retrospect, my friends, that situation turned out very orderly compared to the unpredictability of the current events.

"Once Edward stepped aside, George VI and Elizabeth resumed the proper dignified role of monarch and consort. It was a demeanor Edward never quite grasped, or was beyond his understanding of history. This little Spencer hussy Prince Charles married seems ignorant of history as well!" Sir Warren was relieved to see everyone, except Wilford, finally nodding in agreement.

"So what can we do?" Wilford asked, then provided his own answer: "Nothing! I suspect some in this room wish there was a way to turn back the clock and influence events, a return to happier days when our problems were coping with Princess Ann's speeding tickets or Princess Margaret's infatuation with Group Captain Townsend. But those times can never be again. They're gone, lost, history. Nor should we 'use all our resources' to try to turn back the clock. The royals are the royals and, for good or bad, they were chosen and rule by the grace of God." Wilford declared in pompous tones.

Then, after a brief pause, he added, "We are all aware that Prince Charles' suitability to assume the throne is commonly being questioned. I've personally seen surveys suggesting that fewer than fifty per cent of the British population now thinks him fit to become king. But he will be king, and nothing published by the muck-raking tabloids, or any transcripts of private conversations, not even a divorce, will change that."

"Make your point, Leslie. One minute it sounds as if you're excusing or, even worse, condoning Diana and Charles' conduct, then you turn 180 degrees and point out the gravity of the situation. You can't have it both ways! We've all seen such surveys," Sir Warren grumbled in annoyance.

"I'm just refreshing everyone's memory, Sir Warren, about the inevitability of it all. As you've noted, some surveys indeed report such intense opposition to Charles that it has been suggested the Royal Family should skip a generation, and allow Prince William to ascend to the throne over his father! Would that be such a bad thing?" Leslie Wilford asked.

"I, for one, would have a serious problem with that," Sir Warren shot a weak smile at Miles Blair and continued. "If The

Lord in His Wisdom determines Charles time on earth has been completed and calls the Prince of Wales to His bosom, then it would be right and proper for Prince William to ascend. But to usurp tradition and keep harmony with the masses by denying Charles his birthright in favor of his son, no, that wouldn't do at all. It's a preposterous suggestion. After Elizabeth's time here is done, Charles shall be king."

A majority of those present expressed their agreement with nods, and a few vocally with "Hear, hear."

****

If Diana had been the proverbial fly on the wall, she would have disagreed with Sir Warren, and them:

"William is going to be in his position much earlier than people think now," Diana had said. But when asked specifically if she thought her son should bypass her husband or if she'd be queen, Diana appeared certain about one and, perhaps diplomatically, sent mixed signals about the other with a somewhat confusing and not easily understood answer.

"Well. . . William's very young at the moment. . . My wish is that my husband finds peace of mind, and from that follows others things, yes. I don't think any of us know the answer to that. And, obviously, it's a question that's in everybody's head. But who knows, what fate will produce? Who knows what circumstances will provoke?" Her response to the second part of the question was a bit clearer.

"There was always conflict on that subject with him when we discussed it (Charles as king), and I understood that conflict, because it's a very demanding role, being Prince of Wales, but it's an equally more demanding role being. And being Prince of Wales produces more freedom now, and being King would be a little bit more suffocating. And because I know the character I would think that the top job, as I call it, would bring enormous limitations to him, and I don't know whether he could adapt to that."

And as for herself? "I'll never be queen," she said simply and to the point.

Now, after more than an hour of discussion, Leslie Wilford continued to play the devil's advocate, "So, I repeat what can we do? Nothing really. What will happen, will happen. Oh, go ahead Sir Warren, and whisper your petty little secrets in Prince Philip's ear. Have your faithful servants here and in America, when she goes there, record every word Diana utters. Play your shadowy spy games. Be done with it for, after all, it really is all any of us can do. Beyond that, the situation is not ours to tamper with."

Sir Warren thought, but wasn't sure to what end or hidden agenda Wilford was so strongly campaigning. The man had become a very annoying burr under Sir Warren's saddle and, he correctly concluded, Wilford's last remarks sounded like a meeting-ending statement.

His heart sank as two, then three, then all around the table rose and headed for the door. The gathering was over. Wilford had challenged him and taken control of the meeting. *Damn the little twerp of a man!* Sir Warren turned and faced the window again. The departing attendees were talking softly among themselves as they made their way to the door.

As they did, Sir Warren recognized the unmistakable stentorian tones of his close friend, Austin Smythe-Pembrooke, trailing off as the group made their way through the door and down the long corridor. Though the former government minister had elected to remain rather quiet this day, he bellowed an agitated comment which opened other possible options for Sir Warren and The Committee to consider:

"Doing nothing is unacceptable, we're talking about the rearing of a future king! The Queen and Prince Philip are more properly suited to prepare Prince William for his royal destiny. The Crown, the country, and the Commonwealth would have been better served if Charles and Diana had both been killed in some sort of accident--that ski trip to Klosters for instance--before this disgusting mess became so public."

If only there had been such an 'accident,' Sir Warren thought. If things truly got worse, perhaps, as a last resort, someone might bring such steps into the conversation in a future Committee meting.

But, he admitted, not with Leslie Wilford around. Something severe might have to be done about Leslie Wilford. The man was creating disharmony in the group. He was no longer a team player.

Yes, he thought, if Wilford continued on this disruptive and dangerous course, he'd have to be dealt with. He'd discuss the matter with Smythe-Pembrooke. Austin was a good thinker about such things.

****

As the adults and the Scotland Yard detectives traced the steps of William and Harry to the Montpelier pool, Celia Gaskell smiled and nodded to a staffer who would guide the driver to the cottage. The simple nod was also a signal to disperse the staff.

The blue and white mosaic floor tile pattern gave Montpelier's 60x40 pool a very inviting appearance. The pool itself was rimmed by a wide concrete apron. From Diana's vantage point along the near long side of the pool, the stairs were in the corner directly in front of her.

The location where the group had stopped provided an excellent view. To the left of the pool area, a short breaker wall with a profusion of lush plantings rising perhaps a foot above them and running the full width of the swimming area separated the concrete apron from the ruins of the original sugar mill. The structure rose majestically some twenty feet behind it. Diana silently admired the often-photographed mill ruins.

Three years earlier, Pulitzer-Prize-winning author James A. Michener had admired the mill ruins as well, from approximately the same vantage point, when he visited Montpelier. But he took his interest a step further and traversed the lawn and made his way into it. Michener explored the mill and then seated himself in one of the broad, open window frames while he contemplated his surroundings. The best-selling author was on Nevis finalizing the chapter ,'A Wedding on Nevis' for his 35th book, *Caribbean.*

To Diana's extreme right, slightly behind her and elevated higher than pool level, was the Inn's open air outside serving bar and lounge area which had a permanent cover in the event of rain. Beyond the concrete apron across from where she stood, a five foot high wall was covered by an expansive, several panel mural depicting island life from centuries past in the days 'when sugar was king' in much of the Caribbean.

"It's c-c-co-cold," Prince Harry hammed as he sat near the pool stairs. He had removed a shoe and sock and was feigning horror as he teasingly lowered his foot into the water.

"Is not!" William contradicted his sibling the way older brothers were often wont to. William knelt and agitated the water with one arm up to the elbow. Then, much to Diana's chagrin, in a youthful impulse the child who was destined to one day be the King of England cupped a handful of water and splashed it at his younger brother's face.

CHAPTER TWO

The spray of water tickled Archie Blair's nostrils and formed thin, salty rivulets running down his cheeks as the motor-powered 'Zodiac' skimmed the waves and headed for the quay. Nonetheless, the British MI-6 intelligence officer continued facing land. He was unconsciously scanning the small dockside crowd of locals for anyone or anything out of the ordinary. Though his duties on Nevis had nothing to do with the direct responsibility of protecting the Princess of Wales or her two sons, one of whom was the presumptive future King of England, SIS training habits died hard.

Blair's brief assignment aboard the destroyer sitting a quarter mile off Nevis was quite simple: he had coordinated the installation and initial testing of what was said to be a state-of-the-art communications surveillance system. If the device, promoted by a leading multi-national electronics company, could pass its testing phase during the royal visit, then MI-6 would give purchasing it serious consideration.

The din of the outboard motor decreased considerably when the Royal Navy sailor chauffeuring Archie let back on the throttle as the boat rapidly approached the pier. The dark, leathered faces of the handful of local people busy unloading boxes and bags from an assortment of local boats of various sizes were quite normal. Some of them had even become familiar.

He looked to his left and saw the large, lumbering ferry, the *Carib Queen* from St. Kitts approaching. Archie estimated that he'd be at the quay and off the Zodiac before the larger vessel made it in.

Archie turned his gaze to the large painted sign affixed to the top of the open entrance of the corrugated metal building that identified the pier as the proper landing spot for the daily ferry from neighboring St. Kitts, two miles away at its closest point, as well as sea traffic from other Eastern Caribbean islands. The building was open at both ends so vehicles could drive through and out onto the pier. Actually, it functioned more like a metal bridge. He couldn't think of any logical purpose for it other than as an arrival and demarcation point between Charlestown proper and the dock.

WELCOME TO NEVIS
Birthplace of
Alexander Hamilton

Archie glanced at the sign each time he came ashore in the last week. He smiled to himself thinking of the petty annoyance the greeting caused on a previous trip with Miles Bradley, the destroyer's captain.

"After three centuries of association with us, Blair, surely these people could find and attribute something historic about Britain to post for visitors . . .even on such a tacky sign," Bradley had mumbled. "It strikes me as odd, perhaps even disloyal, that the Nevisian authorities are so keen on mentioning an *American* founding father. You know, don't you Blair, that Nelson was married here? And to a local woman at that! Why couldn't they bang their knockers about that?"

"Tourism," Archie had replied. "I understand they get more Yanks than Brits here. Geographically, Nevis is a lot closer to the States than to Britain. Anyway, no harm done. It's just to make the American tourists feel comfortable." Archie had replied.

The captain raised a suspicious eyebrow at the MI-6 agent and retorted softly. "Quite cavalier about it, aren't you?"

Archie had shrugged off Bradley's feeble attempt to intimidate him and attributed the career officer's bluster more to show, the proper and respected amount of old school indignation, than to a genuine nationalistic concern. He was certain Bradley repeated his consternation to whomever was in earshot each time he came ashore. Save for the Royal Navy enlisted man tendering the Zodiac, Archie was pleased to be solo on this trip.

Archie Blair was lanky and tall at six feet two inches and not a pound overweight. He was one of those people who could eat just about anything without it ever adding pounds or inches and had maintained his weight throughout his adult life. His slightly long, beaked nose, oblong face and prematurely receding hairline gave him more the appearance of a university professor than a career officer in intelligence.

"Hello Archie," a young local boy about ten years old called out from the quay and gave him a broad toothy smile.

"Hello Raymond! I'm starting to think you live here on the dock!"

The boy caught the Zodiac's rope from the sailor, and asked, "You need a car today to go sightseeing?"

Raymond, wearing long pants that had been cut at knee length and held up by suspenders, was both barefooted and bare-chested.

"No thank you, Raymond, I'm using Captain Bradley's rental. It should be parked behind the Ministry of Tourism office." He pointed in the direction of the building at the landside end of the pier. Archie gave the sailor an appreciative wink and a 'thank you' as the Zodiac's line was secured.

In truth, the vehicle he would be going to was for use by the ship's senior officers and MI-6 personnel when they were ashore on business, not exclusively for the captain, despite the senior officer's pronouncements to the contrary.

"Okay," Raymond replied. "Want me to go with you? I am a good guide."

"No, thanks again. I'm not sightseeing or shopping today. Just headed to Newcastle Airport to pick up somebody. I know the way."

"Perhaps next time, but thanks for asking." He selected two 'bee-wee' quarters and handed them to Raymond. The British West Indies coins were used on St. Kitts and Nevis and other British islands in the Eastern Caribbean.

He felt a tinge of insincerity the moment he uttered the words. There would be no next time, but he was in a hurry and felt no need to explain. His work setting up the surveillance system was finished and Archie was scheduled to leave the following day.

The trip to the airport this afternoon was to collect the MI-6 agent who would replace him and test-monitor the device for the duration of the royal visit. The Admiralty felt testing the system during the royal visit would be a good opportunity to evaluate the gear and had dispatched the destroyer to Nevis for that purpose.

As the rubber boat heaved and rocked in response to the tide surge smashing against the concrete pilings Archie climbed up to the dock. "Thanks for being so willing to help. Merry Christmas. I hope you are enjoying Carnival!"

"Thank you, Archie!" the young boy said as he snatched the cash. "You're a good man. Merry Christmas *yesterday* to you and happy Boxing Day too!" Raymond's reference was to the December 26, holiday celebrated throughout the British Commonwealth. The smiling MI-6 agent was already briskly walking toward the 'Welcome' sign on the corrugated building.

Much as this assignment in the Caribbean had been an agreeable mix of work and pleasant beach time, Archie was looking forward to returning home. He had missed celebrating Christmas with his sister and her family but he looked forward to being with them for the New Year.

Once through the structure, Archie spotted the Land Rover where it was usually parked in the alley behind the building that housed the local tourism office. He continued walking around to the front entrance to get the key.

Upon entering, he was taken aback to hear a familiar voice addressing questions to the tourist board officer behind a desk. The build was right, so was the color of the hair, but the profile was wrong. The man he remembered was in the military and didn't wear a beard, and this chap had a very full one at that. Archie paused briefly and listening a bit further to the exchange. When it appeared over, he spoke.

"Bat Lynch? Could that be U.S. Army Captain Bat Lynch, of all people?" he exclaimed.

With a remarkable swiftness, the man turned to face him even as Blair's words trailed off.

"Yes it is!" Archie continued. "You bloody Yank, hiding under all that fuzzy! What are you doing here?"

Lynch's reaction immediately relaxed and appeared relieved.

"Archie. . .Blair! Holy cow. What an unbelievable surprise! You're a sight for sore eyes." The two had met and become something akin to fast friends during Operation Desert Storm. Lynch was a Public Information Officer (PIO), while Blair was a British intelligence liaison at the American command post.

The two hugged and back-patted briefly then broke the clinch as quickly as it had occurred.

"Here on holiday?" Blair asked, as Lynch smiled and nodded a thanks to the woman who had helped him. She smiled back as she rose and went into the office's back room.

"Not quite, but then, what I do can't really be described as work," Lynch lied. "I'm updating information for a travel guide book. Spending time in paradise is one of the perks. I'm a poor-man's editor, but a cracker-jack photographer." Bat jiggled the strap on the 35mm camera hanging from his shoulder. "It's what I do now for a living. I think the beard makes me look scholarly, like an editor should look. What do you think?"

"A photographer I could believe based on what I remember from your desert landscapes in Iraq. Very good indeed. But you're an editor? A writing editor? Sure you are. You don't expect me to believe that tommyrot, do you?" Blair chided in a near whisper. Then added. "I suspected you were CIA in Iraq and now, seeing you here, and hearing your lame cover story, I'm certain of it, your piss poor disguise notwithstanding."

"No, Archie," Bat protested in equally low tones. "Honest Injun. This former Army PIO is a professional photographer and travel editor now. And the beard is real. Give it a tug. . . but not too hard."

Blair rolled his eyes to underscore his disbelief. "You may have been a PIO, but you were one handy chap to have around when things got dicey. You exhibited all the movements and traits of a dangerous field agent." Both men chuckled. Archie's reference was to a roadside ambush on the outskirts of Baghdad, during which Bat seemed to be all over the place firing at attackers.

Compared to Blair's scholarly appearance, Lynch was rather pedestrian at first glance. Nonetheless, women often found Bat ruggedly handsome, though a bad basketball fall in high school nearly two decades earlier left him with a somewhat pudgy nose that to some suggested a much more menacing individual. At five-feet-ten-inches tall he carried the bulk of his weight in his upper torso. It belied a more muscular build than he had. He now wore his once thick and unruly hair in a military style short crop, which with his brown, darting eyes hinted that the man behind them was bright, agile, and able to react fast to vocal or physical situations. The overall effect was that Bat was usually taken to be four or five years younger than 36.

Lynch took in Blair's tropical civilian clothes and asked the obvious. "And what about you? You're here on holiday, right?"

"No, no, far from it. I'm just in mufti. Still with MI-6. This is a working trip for me as well. You must have heard that Princess Di and the future king arrived on island today. Surprise! Surprise!" Like so many people did, Blair had unintentionally dismissed the existence of Prince Harry.

"Don't tell me they have you pulling guard duty to that good looking young blond and her children?"

"Certainly not. I go nowhere near the Princess and princes. I have other chores, full time chores, far removed from the royal presence and frolicking on this island. Now there's something for your travel guide book, Mr. Editor," Blair said mockingly. "I'll bet this royal visit puts this little island on the map! Where are you staying?"

"I'm at Hermitage Plantation." Lynch did his best to conceal his relief. Archie's baby-sitting duties with the royals would most probably keep him pretty busy. The last thing Lynch needed was a Gulf War colleague on vacation wanting to spend days and nights together.

"Oh, this is going to be a better week than I expected," Lynch continued the charade, half-heartedly.

"Well, not if you're counting on me to knock back a few pints. I leave tomorrow, returning to old England and back to the grind," Archie said with a forced look of mock sadness.

"You're leaving? But you said the royals arrived today . . . "

"Yes, they have. They're staying up at Montpelier Plantation. A beautiful place. Very British. But I'm done. I've spent three days doing some very hush-hush stuff on the Royal Navy destroyer, the *HMS Bedford*, sitting some distance off the pier. But I'm done with it, and heading toward the airport to collect my replacement,

31

Malcolm Fletcher. 'Big Mal,' he's called, but not to his face. A runt of a man, as one might expect. Didn't you meet him in Iraq?"

Bat searched his memory. "I think I remember hearing the name, but can't put a face to it." Bat had absolutely no recollection of the man or the name. He was certain he had never met or even heard of Fletcher, but it was easier, and polite, to be vague.

"Not to worry. Most people would agree he is very forgettable. All work, no play, no social life I've ever heard about. Seems out of place in the spy business," Archie offered.

"Really? Sounds to me like excellent credentials for the spy business. Especially the 'forgettable' part." At just under 6 feet tall with an athletic, muscular body, ruggedly handsome looks, Bat would hardly be called 'forgettable.' He hoped no one, Archie not withstanding, suspected he was in the 'spy business,' and had been even before he first met Archie in Kuwait.

"Where did you say you're staying, somewhere on the beach?" Archie asked as he glanced at his watch.

"C'mon Blair. You heard what I said. Trying to trip me up? I'm part way up on the mountain, Nevis Peak." Lynch paused for an instant and pointed South, "That-a-way, I think."

"Yes, that way. Very good, but who would expect less from a travel guide editor?" Archie grinned broadly. Lynch returned a weak smile. The Brit was sharp and suspected his cover, he thought.

"Are you free at the moment?" And before Bat could answer he added. "Come with me to the airport, it's a delightful ride, bucolic and all that, and we can chat about 'old times' and bring each other up to speed on current things."

"Free as a bird." Lynch smiled, "I got in earlier today and just stopped here to pick up some brochures to plan my sightseeing over the next few days, things I need to see and photograph for the book."

Realizing Archie Blair would be out of his hair on the morrow, Lynch could spare the time to be gracious today. Besides, the informer Lynch was on Nevis to meet wasn't supposed to come over from St. Kitts till the last ferry the following evening. Always cautious, Lynch arrived a day early to get the lay of the land, and it seemed as if Archie was unwittingly going to help him do that.

The purpose of Central Intelligence Agency field officer Bat Lynch's visit to the Federation of St. Kitts and Nevis this holiday season was to meet a young St. Kitts man involved in drug traffic from Columbia. With threats to expose his homosexuality, the man had been turned by the CIA and was now prepared to finger higher-ups in the organization. Though accepting people who were openly gay had become 'politically correct' in many countries of the world it was still a stigma to be avoided in most parts of the West Indies where it was met with ridicule and scorn. It could be a fate worse than death in many Caribbean islands.

One need only glance at a map to notice St. Kitts and Nevis are positioned about midway between Columbia and the United States. In recent years the sister islands, larger and busier St. Kitts in particular, had become the favored drop for drugs en route from South America. Serving as something akin to an airline hub, the illegal cargos could then be dispensed in any number of ways from St. Kitts to Miami, New York, or elsewhere.

The CIA wasn't interested in drug traffic per se. It was who was buying the drugs that they wanted. The agency had learned that in recent months terrorist cells in the U.S. had become a heavy buyer. Agency analysts determined that the drugs would most likely then be sold to middlemen or others. Based on what the CIA could piece together, the profits the terrorists made from the drug trafficking would have been considerable already.

But were they sending this money back to their cohorts in the Middle East, or acquiring it for some operation they intended to launch in America? A number of things suggested a terrorist cell was planning an attack in America.

Once the informer fingered the drug dealers on St. Kitts to Bat, it would still be a long and delicate process connecting them and identifying the U.S.-based terrorists. But it was a first step, a necessary first step that had to be taken.

"Good. Then it's off to the airport for us," Archie declared. "I have to collect a key for a rental car around back. We should have plenty of time and be a wee bit early. I absolutely hate being late for anything. We should have time for a cold beer once we get there."

Archie turned on a big grin in recognition of the tourist board office manager who had returned to her desk from the back room in the ground floor office. She smiled back and pointed to a hook on the near wall.

"How've you been, Elmeader?" he asked, making small talk as he walked over and removed the keychain.

"Oh, same as yesterday, and the day before, and the day before," she laughed.

"Well, that sounds pretty routine. Good for you. Stay well," he said, darting his eyes toward Bat. "We're off!" he announced as both men headed for the door and departed.

Once outside they rounded the corner and briskly headed in the direction of the pier to reach the alley behind the building.

"Hello Archie," Raymond, who was sitting on the curb, smiled.

"Raymond, my good man!" the intelligence officer replied as he kept moving. The boy bolted up and fell into step with Archie and Bat.

"Bat, permit me to introduce Raymond, the best guide on all of Nevis. Once he's met you he's like glue, in a good way."

The American smiled and gave the young boy a wink. "Well, the best guide on Nevis, are you?"

"Yes sir, and inexpensive also."

"So I take it you're not in school because of Carnival?"

"That's right. No school during Carnival. Everybody is celebrating."

"Any chance we'll pass Montpelier, where the royals are staying?" Lynch casually asked as he kept pace with Archie. If they were going to be early at the airport, he didn't understand the Brit's hurried pace.

"Do you know the place?" Archie asked. "Are they the reason you are here?"

Bat shot a sideways glance at Raymond but realized the boy had no idea what Archie was insinuating.

"Montpelier? Not really. Not in person, just what my predecessor wrote about it. This is my first trip here. And, no, they

34

are not the reason. I'll tell you later." Bat realized playing cat and mouse with Blair was futile. He'd have to confirm the British agent's suspicions without saying anything but the barest details about his mission.

"Well, we'll not pass Montpelier on the way to the airport, we're closer going north, and it's only a six minute flight over from St. Kitts. Think of looking at an egg standing up: Newcastle Airport is at 12 o'clock, and here, where we are..." he broke the sentence midway "...that's the car" and pointed to a new white Land Rover which they both headed for as Archie continued where he left off "...we're at about 8 o'clock."

"Okay, okay, tell me why you're rushing so much," Lynch finally asked. "You said we'd get to the airport early but you're trotting along as if your pants were on fire."

Archie shot an arm toward the shoreline as he reached the car. "Did you notice that boat docking? It's the ferry from St. Kitts. Think of it as the London Underground, or in your case the New York Subway at rush hour. I guarantee it's loaded with a zillion local people, perhaps a few tourists as well, who'll be clogging our passage to the street if we don't get a move on."

He was behind the wheel and turning the engine over before Lynch had closed the door. An instant later he was carefully pulling out of the alley and slowly turned onto the short street it intersected. Both of them waved to Raymond who responded in kind.

Lynch looked in the side view mirror and, as Archie had foretold, a multitude of people, many carrying packages and cartons of various sizes were already passing the alley where they had been only seconds before.

"Good call." He uttered.

Archie let out an audible sigh as he turned left onto the island's main road and looked into the rear view mirror, "We made it, thank goodness." Then continued, "So we're going this way...it should be less crowded and obviously quicker when one is pressed for time. But we can certainly go round and come back here the other way past the road leading up to Montpelier, if you want to see the cutoff. It's an island, you know. One main road circles the whole thing."

Lynch nodded in approval. He couldn't help notice there were several vehicles moving on both sides of the two-lane road. Before he could ask if this was normal daily traffic Archie spoke again.

"Actually, your place, the Hermitage, is in the same area as Montpelier, but up on the other side of the main road." He paused waiting for a response from Lynch but other than another nod, none came.

"But you must have already known that, Bat. What being a travel guidebook editor and all," again with a patronizing mock.

"Well, yes and no. From what I've read I knew they were the closest plantation inn properties but as I said, it's my first trip to Nevis and I only got here a few hours ago. I don't have the lay of the land yet." Which was all truthful. There was an unusual silence for several seconds, as if Archie was considering what Bat had said. Finally, Bat figured it was time to end the charade.

"Archie, I need your promise you will not repeat what I'm going to tell you to anyone. Absolutely no one."

"Of course, you don't even have to say that. In case you forgot, I'm a professional."

"Okay," Bat let out a sigh and continued. "You're right. The travel editor thing is a cover. Yes, I'm with the agency. But no, Princess Diana and her sons are not the reason I'm here. I swear to God." Bat paused.

"Go on," Blair urged.

"We, the agency received a tip that drugs coming up from Columbia pass through St. Kitts on their way to the U.S. But we couldn't care less about drug trafficking . . . unless the buyers were connected to international terrorists. That's why I'm here, to check and confirm some details. That's the truth. Honest to God. But that's really all I can say."

"Bartholomew, I believe you. This travel editor thing is an excellent cover for a field agent. I have to mention to our chaps that we should use it more. But why are you on Nevis if the conduit is through St. Kitts?" It was a sincere question, without a trace of doubt.

"Not a room to be had on St. Kitts. This is as close as I could get. It's only two miles across the channel and it also provides me with something of a safe haven. And you wouldn't believe the crap we, the agency, had to go through to dig up a room here."

"I can imagine. What being between Christmas and New Years."

They both fell silent for several seconds, Archie replaying what Bat said about terrorists and the plausibility of it all, and Bat wondering if he had revealed too much.

Finally Bat spoke. "Is this normal Nevis traffic?"

"No, I'm afraid it's busier than usual. This is the island's Carnival period, a holiday celebration that begins before Christmas and ends...."

"Yes, shortly after." Bat interrupted, then continued. "It's in the guide book. I did my homework. A real travel writer skirted over it by making a comparison to 'Mardi Gras in New Orleans with steel bands and island music.' But I've heard it's really a lot more than that."

Archie shot him a sideways glance, "Speaking of which, without giving away any additional secrets, how in the devil did you manage to get a room, let alone an airline flight, here? Just about everybody is booked solid for Christmas, some well in advance, and, what with the royals visiting, I would have thought you'd have to sleep on the beach. . . under a swaying palm tree, or something, with carnivorous land crabs nipping at your toes," Archie joked.

Bat wasn't sure if Archie was just being curious or if he thought Bat's trip was connected to the royal visit. So he made a joke "Never underestimate the power of the press, Archie, especially the travel press in a tourist destination!" Bat laughed, but Archie only smiled. So he told him the truth.

"Actually, an elderly, wealthy friend of the deputy director, a guy like those people who book their Christmas vacations a year in advance, is a regular at the Hermitage and until about a week ago was all set to come when we got this hot tip.

"Now this poor fellow's 'cover story' is that he slipped on some ice and bruised his hip badly and needs bed rest for a few days because of the pain. A quick change of my own personal holiday plans with my sister and her husband, and here I am, using his reservation. Under the circumstances, the Hermitage was agreeable to doing that."

"Very good. I guess you could say you got lucky," Archie replied, and changed the subject. "So what's happening in your love life, still single?"

"Yes, unfortunately or fortunately, depending upon how you look at it...." His words trailed off as Bat began vigorously scratching his beard. "Damn! This is what happens when you loose an office bet on the Super Bowl. I've got to wear this damn thing until the next one. And believe you me, it'll be off before the kickoff."

"Well, I'll say this, it certainly changes your appearance while you're undercover. Gives you a rounder, fuller face."

"Thanks. In the future if I need a beard I'll put on one I can peel off in the privacy of my hotel room!"

The conversation during the remainder of the ride was confined to each telling the other about their life since the Gulf War. Bat was certain that Archie had glossed over and omitted things relevant to his duties at MI-6, but that was to be expected. He, on the other hand basically told Archie the truth. In his wildest dreams he never thought he would accidentally meet someone he knew and have his cover story fall apart on this trip.

Anyone landing at Newcastle Airport on the Northern tip of the tiny island of Nevis in December 1992, really wanted to go there. In actuality it was not much more than a paved landing strip with a single one story wood frame building for check in, customs arrivals and all other procedures related to the infrequent arrivals and departures of aircraft. There were no landings at night, because there were no lights.

Having already claimed her luggage, Megan Price was standing in the shade under the overhanging roof of the airport building. She had just put away her cell phone and was debating whether to try reaching Archie Blair again or simply accept a taxi to the pier from the handful of drivers who remained when a Land Rover pulled into the lot and she heard a familiar voice call out her name.

"Megan? Megan Price. . . over here!" Archie called out waving rapidly as he continued driving toward her. "Did you come with Big Mal?" he asked as he brought the vehicle to an abrupt halt parallel to where she was standing and, without giving her time to reply, continued "Why in God's name would they send *two* of you?"

Bat was as surprised at the sight of her as Archie, but for different reasons. The woman Archie was addressing was wearing a figure enhancing tan sheath skirt and a short-sleeved white blouse that complimented her statuesque figure. Her high heels betrayed her as a visitor but Megan was not the bookish, matron-like bureaucrat one might expect to find in the halls of MI-6. Her flowing wavy red hair, actually almost crimson, gave her a vivacious attractive look and suggested she was accustomed to being a bit of a head-turner. And from the way the taxi drivers were appreciating the view, she knew it. She was certainly a woman men would pause to look at. No raving beauty, Bat thought, but striking nonetheless. She was the kind of woman who, with mousy brown hair and in different clothes, would attract far less attention.

"Hello Archie, no, Mal's not here. I'm his eleventh-hour replacement. He had some sort of mishap, a little accident, on the eve of the flight." She gave Bat a quick but inquisitive glance and figured he might be an officer from the ship. But she'd wait for a proper introduction.

"Nothing serious, I hope?" Archie asked. "Big Mal's a little odd sometimes, often unkempt, but otherwise a nice enough chap, poor sod," he added.

"No, I really don't think so from the little I was told," she replied, "which wasn't much, no specifics, but it wasn't anything major. I understand he was pretty shaken up and is having a difficult time walking at the moment. Just enough to ground him for this job. Anyway, they say once the aches and pains subside, he'll recover just fine. So here I am, ready for some electronic skullduggery." This time she looked directly past Archie and at Bat. Archie immediately picked up on her stare.

"Megan, I'd like you to meet a wartime chum of mine, a

Yank," he said. "We stumbled into each other at the tourist board office when I went in to collect the key for the Rover. He was thumbing through some brochures. Fancy that?"

She smiled, tilted her head slightly as if waiting for Archie to continue with the obvious.

Archie gave her a blank stare then stole a quick look at Bat who had a look in his eyes that screamed get on with it!

"Oh, of course, of course. . . Megan Price, I give you former U.S. Army Captain Bartholomew Lynch, and vice versa, et cetera, et cetera. . . but everybody calls him Bat, like that old west marshal on the U.S. frontier."

Bat smiled broadly, nodded and gave her a 'Hello.' He was inclined to extend his hand but saw no indication the woman was prepared to do likewise.

Megan appeared to be forcing a smile and returned the sentiment. "Well, what a surprise. With that manly growth, I would have taken you for a senior naval officer." She paused, then added "A wartime chum? Here on Nevis?" she asked. The question wasn't directed at either one of them in particular, but she hoped the Yank wouldn't be as tight-lipped as Archie often was.

"Yes," Archie replied, much to her surprise. "I was liaison with the Americans and Bat was the headquarters public information officer, the PIO they call it. We saw a lot of each other and became quite friendly," he said as he exited the vehicle.

"Luggage?" He queried, looking around.

Megan pointed to a single, ordinary black suitcase with wheels up against the building wall nearby. It was the kind travelers all over the world were wont to have.

"Not to worry. I can handle it." She spun around and headed toward it before Archie could protest. By the time he'd gotten around to open the back of the Land Rover so Megan could stow the case, she was already beside him and with a solid heave easily manhandled the luggage into the vehicle. Bat had gotten out of the front passenger seat and was holding the door open for her as she and Archie came around.

"Thank you, Captain Lynch," she smiled, this time a bit warmer and feminine, Bat thought. Nonetheless, Megan Lynch just wasn't really Bat's type. That vague word 'type' meant different things to different people, he knew, but in most instances you knew, or felt, if someone was or wasn't your 'type' within minutes of meeting them. It didn't take long. First impressions usually don't.

There was an air of professionalism and all business about her, Bat thought. He knew women like Megan in the business world, and in the intelligence community, and for him those attributes were a turn-off. He had little interest in any of them. They struck him as totally career-oriented and defensive, and this British MI-6 agent seemed to be cut from the same mold. Bat found her attractive enough to appreciate, but at arm's length, nothing more.

As Bat took the back seat behind Archie, he reckoned Megan had expected he would move so she could ride in the front. He positioned himself so that his view would mostly be her profile rather than the back of her head and wondered if addressing him as 'Captain Lynch' was intended as playful or sarcastic.

"And so we're off!" Archie announced with something akin to glee. With his replacement in place on island, Archie was now less than a day away from returning home.

"We're returning to the ship in the other direction from whence we came," Archie said for Megan's benefit. "It's a wee-bit longer than the other way, but there are some interesting sights and sites I can point out along the route. And, Megan, Bat's a travel guide book editor, who's never been here before, and I'm guessing this is your first trip too, so our little sojourn should be somewhat interesting to you both. I hope."

"Oh Archie, will we be passing Montpelier? I have an envelope to drop off with one of the detectives," she queried.

"Yes indeed. It is on this route back. We came to the airport the other way, but we'll certainly go past Montpelier going back this way. An envelope? For one of the Special Branch detectives guarding Diana and the princes?"

"Correct. Scotland Yard approached the director and asked if Mal could deliver it. So now it's my job."

"Is it something we should know about?" Blair asked.

41

"I have no idea, but I think not. I got the feeling it was something totally unrelated to the royal visit. Probably a personal thing. Anyway, if we were to know anything I'm sure I would have been told."

For several seconds no one spoke, or seemed to know what to say next. The Land Rover leaned slightly from side to side as Archie followed the road as it wended its way past clusters of Palm trees, occasional local dwellings, and outcroppings of rocks and sand along the shoreline before turning inland.

Archie broke the silence. "You're flight obviously arrived early, Megan. Bat and I were planning on hoisting at least one cold beer before you landed."

"Really?" she replied, "Once the plane was full they took off. Apparently the pilots in these puddle jumpers don't pay much heed for schedules, and I hadn't bothered to look at my watch. The other nine passengers were all media types coming over here to pester the royals and anxious to get going."

"We're you waiting long?" Bat put in, just to contribute something to the conversation.

"Not really, perhaps 15 minutes," she lied, never turning to face Bat. "Maybe a little more. I tried to call you but couldn't get reception," she lied again. This time to Archie.

"What? No reception on that old, dependable government issue giant you have?"

"Well, actually, I failed to pack my phone and had to purchase one of those throw-away phones they sell at airports."

"That explains it," Archie replied nodding. Then, half turning sideways and rolling his eyes so Bat could see the gesture, added "Bat, you should see the mobile phone she usually carries. It's like a bloody brick! Heavy and big . . . but it's powerful. I think she could talk to people on the moon with it! The only nice thing I can say about it is that the ringer is disabled but it vibrates violently."

"Ignore him, Mr. Lynch. He's jealous. The phone was a special project of our electronics people a few years ago. They tinkered with it and did all sorts of things to make it a safe line. I did a lot of testing with it and took a fancy to it. But I must admit the reason it

42

wasn't put into service is because by the time the project was finishing, the newer, smaller mobile phones were available and reworking them was much easier. Besides, everyone thought the original test phone was too bulky. When the project was done I managed to inherit it. Archie wishes he had thought of it first." Bat and Megan smiled and Archie rolled his eyes as if saying *not true.*

"Megan, dear, it wouldn't have made a difference if you did have it with you, I don't have my cell with me anyway. I'm sorry I wasn't here in advance of your arrival. But then perhaps I never would have run into Bat. Problem is we had a situation aboard ship which delayed my departure just as I was about to leave."

"What kind of situation?" she asked.

"Something of the sort we," he corrected himself ". . .*you*, will be monitoring. As I was preparing to leave to pickup Mal... I mean you, that wonderful equipment I spent several days helping to install tracked an incoming scrambled telephone message, originating overseas. Besides local messages it's exactly the kind of thing we're supposed to be on the lookout for."

Both Megan and Bat listened with interest, for different reasons.

"The blasted thing avoided routing to the ship's authorized frequency and was instead directed to someone elsewhere on the island, not to the Montpelier Plantation Inn, where the Royals are staying, and where a number of the calls we've monitored have been to and from, even before they arrived. " He paused, for another few seconds, and again Megan and Bat remained silent.

"All this expensive hush-hush equipment on board," Archie resumed, "and you can't even get reception on this island! Some testing exercise this is going to be. We'll have the 'computer geeks' take a look at your phone and see if what you experienced is an isolated problem or if these chaps need to return to their drawing boards. I recommend you keep an eye on it, Megan. We can't sign off on something that's not picking up all the chatter."

Megan simply nodded slowly, responding. "Not to worry about my phone. As I said, it's a cheap throw-away I purchased at Heathrow when I realized silly me had forgotten my own. It is little more than a tourist toy. I didn't expect much from it and it proved me right. I won't waste anyone's time playing with it."

Then once again an awkward silence permeated the vehicle for several minutes.

From time to time, Blair pointed out or mentioned historic sites or attractions. Both Bat and Megan asked questions and commented about various things. Eventually, Blair turned off the Main Road and headed up to Montpelier. A few minutes later, he brought the Land Rover to a halt in front of the wrought iron gates of the property. Megan opened her briefcase and removed a single, large Manila envelope and quickly alighted from the vehicle.

"Thank you," she smiled at Blair and made her way to the closed gate. When she did, a detective seemingly appeared from nowhere. After a few seconds of conversation, during which she presented her security credentials, she was admitted.

"Well, that seemed easy enough," Archie said casually. "Look how easy it would be for an assassin to breech the wall and get inside: some false credentials and a great set of legs and the royals could be compromised."

"Well, the credentials are real, and she's a classy looking woman," Bat offered. "She doesn't look dangerous."

"Ha!" Archie mock laughed. "Doesn't look dangerous you say? Let me tell you something Bat. She is deadly. She may look like someone you'd want to get into the sack, but brother, trust me. I wouldn't make a pass at her for a year's salary. Make that ten year's salary, because if she didn't fancy you, a person probably wouldn't live to spend it."

"Her? You can't be serious. She may be a good field agent, I'll grant you that, but I'd have a hard time thinking of her as a physical threat."

"Really? Sounds to me as if your little head is doing the thinking for your big head . . ."

"No, no, nothing like that at all. I'm just saying, look at her. Except for the red hair, she looks like a refined woman, a physician's wife, a business woman, something pedestrian, a genuine civilian . . . not an intelligence operative." Bat patted his shirt pocket for a pack of cigarettes. "Damn it. Old habits die hard. I keep forgetting I gave up the weeds."

"Well, the red hair is real. When she was an active field agent she always dyed or bleached it to a brownish chestnut color. When it was shorter she always wore a wig. But now it's pretty long." Archie had watched Bat patting his pockets in amusement.

"Sorry, Bartholomew, I can't help you with a cigarette even if you wanted one."

"I know. I recall you don't smoke."

"Never did. It's a filthy habit."

"You still thinking about Megan?"

"Yeah, sort of. I just can't see her as a field agent out there in harm's way. She doesn't strike me as the type."

"Oh, brother. Let me tell you something that should change your mind. I've seen her in action. This is personal experience, mind you. I was a bit smitten by her almost from the first time we met through our families, who were mutual friends of sort. When she came into the Service, our paths didn't really cross for a few years. We were ships passing in the night, so to speak.

"Then we were part of a joint MI-5 and MI-6 team that was working on an IRA terrorist case. I'll make a long story short. There were three of us, a chap named Russell Sharp, Megan, and I, and we had an unexpected confrontation with two of these IRA scum. They were underlings, street soldiers, not chieftains. It should have been a quick and easy take down. Russell went for his gun and was shot dead from the get-go before Megan and I could arm ourselves.

"One of the thugs came at me with a pipe he pulled from his waist band. The other one, the shooter, tucked his gun away and went for Megan. He got her in a bear hug. Perhaps he wanted to cop a feel, who knows? He picked the wrong woman to get frisky with. He never even got close. She spun him off and to the ground then snapped his neck like a toothpick. It was so fast he probably didn't see it coming. Then she proceeded to pull the other chap off me and near pistol whip him to death with her weapon. When he struggled to get up she snapped his neck as well. Dead as door nails, both of them. In less than 15 seconds at most."

"Wow!" Bat sighed. "She sounds like a terror."

"Almost a sociopath, the way she did it. Positively deadly. I saw a rage I didn't believe possible in any human. It scared me. I forced myself to cool my affections for her. We remain cordial and friendly, but I absolutely could not get intimate with a woman who could kill you and then calmly sit in a pub drinking coffee, emotionless, while matter-of-factly writing the incident report."

"Holy cow. Do you think that could have been a fluke?"

"Not at all. I've heard stories from others in the Service who've worked with her. Whenever the IRA is involved, Megan takes no prisoners. The victims are always D.O.A. I think that's why she was rotated out of physical situations after her mentor retired."

"Her mentor?" Bat asked.

"So I heard. She was supposedly a favorite of Sir Warren Wormsley, a deputy director with considerably more authority and power than the title suggests. Talk is, she is still in the service because he still has enough clout to protect her, and I know that's a fact. But she's on desk duty and the like, and more mundane surveillance jobs. She'll receive one or two more promotions and eventually retire. The word is she'll never be out in the field again, unless the service wants somebody terminated. This Nevis trip is probably the most foreign activity she'll ever see again."

"Are you pulling my leg?"

"Absolutely not. She showed no mercy to any IRA sods who had the misfortune of crossing her path. She was bloody ruthless. Without Sir Warren looking out for her, she would have been drummed out of the service."

Some believe her rage is related to Lord Louis Mountbatten's murder by the IRA. Her father and Lord Louis were long time chums. I don't know how true it is, but there are rumors Lord Louis was fond of Megan and, had she been blood, he would have made efforts to pair her up with Prince Charles, as he did with his niece."

"But Charles is so much older than Megan, I'm sure of that," Bat stated.

"True enough. But Megan and Diana are the same age. And the Prince of Wales married her. I noticed you checking her out, Bat, and I strongly urge you to dismiss any thoughts of making her a conquest . . ."

"Cool it. . . here she comes."

Megan passed between Montpelier's gates and returned to the Land Rover. "Sorry it took so long. I thought it would be a simple drop off, but I happen to know this detective, we dated for a short time some years ago. All he wanted to do was reminisce!"

Her explanation given, she changed the subject, and her remarks were directed at Bat.

"A travel guide book editor?" Megan turned halfway in her seat and was facing Bat.

"Seems like a strange transition from being a soldier," she said softly, with an inquisitive smile, as Archie resumed driving.

"Not really. I was a fair-to-middlin writer before going into the service," now he lied, "that's how I got picked as a PIO. But, in truth, I'm much better at photography. So it was quite normal for me to resume my chosen field when I got out." Damn, he thought, I could have been an actor!

"See? There's a good answer and reason for everything, if one just takes the time to ask. Even coincidences such as you two stumbling into each other on a practically unknown Caribbean island," she answered through a stilted smile.

Bat wondered if he was getting paranoid again, but there was something about the look in her eyes that told him she doubted every word he had said.

"Had we gone back the way we came," Archie resumed his chatter, "I would have pointed out the ruins of Cottle Church, the first church on the island where the masters and slaves worshiped together back when sugar was king in the West Indies. I suppose you two will just have to look it up on your own once I'm gone."

"Archie, I know Americans are famous for traipsing through every church and cathedral in Europe, but please, you really don't have to give me your Nevis church tour," Bat quipped facetiously.

"Oh, I like touring churches whenever I go foreign," Megan added.

"I was joking," Bat cut in apologetically, "Of course I want to see the churches, every guidebook reports on them."

"Good!" Archie replied with enthusiasm. "Then you must also see Fig Tree Church, it's Anglican, of course. That's where they keep Admiral Nelson's marriage certificate to the local Nisbet woman on display. And then there's the very unusual Black Jesus at St. James . . ."

****

". . . St. James isn't the closest church to Montpelier," the food service staffer was telling Diana, "but it's only one of three black Jesus Crucifixes in the Caribbean. It's quite special indeed."

The Princess of Wales had asked about Sunday services for herself and her sons. Diana was in a poolside lounge chair sitting in the shade on the left side apron of the deep end while the two princes enjoyed frolicking in the swimming pool, replete with two of their ever watching detectives nearby, but not conspicuously visible.

As a mother, she deliberately positioned herself where she was at the pool in order to protect her sons, should they wander too far into deeper water, which was only 6 feet at most. They had been instructed to stay in the shallow area, but they were young boys having fun. Also, from where she was, Diana could clearly see, and be seen, by the barman if she required service.

"We have five parishes," the staffer continued, "the front desk has a list with times for services." Diana thanked the woman, who smiled and promptly left. Diana resumed sipping her tea.

The visit to the Montpelier swimming pool was something of a consolation prize to William and Harry who had both wanted to go directly to the beach after freshening up in their cottage. But Diana had other things to tend to and arrangements to finalize before dinner. And, at some point, she just wanted to relax a bit before dinner. She promised her sons that a trip to the beach would be the first order of business the following morning. For now, though, they seemed to find the pool an acceptable alternative.

Celia Gaskell had left a photo album on the small table next to Diana. It contained numerous photos taken five years earlier to mark the 200th anniversary of then captain, and later Lord Admiral,

Horatio Nelson's marriage to the wealthy local widow, Fanny Nisbet. The photos showed local residents in period costume reenacting the wedding and reception celebration held at Montpelier.

Diana picked up the album and fingered through it. She couldn't help but be reflective about Nelson's infidelity and adulterous love affair with Lady Emma Hamilton, wife of Sir William Hamilton. Hardly a year after marrying Fanny, Lord Nelson and Lady Emma unashamedly began to live together in England. Though aware of the heartbreaking situation, Fanny refused to divorce him.

Fanny only heard second hand rumors and gossip after their marriage about her husband and that Hamilton woman, from afar. Diana had known of the relationship between Charles and Camilla Parker-Bowles before their wedding. She had been so distressed by it that she considered not marrying Charles in 1981.

As she casually perused the pages of Nelson-Nisbet reenactment photos, Diana moved her thumb to her ring finger and flicked it twice before realizing the gesture was in vain.

Often when her mind was occupied or wandering, the Princess of Wales would unconsciously use her thumb to turn the ring over and over. The engagement ring, with a large oval sapphire as its centerpiece surrounded by 14 diamonds set in white gold, had been worth £28,500 ($54,150) at the time. But the ring was no longer there. Old habits die hard.

Nelson had married the wealthy Fanny because she provided the money and proper social standing the aspiring naval captain wanted so dearly. Charles, it had been said, had only married Diana to provide an heir to the throne. According to Charles' closest friends, Camilla was the love of his life.

But Diana was no Fanny Nisbet. The Princess of Wales had no intention of assuming the role of a proper public royal wife and *stand by her man*, as the popular American country and Western song goes, while he resumed his fling with his married mistress.

Even before the marriage, Diana was certain beyond any doubt that Charles and Camilla were carrying on.

"We always had discussions about Camilla ...I once heard him

49

on the telephone in his bath on his hand-held set saying: 'Whatever happens, I will always love you.' I told him afterwards that I had listened at the door and we had a filthy row. The Camilla thing reared its head the whole way through our engagement. "For example, my husband sending Camilla Parker-Bowles flowers when she had meningitis."

And when Charles would call Diana on the phone, Camilla would somehow manage to be in the conversation.

" 'Poor Camilla Parker-Bowles. I've had her on the telephone tonight and she says there's lots of press at Bolehyde (her home). She's having a very rough time.' I never complained about the press to him because I didn't think it was my position to do so. I asked him 'How many press are there?' He said 'At least four.' I thought: *My God, there are 34 here!* And I never told him."

Diana became so distressed about the obviously ongoing relationship between Charles and Camilla that on the eve of their marriage she considered calling the wedding off, or at least vocalized such thoughts as a threat erupting from frustration. Her sisters talked her out of it. On July 29, 1981, Lady Diana Spencer and Charles, Prince of Wales, 12 years her senior, were married.

"I remember being so in love with my husband that I couldn't take my eyes off him," she recalled. "I just absolutely thought I was the luckiest girl in the world." But Camilla remained the third person in their bed.

"As I walked up the aisle, I was looking for her. I knew she was there of course. I looked for her. Anyway I got up to the top. I thought the whole thing was hysterical, getting married, in the sense that it was just like it was so grown up and here was Diana, a kindergarten teacher. The whole thing was ridiculous!"

"So, walking down the aisle, I spotted Camilla, pale grey veiled pillbox hat, saw it all, her son Tom standing on a chair. To this day a vivid memory."

But that October, in their first year of marriage, Diana became pregnant and would give birth to Prince William Arthur Philip Louis the following June. Then, 27 months later Prince Henry Charles Albert David, known the world over as 'Harry,' was born. The boys became the unquestionable joy of her life. Had two sons not arrived so early on in the marriage, the "Camilla thing" might have come to a head sooner and ended the fairytale before Diana had provided an *'heir and a spare'* to the Crown.

That was then. This is now. And in the years in between the royal couple drifted apart. Both had extra-marital affairs. The marriage between the young kindergarten teacher and England's most eligible bachelor had become a sham.

Consenting to cooperate and tell all in Andrew Morton's book *'Diana: Her True Story,'* was her crossing of the Rubicon, burning bridges behind her. She expected, and wanted, exactly that. Published just six months earlier, Diana was well aware that once it was out, her husband, the Queen, and the Royal Family would know she had been the source, no matter how many times she denied providing the information to Morton.

The several personal and shocking revelations in the book, including suicide attempts, and confirmation of the long rumored love affair between Charles and Camilla Parker-Bowles, were astounding because as many suspected the events and contributing factors of this royal tragedy came from her, in her own words, in collaboration with Morton, not from the sometimes prejudiced pen of a biographer. She had pulled no punches and revealed a wealth of dirty laundry in the royal hamper.

Her unhappiness actually began shortly before the wedding when she became aware of Charles' emotional ties to Camilla, and lingered throughout the years of what eventually became a loveless marriage.

By the late 1980s, the strains in the marriage had been widely publicized. By that time, Diana had already adopted charity work as her royal duty.

The June, 1992, publication of *Diana: Her True Story* most likely guaranteed her forthcoming departure from the Royal Family. But the August 25, 1992 publication by *The Sun* of a monitored telephone conversation between Diana and an assumed lover positively rubbed salt in the royal wounds. Her enemies were vocal, it just wouldn't do for the Princess of Wales, wife of the heir apparent to the throne, to be carrying on like some common harlot, they said.

So it was, hardly three months later, that on December 9, less than three weeks before this holiday trip on Nevis, Prime Minister John Major announced to Parliament that Diana and Charles were separating but there were no plans for divorce.

By the time she arrived in Nevis, Diana had decided that after this trip she would withdraw from public activities for several months, or how ever long it took, to avoid or lessen the negative publicity focused on her separation from Prince Charles.

"Ma'am?"

Diana hadn't noticed a third detective approaching her, she closed the photo album.

"I'll be meeting with the media at Hermitage this evening," the detective told her. "It seems several of them favor the bar there. I've typed up your wishes as we discussed and included the daily time you allotted for public photography, starting on the morrow at the beach. It's based on what was done for the trip to Necker."

The reference was to the candid photo sessions Diana allowed the media when she and her two sons holidayed on Virgin Air owner Richard Branson's private Caribbean island in April, 1990. The thinking was that, by agreeing to throw them some crumbs, the paparazzi would leave them alone, or at least be far less intrusive. It was a truce that didn't always work with her antagonists.

"I've made a goodly number of copies," the detective continued, "and I'm certain other copies will be available for late arrivals." He handed the single page of white paper to her. As he had said, it explained that she and the princes would permit observation and photography for a specific amount of time each day during their stay on Nevis. Beyond that, Diana expected the photographers to respect her and her sons' privacy. The whole thing took up less than the top half of the page. She gave it a cursory glance. Diana knew it by heart. She smiled and thanked the detective, who immediately withdrew.

As he did, a Montpelier staffer appeared and placed a plate of sweets on the table next to Diana's lounge chair. She handed him the photo album and said 'thank you.' As she did, Diana became aware of a commotion as her boys came out of the pool and were quickly beside her.

"Mummy," William said, as he and his younger brother reached for one of the sweets, "When I grow up I want to be a policeman and look after you. . ."

"Oh, no you can't," Harry interrupted, "You've got to be king!"

Diana often told friends she was pleased that sibling rivalry between them was almost non-existent. "Harry's a 'backup' (to the throne) in the nicest possible way." As for her eldest son being a future king, she once remarked "William is going to be in his position much earlier than people think now."

That evening, Diana and her sons had dinner on Montpelier's open air balcony Terrace Restaurant. They chatted among themselves, sometimes whispering, and an occasional low giggle brought smiles from the other hotel guests at nearby tables. No one intruded on their privacy.

Diana would later mention to friends that the trip to Nevis, so close after the public announcement of her and Charles' separation, was a marvelous experience. Not just the obvious get-away-from-it-all aspect, but being someplace where the people treated her and the boys with friendliness and were not intimidated by their royal position. It was all proper and respectful, but much more casual than life in London. She only recalled a few individuals who seemed to "quake in their boots" in their presence. She was particularly pleased that her sons got to experience a slice of 'normal' life on holiday at such a young age and thought it bode well for them.

Whenever adults are at odds in an unhappy marriage, it is inevitably the children of such unions who suffer. Diana had spoken of her concerns about this with close friends, most of whom proffered advice about how to deal with the situation. The princess was wont to tell friends that, more than anything else, she wanted to protect her sons from scars and bad memories about their parents feuding.

Despite the Palace-encouraged rumors to the contrary about

her being 'unstable,' HRH The Princess of Wales proved to be a concerned and caring mother to her two sons throughout the separation and eventual divorce process. Her actions were remarkable considering the personal turmoil and uncertain future she faced. But such things were inward, emotional feelings of the heart. Diana also harbored tangible fears for her sons' physical safety in a world where some put little value on human life.

Though not visible in the outward persona of this very public woman, the Princess of Wales faced more sinister specters and demons begat by a horrific 20-month period of tragedy, death and mayhem preceding her walk down the aisle with Charles. Ever present, these visions percolated just below her public awareness.

She had vivid memories, at age 18, of the 1979 IRA murder of Lord Louis Mountbatten and seeing the deep grief and agony on the face of her future husband, Charles, at his beloved 'uncle's' funeral. She was as shocked and stunned as the rest of the world when John Lennon was murdered in the presence of his wife as he left his New York apartment in early December, 1980.

Then, in March 1981, a month after Buckingham Palace announced that the Prince of Wales and Lady Diana had become engaged, the President of The United States was shot by a crazed assassin wanting to impress a movie actress. Six weeks later, an attempt was made on the life of the Pope while the former kindergarten school teacher was in the midst of making plans for her July wedding.

These four senseless celebrity attacks *within two years* of each other were just the most recent incidents to remind her that fame, celebrity or high office often came with a terrible price. But if such things tempted her to modify her lifestyle and spend more time in the sanctuary of Kensington Palace, or the country estate known as Highgrove, she refused to succumb.

Yet the comfort and security she often felt for her sons in these homes would also be challenged.

Prince Charles loved and had painstakingly refurbished, nurtured, and devoted much time to the estate. It is situated in Gloucestershire, approximately a mile from the town of Tetbury. Its surroundings are bucolic and light years away from the hustle and bustle of London, some 110 miles away.

In 1980, the Duchy of Cornwall acquired Highgrove from Member of Parliament Maurice Macmillan, son of the former Tory Prime Minister Harold Macmillan. The Prince of Wales, who is also Duke of Cornwall, picked the area for his new home because of its easy access to London. The purchase fueled speculation that the Prince was considering marriage.

Prince Charles and Princess Diana took up residence at Highgrove soon after they were married in 1981. It was the first home for Princes William and Harry who spent much of their early years on the estate prior to starting school. Princess Diana frequently made shopping trips to Tetbury and neighboring Cirencester, and the watchful eyes of Sir Warren's spies became used to seeing her and the young princes out and about in the area.

The house, constructed between 1796-98 in Cotswold stone and featuring a stone roof, is a rectangular three-story building with nine bedrooms, four reception rooms, eight bathrooms and a nursery wing built in the Georgian classical style. The façade has an open balustrade surmounted with urns. Ionic pilasters stand at the front of the house. It reposes on 37 acres replete with stable buildings, staff dwellings, parkland and a home farm of nearly 350 acres where Charles promotes his interest in organic farming and gardening.

The Prince of Wales, with a staff of gardeners, was fastidious about the gardens framing the house. Esthetically arranged plantings and shrubs on both sides properly accentuated the dwelling itself in a myriad of color. Towering Golden Yews formed a delightful and picturesque avenue complemented by a profusion of green topiary, multicolored wildflowers and an outstanding field of buttercups.

The landscaping was one of Charles' great joys, and easily among the most pleasant to view anywhere in England. Though he had a qualified staff to attend to such things, it wasn't uncommon to see Charles spend hours digging around, adding personal touches, creating paths, and various other things. It had become an escape haven for him where he could walk the grounds with Tigger and Roo, his two Jack Russell Terriers, and, for a brief time, be the uncomplicated, wealthy 'country squire' with few cares in the world instead of the man who would be king. He often spent upwards of three days midweek there, frequently without Diana, while he entertained guests, including Camilla Parker-Bowles.

In his book *Highgrove: Portrait of an Estate,* Prince Charles wrote: "I had absolutely no experience of gardening or farming, and the only trees I had planted had been official ones in very official holes. I knew I wanted to take care of the place in a very personal way and to leave it one day, in a far better condition than I found it". He reportedly spent £500,000 on the gardens.

Another book *Highgrove, a Prince's Legacy,* showcased a year tending to the garden and estate farm and Prince Charles' efforts to make it a model for traditional and organic growing methods. The private grounds are only occasionally open for public viewing, but there is a five year waiting list to do the tour.

It was to this, his beloved hideaway, that the Princess of Wales also found comfort and safety. But Diana officially moved out of Highgrove following the breakdown of her marriage to Charles in the early 1990s.

Nonetheless, when the Prince and Princess were still living under the same roof at Highgrove, an alarming event took place which reminded her that assassination or sudden death could be lurking anywhere, even at Highgrove.

Much like a suspenseful scene in some 1930's black-and-white movie thriller, the full moon caused the agent to cast a long shadow on the rear of the stone building. With appropriate concern he moved slowly, cautiously, toward the point of entry, for which a key had been provided.

Once inside, he stood perfectly still and oriented himself, bringing to mind every detail of the floor plan he had memorized. That done, he methodically went about his surreptitious work, which he knew he need not rush inasmuch as neither the Prince nor Princess of Wales were presently in residence.

The once-happy royal couple's Kensington Palace residence in London would have been far more difficult to enter and affix eaves-dropping devices. Consequently, no changes would be made in the existing surveillance there, nor in the continued reliance of household staff spies. Furthermore, with ever increasing signs already visible that the royal marriage was deteriorating, Diana was the primary target under observation. Since she spent considerably more time at Highgrove during this period in her life, the country estate was an excellent place to increase surveillance.

Near the completion of his task the man's dark image was observed moving through the light in an upstairs rear window. By chance, the shadowy figure was observed by one of the members of the half-dozen-strong security detail that patrolled the estate. In short order they were joined by a small, but armed, detachment from the Gloucestershire Constabulary, replete with a pair of dogs.

But their quarry was considerably more adept at evading detection than his pursuers were at their job.

The police had alerted Paul Burrell, Princess Diana's butler, the man she called "my rock," at the home where he and his family lived at elsewhere on the estate. Burrell had become Diana's most loyal and intimate confident, and she told close friends he was "the only man I can trust."

Burrell joined the contingent of law-enforcement officers and effected entry into Highgrove through the same rear door the agent had entered. Along with the others, Burrell had been given a bulletproof vest. But, once he quietly opened the door, the butler stepped aside so those trained in dealing with such matters could proceed first.

The police were armed with guns. All Burrell had was the knowledge of the layout. After considerable time was spent exploring every room, closet, under the beds, basement, loft, roof, every nook and cranny, nothing was found. It was as if whoever it was had vanished into thin air.

When they returned to the residence both the prince and princess were informed of the incident. The paperwork filed with the Gloucestershire Constabulary listed the incident as a mistaken report.

Yet the officer who initially raised the alarm by reporting a figure in the house remained steadfastly convinced someone had been there.

In *A Royal Duty,* which Burrell would author some years later, he mentions the incident and recalls his feelings as he slipped the key into the rear door at Highgrove: "Beads of sweat broke out on my forehead, and fear took hold of me."

If her butler broke into a sweat at that incident, Diana's fears and suspicions were more severe over the years.

". . . I really thought there was a conspiracy to get rid of me. I thought my car brakes were being tampered with and I had the apartment swept for bugs and, of course, they found nothing. . ."

Diana called her solicitor to Kensington Palace and signed a will saying that, if she died, Charles would not have the solitary word in rearing their children:

"I express the wish that, should I predecease my husband, he will consult with my mother with the regard to the upbringing, education, and welfare of our children."

More and more, as their marriage continued to spiral downhill, Diana verbalized her fears that 'The Firm,' or those loyal to it, would resort to extreme measures to get rid of her. "One day, I'm going to go up in a helicopter and it'll just blow up. MI-5 will do away with me."

Perhaps, she best expressed her exasperation in the now famous profane comment to James Gilbey on the Squidgygate tapes.

"After all I've done for this fucking family."

****

Archie felt obliged to attend dinner that evening and properly introduce Megan to the ship's officers on her first night aboard. She and Captain Bradley hit it off immediately. From the mutual name-dropping, *ad nauseam*, he was surprised at how many of the same upper-crust people the two of them both knew.

Bat Lynch took an early dinner at Hermitage, the plantation inn he was staying at. Afterward, from the privacy of his cottage, he was unsuccessful in several attempts to contact the informer on St. Kitts who was the real reason for this Caribbean trip and cover as a travel editor. But he gave it little thought since he wasn't supposed to be in the Federation of St. Kitts and Nevis until the morrow and the man was most likely out for the evening. But Bat had no plans, no agenda. He decided to take a nap and dropped onto the bed fully dressed.

When he awoke nearly two hours later, it occurred to him that tonight would be his only free night before work began. He decided to go back to the main Great House building and have a drink or two at the inn's tiny bar. To his surprise the bar and covered open patio adjacent to it was crowded. But by the way they were dressed, and their demeanor, Bat got the feeling this was a transient group, not Hermitage guests. He wondered where they had come from.

The inn's owner, Richard Lupinacci, and a staffer were busy filling drink orders for waiting staffers as others would take full trays to the patio or to the also crowded main public room where someone was playing the piano and singing, both quite badly, the popular English World War II ditty, *Doing The Lambeth Walk*. When Bat finally caught Lupinacci's attention, he ordered a single malt Scotch on the rocks. It was produced quickly.

The patio crowd was getting noisy so, with drink in hand, Bat decided instead to stroll into the main room. The wannabe singer/pianist had ceased playing, probably by popular request, Bat reckoned. All the overstuffed chairs were taken, so he picked a spot of empty wall next to a well dressed man with snow-white hair. Bat correctly assumed everyone in the room was a Hermitage guest. Bat's first impression had been that the man was elderly, but his smooth skin hinted he was prematurely gray and in his forties.

"Quite a crowd out there" Bat casually commented without introducing himself or looking at the man he was speaking to.

"Where did they come from?" Bat took a sip from his drink as he waited for a response.

The man snapped his head sideways and looked Bat over.

"Then I take it you're not one of *them*?" he said with a heavy English accent, and what sounded like relief in his voice. "Yet, with that marvelous beard, I would have taken you for a Brit, probably a naval officer."

"No, no. I'm not one of *them*, whoever they are. I checked in today. I'm Bat Lynch, from New York, and I'm a guest here." He wondered why both Megan and now this Brit thought the beard made him look nautical.

"Well, Mr. Lynch, that very well may be your last drink on this island if these chaps continue at the rate they are going. Less than half an hour ago I heard the owner frantically calling an island liquor distributor, or someone, saying he was running out of booze! Oh, by the way, Lawrence Brinkley, from London, at your service. My wife Maggie and I are also guests here. She's back in the cottage. Can't stomach this boisterous riff-raff. I shall be joining her shortly, but wanted a night-cap first." He tilted and rocked his glass.

They shook hands and smiled at each other.

"But who are those guys? *Them*?" Bat asked, jerking a thumb in the direction of the patio.

"*Them* are the notorious paparazzi who follow celebrities all over the world. Like a proverbial plague of locusts they have been arriving on island all day. They are here to invade the privacy of, and torture, the Princess of Wales and our young future king."

Before Bat could comment the Englishman continued:

"The proprietor says the local Nevisians are already calling them the 'reptiles.' They are mostly an uncouth bunch staying at cheap hotels, or anywhere else they can rest their dirty heads, since good hotels are always full this time of year. They swarmed down on The Hermitage for meals. . . and stayed for drinks. I'm told they all flashed Amex Platinum or Black charge cards and seemingly have unlimited budgets. They consumed champagne by the case till that ran out. Now they appear to be drinking anything with alcohol in it. An unsavory bunch!"

"You should have booked into Montpelier. I think it would be quiet and no paparazzi around. Not with the royals staying there."

"We had no idea the princess and princes would be on island when we made arrangements to come here. My American brother-in-law and his wife stay here every Christmas," then, adding in conspiratorial tones, "They prefer to get away from all the stuffy English back home." He laughed at his own joke. To be polite, Bat smiled and nodded. But the man wasn't finished and had more to say:

"My brother-in-law made this reservation nearly a year ago but managed to get himself in the hospital by making a mess of things testing a new boat. So here we are, the replacement relatives! And as for Montpelier, the space situation is true for them and the few other top notch places on the island: one needs to book next year's Christmas trip before leaving this year."

Bat's eyes widened and he couldn't conceal his surprise. "You're THAT Brinkley, of Brinkley & Cummings, the racing boat builders?

"The very same. Racing boats, pleasure craft, and we dabble in non-marine business interests as well." He made the statement with off-handed casualness, almost self-depreciatingly. The way the very wealthy often did.

Dabble? Bat thought. *If he calls controlling interest in a number of multi-national companies dabbling, what would he call serious work?*

"See, I was almost right about your beard. You seem to know something about boats, Mr. Lynch, you must be a sea-faring man."

Bat nodded and replied "Call me Bat, but my sea-faring experience is mostly from reading and admiring boats, not owning one." He considered boosting his image by mentioning he had a private pilot's license, but there was no reason to.

"All right then, Bat it is. Speaking of boats and ships, did you know England's greatest naval hero, Lord Admiral Horatio Nelson married a local woman from this island and that he frequently watered his ships here? The place where he collected the necessary water is known as Nelson Spring."

"Yes, I did. The marriage took place under a tree up at Montpelier as a matter of fact. That fact, and the spring, are mentioned in every Caribbean guide book, including ours." Bat was thankful he not only read the required background material on St. Kitts where his meeting with the informer was to be, but in his thoroughness, he also included the chapter about Nevis, only two miles across the channel at its nearest point, and the other half of the country that made up the two-island Federation.

"I must visit Montpelier whilst here. Somehow." Brinkley's eyes seemed to suggest he was thinking about things a long time ago. After several seconds, he turned to Bat flush with enthusiasm:

"Can you imagine what it must have been like to see Nelson's *Boreas*, and King William's *Pegasus*, and those other great fighting ships resting at anchor off Charlestown? What a magnificent sight it must have been!"

"Certainly would have been a fine sight to see," Bat thought he should say something, though conjuring up an image of 18th century English men-of-war wasn't high on his list of daydreaming.

"I recall, though, that the fame and recognition both Nelson and Prince William would one day achieve were still in their future," Bat added. "At the time of the wedding here, both were simply naval ship captains."

Brinkley was taken aback and gave Bat a stern look, including a slightly raised eyebrow. "Simply captains? . . ."

"Michener," Bat offered in explanation. "He has a whole chapter about Nelson being here and marrying the widow Nisbet."

"Have you no sense of history, man? You're saying they were just young naval officers? That's almost like saying the Greeks left a child's wooden hobby horse at the gates of Troy!" Brinkley's face was stone serious. But in an instant he burst into a loud belly laugh and slapped Bat on the back.

"I'm putting you on. I was joking."

Bat joined him in a good laugh. He actually thought he had offended the man.

****

The Princess of Wales lifted Harry into the back of the pickup truck while William boosted himself in and quickly found a spot where he wanted to sit. Instead of sitting next to him, his younger brother positioned himself against the side panel directly across.

Diana declined an offer of assistance from one of the detectives and managed to make hoisting herself into the truck appear graceful and something she did every day. Today was the first 'beach day' Diana had promised her sons, but they seemed equally thrilled to be riding in the back of an open truck.

The small caravan of vehicles that pulled away from the wrought iron privacy gate and stone walls of Montpelier was also transporting the Special Branch bodyguards, the Gaskells, and Montpelier staffers. It would wend its way down the curving road to the main island road, eventually dropping 750 feet to sea level. As a 'mountain' property, Montpelier provided guests with daily transportation to Pinney's Beach, where they maintained a hut and area for serving food and beverage.

Despite the driver's care, occasional bouncing from ruts and holes in the road was unavoidable. Early in the trip Diana collected both boys to her, one on each side. With her arms around them the young princes laughed and enjoyed each bounce. The experience was just the kind of exposure to a normal life and jolly good time that she dearly wanted her sons to have and remember. They would certainly never have an opportunity to bounce around in the back of a truck in England. And, she mused, not a paparazzi in sight.

Shaded by towering palm trees, Pinney's Beach is six kilometers long, almost three and three-quarter miles of golden colored sand, and is the tiny island's busiest beach. Nonetheless, it somehow always managed to look relatively deserted. Considered one of the most attractive beaches in the West Indies, it reminded one travel guidebook writer of those pristine, Pacific beaches thick with palm trees so often seen in old war movies.

In addition to Montpelier's compound for guests, there were several beach bars and restaurants up and down Pinney's length. But by far the most dominant structure on the shoreline is the luxury 196-room Four Seasons Resort, replete with its Robert Trent Jones II golf course rising upwards towards the almost perpetually cloud-fringed Nevis Peak.

Several minutes after passing through the center of Nevis' quaint capital Charlestown, the caravan rolled by part of the impressive Four Seasons Resort golf course on the left. The main lobby building could partially be seen in the distance through the profusion of tall palm trees. The grounds appeared meticulous. Diana remembered Oprah Winfrey had told her she stayed there two years earlier and raved about it and Nevis in general. But the

Princess of Wales thought the ambiance, atmosphere, and privacy, for her and her sons would be totally different than at Montpelier, and not what she was looking for on this trip. Perhaps on a future holiday.

After another ten minutes, the caravan swung onto a dirt road that seemed to be in a canyon of trees, bushes and tall grass high on both sides of the vehicles. This was, without a doubt, the bumpiest part of the trip, and the children, especially Harry, loved it, as most 8-year-olds would.

Eventually, the pickup truck and other vehicles were through the vegetation and came to rest in an area with far less growth and which showed previous use as a car park and this day was quite full with vehicles. The beach and the Caribbean Sea were clearly in view. They had reached Montpelier's two-acre stretch of Pinney's Beach, affectionately called Montpelier By The Sea for obvious reasons, complete with lavatory, telephone, sun-shelters, picnic spot, lounge chairs and limited service bar. The Inn's guests were shuttled to the beach each day. But this trip for the royals rolled away from the property an hour and a half earlier than the usual 10:30 AM departure. Diana was intent about making sure the boys were not out in the sun when it was strongest. Hence the early start, which would conclude before noon.

The rules which had been dispensed to the paparazzi the previous evening provided for 15 minutes of candid photography at the beach just before she and the princes would leave. She and one of the detectives would huddle at some point this morning and determine a location and time for another session on the morrow.

Once the tailgate was lowered, Diana and William received assistance from two of the detectives as they disembarked the vehicle. Before he was helped down, Prince Harry asked the driver if they could go back on "that road" again.

Much to her chagrin, Diana noticed the car park was nearly full with vehicles. Apparently the photographers had all arrived much earlier than the proscribed time. Nonetheless, she was intent on having them abide by *her* schedule.

Megan Price was lying on her stomach on a large white beach

blanket on Pinney's Beach when Bat spotted her. Actually it was the rich color of her hair laying in profusion well below her shoulders. She was some 20 feet from the water's edge and her blanket was close to a grove of coconut palm trees which, because of the hour, provided no shade protection whatsoever. She was obviously there to soak up the sun. Bat was accompanied by the young Nevisian boy, Raymond.

Unlike most women with good figures, wont to wear revealing two piece swimsuits, Megan wore a one piece form fitting navy blue Latex suit with bold white stripes flanking both sides. It resembled the kind of swimsuit Bat remembered girls wearing in those beach party movies from the 1960s, before bikinis became the rage. And from what he could observe, the suit hugged every curve on Megan's body.

As soon as he was close enough for her to hear him, but not loud enough for others nearby to hear, he spoke.

"Hello *Miss* Price, fancy meeting you here. I would have thought you'd already be busy doing whatever MI-6 skullduggery you were supposed to be doing as Archie's surrogate." Bat let the shoulder strap of his camera case slip down and put it down on the edge of her blanket as she half turned and propped herself up on one elbow, and smiling replied.

"Good to see you as well, *Mr.* Lynch . . . no, nothing for me to do until tonight, someone else is doing the royal eavesdropping at the moment. And probably not very busy at that since the royal travelers are here at the beach this morning."

"Good for you. Archie said you were a smart one."

"Actually, I just pulled rank and took the night shift. You don't think for a moment I intend to work away these beautiful days out there rocking on a ship, do you?" Before he could respond she continued.

"And, speaking of your war buddy, I just drove Archie to the airport to catch his plane."

"I'll bet he talked your ear off with all that technical gibberish he loves so much." Bat dropped to his knees onto the blanket.

"Some, but more importantly he gave me the inside scoop on

all those gallant, and randy, Royal Navy officers I met at dinner last night. . .and other than the ship's old salt captain, none of them had beards."

"Beardless, horny sailors, on HMS Bedford!" Absolutely shocking Bat laughed, "So old Archie has really gone. Flew the coop..."

"Yes, but he's not going right back to work. He told me he had some accumulated time coming and he was going to take a few days of private time and just do nothing," she said casually. Then looking at Bat in an exaggerated conspiratorial way added:

"I'll let you in on a secret if you cross your heart you won't tell anybody!"

"Uh oh, this sounds serious."

"Promise you'll keep it to yourself?"

"I promise, I promise. What is it already?"

"The ship isn't the *HMS Bedford*. I have no idea what its real name is, if it even has one or just a number."

"So why do you call it *HMS Bedford*?" Bat queried.

"That's for local consumption. The captain figures people always ask the name of a ship they see in port, so this trip it's the *Bedford*. It's easier than just saying its number 007 or whatever is on the hull."

"Why did you use those numbers?" Bat asked.

"Because, with all the electronic eavesdropping equipment on board, she's a bloody spy ship!"

They shared a hearty laugh. Bat wasn't sure if she was pulling his leg or not, but it didn't matter. He was enjoying her company. Megan pushed herself up and turned around facing the water. She raised both knees and pulled them toward her chest and wrapped her arms around them in a hug. She locked her fingers together. Bat followed her lead and made himself comfortable seated on the blanket next to her.

"Excuse me Bat, and Misses, I'm gonna go in the water a bit to see the Princess and Princes better," Raymond announced. The boy peeled off his suspenders and let his pants drop in the sand, revealing a bathing suit, and dashed off for the water line.

"I see you've made a friend, *Mr.* Lynch," Megan proffered, "and he's one who appears always ready for a dip into the sea!"

"I guess it comes with the territory, *Miss* Price, living on an island and all that. I inherited him from Archie. He spotted me as we drove through traffic in town and convinced us to give him a lift. He keeps reminding me he's the best guide on the island," Bat paused briefly to change the subject.

"We're going to beat this *'Miss Price'* and *'Mr. Lynch'* stuff to death, if we haven't already, even if we're both being facetious."

"You're right," she laughed. "I was wondering how long you'd keep that going." It was genuine and Bat realized she seemed much more relaxed than she had been when they met yesterday.

"Make it just plain old 'Meg' or Megan if you prefer from now on and I'll get used to calling you Batty," she giggled. "How did you get here? Rent a car?"

"Just plain Bat will do fine, thank you. No 'Batty' please," he was grinning broadly. "Actually, I met one of your famous countrymen at Hermitage last night."

"Really, who?

"Lawrence Brinkley of Brinkley & Cummings, and, by the way, he's a big fan of Admiral Nelson."

"Oh, he's not famous, not like a celebrity or anything like that. He's just filthy rich and a royal insider. Did you know Nelson was married at Montpelier? Of course, you must know, what with editing the Nevis material for your guidebook."

"Yes, I knew it, but it seems like every British subject wants to tell me about it anyway. You may recall Archie mentioned it yesterday on the way back from the airport?" Bat paused then added, "I even know the names of Nelson and Prince William's ships . . ."

"*HMS Boreas* and *HMS Pegasus*," Megan chimed in. "We take our history seriously in Britain,"

"You certainly do," but Bat was in a playful mood and wanted to tease her.

"Okay, how about this: Do you know the name of the tune the British military band played when General Cornwallis surrendered to Washington at Yorktown?"

Without missing a beat Megan replied, *"The World Turned Upside Down*, and so it was." She gave him a devilish smirk.

Bat knew he was jousting with an equal so he resumed where he had left off earlier.

"Well, in the U.S. you can't talk about racing boats without the name Brinkley & Cummings popping up. It would be like talking about the Indianapolis 500 without mentioning Penske."

Megan gave him a puzzled look. She didn't have a clue what he was talking about.

"Anyway, we spoke for quite some time. He's very opinionated about the royals, or I should say the monarchy."

"Really, pro or con?" Megan asked.

"Oh definitely pro. I had the feeling he still hadn't forgiven Americans for the hard time we gave King George way back when."

"Sounds like a proper Englishman, I would think," Megan gave him a teasing smirk again.

Bat took her comment as humorous but instead of saying something cute in response he returned to why he was on the beach this morning.

"Brinkley told me he overheard paparazzi at the Hermitage bar saying the princess and the princes would be on the beach this morning. And, since I have to check out the beach anyway for the guide book he was kind enough to drop me off here while he visited the philatelic bureau in town. He's big on collecting stamps. So here I am."

"Ah, you're a 'royal watcher,' too, then?"

"Not really, just curious. I'm on this island the same time they are," he shrugged, "And I figured I might get a tidbit or two for the book, a little color, and I wanted to see what all the fuss is about with the paparazzi."

"Well, take a look, that's them, that herd with their cameras," Megan tilted her head to the right indicating an obvious crowd clearly within shouting distance. "They've been clicking away for about 15 minutes straight now. God, they're insufferable." There was a noticeable tone of revulsion in her voice. She obviously shared Brinkley's opinion of the press.

"Have you been in the water?" Bat asked.

"No. I rarely go into the ocean. I'm just here to catch some rays. I hate the sticky feeling of salt on my body. And my hair! Goodness, the salt water makes it thick and bunches clumps of it together like rope. No thank you. I'm a freshwater pool person, and even that's rare.

Bat smiled and nodded as if he understood. He again looked over in the direction of the Princess and her sons. "I think there are more photographers here on the beach than tourists." Bat was surprised people were permitted within such close proximity to the royals, but let the thought pass.

"He's in trouble!" Megan said softly. She was looking into the water ahead.

Before Bat could associate what she had said or whom she was talking about, Megan had sprung up from the blanket and was already several paces away running toward the water. He rose and turned to follow her. She was already in the surf.

She quickly realized the water was well over the boy's head and as she moved closer to him the sand beneath her feet suddenly dropped off and her own mouth and nose were now below water as well. In the few seconds it took to reach him, she had to bounce up from the bottom and physically manhandled him into a lifesaving grip.

Raymond was nearly limp, gasping, coughing and appeared disoriented. She bounced off the bottom again and thrust out an arm pulling water back toward her as she rolled onto her back and began kicking rapidly. In a few strokes they were out of the deep water and she was able to drop her legs and touch bottom.

Bat was in the water up to his knees approaching her and Raymond as she reached him on her way back to the shore. She shook off his offer to carry Raymond out of the surf and onto the sand.

Bat was impressed by her quick reaction and stamina. Instead of stopping, Megan carried the boy back to her blanket and gently seated him on it, supporting his back. Bat was at her side and they both dropped to their knees. Raymond had stopped coughing but his breathing still seemed labored and he was still not fully alert.

"I think he had a seizure, or something. Maybe he's diabetic and it's low blood sugar," she said. "It wasn't a cramp. . . hold him, keep him upright," she ordered Bat. "What did you say his name is?" she asked.

"Raymond," Bat had moved behind the boy and, kneeling on the blanket, braced his body.

"Raymond, don't move your head. I'm going to have my fingers near your eyes. I want to keep your eyelids open so I can look into your eyes. Do you understand me? Don't move your head. I'm not going to hurt you. Stay still." She was in control and Bat realized she apparently knew what she was doing.

The boy made a grunting sound that resembled 'yes' and did as she had told him.

As Megan gave him a cursory exam, she asked Raymond if he was diabetic and he answered affirmatively. Bat became aware of a sound he recognized as a camera motor drive. He looked to his right and less than four feet away a crouching photographer was recording the incident.

"Okay. Bat, please dig into my tote bag. There's a towel and a power bar snack in there amidst all the other junk. Give them to me. It'll do till we get some real food into him." Megan began drying off Raymond as Bat produced the unwrapped bar and handed it to him.

When he had moved her blouse to locate the towel in the tote bag he was surprised to notice a larger than normal cell phone. It was obviously not the small, plastic 'throw away' kind she said she purchased at the airport. He figured she had forgotten she had packed it.

"Eat it all," Megan ordered. Then she noticed the photographer.

"Stop it! And get the hell out of here, damn you" she practically screamed at the man as she continued drying off the boy. "Go back with the rest of the vultures and bother your royal victims!"

"Beat it, buddy, or . . ." Bat began to utter a threat he fully intended to carry out if the man persisted and locked a menacing glare on the man.

"Okay! Okay! No more pictures. I was just doing my job. The photo session with the royals is over now and I just thought you and your wife might want something to remember how she saved a kid's life. That kind of stuff doesn't happen every day."

Neither Bat nor Megan corrected the man's assumption that they were married. Bat locked a stare on him again and the man seemed to wither in the glare.

The American accent suggested the man was obviously not British. The use of 'vacation' instead of the 'holiday' confirmed it. Bat looked over at where the royals were and noticed that all but a few of the photographers had already departed and those few that remained appeared to be preparing to leave.

"Well, go, be gone, anyway. We don't want your pictures," Megan said gruffly though her attention was fixed on examining Raymond. Bat continued to glare at the photographer.

"How about a can of soda for the boy?" the photographer inched closer and produced one from his large camera case.

"It's not diet soda. Plenty of sugar in it. I'm a little diabetic myself sometimes. I heard what you said. By the way, I'm Tony LaRocca." He seemed concerned and sincere.

Megan snatched the can from his extended hand. Her 'thank you' was less intimidating than her previous remarks. She opened and gave the warm can to Raymond who began eagerly drinking it in large gulps. She handed the damp towel back to Bat who almost stuffed it in the satchel on top of her blouse. Instead he held it.

The boy seemed to recover quickly. He smiled and thanked the photographer for the soda, and introduced himself. "I'm Raymond. I live on Nevis," he announced proudly.

Neither Megan nor Bat felt obliged to exchange names with Tony LaRocca. Bat was tempted to ask the man what exactly *'a little diabetic'* meant but decided not to encourage further conversation. It reminded him of the adage that a woman can't be 'a little pregnant.' You either were or you weren't.

Megan looked at Bat, "I think we should get him something to eat." Bat nodded in agreement.

She rummaged through her tote bag again and removed another towel with which she began vigorously rubbing and drying her hair.

"See what I mean about the salt water and long hair?" she asked Bat without looking up at him. "It's now all matted and knotted into bloody, sticky ropes!" She continued her drying efforts for another half minute before converting the towel into a tightly tucked turban. When she finished applying it her hair was totally concealed.

"Nice job." Bat thought it was the appropriate thing to say.

"It'll have to do. Couldn't go anywhere to eat, or even back to the ship, looking like something from a Gothic horror movie." She looked around, taking in the scenery one last time and at her sun tan oil and other contents spilled on the blanket from her tote bag and announced. "Well, let's get this show on the road".

Neither said anything else to the photographer as they began collecting Megan's things and Raymond's pants, which she handed him. "Don't put them on yet. Your swimsuit is wet. Wait till it's dryer," she advised as the trio prepared for the trek towards her vehicle.

The photographer understood he was being ignored, took the hint and wandered away. Besides, he had more pressing things to do than chit-chat with strangers. Like most of the other paparazzi who followed Princess Diana and other celebrities on trips, he had state of the art electronic transmitting equipment which could send photos over phone lines. The photos most of them had taken could be published in London or elsewhere in the world within hours.

"That's all of it, we're ready to go. I've had enough of the beach today. And it's almost 11:30 anyway."

"At twelve noon, the natives swoon, and all the work is done. But mad dogs and Englishmen go out in the midday sun," Bat affected a poor English accent.

"Very good, a colonial familiar with Noel Coward. There may be hope for you after all, Mr. Lynch," she chided. "Ops! Sorry about that," instantly realizing she'd used Mr., then added *"Mr. Bat!"*

"What am I going to do with you," Bat shook his head in mock frustration.

"Take me to lunch, that's what. And young Raymond here as well. After that I can drive you to your hotel or to a car rental agency if you wish."

"As a matter of fact, getting a car would be a good idea," he lied, since he expected to be leaving for St. Kitts and his appointment with the informer that evening or in the morning. ". . .but I can order one through Hermitage and have it delivered there."

"Whatever. Suit yourself. Either way is fine with me." She shrugged.

"So, Raymond, tell me about yourself, your family, where you go to school . . ." Megan engaged the boy in conversation as they began walking toward the car park. Bat thought her concern and kindness confirmed the protective motherly instinct he had seen on the beach. His first impressions at the airport were way off base, he thought. Bat half listened to Megan and Raymond's exchange as he stole a glance at Princess Diana watching her boys frolicking in the low surf.

As the three of them came abreast of the Princess, Bat and Diana's eyes locked for an instant. He nodded and smiled and she did likewise. If he could tell his younger sister back home about this brief encounter with the Princess of Wales, she would either think this was 'very cool' or she wouldn't believe him.

The car park area was nearly empty now with nearly all the paparazzi having departed. The HMS Bedford's white Land Rover rental that Captain Bradley considered his personal vehicle, but which all the ship's officers and MI-6 agents had use of ashore, was parked next to the pickup truck which transported Diana and her sons to the site.

Megan's Land Rover and the other few remaining vehicles were parked with their fronts up against a long hedge row. When they reached the car Megan took the towel from Bat and quickly dried herself off, then retrieved her khaki Bermuda shorts and a white blouse from the satchel.

As Bat listened to the again talkative Raymond touting all the sites on Nevis that he could be their guide for, Megan moved towards the high hedge at the front of the Land Rover. She opened the vehicle's door and, with the hedge at her back and another vehicle alongside, she had transformed the small area into a make-shift dressing room, albeit an open air one.

"Excuse me," she looked directly into Bat's eyes. He obviously didn't have a clue about what she intended. She raised her hand, the one holding the blouse, and shook it.

"Oh, of course," Bat felt his face blush slightly, "C'mon, Raymond, the lady needs some privacy," he said as the two of them moved around to the rear of the vehicle.

"On the way here, we passed Four Seasons," Bat said after several seconds of silence, "It's perhaps ten minutes, more or less, heading back towards town. According to what my predecessor wrote, they have a pretty good beach restaurant there."

"That'll do nicely," Megan replied, adding "I certainly don't think we could get into their regular restaurant the way we're dressed." A short time later Bat heard the Rover's door close and she emerged from between the vehicles. She glanced at Bat's pants legs, which were wet just past the knees, and his soggy shoes.

"If it was a bit closer, say three to five minutes away, we could have walked to Four Seasons via the beach and your pants and shoes would dry out a lot quicker," she suggested.

"I said it's about a ten minute *drive*. The guide book says it's four miles distant. Too much of a beach walk in sand for Raymond, or me. Besides the shoes are shot anyway." He told her.

As at the airport in the fitted skirt, Megan again struck Bat as attractive. In fact, he thought, she was looking better the longer he was with her. But he had been most impressed by her speed, agility and strength rescuing Raymond. Archie was apparently right. She had the characteristics of a very able field agent.

****

The Princess of Wales agreed with Noel Coward's assessment about being out in the midday sun. Consequently, even as the last photographers were driving out of the car park and the sun neared its zenith, she had coerced her sons to go under the protection of the Montpelier beach site's shaded food serving area by tempting them with hot dogs, and all the trimmings, followed by a real Caribbean parade. Diana joined them and enjoyed watching their feasting while the detectives and Montpelier staffers collected all their belongings and took them to the vehicles.

Before the boys were fully aware that beach time for today was over, she was telling them of the many colorful things, oddly dressed people, and steel drum bands they would be seeing. Also, perhaps, the 1992-93 Carnival Queen, Uazel Glasford, would be riding by on a brightly decorated float.

When she received a nod from one of the detectives indicating that the vehicles were packed and ready to roll, Diana encouraged her sons to take their hot dogs and drinks and head for the pickup truck.

"You know what?" Bat asked as Megan cautiously moved the vehicle over the road that brought such joy to Prince Harry, "If you think it wouldn't be harmful to Raymond, perhaps we should forget about Four Seasons and go right into Charlestown. We can catch something to eat there. I need to stop by the philatelic bureau and let Brinkley know not to go looking for me."

"Do you think he'll still be looking at stamps?" She queried.

"He said he could spend a day in such places. And, again according to our guide book, the Nevis stamp bureau has quite a selection."

They had hardly gotten onto the main road when Bat recognized Brinkley's rental car approaching them from the opposite direction. Megan pulled over and Bat went several paces in front of the Land Rover to flag him down. Megan reached into her tote bag and fumbled for her sun glasses.

As what should have been a few second stop turned into more than a minute, the two men seemed to be involved in an extended chat, Megan thought. Whatever they were talking about was obviously beyond a simple 'No need to come fetch me. I've got a ride.'

As she began tapping her fingers on the steering wheel, the

royal caravan passed by. En route to Montpelier, she reckoned.

A few seconds later Bat was back in the vehicle and they were on their way. Megan turned her head toward Bat and spoke as they drove off.

"So much for your new friend spending all day perusing stamps," she said with a smile, adding, "Oh, by the way did you know that Charles and Diana were actually cousins several times removed?"

"Really?" Bat seemed surprised. Actually, his surprise was at suddenly seeing her in sun glasses here in the car instead of at the beach.

"Yes," Megan said as she returned her attention to the road ahead. "Diana's father, Johnnie, was the godson of Queen Mary and his family included a line of earls, dukes, and duchesses back to King George III in the fifteenth century. The monarch conferred the title of Earl Spencer on one of Diana's ancestors. It passed down to her father."

"Thank you for that tidbit of royal trivia. I'm sure my sister already knows it," he laughed.

Bat didn't have a clue she had turned toward him to avoid eye contact with Brinkley.

"What took so long?" she continued, removing the sun glasses and ticking them in her blouse pocket.

"He insisted on telling me about his 'absolutely wonderful experience' at the Nevis Philatelic Bureau buying stamps for several friends back home. The man is a chatter-box." But, Bat realized, Brinkley seemed to have said an awful lot about the stamps he had supposedly seen in a relatively short time.

He paused and withdrew a handkerchief from his pocket, "Damn, it's hot out there, even in the shade."

****

The Carnival on Nevis is quite similar to such celebrations throughout the West Indies. Street parades, costumed celebrants, dancing, singing, playing calypso and other music, performing short dramatic presentations, Jam sessions, and Carnival queen shows have been shaped by a number of other carnivals especially Trinidad's, the African ancestry of a majority of local residents, and changing trends in music. Much of it can be traced to folklore, traditions, beliefs and customs which are passed from one generation to another and celebrated from Christmas Eve to New Year's Day.

But more than the Carnival Parade, which Diana promised her sons they would locate, young Harry was excited as his mother lifted him into the back of the pickup truck at the prospect of another bumpy ride on "that road." Harry still had two bites left as the caravan left the car park.

As promised, the caravan came upon an impromptu Carnival celebration as it entered Charlestown and speed was reduced to a crawl, eventually a halt. Such things often flared up during Carnival with little advance warning. It wasn't the foretold 'big parade' or a major celebration, but when you're 10 and eight years old, music, noise, and gathering of costumed people blocking traffic was an extraordinary event.

The center of attraction at this place this day was a dramatic street presentation, with locals dressed in faux period attire as white English plantation owners from the days when sugar was king. The series of quickie vignettes performed was more akin to 'Punch 'n Judy' satire.

The children stood up in the back of the truck, and their mother joined them. From their vantage point, the performers were clearly visible, though all their spoken lines were not. Nonetheless, the slapstick antics were in the language understood by children the world over and brought giggles and laughs from the young princes.

One sequence proffered a character decked out as an overly dressed and medaled navy officer taking the hand of a woman shading herself with a parasol. He executed a very deep bow and as he did his long sword rose and struck the groin of another officer behind him who made an exaggerated fuss over the injury. The comical display obviously depicted the captain of HMS Boreas and England's greatest naval hero, future Admiral and Lord Horatio

Nelson meeting the widow, Fanny Nisbet.

Nelson's graphically injured comrade in this scenario was taken to be England's future King William IV, then commander of *HMS Pegasus*. At the wedding, the future king gave away the bride to the officer who would become Britain's greatest naval hero. Prince William Street in Charlestown is named in his honor.

As she and her sons watched the farce, Diana later told friends she found the social contradictions between the street spoof performed by Nevisians of African ancestry and the elaborate and respectful reenactment by the white Nevisians of English ancestry, captured for posterity in the Gaskells album, somewhat amusing.

Because her Nevis visit came so close after the royal separation, she wondered if years from now locals would be prompted in some future Carnival Parade to mimic her, Charles, and The Rottweiler in a 'lovers' triangle' skit. Perhaps not, she thought, because the people she'd met here seemed genuinely kind and friendly, and devoted old Fanny was a local lass who would always merit their attention.

A few minutes later, Diana felt the truck lurch slightly and thought for an instant they would be moving. It was a false alarm. The actors who had portrayed Nelson and Fanny Nisbet, et al, were now dressed in different costumes and playing other roles.

****

"This is a first-rate traffic jam," Megan said softly, "Looks like a celebration in the street ahead." The Land Rover was rolling, inching along so slowly that people passing by were moving faster.

"I know how to go around it. Make a left turn at this street right there!" Raymond indicated a cutoff only three cars away. In less than a minute Megan turned into the street and was able to drive at a safe speed.

"Now turn right, up there, no the next block, the next block, at the blue house with the metal roof."

She did, and again they were on a street with few moving vehicles. Both she and Bat smiled.

"Well, Raymond, Archie was right. You *are* the best guide on Nevis!" The boy grinned broadly at the compliment from Bat. With a few additional turns, they continued driving parallel and west of the congested main road through town which they had been on. In a relatively short time, Raymond shouted "Stop! That's where I live. Let me out, thank you." He indicated a brightly painted yellow, wood-frame, one story house. It had a short front yard with several potted flowers. Megan pulled the vehicle over.

"But we're going to take you someplace for lunch…" Megan was saying when he interrupted.

"No thank you. My momma knows what to make me eat to make my sugar okay. I always come home for special lunch every day." Raymond managed to open the passenger side door.

"Are you sure?" Bat asked, "We can have lunch at Hermitage. Did you ever eat there?"

"Yes, my brother's band plays there sometimes. They pay him, and we eat there too." He was out of the car. "The Main Road is just down there," he indicated the direction, by extending his right arm and twisting it in a snake-like fashion several times. Both Bat and Megan took that to mean there were most likely a few curves or turns to take, ". . .and it will take you to Hermitage." He finally stopped twisting his arm.

"Oh, and no charge for sightseeing today because Misses Megan saved my life… Bye." Raymond bolted across the street and entered the house.

"Do you think we should go in and have a word with his mother? Tell her what happened?" Megan asked.

"We could, but from what he said I gather she's aware of his condition and things like this have happened before," Bat replied, adding, "Kids are kids. He probably skipped breakfast this morning. If we go in and make a big thing about it, she might be insulted and think we are saying she isn't a good mother, or punish him, or something. Best to leave it as it is."

Megan thought for a second and nodded agreement.

"Misses Megan," Bat mimicked, "may I come up now and sit in the front with you?"

"You'd better, *Mr. Batty*, or the local folk will think you're some big-shot with a female chauffeur."

"And what would that photographer on the beach think? He thought we were married. What kind of married couple drives around with one in the front and one in the back," Bat chided. "It's almost as unholy as a married couple having twin beds!"

"Bat Lynch," Megan scolded, "You're starting to sound as horny as those degenerate officers and gentlemen on *HMS Bedford*!"

Despite Raymond's ambiguous sign language directions Bat and Megan managed to find the Main Road with little difficulty. They reached Hermitage in several minutes. The central building of the restored 350-year-old plantation property is the Great House with its dining room, large sitting room with a small library off to the side, a powder room, and a small bar, plus the kitchen. A covered open-air patio terrace overlooks lush tropical foliage and gardens. Built of Lignum Vitae, the hardest wood in the world and called Iron Wood in the U.S., the Great House is the oldest standing wooden structure on Nevis. Some historians say it's the 3rd, if not the oldest, in the Caribbean and Western Hemisphere.

The casually elegant 15-room inn is nestled on a hillside. Elegantly furnished one and two-story cottages dot the property and serve as guest accommodations. Many are former local Nevisian homes which were purchased and trucked to Hermitage. All proffer four poster canopy beds, oriental rugs and hard woods, baths and private porches or verandahs. Overhead fans circulate the cool mountain trade winds, providng natural air-conditioning.

There were two other couples taking lunch on the terrace dining porch. Once seated at a table, and while Megan continued perusing the wine list, they placed drink orders. Bat checked his watch and excused himself. Instead of going to his cottage he went to the small outside building that served as the inn's check-in office next to the Great House. He placed a call to the informer he was to meet on St. Kitts. As had happened with his attempts the previous evening, the phone rang to no avail. He realized this wasn't a good sign and he grew concerned.

Before leaving the U.S., the man had been told Bat would contact him by phone when he arrived on St. Kitts on December 28, though Bat arrived on the sister island of Nevis two days earlier. The informer wasn't told which flight Bat would be on, just to wait for it sometime between 12:45 and 5:30 PM. Bat checked his watch again. It was 1:15. There was absolutely no question the man should have been glued to the phone during this time. Had the man been compromised? Would Bat be walking into an ambush if he flew into St. Kitts today? With the limited number of daily flights into St. Kitts, it wasn't rocket science to post people to watch the airport all day.

Bat made a second call, this one to his Central Intelligence Agency control officer at a safe house in New York. In what to outsiders would have sounded like an innocent conversation between friends, he included the phrase indicating the informer was not answering his phone. There was a pause as the control officer discussed the situation with others. In equally innocent sounding conversation, Bat was told to make a final attempt an hour from now. If contact wasn't made he should consider the mission scrubbed and leave the island at the earliest possible opportunity.

As he took the short walk back to the patio, Bat silently thanked his lucky stars that he had not been able to book a room on St. Kitts for arrival today but instead had to arrive on Nevis a day earlier.

"Well, you look relieved," Megan said teasingly. He was anything but. Though she assumed he had visited the toilet he didn't want to chance being caught in a lie.

"No, not that. I went to the front office to check in with the publisher in the States." Then added, "If I needed a restroom it would have been just as easy to go to my cottage. It's the Blue Cottage, right there behind you."

She turned and saw a quaint, balconied, two story old colonial gingerbread cottage with flowered trellises amid a profusion of tropical plants and fruit trees, approximately 75 feet away. A vervet monkey, one of the hundreds that roam free on Nevis, was perched on the balcony rail observing Bat, Megan and the other diners lunching on the terrace.

A Hermitage staffer came by and took their meal orders. When she left Bat looked across the table and his and Megan's eyes locked.

"I have to tell you, I was very impressed with your agility and strength pulling Raymond out of the water. You made it all look almost effortless. You're a regular fish!"

Megan shrugged his comments off, "I medaled in golds and silvers for track and swimming and various other sports, throughout my school years. Athletics always came easy to me. I guess I was what you Yanks would call a 'Tom-boy.' Something in the genes they say, could be," she paused in reflection for a few moments before continuing.

"My father was a bull of a man: rugged, outdoors-ish with strong hands the size of hams. Looked more like a burly dock worker or prize fighter than a retired naval officer. He was a young leftenant attached to Lord Louis' staff when Mountbatten was overseeing the creation of independent India and Pakistan after the war. They hit it off smashingly well and became lifelong friends. Lord Louis treated my father like an adopted son. "

"Your father must have taken it hard when Mountbatten died," Bat thought it was an innocent and proper comment. He never expected what followed.

"Hard? He and Lord Louis were *killed* the same day. They didn't die, they were killed. The IRA blew up Mountbatten's boat while he was sailing near his holiday home in County Sligo, Ireland. Killed him, his 14-year old grandson, his eldest daughter's mother-in-law and a local teenager. They never gave a reason why they went after him. He was nearly 80 years old and had never been involved politically in the Irish situation. Senseless." She paused again.

"We, my parents and I, were on our way to visit Lord Louis. The news came over the car radio while we were stopped for petrol and out of the car stretching our legs. I swear the veins in my father's head were throbbing so much with rage that he went into absolute shock and keeled over, dragging me to the ground with him. His last words were, 'Dirty IRA bastards.' He was pronounced dead when the ambulance arrived. I was fourteen. I can remember it, every detail, as if it just happened. They killed him too."

She and Bat again locked eyes. Hers were dangerously aflame with hatred. He reasoned this wouldn't be a good time to try changing the subject by telling her he was named after his paternal grandfather's brother, Bartholomew Lynch, a member of the IRA during the 1916 Easter Rebellion.

At that instant their lunch plates arrived. Bat did change the conversation as they began eating. In the relatively short time he had been with her this day, he had seen multiple sides of Megan Price, and he liked the most recent one the least.

He kept the conversation light and tried to anticipate provocative or disturbing issues as they ate. When they were finished, Megan asked if he would mind showing her his cottage.

"And if it's not an imposition, could I use your shower? I can't stand this hot turban or the salt all over my body."

"Yes, certainly. Be my guest. He correctly understood her request as genuine. She had made it clear earlier how much she disliked the feeling. It was not a forward pass by a sexually liberated woman. As he rose from the table he noticed a smile on her face.

"What's that all about?"

"You and Archie as friends."

"Why? We worked together as military liaisons during Desert Storm."

"Yes, but I've known him for several years. In fact, we once did field work together, and he can be such a proper snob. He comes from old money, a titled family and he's very class conscious. Not the kind of person you Yanks would be keen about."

"Our Archie? You must be mistaken. I never found him hoity-toity or looking down on anybody."

She shrugged. "No matter. We apparently both know him under different circumstances."

Bat thought about that for a moment then replied somewhat reflectively: "So his family has friends in high places . . ."

"Like Buckingham Palace," she replied. "The whole royal lot of them."

"You're kidding! He's chummy with the Royal Family?"

"Well, we wouldn't say *'chummy'* but it would be accurate to say they all know him, some quite well."

Bat shook his head in amazement as he tried to connect his beer-drinking, rowdy wartime companion with someone who would have been comfortable sipping tea and chatting with the Queen.

"He never mentioned a word. I never would have guessed in a thousand years that Archie Blair was a genuine blue blood."

"Well, that depends how one defines 'blue blood.' His family is wealthy, granted, and he went to the best schools. But his family's association with the royals goes back to George VI, the Queen's father. Archie's grandfather, or is it his great-grandfather? I can never get that straight. Anyway, he was an earl and one of the King's card-playing mates."

"And yet Blair couldn't wait to get off this island and get back home, even with a future king of England and his popular Princess of Wales mother here," Bat reflected.

"Diana? Don't be silly, she won't be the Princess of Wales once the divorce goes through. Her adoring public will drop her like a hot potato, once she's on the outside looking in. And as for Prince William, he'll have to wait until both Elizabeth and Charles pass on. It could be a rather long wait, if Charles inherited his mother's longevity genes."

"You don't seem to like Diana very much," Bat said.

Megan stared blankly at him. He wondered what was going through her mind.

"It's not a matter of 'like' or not. I think it was a mistake for Charles to marry her in the first place. She was too young and hadn't been properly trained about what to expect. I think of her, many of us do, as just someone who was necessary to provide an heir to the throne. Plain and simple, period." Then quickly added, "You know Charles' father, Prince Philip pushed him into it, don't you?"

"Well, in America the public loves her. It was a fairy tale wedding."

"It's the same in England, too. Unfortunately the bride and her Prince Charming didn't live happily ever after, to say the least. But all this adoration, it's just a fad. Her conduct in recent years has tarnished her image. All this celebrity watching will vanish once she's off the public stage. She produced two sons, but now she has outlived her usefulness to the Crown."

Just as they were leaving the patio, one of the servers approached them and told Bat he had a telephone call. Megan slowly strolled around the area and examined the flora as Bat went to the check in desk again.

What he heard was not totally unexpected. His control officer told him the mission was aborted and he should get out of the country, now. Something had apparently gone terribly wrong.

"Back already?" Megan quipped, "You're certainly a man of few words."

"Well, fewer than you think. That was my publisher he just told me to drop everything here and get back to New York as quickly as possible, some sort of serious family crisis and he needs me to run the show while he's away. They've actually made plane reservations for me to be on my way this afternoon." He looked at his watch.

"Holy cow! I have to be on the LIAT flight from here to Antigua in two hours. Then a quick connection to New York on American. My little visit to paradise is over."

Megan appeared surprised and crestfallen.

Don't worry. You'll have time to take that shower while I pack my things and go to the desk to check out. But let's move now."

They resumed walking across the grass lawn, this time a bit more briskly, and as they neared Bat's 'Blue Cottage' the audible sound of monkeys scampering away broke the silence.

"Roommates of yours?" she asked jokingly.

"Not exactly, but I did find one sitting on the rail of the back balcony. Just sitting there, watching me through the open door as I got dressed this morning." That was the extent of their conversation. She did make few comments as she very quickly toured the cozy little cottage and clearly observed everything in the place.

"Now it's into the shower with me. I trust you have shampoo and a hair dryer?"

"Yes to both, take your pick. There are four or so small plastic bottles in my toiletries case on the sink, all liberated from various hotels" He was going to add *There's also a comb,* but had seen hers in the tote bag when he noticed the phone.

Bat collected his clothes and packed them in very short time. Since he could still hear the shower running, he left the cottage and made his way to the property's front desk to settle his bill.

When he returned to the cottage, she was dry, dressed and coiffed and on the back balcony watching a trio of monkeys frolicking in the trees.

"Well, that's the Megan Price I remember from yesterday! You certainly put the repair all together in a hurry."

She smiled but didn't comment. Instead she extended her hand, "Thank you. I needed that. And thank you also for a pleasant day. I've enjoyed it and your company. Perhaps, if you weren't leaving, we could have done it again in the week ahead."

It was as platonic as any such parting could be. Similar, in a way, to seeing a casual friend depart on a trip.

"Do you need a lift to the airport?" she asked.

"No. No thanks. The desk called a cab for me and they'll ring me when it arrives. But perhaps I'll go down with you and wait outside in the car park."

"No need. Stay here it's cooler. It's not necessary. Goodbye Captain Bartholomew Lynch." She leaned forward and pressed her cheek against his, instead of planting a kiss, as she grasped his shoulders.

"Goodbye, Megan Price. It was a pleasure meeting you," he smiled.

She gave a weak smile back. Then, without further fanfare, she turned and went down the stairs and exited the cottage.

As she walked across the grass back in the direction of the Great House terrace and the car park area beyond that, Bat watched her from the second floor front window. He couldn't explain why, but for some reason he had the feeling they would indeed cross paths again. He hoped the next time would be just as pleasant as this brief encounter had turned out to be.

Back at Montpelier Diana had little difficulty convincing her sons that an afternoon nap would be quite appropriate after the morning at the beach, the ride in the back of the truck, and the surprise stop at the Nelson Museum with its extensive collection of artifacts. She could have passed on the museum, but the boys had enjoyed the street actors' slapstick sketch so much that when someone asked if they wanted to see what the real Admiral Nelson looked like, and see his real fighting sword, William and Harry were beside themselves with excitement.

Thrilled as they had been to go there, the glamour wore off quickly when none of the adults in the group were able to locate Nelson's sword for them. For, as a matter of fact Nelson's actual 'fighting' sword is in a Wales museum.

However, once there, the Princess of Wales couldn't very well throw up her arms and declare "Well, that's it boys! No Nelson sword, so we're out of here." Even a more lady-like and refined rapid withdrawal would be taken as bad form. After all, Nelson was married to a local woman and he became a great English hero, despite his philandering. Nelson was the closest thing England would have to being a saint. Not only would a quick exit by her and the boys be an affront to the Nevisians charged with the care of the museum, but the scandal-hungry press would beat her up for such a misstep. She could imagine the fantasy tabloid headlines now:

'HELLO HORATIO ... GOODBYE HORATIO'
DIANA WAS IN AND OUT OF "NELSON THE CHEATER" MUSEUM ON NEVIS FASTER THAN CANNON BALLS FLEW AT TRAFALGAR!

Diana would later confide that she had a difficult time suppressing a giggle thinking about such bogus headlines. Consequently, she and her sons spent a respectable amount of time touring the site.

As her sons napped the Princess of Wales took the opportunity to make some personal telephone calls back to the U.K. Instead of using the secured lines and electronic scrambling equipment provided by *HMS Bedford* resting at anchor less than a half-mile off Charleston, she opted to use the normal phone connections available through Montpelier.

Then, as she did every afternoon, she briefly went over and signed off on the following day's schedule and time allotment for press photography during their periods of island sightseeing and other beach trips. This routine was dutifully performed each remaining day of the trip and, for all intents and purposes, worked well. Despite some expected grumblings, the press appeared happy, and she and the boys were happy. The rude intrusions at other times were minimum and manageable. But never at Montpelier. That was their safe haven.

Soon, far too soon, she would later say, the holiday on Nevis was over and Diana and her sons were winging their way back to the U.K. She made a promise to them that they would all return one day.

Three years later, in December 1996, Diana made inquiries about again returning with her sons to Nevis for the holidays. Oprah Winfrey, she recalled, had visited Nevis prior to Diana's trip and spoken highly of the modern amenities, and privacy, proffered at the Four Seasons. It would be a totally different experience from the quaint plantation inn atmosphere at Montpelier to be sure.

Unfortunately, her 1996 inquiry was last minute and far too late. In the years since her 1992 Christmas-New Year's visit, Four Season's on Nevis had become one of the most desirable resorts in the West Indies. Along with all other quality accommodations on tiny Nevis -- throughout the Caribbean for that matter -- the holiday season had been booked solid for several months.

So it was that on January 4, 1993, the Princess of Wales and her young sons, 8-year-old Prince Harry, 'the spare,' and Prince William, the 10-year-old who had proudly announced he wanted to be a policeman so he could take care of his mother, departed in business class on a commercial flight for London.

Princess Diana would visit the Caribbean and West Indies on future holidays again.

But she would never be back to Nevis.

CHAPTER THREE

Weather permitting, Austin and Madge Smythe-Pembrooke regularly spent from late Friday afternoon through Monday morning at *Mora*, their very large, three-story fieldstone and wood Tudor-style estate outside London. Madge considered herself one of the British Establishment's leading social hostesses and the expansive estate with its rolling forest acreage, a former hunting lodge built during the twilight years of Queen Victoria's reign, was still preserved in its original medieval theme. An invitation to spend an overnight at *Mora* suggested the guest was part of a very elite coterie to whom loyalty to the monarchy was an undisputed act of faith. The original name of the estate was one of those multi-syllable Germanic words that few people pronounce correctly. The Smythe-Pembrookes had renamed the estate *Mora* in honor of the flagship of William, Duke of Normandy, for his 1066 invasion of England.

The main building proffered a large dining hall dominated by a 23-foot long, ornately carved, oak table with matching decorated high-back arm chairs. Four highly polished full suits of armor were decorative sentinels in the various corners. Elsewhere, richly colored tapestries depicting hunting scenes and myriad large framed oils of dukes, counts, earls, and other nobles adorned the mostly paneled walls throughout. As one might expect, the dining hall itself featured a very large portrait of William The Conqueror.

Elsewhere on the spacious ground floor was a library containing part of Smythe-Pembrooke's collection of rare and first edition books, a smoking room with a fully-stocked bar decorated by numerous free-standing bronze nudes of various sizes, an auditorium style theater for viewing films or videos, and a huge kitchen sufficient for banquet-style repasts.

The second floor was mainly guest rooms which could accommodate upwards of 15 couples, but the Pembrookes rarely entertained more than ten at a time. More often than not they would host from a few to several couples for overnights on 'escape' weekends, as Austin liked to call them. With few exceptions, most guests would arrive early Saturday and depart Sunday evening.

Mora was a welcome retreat from the pressures and tumult of city life.

Nearly a third of the top floor was devoted to the Pembrooke's private penthouse-like living quarters, which Madge had redecorated as modern. The remainder of the floor had been bordered off with floor to ceiling paneling and used only for storage.

Modern staff quarters were in what had once been the property's large stable. The interior of the estate's former green house had been gutted and paved to serve as a protected garage for guests' cars. Both buildings were attached to the rear of the main lodge by extended enclosed walkways.

It was a pleasant Friday afternoon in advance of one such weekend that Smythe-Pembrooke, Miles Blair, and Sir Warren sat casually chatting and sipping drinks on the farthest point of the elevated, richly planted, terrace patio on the west side of the lodge. Access to this perch, overlooking the sloping grounds below, was through tall wrought iron and glass French Doors from the smoking-room. Where they were seated extended some 30 feet away from the lodge's wall.

"Hello, everyone," Archie Blair beamed as he crossed the patio to join them. He was casually dressed in tan slacks, a solid white V neck shirt and a green blazer. Much to his father's chagrin, Archie wore no socks just leather moccasin-style loafers. Miles Blair was a stickler for proper attire. Going 'sock-less' was just something one shouldn't do when socializing. But he would never publicly embarrass his son by commenting about such things in front of Sir Warren and Smythe-Pembrooke.

"There he is, the man of the hour. The junior James Bond himself!" his father quipped.

Archie was carrying a thin attaché case and had a well worn hard-cover book about heraldry tucked under the same arm. In his other hand he carried a crystal water glass, half full. He made the crossing in considerably fewer strides than it would have taken the others.

"No, Miles. He's better than Bond, he's real." Smythe-Pembrooke added.

Archie took a seat directly across from the trio, who were clumped rather tightly together despite the considerable room around the circular glass-topped patio table. It could seat eight comfortably. The MI-6 agent placed the attaché case on the redwood timber floor beside his chair and put the book and glass on the table's surface, directly in front of him. As he smiled at his companions, Archie rested his elbows on the table and linked his fingers as if preparing to pray.

"Yes, indeed he is real, and unlike the fictional Mr. Bond. . . Mr. Blair works for *us!*" Sir Warren added with a sinister grin.

Archie simply smiled and took a sip of his water. He didn't like the air of possession Sir Warren's comment suggested, even if jokingly. Archie Blair considered himself a loyal SIS operative, devoted to the monarchy. He justified the occasional work his father asked him to do for The Committee, and the sharing secret information with them, as akin to that.

"So, Archie, what are you driving these days," Smythe-Pembrooke chided, ". . . an Austin-Martin, like 007, or that old green Morgan, if it's still running?"

"The Morgan. I love it . . . it's a classic 1964. And yes, it is very much still running. Quite perfectly I might add."

"Don't josh with the lad," Sir Warren interrupted with a broad smile. "I predict a bright future for our young Archie in the years ahead. Possibly a deputy director's chair, or the top job itself," he paused ever so briefly, winking at Miles and Smythe-Pembrooke.

"Of course, he'll need to watch his p's and q's and develop a proper waistline," Sir Warren patted his own belly, adding, ". . .and even earn some gray hairs to prove his worth!"

The remark brought the expected chuckles, for no apparent reason.

Archie knew that such laudatory praise from Sir Warren was very good, even in a jocular vein.

"By then, perhaps, he'll fancy a Bentley."

The last comment brought yet another undeserved round of laughs from all of them.

At that moment, a liveried butler appeared holding a silver

serving tray and replenished the drinks for the others. He turned and was about to remove Archie's glass and replace it with a fresh one. A polite, but firm, 'no thanks' dismissed the man, who immediately retreated.

"Well, Archie, what's this good news you're so secretive about that you encouraged your father to have Austin gather here a day ahead of the rest of the weekend's guests?" Sir Warren prodded. "You said you'd be giving us a demonstration. Carry on" he added.

"A spectacular piece of technology. Revolutionary, actually. It takes surveillance to a level never dreamed of. And we now possess it! This will give our agents an unprecedented advantage over every country in the world."

"Pray tell, man, what is it? Some new parabolic audio thing? The smallest video camera ever invented? What?" Smythe-Pembrooke fancied technical and electronic devices as much as Sir Warren.

"Close, in a related sort of way, but no cigar. It's beyond belief." Archie replied.

"Tell us already, Archie," his father demanded. Sir Warren's long experience and skepticism in such matters kept him silent.

As the younger Blair individually looked at each of his seniors, a sly grin creased his lips.

"It's called FOTT. Well, that's what we're calling it anyway. The Chinese have another unpronounceable name for it, but FOTT works for us, for now. The initials F-O-T-T are short for *Fiber Optical Tape Transmitter.*"

His revelation was met with blank stares. The words meant nothing to them. Now Sir Warren spoke.

"The Chinese, you say? What have they got to do with it?"

"One of our people in Korea heard the technology was in development, about six months ago. He was able to turn a Chinese scientist whom he learned was actually a double agent for the North Koreans by threatening to blow the man's cover. As a result he got actual, working samples."

"What is it and what does this 'foot' do?" Smythe-Pembrooke asked.

"Not 'foot' It's FOTT, sounds like cot." Archie corrected.

"Get on with it, we're waiting. Tell us. Show us." Sir Warren's tone suggested he was becoming impatient.

"Okay. Without going into all the chemistry and technical details, which are way above my head anyway, FOTT is an extremely small, thin piece of transparent fiber optic tape. It works as a video transmitter. It's no bigger than the period you'd make when you write on paper. Devilishly small and so thin and transparent it is virtually invisible when applied to anything. I've tested it and, in my opinion, it *is* invisible to the human eye. I should add that because of its size it is excruciatingly difficult to work with. We have to use powerful magnifying goggles when we do." He looked around and was satisfied he had their undivided attention.

It can be attached to clothing, wallpaper, metal, ceramic, anything. It's adhesive on one side and sticks. Water and other liquids will not remove it. I had to scrape my test piece off with a sharp pocket knife and wasn't sure I had succeeded until the video transmission stopped!"

"You've tested it, you say? How and what were the results?" Sir Warren asked.

"I fixed a piece onto the boarding rail of a double-decker and was able to see everyone who boarded that bus for several days. Clearly. During the day, at night, in rain. It transmitted a wide image back to my laptop. If it's still on the rail, and I have no reason to think otherwise, it's still working. All I have to do is activate it. I copied the files onto my laptop. I can get the laptop, it's inside, and show it to you."

"But why can't you say for certain it's still working? Why don't you know if it is still transmitting?" Sir Warren asked.

"It's activated by GPS. You need to know the coordinates when it is applied and then some keystrokes on the laptop and you've got surveillance. I stuck it on the bus rail at Charing Cross Road, activated it then we sat at a café table sipping coffee and watched the bloody thing for nearly an hour. Absolutely fascinating!"

"We?" Miles asked.

"Who else knows about this at SIS?" Sir Warren asked.

"Nobody. We wanted to present it to you, the Committee, first and get some guidance to proceed."

"You said *'We.'* Who are your confederates?" Smythe-Pembrooke asked, even as Sir Warren was preparing to.

"Only two of us. Myself and Megan Price, and our man in Korea, obviously, knew also. Unfortunately, the poor chap was found dead in his bed the day before yesterday. Natural causes, nothing sinister. He had a bad ticker, Megan told me. Actually, she had contact with him and deserves the credit for bringing this to us."

"And you want us to pass judgment on this device rather than immediately turning it over to your proper superiors? A bit odd, don't you think?" His father's tone suggested that the elder Blair was somewhat disappointed in his son's behavior and priorities, Archie thought.

Archie felt his face flush from the reproach, bordering on disapproval, in his father's remark. He looked at Sir Warren and Smythe-Pembrooke for any indication that they agreed. But their poker-faced demeanor revealed nothing.

"I'm sorry if my actions, our actions, do not meet with your approval." He shot a passing glance to his father.

"But must I remind you that everyone in SIS and in the military swears an oath to the *monarch*, not the State? That notwithstanding, I'm sure you know we have some people in our ranks who seem to forget that from time to time, or outright have a lapse of loyalty. And some of those people are in high enough places which would make them privy to this extraordinary technology." Archie paused briefly and was relieved to see slow affirmative nods from the trio he was addressing. He continued.

"The first thing that struck me was the enormous application this will have in our surveillance of the Princess. Yes, it offers the same benefits for much of our other covert work also. But, unless I've misread the direction The Committee has been vigorously pursuing these several years since I joined the intelligence service, the primary concern has been the God-awful actions of the Princess of Wales." He paused again to a chorus of affirmative nods.

"FOTT is virtually undetectable! It decreases our personnel security risks tremendously. It's a godsend for collecting the kind of information you want about Diana."

"Quite. A remarkable innovation!" Smythe-Pembrooke said enthusiastically.

"We will, of course, inform SIS. We just want your direction and input, that's all." Archie declared. "It's just that Megan and I both feel that, of everyone on The Committee, you three probably have the best knowledge of whom we should approach, which people can be trusted to permit us to use FOTT for our purposes." He included his father as a courtesy, knowing well that though Sir Warren and Smythe-Pembrooke were friendly with Miles Blair, he was not at their decision making level with regard to privileged information

"Very good. Clear thinking." Sir Warren cut in. "No need to explain your motives any further. This is just the kind of thought process I was alluding to earlier." He leaned slightly forward and spoke to Miles Blair. "This sort of thing augurs well for our Archie. The man doesn't miss the forest for the trees!" Then, facing Archie, he added. "And don't worry yourselves about informing the hierarchy in SIS. We'll take care of that: it will be better that way." He looked at Smythe-Pembrooke.

"I'm sure Austin here can create a believable scenario crediting the discovery and control of the technology to The Committee. That will insure our position in the pecking order for usage." He smiled broadly.

"And, being loyal subjects," Smythe-Pembrooke added, also smiling, "we obviously want to share our find with the services."

Archie shot a side look at his father, who seemed in accord with what the other two had said.

"So? The demonstration you promised?" Sir Warren asked.

Now Archie smiled. He half turned in his chair and made a broad wave at the corner window on the second floor above them. When the others looked up they caught a brief glimpse, before she vanished from view, of the unmistakable brace of red hair which they knew belonged to Megan Price.

95

"I couldn't be more pleased to know this entire thing is in the good hands of you and Megan," Sir Warren told Archie. The comment was absolutely true, and one of the rare times no one needed to wonder if what he said had a hidden meaning.

"You know, Sir Warren, Archie was once taken by her. She made his heart flutter." Miles commented. "Pity that didn't work out. She has proper breeding and is a good looking, robust looking woman, quite attractive in an Amazon sort of way" he looked warmly at his son. "You two would have made a handsome couple . . . and I'll bet that by now I'd have several grandchildren."

Archie smiled weakly. "Just wasn't in the cards, I guess." He had been through all this with his father more than a few times and didn't want the subject resurrected here.

"Here she comes now! The 'Cat Woman' who manages to collect what sounds like marvelous, albeit still mysterious and unseen, technology from the Chinese and is able to move through my estate undetected." The other three joined Smythe-Pembrooke rising from their chairs as she reached the table. She was carrying a laptop computer.

"Fiddlesticks. Stop making a fuss over me, all of you. I'm just a simple civil servant doing my job." She seated herself in one of the empty chairs and without waiting for any witty replies, announced "It's show time everybody."

Megan put in a few keystrokes and turned the computer around so the four men could see the 17" flat-panel screen. What they saw playing out before them left all of them in total awe.

They *were* the visions on the screen. Everything that had transpired from the moment Archie entered the terrace through the double French doors. There they were, the three of them, sitting at the table talking. Only Archie himself was not seen on camera, but his voice, and theirs, were all heard.

"Hello, everyone."

"There he is, the man of the hour. The junior James Bond himself!"

"No, Miles. He's better than Bond, he's real . . .and he works for us."

They watched, spellbound, as the video playing recreated Archie's arrival and the conversations which followed. Several times each of them took their eyes off the screen and scrutinized Archie, looking for the slightest clue of where on his clothes or body the FOTT might be.

The video played for a few minutes more and the trio continued examining Archie's person to no avail. Smythe-Pembrooke actually got up and went behind him, leaning over so close that Archie could identify the brand of single malt Scotch he was drinking.

"Ah-ha!" Miles exclaimed as he snatched the book and began vigorously examining it and running his fingers over the spine. "Nothing!" he uttered in almost a whisper as he put the book down.

Archie and Megan exchanged glances and she gave him a friendly wink.

"There's only one possible place your FOTT could be," Sir Warren concluded. He had been the least animated and least physically curious of the three. Sitting back and observing instead.

"And where do you think that is, Sir Warren," Archie asked.

"That water glass you declined to have replaced. It's sitting in the right place to capture the three of us in the frame, and from the high positions of our heads in the video, related to the top of the screen, that must be it."

"Very good, Sir Warren!" Megan said with obvious admiration in her voice. She turned the computer to face her, introduced a few keystrokes, shut it down, and closed it.

"Yes, very good indeed. But did you actually see the FOTT or deduce where it was because of what you observed on the screen?" Archie asked.

"The latter. I've moved my eyes across every millimeter of the glass and from this vantage point I am unable to see anything on the surface that looks out of the ordinary," he admitted.

Smythe-Pembrooke had picked up the glass and carefully examined the surface before shrugging and passing it to Miles who went through the same motions.

"Right. Remember I said it was clear? It's also non-reflective. Even if you were holding the glass you'd be hard pressed to discover it. Perhaps by feel, if you have sensitive finger tips, but very unlikely by eyesight alone. Had we played the video all the way to the end, you would have seen a lot of movement and sky when I lifted the glass to take a sip."

The glass finally reached Sir Warren who, in turn, mimicked what his colleagues had done. He held the base of the glass in his right hand and used his left hand to rotate it clockwise. Then he went a step further and checked the rim for a pressure print from Archie's lips. When he found it he lined up the glass to approximately where it had been on the table, taking care to have the lip print relatively lined up with Archie.

Miles, Smythe-Pembrooke along with Archie and Megan watched him in silence. Once he felt he had the proper alignment he again lifted the glass, holding it in the proper perspective and brought it forward, very close to his face at eye level. Nearly a half-minute passed as he darted his eyes from one place to another.

"I've got it," he announced ". . .right . . . here ..." and began moving his finger to ward the spot.

"Wait, Sir Warren. Hold that pose." Megan interrupted as she opened the computer and entered the coded keystrokes again. The screen was practically full of his nose and partial right and left eyes.

"You should come around here and watch this," she said to Miles and Smythe-Pembrooke. In an instant they were leaning over her shoulder. Archie simply inclined his body toward her.

"Go ahead, Sir, carry on. Touch it," she said.

Sir Warren slowly advanced his left index finger toward the spot. As the tip of his digit closed in the center of the screen, it grew very dark until it was totally covered. When he removed his finger he turned the glass toward the other four and asked, "Is it still working? I tried not to press very hard."

"Yes, yes indeed" Archie replied, pointing to the screen. We're all there, sharp and clear."

Sir Warren handed the glass to Archie, who promptly deposited it in his attaché case as Megan once again shut the computer down.

"I'll go through the laborious task of trying to remove the FOTT for reuse later," he explained.

"I trust that's not the only one you have?" Miles asked.

"No, father. We have a sheet of them about the size of an index card. Perhaps 500 or so on it. I haven't counted them, but I think that's a good ballpark figure. I suggest we retrieve and reuse them whenever possible. Once these are gone, that's it."

Sir Warren turned to Megan. "Did your man know how far along the Chinese are with this? From what we've just seen, it seems quite ready now."

"Actually the Chinese abandoned this model and are trying to develop a larger one of the exact same composition that's easier to handle. This size is a devil to work with, and it doesn't have audio capabilities. The one they are replacing it with will."

"No sound? But we heard sound." Smythe-Pembrooke noted.

"Only because Megan was using a parabolic receiver we synchronized with the FOTT. That's the drawback. With this we can see anything we want once it is in place wherever. But if we need to hear what's being said we'll have to have an audio receiver shoot the signal to a relay transmitter and do the sync in a mobile unit."

"Why a mobile unit?" Sir Warren asked.

"Well, it makes sense, and provides the kind of personnel security we spoke of earlier. For instance: suppose we plant four or so FOTT dots in Highgrove to pick up the princess in the rooms she most frequents. Each would have its own digitized GPS code and could be projected onto a bank of screens. It would be like the control room at a TV station. We already have a stationary parabolic, permanently nested in a tree facing the residence, which picks up conversations anywhere in the house. The mobile unit, a medium size lorry, could even be ten or more miles away. The video feeds and the audio would be matched in the lorry."

"I'm very impressed, not only in what you have brought us, Archie and Megan, but with your technical expertise and creative endeavors to make this functional for our purposes." Sir Warren said. He shook both their hands, as did Miles and Smythe-Pembrooke. The group returned to their individual seats.

"I wish I knew how far along the Chinese were with their larger model, and when they intend to put it into service. If the North

Koreans had a mole in their system you can bet the Russians and Americans are there too, or not far behind. Once Beijing has the larger model up and running the spy game becomes a different animal for all of us."

For the first time since Archie arrived, there was absolute silence on the terrace as each of them contemplated the implications of what Sir Warren had just said. During the lull the butler returned with a tray of drinks, including a Bloody Mary for Megan, remembered from a previous trip. Once served, he again departed.

"Sir? I think we should waste no time getting FOTT dots in as many prime locations as we can as soon as possible. And Highgrove would be first on my list." Megan said.

"I agree," Sir Warren replied without hesitation. He usually took suggestions, no matter how sound, under consideration and afterward dissected them every which way from Sunday with Smythe-Pembrooke and a handful of others on and off The Committee. But Megan's suggestion to quickly install FOTT dots in Highgrove and the urgency to have seemingly unlimited access to Diana, the so-called 'enemy camp,' was paramount now. Developments were rapidly racing downhill to an inevitable disaster. She seemed hell-bent on embarrassing the Crown.

"How soon can you accomplish that?" he asked Archie, and added, "Without Megan. I understand SIS has her scheduled for something significant, in another security area, and she won't be available to you." He turned to her.

"I'm sorry, my dear. I'm sure you'd prefer to continue with this and see what develops, but my hands are tied. You're needed elsewhere for something the director is keen about."

Megan was stunned by the disclosure, but knew better than to question it. The vagueness of Sir Warren's comments meant that whatever the assignment was it was obviously on a 'need to know,' and that excluded the other three people on the terrace. And though she felt certain Sir Warren knew more than he was saying, Megan knew even she wouldn't learn the details till the director told her.

Likewise, Archie was surprised at the announcement but didn't hesitate to respond accordingly.

"I believe we can do it very quickly. Diana won't be back in the country for a week. Just as soon as I can get into Highgrove, it'll be done. Could be a day or two."

"Good, get hopping on it. Have some trusted people carry out the actual leg work, getting into the place and all that, while you supervise from a distance and work up a list of other locations. We'll do likewise at our end," he indicated to Miles and Smythe-Pembrooke then glanced at his watch.

"Now, you two should make your departure with as much stealth as your arrival. Our wives will be returning shortly from the shopping spree they've been busy with." Then directly looking into Archie's eyes, he added. "I trust I made myself perfectly clear about your role: I don't want you physically involved or even anywhere near Highgrove when your man installs these FOTT things."

Archie concurred, then, he and Megan bid their final goodbyes, collected their gear and were gone. Once they were off the terrace and out of sight, Sir Warren told his two companions.

"I think we're going to have a marvelous weekend." He hoisted his glass with a smiling "Cheers!"

****

As he was wont to do, Bat picked up the desk phone in his New York office on the second ring and learned from Charlie Stone, the senior agent he reported to, that his long-missing informer on St. Kitts had finally been located. The badly decomposed and charred bodies of the 23 year old son of a local politician, and the man's lover, had been discovered.

For Bat, so much time had passed and so many other assignments were wedged in his mental file between that Nevis trip and what he was presently doing the that revelation caused far less excitement than it would have two years earlier.

The bodies, actually skeletons, had been found in a burnt car hidden under the rubble in the ruins of an 18th century sugar mill in a highly grown cane field. Both had died from gunshot wounds to the backs of their head. The disclosure had come from regular Scotland

Yard detectives who had been on the island for some months tracking down drug traffickers. DNA had been employed for positive identification.

Nonetheless, in the days and weeks which followed Charlie Stone's call, this new information permitted CIA teams to resume chasing down a number of leads in the original case. But once again their efforts all came to one frustrating dead end after another. Soon months and seasons also passed and another year had fallen from the calendar. And despite their best efforts, and with the assistance of Interpol, so many promising leads came up empty.

But this day, after finishing the conversation with Stone, Bat felt restless. He couldn't put himself in the necessary mental state to concentrate on the work at hand. Instead, he decided to tend to some 'house cleaning' and put a serious dent in the pile of unread newspapers that his secretary always collected and saved when he was away on a trip. The pile had become formidable. He rarely touched it.

Besides being useless for information of value, it was a blight to his otherwise neat and orderly office. He separated the stack into two piles and lifted what had been the bottom to his desk, face down, so he could quickly glance at and dispatch the oldest papers first.

Before beginning the task, he poured himself a cup of coffee from the little machine within reach on the wide window sill behind his desk. Then he turned the pile of newspapers over and began flipping through them. He noticed, but didn't read, an item mentioning Prince Charles and something called 'Camillagate.' Though celebrity gossip was of no interest to him, Bat was sure that whatever it was his sister would surely know. Peggy was what Megan Price had called a 'royal watcher'.

Without deliberately recalling it, his mind produced the image of Megan, her red hair aflame in the sunlight, crossing the lawn toward the terrace and car park at Hermitage Plantation the last time he saw her. It was a pleasant image.

But now that Caribbean interlude all seemed so long ago. Bat wondered if SIS was still misspending Megan's field agent abilities on their petty surveillance of Princess Diana?

****

Archie Blair prided himself in keeping physically fit. Fortunately, he was one of those people nearly everyone resented because he had the ability to eat as much of anything he wanted without ever gaining a pound. Some called him thin or skinny or, because his weight was accented by his height, 'a tall drink of water.' But according to the actuary charts, he was carrying the proper weight for his six-feet-two-inch frame.

Nonetheless, he worked out at a gym regularly to keep his muscles toned and his reflexes ever at the ready. Though Blair lived not far from Kensington Palace, the gym that he went to was, by intent, not Earls Court Gym, nor Chelsea Harbour Gym or any of the others reportedly frequented by the Princess of Wales.

Archie was on the weight bench doing repetition sets when Leslie Wilford came over.

"Hello, Archie. Seems you're here as much as the owner."

"Hi Leslie. I don't know about that, but more often than you, I'm pretty sure of that." He exhaled several short puffs before continuing, "And with that pot belly you're growing, you should be more often."

"No thank you. I'm nearly your father's age. I don't ever recall seeing him here. And the last time I saw him he was starting to sag around the middle. As for me, I have no desire to be the healthiest man in the cemetery."

"And how is dear old dad? I take it you see more of him than I do."

"I sincerely doubt that. After all, you're in the intelligence business, and your father, along with Sir Warren Wormsley, Smythe-Pembrooke, and the rest of that bunch who consider themselves the Praetorian Guard, are very keen about intelligence matters. Especially matters concerning the Prince and Princess of Wales."

Archie hoisted the barbell to its rack and snapped up into a sitting position. He looked around, unsuccessfully, for his towel. Wilford pulled his own towel from around his neck and handed it to him. Archie grunted a '*thanks*' as he wiped first his face and neck.

"Leslie, I have no idea what you're talking about." Blair vigorously rubbed his hair with the towel. "If you know anything about the intelligence community, and I suspect you do, you know we do not discuss such matters with civilians, or even others in the service, unless they have a 'need to know.' He quickly ran the towel across his chest, then moved it vigorously over both arms.

"Oh, come now, Archie. I've seen photocopies of the reports with the agents' names blackened out . . . well, at least those reports Sir Warren wants to share with The Committee. Anyway, I can understand why the authors' names are kept secret."

"Really? You know more about all this than I do. Suppose other agents do in fact file such reports, what's it to me? My father never mentions what he does, or even who he sees, when he goes to his club, or wherever it is you seem to think he and Sir Warren are discussing affairs of state."

"Affairs of State?" Wilford gave him a sarcastic smile raised an eyebrow in amusement. "That's a proper thing to call The Committee's machinations. . ." His words trailed off.

Archie lifted himself up from the bench and began walking toward the registration desk with its several bottles of water on the counter. Leslie kept pace with him.

"You keep referring to some 'Committee.' What's that all about? I know the clubs and boards my father belongs to and none of them have any sort of ominous agenda such as you are suggesting." Archie grabbed two bottles and offered one to Wilford, who declined. He twisted the cap on his own bottle and took several short gulps.

"You know perfectly well what I mean. You know what The Committee is, and that your father is part of it, as am I."

Archie removed the bottle from his lips and tapped it on Wilford's chest.

"You might want to be more careful about what you admit to, Leslie. Assuming, of course, such a group exists." He turned and walked to an area of the gym where no one else was. Wilford stayed with him.

"Alright Archie, I'll cut right to the chase: I'm convinced you are one of the rogue agents in Sir Warren's stable doing surveillance on Diana."

"Just Diana, not Charles as well?" Archie tried to make light of the comment.

"Don't play coy or cute with me, Archie. Your father, and the rest of Sir Warren's gang, are on a dangerous course. I suspect it's because of much of what's being reported to them."

"You are obsessed with this imaginary 'Committee' thing, Leslie. Such delusional fantasies are not good for a man of your age. It makes you appear irrational. And keep your voice down."

"Obsessed? Irrational? That's odd, those are the exact words I would use to describe what your father and the others!"

"A few moments ago you said you were a member, too, remember?"

"Yes, I am. And I'll admit participating in some downright horrible and dishonorable things over the years. The kinds of things civilized gentlemen do not do. But that's in the past. I'm willing to pay the piper for my indiscretions. Better late than never, they say. However, I won't sit silently by and be part of a conspiracy to have the Princess of Wales labeled insane so she can be taken away from her children and committed to an asylum. That was actually suggested at a recent meeting."

Archie looked deep into Wilford's eyes. "Surely you must be mistaken, it was probably said in jest, a sick joke." What he saw was a man desperately wrestling with his conscience.

"How could such an outlandish thing be accomplished?" Archie asked.

"With drugs. One of your MI-5 or MI-6 confederates, I never know which, could introduce an untraceable drug over a period of time. Slowly but surely, Diana would fall into an increasing stupor. After a few well arranged public instances, perhaps even a faked suicide attempt, the Palace would announce she had a breakdown and have her sent to a private sanitarium. I won't have any part of that, I tell you. I won't!"

"Leslie, Leslie, it's a nightmare. That's all." Archie grabbed Wilford by the shoulders and shook him gently.

"You had a nightmare. Nothing like that could ever happen. . ."

"Tell me such a drug doesn't exist. Tell me you've never heard about it." Wilford demanded.

Archie blinked in surprise. "No, I've never heard about a drug like that, or such a plan to dope up somebody."

"Well, I have. It was in a report. The drug, and the scenario I just mentioned, in a report I saw at the last Committee meeting." Wilford declared.

"Was my father there?" Archie asked.

"Yes, but he didn't see it. None of the others did with the exception, perhaps, of Smythe-Pembrooke. Warren shares a lot with him that the rest of us are not privy to. It was when we had broken for lunch and everyone else had left the room for the dining area. I'm nosy and I happened to see there was still something left in the Manila folder where Sir Warren sits. He must have mistakenly picked it up with other papers when he prepared for the meeting. They're certainly capable of doing such a thing, or worse. Remember what they did to that policeman."

"What policeman?"

"That bodyguard she carried on with, before Gilbey or Hewitt. Mannakee, his name was. He was a sergeant."

Archie furrowed his brow in thought but couldn't connect the name and a face. Though he vaguely recalled hearing several years earlier about a former security staffer being killed in a car accident.

"Leslie, I'm certain I have absolutely no idea whom you're talking about. I'm drawing a complete blank."

"You must remember. How could you forget something like that?"

"I didn't forget about it, I never knew about it!"

Wilford looked deep into his eyes for several seconds and, just as Archie was about to break off the conversation, something occurred to Wilford.

"When was your active service in the military?" he asked.

"1985-88, and I joined SIS as soon as I got out" Archie responded without hesitation, adding "But I was also reactivated, at the behest of SIS, for intelligence work during the Gulf War."

"That's it! The poor sod was killed back then, around '87, while you were away soldiering, before you were in SIS."

"Thank you, Leslie, I was starting to wonder how I could not recall anything like that. Tell me what you know, and why you think this man's death has the imprint of your so-called Committee."

"It was simple enough, actually. Diana used this fellow as a shoulder to cry on," Leslie replied "By this time, surveillance on her was already substantial. She told him everything. They became close, even members of the Kensington Palace staff were saying it was odd and not proper. I heard the tapes, your father did as well. The whole thing was the subject of scandalous conjecture on The Committee. Prince Charles got wind of it. I believe Sir Warren made a point of personally delivering copies to Buckingham Palace."

He paused briefly then added, "Anyway, the upshot of the thing was Mannakee was relieved of any royal duties and assigned to other police work. He was killed in an automobile accident not long thereafter. Absolutely criminal, that."

"And this 'Committee,' your committee, you say they arranged the accident? They did away with this man?"

"I can't prove it. No vote was taken to terminate him, just a lot of outrage and disgust in the Committee over his carryings on with Diana . . .and even that left considerable room for doubt."

"So you're saying no order was ever given to murder the man and make it look like an accident?"

"That's right. But I've always had my suspicions. Others have too."

"Well, Leslie, as much as I doubt that there's anything to the whole story, if it makes you feel any better, I'll bring it up with my father, along with the subject of this mystery drug report you saw in Sir Warren's folder." Archie and Leslie had begun walking towards the men's dressing room and gym's showers.

"Yes. . . you must. He'll believe you about the plan to drug Diana. Tell him exactly what I told you I saw. With him as an ally, I'm certain the two of us can convince the others on The Committee that Sir Warren is entertaining wild and dangerous suggestions from rogue members of the intelligence community."

"Okay, then, but promise me something, Leslie." Archie had his hand on the door to the dressing room, "Keep this to yourself. Don't whisper a word to anybody. If the report you speak about is genuine, I'll have my father find out. Then we can put our heads together, the three of us, and decide how to resolve this for everyone."

Leslie Wilford, smiled for the first time all day, albeit a weak smile. He gave Archie an appreciative 'thank you,' turned and left.

Archie watched the older man make his way to the exit. He didn't need to shower. Though dressed in a jump suit, Wilford had not exercised. The towel he removed from his neck and handed to Archie was fresh and clean. His reason for visiting the gym was to approach Archie. And it was obvious he expected the information and suspicions he voiced to be passed along to the elder Blair. Which was exactly what Archie intended to do.

****

The holiday respite in the Caribbean with her sons seemed like ages ago to Diana as well. A fantasy escape from reality in an earlier life. From the moment the plane carrying the Princess of Wales and her two sons touched down at Heathrow Airport, the media were once again all over her like a rug. Unlike the arrangement she had with the paparazzi on Nevis, the competitive, insatiable clamor for royal photos and news was far greater here in the U.K. And as more and more lurid details of the deep chasm in the royal marriage surfaced, it seemed to feed off itself and actually increase. It was no longer just the scandalous tabloids framing the obvious breakup of the royal marriage as Britain's greatest soap opera. Mainstream media couldn't resist the temptation to increase circulation with this gift from the House of Windsor.

Briefly, early on in the marriage, trips abroad and holidays had been a marvelous fantasy escape from the crushing pressure of life in the royal fish bowl. But always, the moment Diana set foot again in the land and world her mother-in-law ruled, she was confronted by reality. As the flame of fairy tale romance noticeably flickered in public, arriving home after being abroad always brought a barrage of media questions and accusations.

Actually, the speculation had been brewing for some time before the separation was announced. When Diana and Charles were photographed seated together, but with space between them, during an official visit to Toronto in October, 1991, the press said it suggested they were cool towards each other and not on the best of terms. Questions followed upon their return.

When Diana and Charles visited India in February, 1992, and photos were taken in front of the Taj Mahal, the press questioned if there was a hidden message in the fact that instead of a lovey-dovey photograph of a romantic royal couple at the world famous monument to love, the Princess of Wales was alone.

In May, 1992, she was photographed alone in front of the Pyramids of Giza during her first official trip to Egypt. It was two months short of her and Charles' eleventh wedding anniversary. Media pundits pointed out that the Princess was making more and more trips abroad without her husband and quipped that their expressed 'eternal love' for each other wouldn't endure the way the pyramids had.

At first, the shouted questions were the same ones hurled at her immediately after it was announced that she and Charles were separating. But as time went by they became more profound and speculative: *Are you getting divorced? . . . Who asked for the separation, you or Prince Charles? . . . Have you spoken to the Queen about a divorce? . . . Do you think Charles and Camilla will marry once you're divorced? . . . Tell us about* (they would use the name of whomever she was currently seeing or seen in public with). *Do you love him? Will you remarry someday? Will the boys live with you or Charles? . . .*

If Diana had been relieved to see the year 1992 come to end while she and her sons holidayed on Nevis, her mother-in-law harbored the same feelings. The Queen had called 1992 her *annus horribilis*, her horrible year, and with proper cause. During that year, Elizabeth II had to suffer through announcements that all three of her married children were headed for divorce.

Prince Andrew and Sarah separated after the press ran stories about her infidelity, but not a word about his philandering.

As early as March, nine months before it was officially announced, *The Sun* published a story that Diana and Charles would separate as well.

Anne, the Princess Royal, and Mark Phillips were the first to be divorced after a two-and-a-half-year separation. Both had taken up with lovers.

Then, days before the newly divorced Princess Anne was to marry Royal Navy officer Commander Timothy Lawrence, with whom she had carried on a five year affair, a disastrous fire at Windsor Castle added a public royal sorrow to the Queen's personal discomfort.

But the final, and perhaps most stunning and embarrassing blow came that last month of the year when *The Mirror*, one of the U.K. scandal tabloids, published transcripts of a lurid New Year's Eve 1989 secretly taped conversation between the Prince of Wales and his married mistress. The shocking record of their intimate conversation was quickly called "Camillagate." These transcripts followed by four months the publication of the illegally monitored romantic phone conversation between Diana and James Gilbey, friend, admirer, and wannabe lover. He called her 'Squidgy' on the secretly recorded phone call, which instantly became known as "Squidgygate". In the conversation, Gilbey called the princess "Darling" 53 times and "Squidgy" 14 times. Not even Sir Warren's vast surveillance capabilities could say for sure if Diana and Gilbey's relationship remained platonic or ever became intimate.

An automobile salesman by profession, what Gilbey lacked in prominent social standing meant little to Diana. She found Gilbey to be humorous and fun loving, quite different from her usually stiff and serious husband's public, and private, persona. Diana counted on Gilbey to be a sounding board, someone she could pour her heart out to, during her frequent lapses into depression and personal crisis.

But the revelations and innuendos in the Princess of Wales' 'Squidgygate' telephone conversation were mild in comparison to the raw and uncensored utterances the Prince of Wales and his married mistress had over the burning phone lines.

In the heat of passion, some would reason, lovers often make very detailed, intimate, sexual comments to each other during foreplay or as pillow-talk. Sometimes, when they are apart and as preamble to a rendezvous, they commit such things to the telephone.

But no matter, supporters of Prince Charles said in his defense, these intimacies should rightfully be shared privately by the two parties concerned, not scandalously published by the media. Yet, for a media bent on a royal feeding frenzy nothing was considered private any more, especially if the subjects were members of the Royal Family.

As the 'Camillagate' transcript revealed, there was some pedestrian chit-chat during Charles and Camilla's phone call. But it was the vividly detailed carnal conversation that dropped the bomb.

What Diana, the Queen, and the rest of the interested world of 'royal watchers' read brought the Princess of Wales to tears and her mother-in-law to a near fit of rage.

The intimate conversation was recorded during Charles' visit to the Duchess of Westminster's Cheshire home. She is the 'Nancy' who is mentioned. Camilla was at her home, Bolehyde Manor. The recorded portion of the conversation lasts six minutes. Sir Warren felt if anyone believed the conversation had been a chance accident they were naive. The tape was recorded on Monday, December 17th, 1989, verified by Camilla mentioning her son Tom's birthday the following day, December 18, 1974. This suggests MI-5 recorded it at that time and then broadcast it so some ham-radio operator would pick it up and make it public. Whoever authorized its release was no friend of The Committee. He read the excerpted transcript again:

Camilla: Mmm. You're awfully good at feeling your way along.

Prince Charles: Oh stop! I want to feel my way along you, all over you and up and down and in and out.

Camilla: Oh.

Prince Charles: ... particularly in and out.

Camilla: Oh, that's just what I need at the moment.

Prince Charles: Is it?

Camilla: I know it would revive me. I can't bear a Sunday

night without you.

    Prince Charles: Oh god.

    Camilla: It's like that program *Start The Week.* I can't stand the week without you.

    Prince Charles: I fill up your tank!

    Camilla: Yes you do!

    Prince Charles: Then you can cope.

    Camilla: Then I'm all right.

    Prince Charles: What about me? The trouble is I need you several times a week.

    Camilla: Mmm. So do I. I need you all the week. All the time.

    Prince Charles: Oh, god. I'll just live inside your trousers or something. It would be much easier!

    Camilla: (laughs) What are you going to turn into, a pair of knickers?

    (both laugh). Oh, you're going to come back as a pair of knickers.

    Prince Charles: Or, God forbid, a Tampax. Just my luck! (laughs).

    Camilla: You are a complete idiot! (laughs). Oh what a wonderful idea!

    Prince Charles: My luck to be chucked down a lavatory and go on and on forever swirling round on the top, never going down!

    Camilla: (laughing) Oh darling!

    Prince Charles: Until the next one comes through.

    Camilla: Oh, perhaps you could just come back as a box.

    Prince Charles: What sort of box?

    Camilla: A box of Tampax so you could just keep going.

    Prince Charles: That's true.

    Camilla: Repeating yourself. (laughing) Oh, darling. Oh I just want you now.

    Prince Charles: Do you?

    Camilla: Mmm.

    Prince Charles: So do I.

    Camilla: Desperately, desperately. I thought of you so much

at Yaraby.

     Prince Charles: Did you.?

     Camilla: Simply mean we couldn't be there together.

     Prince Charles: Desperate. If you could be here, I long to ask Nancy sometimes.

     Camilla: Why don't you?

     Prince Charles: I daren't.

     Camilla: Because I think she's so in love with you.

     Prince Charles: Mmm.

     Camilla: She'd do anything you asked.

     Prince Charles: She'd tell all sorts of people.

     Camilla: No she wouldn't, because she'd be much too frightened of what you might say to her.

     I think you've got, I'm afraid it's a terrible thing to say, but I think, you know, those sort of people do feel very strongly about you. You've got such a great hold over her.

     Prince Charles: Really?

     Camilla: And you're . . . I think as usual you're underestimating yourself.

     Prince Charles: But she might be terribly jealous or something.

     Camilla: Oh! (laughs) Now that is a point! I wonder, she might be, I suppose.

     Prince Charles: You never know, do you?

     Camilla: Darling . . .

     Prince Charles: But I, oh God, when am I going to speak to you?

     Camilla: I can't bear it. Um . . .

     Prince Charles: Wednesday night?

     Camilla: Oh, certainly Wednesday night. I'll be alone, um, Wednesday, you know, the evening. Or Tuesday. While you're rushing around doing things, I'll be, you know, alone until it reappears. And early Wednesday morning, I mean, he'll be leaving at half-past eight, quarter-past eight. He won't be here.

     Camilla: It would be so wonderful to have just one night to set us on our way, wouldn't it?

Prince Charles: Wouldn't it? To wish you a happy Christmas.

Camilla: (indistinct) happy. Oh, don't let's think about Christmas. I can't bear it. (pause) Going to go to sleep? I think you'd better, don't you? Darling?

Prince Charles: (sleepy) Yes, darling?

Camilla: I think you've exhausted yourself by all that hard work. You must go to sleep now. Darling?

Prince Charles: (sleepy) Yes, darling?

Camilla: Will you ring me when you wake up?

Prince Charles: Yes I will.

Camilla: I do love you.

Prince Charles: (sleepily) Before . . .

Camilla: Before about half-past eight.

Prince Charles: Try and ring?

Camilla: Yeah, if you can. Love you darling.

Prince Charles: Night darling.

Camilla: I love you.

Prince Charles: Love you too. I don't want to say goodbye.

Camilla: Well done for doing that, you're a clever old thing. An awfully good brain lurking there, isn't there? Oh darling, I think you ought to give the brain a rest now. Night night.

Prince Charles: Night darling. God bless.

Camilla: I do love you and I'm so proud of you.

Prince Charles: Oh, I'm so proud of you.

Camilla: Don't be so silly, I've never achieved anything.

Prince Charles: Yes you have.

Camilla: No I haven't.

Prince Charles: Your great achievement is to love me.

Camilla: Oh, darling. Easier than falling off a chair.

Prince Charles: You suffer all these indignities and tortures and calumnies

Camilla: Oh, darling, don't be so silly. I'd suffer anything for you. That's love. It's the strength of love. Night night.

Prince Charles: Night, darling. Sounds as though you're dragging an enormous piece of string behind you with hundreds of tin pots and cans attached to it. I think it must be your telephone.

Night night, before the battery goes. (blows kiss) Night.
>Camilla: Love you.
>Prince Charles: Don't want to say goodbye.
>Camilla: Bye.
>Prince Charles: Going.
>Camilla: Gone.
>Prince Charles: Night.
>Camilla: Bye. Press the button
>Prince Charles: Going to press the tit.
>Camilla: All right darling, I wish you were pressing mine.
>Prince Charles: God, I wish I was. Harder and harder.
>Camilla: Oh darling.
>Prince Charles: Night.
>Camilla: (yawning) Love you. Press the tit.
>Prince Charles: Adore you. Night.
>Camilla: Night.
>Prince Charles: Night.
>Camilla: (blows a kiss).
>Prince Charles: Night.
>Camilla: G'night my darling I love you.

This newly revealed eavesdropping, coupled with the shocking dialog in the illegally gotten phone tap of Diana's romantic phone transcripts, left no doubt that there truly was, as the popular West Indian song Diana had heard and laughed at on Nevis, a *Scandal In The Family.* And such unpleasant things only exacerbated Sir Warren's blood pressure.

He neatly folded the newspaper and tucked it under his arm. He wanted to get this meeting with Austin Smythe-Pembrooke over with as quickly as possible. Though Sir Warren was comfortably seated in the rear compartment of his Rolls, he anticipated the sudden chill that would blast his face when he exited the car. Even as he was thinking this he recognized the moving profile of the sleek Jaguar crossing Westminster Bridge and making an immediate right turn. The driver pulled up to the curb in the opposite direction, perhaps five car lengths across the way. Unlike Sir Warren who was chauffeured everywhere he went, Smythe-Pembrooke preferred to drive his own car.

It was becoming late in the day, and dusk would be upon them shortly. Though Sir Warren was certain the Jaguar was Smythe-Pembrooke's, he nonetheless told his chauffeur to flash the Rolls headlights in the usual way. *If you expect people to follow rules you must be prepared to follow them yourself!* He told others, that when dealing with subordinates, he always lived by that code. . . when it was convenient.

The expected headlight response came from Smythe-Pembrooke's vehicle and both men left the comfort of their cars for the cold January embrace of a meeting along the Thames. Both walking briskly, they were upon each other in short order. Sir Warren had left his gloves on the seat of the car. He shoved his chilled hands deep into the pockets of his Cashmere topcoat.

"Really, Warren, this is a bit melodramatic, don't you think? Meeting by the river, in the shadow of Big Ben on a January day cold enough to freeze one's balls off?" A continuous volley of white steam rolled from his mouth.

"What I'm going to tell you requires the utmost secrecy," Sir Warren replied without having taken any offense to Smythe-Pembrooke's remarks. His words and breath also turned to telltale steam. "We can't be casual or lackadaisical about such things." He pulled the copy of *The Sun* from under his arm and proffered it.

"Have you seen this smut?" Sir Warren asked.

"Charles and Camilla's telephone sex?' Smythe-Pembrooke asked.

Sir Warren simply nodded rapidly. The cold was getting to him much faster than he thought.

"No, but everyone in the office seemed to be talking about it all day so I know the juicy details," he said gruffly, adding, "Some bugger snatched my paper before I got to read it." He accepted the copy Sir Warren had offered, then added "Christ Almighty, Warren, is *that* what this meeting's about. . ."

"No, no, certainly not. We'll discuss this new royal information at the next Committee meeting. I called you about something of immediate and dire consequences to the Crown and The Committee: something that borders on treason . . . dangerous to the monarchy, by one of our own."

Smythe-Pembrooke stopped in his tracks and half turned to face Sir Warren.

"Treason? Are you serious, man? Who?"

"I have it from unimpeachable sources, actually monitored telephone conversations between our Leslie Wilford and inside contacts at *The Sun* and other papers. I've suspected this for some time, even before the Morton book came out. But I wasn't able to prove it and confront him." Sir Warren paused briefly for effect. Very briefly, the cold was causing his teeth to start chattering. The tale he was telling Smythe-Pembrooke was pure fabrication. But it was the necessary prologue for the real information he was about to reveal. Sir Warren wanted an iron-clad reason to collect Pembrooke's support for what Sir Warren had in mind.

He resumed his accusations, "It seems our Leslie has been feeding the media the most sensitive information The Committee has been privy to," Sir Warren continued "I suspect the poor man's gone daft. He recently confronted young Blair at the gymnasium they both frequent and mentioned he'd been sneaking around my office and seen that drug report. Furthermore, he blabbed his suspicions about the policeman, Mannakee, who died in a motoring accident several years ago. He told Blair he suspected we, The Committee, were behind it."

"Oh my God. The man has truly taken leave of his senses," Pembrooke was stunned.

"My great fear is that when nothing comes of his tattling to Blair, he'll run to his cronies in the media and repeat such things to them! It is unlikely they will be unable to substantiate anything at first. But if some busy beaver really does some digging, who knows what can surface under dedicated scrutiny? Even just the rumor of these things could bring us all to ruination, perhaps some even to prison."

"Prison? What could he tell them, and prove that would threaten us with that?"

"Oh, just a few other sudden and unexpected 'accidents,' over the years, which, I remind you The Committee considered totally justified as clear and present dangers to the image of the monarchy."

Smythe-Pembrooke reflected on what Sir Warren had said. "My God, man, we've always covered our tracks . . ."

"Perhaps," Sir Warren interrupted. "But with a little effort, Wilford is capable, and apparently willing, to explain in precise detail how even that was accomplished. You'll recall that, before this sudden change in him, Wilford was a very active and trusted member of The Committee." In the short time they were together, dusk had drifted closer to night.

"Why would he betray us? What possible reason could Wilford have for destroying us, and implicating himself as well?" Smythe-Pembrooke asked, "Surely, himself as well!" he added

"Maybe he's having some misguided conscience issues, that's what Archie told his father, or pangs of regret, or guilt feelings, or perhaps he hopes to cut an amnesty deal for himself, whatever. Miles was outraged when he repeated to me what his son told him."

"I could imagine, as I am now."

"But, Austin, you've certainly observed Wilford's obvious hostility and eagerness to challenge even the most trivial items at Committee meetings. Could be he now fancies himself as a reformed moderate. If I didn't take the precaution of having the room swept for surveillance recording devices at the start of our meetings I'd think there were times he was wearing a wire."

"He has to be out of his mind to betray us, are you certain?" Smythe-Pembrooke asked still in partial denial.

"As certain as I am that Elizabeth is our Queen and we've inherited the mantle to protect the monarchy from those who came before us. I absolutely trust Miles and Archie Blair, none of this is fabrication or nervous Nelly stuff." Sir Warren kept silent for several steps as they walked. He wanted his words to sink in. Then when he thought he had given Smythe-Pembrooke sufficient time to reflect on what he had said, Sir Warren continued:

"Wilford has been more of an obstruction than a team player for some time now. I really don't care what trumped up reasoning he is using to justify his deplorable conduct. He's now our very dangerous and very loose cannon and must be warned in no uncertain terms. Something shocking. Something to shake him up, wake him out of this insane stupor. If that fails to bring him around, we'll have to consider other ways for dealing with him once and for all. And all options, all solutions, are on the table."

"Why wait? We need to ring the little bastard's neck!" Smythe-Pembrooke had taken the bait, as Sir Warren knew he would. Next to members of the Royal Family, Sir Warren was regarded with enormous respect in proper circles. His thoughts and opinions were almost always readily taken as absolute fact by The Committee members and were rarely questioned, and never challenged. Except, in recent memory, Leslie Wilford.

"I can have some blokes way-lay him and beat the stuffing out of him before knocking him off!"

"No, Austin, that would obviously be murder and Scotland Yard would certainly thoroughly investigate the killing of a prominent former Member of Parliament. No, I think we should try to bring him around to his senses without actually getting physical.

"And just how could that be accomplished?" Pembrooke asked sarcastically.

"With a deliberate near-miss event. Something that makes him realize he is lucky to be alive and could have been killed if that had been our plan." Sir Warren paused. "Of course to achieve the results we want he will have to strongly suspect that someone on The Committee, most likely Miles Blair with help from his son Archie, was involved but cooler heads, probably yours and mine, intervened and prevailed at the last moment.

"Damn! Suppose he continues his blabbing?"

"Let's not mull over theoretical situations or things which will, hopefully, never come to pass. That's not what we're talking about today. We need to scare him so badly and so shockingly that temptations to continue misbehaving will never enter his mind again."

Pembrooke shook his head from side to side slowly. "It's risky. If you're positive he's betrayed us, we should do him in and have it over with."

"No Austin, I've thought this out and I'm convinced we should first try it my way," he demurred insincerely. "If I've miscalculated, then, when Leslie departs this world he should succumb in an accident. A neatly arranged and proper accident." Sir Warren could hardly stand the cold now. He had made match point, now all that remained was a final suggestion to push Smythe-Pembrooke to do it the way Sir Warren wanted it done, and the only way a hot head like Pembrooke would ever handle this kind of situation: termination.

"Are you still able to reach that rogue IRA chap with the electronic talent to remotely control one's car? O'Connor, I think his name is?"

"Oh, it's been three, maybe four, years since I learned about him, or even thought about him." Smythe-Pembrooke was impressed by Sir Warren's recall.

"He's a member of their lunatic fringe. A lot of the IRA wants no part of him. He's not really a regular in the accepted sense . . ."

"I don't care if he is a member of the Pope's bodyguard. Can you make contact with him?"

"I've never met him personally. We just reached out to him that other time through a Constable who knew him. But the man is dead now." Smythe-Pembrooke paused, obviously in thought, then added:

"Wait a minute. There just may be a way. I think I have somebody who might very well be able to make contact," Smythe-Pembrooke continued ". . . yes, I think we can reach him. But I don't fancy us getting involved with those IRA killers again. Especially O'Connor. We really can't trust them. And O'Connor, I don't doubt for a moment that he'd pop any of us off if he had the inclination."

"It's a risk, to be sure, but at times like this they can be terribly useful. Use caution and create some kind of story about Wilford being an immediate threat to them. Impress upon your man that it's imperative O'Connor believe what he tells the bastard. And then we'll make sure Leslie learns of the assassination attempt at the very last minute so, when O'Connor's plan goes amuck, then it's publicly reported as just an unsuccessful terrorist incident. And, to Leslie, we are heroes for saving his life," Sir Warren lied.

Pembrooke stopped walking and turned toward Sir Warren. "Of course, right and proper heroes. I think I have someone O'Connor will trust to pass along 'inside' information he'll be certain to act on. . ."

"Good. . . good." Sir Warren quickly cut off the conversation. "I'll leave the details and arrangements in your capable hands. Let me know when things are in the works." Then, without missing a beat he changed the subject.

"I want to call a full Committee meeting once we know how this latest royal scandal is unwinding," he tapped *The Sun*, now under Smythe-Pembrooke's arm, then added with a shudder. "I'm freezing."

"Me too." Pembrooke admitted.

Sir Warren turned away and rapidly headed for the warmth of his car. Pembrooke did likewise.

As Sir Warren's chauffeur came around and opened the door for him, Big Ben tolled the hour and a flock of pigeons suddenly took flight from the barren trees nearby and arched into a wide circle as they flew out over the Thames. As many Londoners were wont to do, Sir Warren glanced at the clock and checked his watch to confirm the time. Old pennies act as counterweights to ensure Big Ben keeps time to the nearest second. When Parliament sits by night a light in the Clock Tower burns above Big Ben. This night there was no light.

Once comfortably seated in the Rolls and vigorously rubbing his hands together to generate warmth, Sir Warren noticed bird droppings had soiled one of the sleeves on his Cashmere topcoat.

Filthy little winged bastards, he thought.

****

Bat Lynch, continuing his ongoing cover of a travel guide book editor, was in his private office at the publishing company's Manhattan office complex in the Empire State Building and, with nothing urgent on his plate, he was daydreaming.

In the years which had passed since Bat Lynch's aborted meeting with the missing informer on St. Kitts, he, and other members of the small CIA anti-terrorist unit were now occupied with other duties. However, from time to time, they would assess other possible avenues and leads on what had become a very cold trail. The beard he had worn on Nevis so many years ago was now just a humorous memory. In many ways, his work at the agency had practically become clerical and he was bored. He rarely received undercover assignments anymore and he wondered if the botched and aborted assignment in St. Kitts and Nevis had been the reason, though he couldn't put his finger on any event or particular thing that could have provoked a change in his active status.

He found himself thinking about what it would be like to have a normal life, one out of the spy agency. He'd certainly have more time to date and be relaxed about making long-term commitments, perhaps even get serious with someone and marry. Life outside the CIA would be a life without fear of making a mistake or getting caught up in the litany of lies he was forced to tell to maintain his cover, he concluded. At least, he owed it to himself to explore the possibilities.

After all, he was a licensed pilot. It wouldn't take a lot to get a rating to fly corporate private jets, and the money was good. Then, too, with some five years undercover working on travel guides, he had learned by osmosis and proven he was a capable writer. Maybe a job as a real travel guide book writer or editor could be his niche.

Then there was photography, which he really enjoyed and was innately good at it. But could any of these careers provide the kind of income he had become use to? One way to find out. He telephoned an old colleague from before his days as a CIA operative.

"Higgins," The voice at the other end answered.

"William Himself. Bat Lynch here. How the hell are you?"

"Hey! Bat the Travel Editor, alive and well. Good to hear from you. What's up?"

"I caught a glimpse of you at the other end of the room a few months ago when I was leaving the Mexico Tourist Board reception early. But I was in a hurry to catch a plane and didn't have time to stop. I reminded myself to give you a call. So here it is."

"Damn it. Wish I had seen you earlier, we could have had a nice chat."

"Yeah, me too. But I just stopped in to make a brief appearance and stroke the U.S. manager. In and out. It was a quick stop. I was going down there, at their expense, to get some fresh photos of Chichen-Itza for the guide revision and the publisher thought a little ass-kissing was in order." In fact, the Chichen-Itza stop was the cover for Bat's real reason to be in Mexico, but Higgins would never know that.

"I saw a few flashes during the reception. Were you popping pictures there?"

"No, I don't do that kind of stuff. They hired Cancellari to get reception shots to send to the travel trade papers. That's his forte." Then, as an after thought, Bat added. "But I had my camera with me. Always do."

"Shucks, I wish I had seen you there. You could have told Cancellari to get a shot of me for the industry trade publications."

Bat made what sounded like an affirmative grunt. *How could I have missed you?* he thought.

Bill Higgins was a big man by anybody's standards. His 6' 3". height wasn't unusual, but his upwards of 350 pound girth made him a standout in any crowd. Before his military service Bat had been a novice photographer and Bill, a fresh out of college young writer with an entry level job at the same magazine. Now, a decade later, Higgins was managing editor at a men's outdoor adventure magazine.

"How did your Mexico trip go?"

"Okay, I guess. I got some good stuff, but that site has been photographed so much from just about every possible angle, and at different times of the day under every light condition, that I doubt anything I got is really new or original. Nonetheless, it was a good trip. I also shot a few rolls for an auto club magazine."

"Really? You do freelance? I didn't know that. I thought you just worked full time with the guide books."

"Most of the time that's all I do. But whenever I can piggy-back a freelance job onto something I'm traveling for anyway, then I do it if the bucks are right." Not said was that such 'freelance' work was also an excuse for Bat to wander around to other areas for his spy work.

"So what's new with you?" Bat changed the subject. Higgins, though quite likeable, had a tendency to brag and blow his own horn a lot. Bat gave him the floor."

"Well, something pretty flattering, actually. The communications office in The White House is dangling a writing job in front of me. They want my talent to help make The Man in the Oval Office sound more erudite when he opens his mouth, more Eastern Establishment. A truly impossible task for that Arkansas hick, don't you think? What they really should be doing is teaching him to keep his hands off every skirt that passes by."

Bat was a bit surprised at Higgins cutting reference to the President. "He seems to have done pretty well up to this point without you," Bat teased. "Furthermore, the guys writing for him now are not slouches." Bat's reply was intended to send Higgins a message that Lynch was the wrong person to join him in beating up on the President.

"True, Bat. But in politics you need to have backup people who are just as sharp as your first line. I think they'd like to get me on the team as insurance." The subtle message Bat Lynch had sent was not lost on Higgins.

"So are you going to do it?" Bat seriously doubted Higgins had a serious offer but he played along.

"Not on your life. I'm flattered that they would approach me, and I refuse to admit to myself they are probably talking to a half dozen other people, but no thanks, Charlie, political jobs are too risky. You're their darling one day and a bum they kick out the door the next. Anyway, Clinton is in his second term. I accepted the invite to go for an interview, because it pleases me and fits into my traveling schedule. And, confidentially, it could only improve my stock here at the magazine if the publisher gets wind that The White House is courting me."

"Now how, pray tell, could your publisher *ever* find out something like that?' Bat's facetious question caused both of them to chuckle.

Higgins let a few seconds pass then asked. "Bat, any chance you might want to pick up some more freelance money by shooting a role of film of some still life for my magazine? It's a rush job. I need to get someone real quick, if your work has gotten better. I just got a call that the guy I had can't make it. And I'm kind of out on a limb . . ."

Bat cut in before Higgins could finish: "Rush job? How rush?"

"Pronto. I need the pix in the next week."

"No thanks. A trip isn't possible now. I'm stuck in the office for the immediate future, tied up with galley revisions, cover art, etc. for two guides that are going on the press next week. Bad timing. Sorry," Bat lied. But it was the kind of suggestion or invitation he was hoping to get from this phone call. He felt good that Higgins would offer him freelance work. But if he left the agency would a full-time job be an option?

"Are you sure? It could be a good payday." Higgins added

"Yes, I'm sure. There's just no way I can do anything now. But please keep me in mind if anything else comes up. I'm seriously thinking about going into photography full-time. I'm better at it than writing."

"But you didn't even ask what the assignment is, or where it is! It's Belize. You can fly there, shoot my film and probably be out and back the same day."

"It's tempting, but I have an obligation here. It wouldn't be right to slip away, even briefly. I just couldn't do that." *Doesn't hurt to show the man you are a loyal employee,* Bat thought.

"Okay. I understand." Higgins conceded.

"You said Belize. Curious, what's the job?"

"It's a super photo op. Still life. No models, no kids, nothing moving. Just an enormous Mayan Jade head discovered near an archaeological site. You shot Mayan stuff in Mexico, right? You know the light, texture, the whole nine yards."

"Yeah, but Jade has different reflective properties than stone. Time of day you shoot is critical."

"See? That's the kind of experience I want. You don't just point and shoot and hope for the best. You're a natural with a camera. You always were." There was enthusiasm in Higgins voice.

"Thank you, I'm blushing. But like I said, keep me in mind next time. Who knows? I might even chuck it all over here and come to you for a job, if you'd have me."

"In a heart beat!" Higgins replied. The two chatted for a few minutes more, then Higgins had to take another call. They ended their conversation with a promise to get together shortly for lunch.

Bat was satisfied he had options. He could fantasize about a life outside the agency, if he wanted out. A life with a semblance of normalcy without guns, disguises, or a persona built around lies.

He no sooner hung up with Higgins when the phone rang a second time.

"Hello, Ba. . ."

"Bat, it's Charlie Stone," He was surprised to hear the voice of a supervising field agent on the unscrambled line. They both worked out of New York, but in different offices, and Stone was not an undercover operative. Direct line phone contact between both types of agents was almost unheard of with few exceptions.

To his fellow employees at the publishing house, Bat had the 'dream job.' He was one of three senior editors and spent an extraordinary amount of time out in the field, but few people ever knew what book he was working on and fewer still could recall ever seeing him at a staff meeting. He showed up two, at most three days a week when he was in town, never gave any of them work or orders. What ever he did for the company, many thought, was a mystery, though his photos often appeared in various books. Perhaps Bat was the publisher's illegitimate son, one wag had speculated, and his practically no-show job was payback.

"Do you have a TV or radio on?"

"No, I'm. . ."

"The FBI picked up a Saudi in Texas that they say is linked to the 1993 World Trade Center bombing. It's all over the cable news stations. He had a trunk full of cocaine that has the hallmarks of the stuff we were chasing in St. Kitts. Could be a connection to your missing informer who ended up 'well done' in that cane field."

Bat was already out from behind his desk and heading toward the door intent on going over to the regional FBI office when Stone, as if able to see him, stopped him in his tracks.

"You stay put. I'm going there and will fill you in later," The click on the line told Bat that Stone had ended the conversation.

Bat immediately left his office and went through the large common area, where writers and copy editors worked. It was lunchtime and the room was virtually empty. He crossed the area and entered the conference room and turned on the TV.

The local stations all had regular programming. Bat flipped through the dials to determine the best coverage on the cable news stations and settled on one showing the apprehended individual in handcuffs being walked into a building Bat took as a jail.

An FBI spokesman accommodated the TV cameras by making a brief statement that the agency believed the individual was connected to the World Trade Center bombing nearly two years earlier. File footage showed the confusion and rescue of people from the building. The voice over gave generalities but Bat, Charlie Stone and the Agency team were aware of more, but not all, of the details and evidence collected by law enforcement authorities.

On February 26, 1993, a Ryder truck filled with 1,500 pounds of explosives was detonated in the underground garage of the World Trade Center's north tower at 12:17 PM. The resultant blast opened a 98 foot hole through 4 sublevels of concrete. Six people were killed and more than a thousand injured.

What wasn't known by the public is that the conspirators' chief aim at the time of the attack was to de-stabilize the north tower and send it crashing into the south tower, toppling both landmarks.

Another piece of information not emphasized to the media, was that underneath the World Trade Center was one of the world's largest gold depositories. The vault withstood the explosion, as did the towers. The 1993 value of the gold was said to be more than one billion dollars, believed to be owned by Kuwaiti interests.

Hundreds of individuals were questioned in connection with the bombing, including Emad Salem, a former Egyptian Army officer who would become the government's star witness against Egyptian cleric, Dr. Omar Abdel Rahman, whom the FBI charged was the ringleader in this and other several bombing plots. Shortly after the Twin Towers bombing, the government put Salem into the Witness Protection program. To Bat, one of several CIA agents privy to the investigation, Salem was just a greedy opportunist who was in the right place at the right time.

Bat learned from the FBI that Salem was aware of the Twin Towers plot because he had infiltrated Sheik Rahman and his associates' inner-circle. Salem traveled in the cleric's inner circle and surreptitiously recorded more than 1,000 conversations. He then sold this information to the FBI. But Salem was also recording his conversations with the Bureau, most likely to protect himself.

Bat's interest was in anything that might tie the Twin Towers bombing with the revenue generated from the drugs going through St. Kitts. Months went by and he discovered nothing of substance. It appeared the two operations were not connected.

Yet something nagged Bat and it kept him looking for a thread connecting the two, if not specifically to the Twin Towers terrorists, then to other cells planning an unthinkable attack on America.

That money, large sums of it, was being generated into the coffers of terrorists here in the U.S. because of the drugs coming North from Colombia was a minority opinion shared by Bat and a handful of other CIA agents. Because terrorism at this level was a new and strange war for the agency, and because nothing could be automatically ruled out. He had *carte blanche* to follow leads wherever they took him. But he knew the clock was running and if he didn't soon come up with proof soon that the drug trafficking was a legitimate link to terrorism, the agency would pull the rug out from under him. He had been given enough rope to hang himself.

Instead, he nearly worked himself into exhaustion. Eventually the team had run out of leads and other more pressing matters took center stage. As expected, he and the others were reassigned to other duties and the team disbanded.

CHAPTER FOUR

Cormick O'Connor pedaled his bicycle up and down the undulating hills along one of the newly paved roads in the county. He had an excellent reputation as the local tinkerer in a small village not far from the border separating Catholic Ireland and Protestant Northern Ireland. If something electrical needed fixing, people called him and he'd mount his old American made Schwin to make house calls. He had a car, but he believed the bicycle provided exercise he otherwise didn't get.

His electrical and mechanical talent was so widely known that some said electricity, not blood, ran through his veins. Unbeknownst to all but a few confederates, O'Connor was among a handful of IRA moles in the predominantly protestant region.

A solution to the problem that Sir Warren hoped would be resolved soon was the one he and Austin Smythe-Pembrooke had discussed in the shadows of Big Ben and Parliament that bitter cold January evening a few weeks earlier. The mechanics of it were to be dropped on O'Connor by a surrogate employed by Smythe-Pembrooke.

After traveling nearly half an hour he pulled up in front of *The Pig & Whistle* pub. It was a favorite watering hole and rest stop for the Sunday and Wednesday twice weekly tour busses filled mostly with foreigners traversing the historic sites in the three county area. At other times during the week, it was frequented sparsely by locals.

The pub was the only building one could see in the middle of flat grasslands, save for the partially overgrown ruins of St. Mary's R.C. Church some 100 or so feet behind it. St. Mary's had been bombed and destroyed during "The Troubles" in 1916 and never rebuilt when the Catholics who had worshipped there all left the area. The majority Protestant community preferred to let the ruins and pile of rubble remain as a lasting message to the despised Catholic riff-raff. *The Pig & Whistle* had been the original rectory and for some unknown reason it had been spared. It wasn't until the outbreak of World War II that the rectory was taken over and converted into a public house, mostly to accommodate the business of the German Kriegsmarine U-boat sailors who often made port in the protected bay on the Catholic side hardly a quarter mile away.

O'Connor walked into the pub and stopped dead in his tracks. He nodded to the barman. Two elderly customers, locals he recognized, were occupied arguing about the merits of a regional championship football game on the pub's television. With their backs toward him, O'Connor stealthily headed for the two water closets at the far end of the room, marked LORDS and LADIES.

As O'Connor began to slowly and quietly move, the barman drew and planted two new pints in front of the pair and engaged them in conversation about the game. O'Connor entered the WC marked LADIES, with its 'Out of Service" sign hanging on it and quietly closed and locked the door.

When the building served as a rectory, this particular toilet had a sturdy side panel which, when removed with some difficult but silent manhandling effort, revealed a steep wooden staircase leading to a brick tunnel passage. O'Connor twisted an inside wall switch and a series of dim overhead lights stretched the distance from the bottom of the stairs to the basement of St. Mary's. Before descending he re-secured the panel. Odd how it was always easier to do this from inside than from the WC itself, he thought.

The tunnel passage had been a convenient way for the parish priest and sometimes others to go between the two buildings in inclement weather. Such trips could be done in less than two minutes. With tons of rubble from the destroyed church preventing any entrance from above ground, the passageway now served the IRA for it's less than godly purposes.

When preparing to leave the church basement those down there pressed a button which would ring the phone in the pub to make sure the LADIES WC wasn't occupied, the "out of service" sign not withstanding. If there were patrons at the bar another panel in the WC provided an exit to the outside without going through the pub. This could also be used for entering the WC if necessary.

When the barman left the innocuous message for O'Connor, it included code words indicating he should come to the Pig &

Whistle. As he entered the basement proper O'Connor was surprised to see a badly beaten man tied to a chair while two rogue IRA members hovered over the victim. O'Connor had expected a meeting, not a bloody interrogation, and by *these* two at that.

The pair had been effectively removed from active IRA lists for a variety of reasons, not the least of which was an inability to follow orders instead of going off on their own to cause mayhem. Despite not being asked to participate in any covert activity for some time, they were unaware of their status and situation. Recently, when they did ask about why nothing was happening, the question was handled nicely:

'It's been awful quiet for some time now, Fin, isn't there something the boys need us to do?'

'It's quiet on purpose,' the barman had told them with an exaggerated wink. *'Something big must be in the works, and some of us* . . . he darted an index finger at himself and then them, *'* . . . *and Cormick O'Connor as well, are being kept low for a good reason, I suppose. Don't worry, before the shit hits the fan we'll all be in on it.'* That somewhat simplistic excuse seemed to mollify them.

"What in God's name do we have here?" O'Connor asked as he drew closer to the limp man tied to the chair.

"Hello Cormick," Shamus Boyle, the burlier of the two, replied. "We have us a genuine English spy who thought he could dupe us into revealing where he could locate you," he added somewhat self-assuredly.

"And the bugger actually thought we'd believe his blarney about having, quote, 'some important information,' unquote,' you needed to know. But we got the truth out of him. Yes sir, we did," Billy Kelly added proudly.

"A spy? An *English* spy? To what end? And start from the beginning," O'Connor stepped closer and examined the unconscious man's bloody facial features, or what was left of them. His nose was obviously broken, and likewise his jaw. Red bruise welts on his face had nearly closed his eyes. When he coughed the victim regurgitated more blood. Rivulets of it ran down his chin and neck. O'Connor noticed several teeth in bloody goop stuck to his bare chest. O'Connor couldn't shake the feeling the man looked familiar. He focused his attention on the man's captors as Billy began to speak.

"Well we, Shamus and me self, was up at the pub hoisting a few pints. There was nobody else in the place, just us and Finnegan. . ." [the barman, who was also an IRA operative] ". . . when this fellow saunters in and strikes up a conversation, saying something about needing to see you and wondering if we knew your whereabouts. He said he had been by your cottage but you weren't there. . ."

O'Connor abruptly turned his attention to the man in the chair again and examined his features more closely.

"Jesus, Mary, and Joseph! I know this lad. I don't recall his name, but he was a part-time letter carrier in our district during the holiday season for a few years. He was attending university and supplementing his tuition," O'Connor nearly shouted. "You've nearly killed him!"

"He said his name was Anthony Pickelton. . ." Shamus put in. ". . .but the photo ID in his wallet says he's Michael Walling. He's a bloody English spy, Cormick!"

"Tell me why you say that, and be quick about it. And if your reasons don't prove out, I swear I'll work the two of you over so badly that this poor sod will look handsome the way he is!"

Billy and Shamus knew well that Cormick O'Connor could do it. Though each of them outweighed him by nearly 50 pounds, O'Connor was a ferocious and merciless fighter with extraordinary strength. He was not someone you wanted angry at you.

"Take it easy, Cormick," Billy said. "In the interest of brevity I'll skip the details and go right to the heart of the matter, the reason we knew he was a spy. And an English spy at that!"

The former letter carrier groaned and through one squinted eye saw O'Connor. "Mister O'Connor, please. . ." was all he could say before passing out again.

"Christ Almighty! He recognized me, you stupid bastards. You know what that means, don't you?

He knows this place and he knows me. Shit! Now we'll have to kill him."

With his head bowed, Shamus moved one foot around in the basement's dirt floor and looked like a puppy who had been scolded for a miscue. Billy, frightened at what O'Connor might do was nonetheless less intimidated.

"Cormick, calm down. We all know the consequences of what's been done. He'll never leave this place. We'll do him in and put him to rest right down here with the others."

"I still haven't heard a single word about why you've tortured this man or why we'll be murdering him," O'Connor replied.

After Billy had explained the details to him, O'Connor realized they hadn't just gone off on another of their murderous sprees. The man, who's image as a letter carrier was etched in O'Connor's mind, but who's name still escaped him, had been caught in a lie. A big lie. And was most likely the lackey of the English. Shamus and Billy had been keenly observant and he apologized for berating them earlier. He actually felt somewhat relieved that they had intercepted the man.

"We thought you should know about this," Kelly told O'Connor. "Seems like the Protestant bastards were laying a trap for you, Cormick."

O'Connor thought about what had just been said and added. "Finish him off. Then stay away from here, stay out of sight till someone contacts you."

As he made his way through the passage and back up into the WC, O'Connor decided something had to be done about Billy and Shamus. This time their intervention proved useful. But they were dangerous, and the rotten spy bastard on the chair could have easily been some innocent sod who simply said something they took the wrong way. He admitted to himself they were bullies who enjoyed inflicting pain and murdering people, not patriots fighting for the cause. They had to go.

As he pedaled toward home, Cormick O'Connor reflected on what Shamus and Billy had told him. Walling had said he wanted to find O'Connor because he had important information that 'friends' in London wanted to share about a leading London businessman, Leslie Wilford.

The man said O'Connor would find what he had to offer very interesting. Wilford, so Walling had said, was actually an undercover operative for MI-5 and was about to blow the whistle on IRA cells in London. The man mentioned two IRA names which Shamus, Billy and O'Connor indeed recognized.

Walling also said the IRA's 'friends' in London thought it might be a good idea for O'Connor to come to London and fix Wilford's car so an accident could happen by remote. An accident would protect everyone.

Problem was that one of the men whom the man said Wilford had turned as an informer had died of a heart attack at home in Ireland last month. He only made infrequent trips to London as a courier. For Walling and others to know his work with the IRA was a surprise. But, O'Connor thought, for the Limeys not knowing he had died was a bigger surprise. It was obviously a trap to lure him somewhere.

"When did you say this Wilford turned him?" Billy asked.

"Day before yesterday," Walling said. Unfortunately, to make the story more believable, he added an ad lib comment on his own initiative.

"An influential 'friend,' high up in government by the way, and I met for lunch and happened to see them huddling in a corner. Our friend is very knowledgeable about such things and, shortly after he got back to his office, he called and asked if I could do him a big favor. I presume he discussed the clandestine meeting with others and discovered what Wilford was up to. That's how I got dispatched here to locate O'Connor. I'm just doing the man a favor. . . and helping the cause."

"Oh, you're a sympathizer to the cause as well, are ya?" Shaun asked somewhat sarcastically and buried a beefy hand into the man's stomach.

Walling doubled up. The punch had knocked the air out of him. He immediately realized he had played his hand badly. He should have stuck to what Smythe-Pembrooke had told him.

Under interrogation in the church basement, the man confessed he had not witnessed any such meeting, and identified the 'friend' as Austin Smythe-Pembrooke: Someone O'Connor, and many in the IRA knew had a reputation as a staunch monarchist, and certainly no 'friend' of the IRA.

O'Connor, deep in thought, almost cycled past his own cottage. As he put the bicycle under the overhang and against the rear wall near the exit door he felt a surge of alarm that Walling and his cohorts knew about his other talents. He concluded it had been a poorly plotted trap to entice him to go to London.

After Billy and Shamus each took turns trying to break Walling's neck by violently snapping his head from side to side, the popping sound they wanted to hear eventually came. They decided not to bury the body in the basement but instead to deposit it on the road leading to the British military garrison a few towns over. Shamus and Billy loaded the corpse into the trunk of Billy's car, parked at the back of the pub, and in the middle of the night they would deliver it.

Twenty-four hours later, Smythe-Pembrooke was informed that the body of his son-in-law, Michael Walling, a rising star in the Foreign Office, had been dumped near the British Garrison in Northern Ireland. To make certain their message made it's point, the brutally beaten and murdered man had been castrated and his genitals were stuffed in his mouth.

When informed that Smythe-Pembrooke's attempted recruitment of IRA involvement to solve the Leslie Wilford problem had gone horribly amuck, Sir Warren was annoyed and disappointed. Eventually, he fixed his attention to his second, and lesser favorite of the two alternatives: Using rogue agents from MI-5 or MI-6 to accomplish the same end.

****

"I'm delighted you're able to join me for lunch," Sir Warren told his companion at one of the private London clubs he was a member of and simultaneously signaled a waiter. He had selected a corner table and given instructions that, for as long as possible, the tables around them be kept empty. As a club director, such requests were unquestionably honored.

"I read your report about the subject's trip to America. Quite detailed, and very good observations, indeed. Sorry it has taken so long to get back to you about it," he added.

The waiter appeared promptly and Sir Warren and his guest placed drink orders.

"I've taken the liberty of ordering lunch for both of us earlier. Today's special is stuffed salmon, absolutely marvelous. You'll love it."

"Thank you, Sir Warren. I had so much fish when I was on Nevis I thought I would have grown gills by now. But enough time has passed, and now I look forward to English cooked fish."

"Yes, indeed, good observations," He ignored the agent's remark and continued as if he hadn't heard it. It was a clear message that Sir Warren didn't want to drift from the subject. This meeting was not about fish or culinary choices, or ancient history such as the Nevis trip.

"Thank you, sir. There was nothing extraordinary, rather routine, actually. Just old fashioned spying on the royals."

"Ah, that's the best kind. And I'm delighted that all that new fangled electronic gear we tested on *HMS Bedford* works as well in close quarters on land. It serves a purpose of a sort, I suppose, but nothing compares to the nitty-gritty work of having an actual agent keep tabs on the goings on, don't you agree?"

"Yes. . .with some reservations," the agent replied.

"How do you mean?" Sir Warren asked curiously.

"Oh the 'nitty-gritty' work, as you call it, gave us the proof positive that the princess had a fling with the American prince in the Carlisle Hotel, which is the same hotel where his father slipped between the sheets with Marilyn Monroe."

"You know that for a fact?"

"Well, if we can believe our CIA colleagues, yes, it's a fact. But it was the electronics, especially that new, miniature parabolic receiver, that clinched it."

"So," Sir Warren mischievously rubbed his hands together. He loved good gossip, especially if it involved sexual indiscretions by famous people, "John F. Kennedy, Jr. and our Princess of Wales, tumbling around under the sheets, eh?" Who knows about this, besides you?"

"Only me, and the Yank who was on shift with me."

"Why, in God's name was he there?"

"She, Sir Warren. It was a female agent. Once it appeared the loving couple was going to be in the same hotel room together it was a mad dash to get the equipment in position. Without her influence and credentials I wouldn't have had access to the room we worked out of. It was an excellent vantage point."

"Did you get any photos?"

"Yes, but sorry to say by the time I had the parabolic set up, you can't identify individual faces, only occasional body parts, limbs mostly. They did most of their gymnastics on the floor, totally out of view."

"Pity," Sir Warren sighed. "All serious business aside, they truly make a very handsome couple, don't you think? A clear photo of them copulating would end all our problems with the wayward Diana."

"You'd release such a photo?" the surprised agent asked.

"No. Certainly not. We'd simply pass prints on to Prince Philip. He would make sure she was out of the family, and without the two princes, in short order."

Based on the extensive use The Committee made of wire taps and other electronic eavesdropping, the agent had little doubt about the sincerity of Sir Warren's comments or his ability to do what he claimed.

Since Sir Warren was considered the leader among equals on The Committee, few things were done without his advice and consent. As the agent considered a response, Sir Warren continued, changing the subject slightly.

"Not a single one of our private transatlantic telephone conversations was broken by the CIA! Thanks to our deliberate improper setting of the bands. So much for that 'wonderful' technology we shared with the Americans."

"But, sir, as the field report notes, every other exchange between New York and London was snatched."

"True enough, and that's what it was intended to do. Sometimes you have to throw them a bone." Sir Warren reflected for a moment. "Had I not taken steps to insure that the reception and transmittal bands be discretely set to a narrow frequency before the equipment left London, perhaps our conversations would have been compromised." He paused, deep in thought for a few seconds.

"Well enough said about all that. Marvelous job, you did. You have our deepest appreciation."

The agent accepted the compliment but was confused about the apparent importance Sir Warren had placed on the assignment.

"Now we're going to pick up the pace and keep even closer tabs on the Princess and her dangerous carryings on.

"Dangerous? I would think promiscuous would be more descriptive," the agent proffered.

"Well, that too, of course. But The Committee is more concerned with her mental state," Sir Warren lied. "You recall she's attempted suicide three times, and that bulimia thing. Certainly not conduct becoming the mother of a future king. We'll need to watch her ever so much more closely."

Sir Warren leaned in a bit and in conspiratorial tones, as if he were dispensing very private information spoke in nearly a whisper: "Even the Queen blames Diana for the shambles the marriage is in. And, God forbid, if the Princess is successful in her next suicide attempt it would not only be unbearable for Princes William and Harry, it would threaten the very monarchy itself! She, Diana, is quite popular with the masses and those cads in the tabloids are not above accusing the royal family as having driven her to it."

"My goodness. I'd not thought of it that way. I thought the suicide attempts were all in the past. I've heard recent gossip, but I took them with a grain of salt. . ."

"Oh, gossip and rumors they're not. And The Committee has the tapes of conversations between various of the royals to prove it. If it interests you, and it probably should, I can make the tapes available to you to hear. In the privacy of my office, of course."

"I'd certainly be curious to hear them, but perhaps that would be an invasion of her privacy," the agent answered.

"Well, you'd better get used to it, and put all concerns of conscience aside. Based upon my recommendation, at the next gathering of The Committee, you will be put in charge of all such efforts to keep track of her, what she does, who she sees, talks to. Everything. We've got to know what she's up to. For her sake, yes, but more so what it would mean to the Crown," He then sat back and resumed speaking in more audible tones.

"How does that suit you, eh? Quite a feather in your cap! The Committee is prepared to entrust you with this very, very top priority and hush-hush mission. What have you got to say about that?"

The agent looked at him with wide eyes. It took several seconds to regain composure.

"I'm flattered, of course." The suggestion had come out of the blue, and the agent tried not to appear unprofessionally surprised. "But certainly you have people closer to Diana who could pull off keen observations without attracting any attention."

"Not to worry. Believe me, I've given this great thought and you fit the bill perfectly. You'll be responsible for directing the activities and rotating a small hand-picked group of MI-6 and MI-5 people whom The Committee has worked with previously. All solid chaps, experts in various clandestine disciplines, loyal monarchists to the bone.

"This is a priority assignment, high on The Committee's agenda. At the very top of the agenda to be blunt. Are you up for it?"

"Certainly, Sir Warren," the agent responded unhesitatingly. "It would be an honor to be singled out by The Committee for such a task." It was an appropriate response, one the agent knew Sir Warren wanted to hear. Yet even though agreeing to assume this unusual responsibility, the agent couldn't fathom what the long range consequences or outcome would be.

"I trust I'll be reporting directly to you?" the agent asked.

"Certainly. But without question or reservation, it's all your show. You'll be my conduit through which everything from The Committee passes down and, in turn, I'll introduce your reports on progress up the other way. Here are the names of the MI-5 and MI-6 agents you'll be working with. They are all presently involved in one or another aspect of keeping tabs on the Princess of Wales, discreetly, of course."

As the agent perused the list, the stuffed salmon arrived.

"I have to remove myself from the day to day operations of this thing," Sir Warren announced. "I'm embroiled in a possible security situation I thought was being handled, but something unforeseen has come up and it needs my undivided attention. . . hopefully that will be resolved very shortly."

While placing the napkin on his lap and lifting his flatware as if preparing for an assault, he added, "One final comment on the matter before we become involved with our meals. Henceforth, when you need to reach me simply call my service number and leave a message under a pseudonym always ending in the letter 'L' as in Michael, Paul, Mitchell, you get the idea. We'll change that coding every so often, no need to raise any eyebrows if someone happens to be listening. But we need one to begin with." He paused and lifted his eyes toward the ceiling, for an instant, as if the answer was written there. Then he looked across the table and directly into the agent's eyes. "I can't believe it. I'm stumped! How shall we identify your phone calls? Is there a secret nickname you favor?"

The agent shrugged indifferently.

****

Diana's father had been an equerry for both Queen Elizabeth, and her father George VI. As a child she had often played with Prince Andrew and Prince Edward. If she ever married either of them, the inside family joke reasoned, she would become a duchess. Her sisters began calling her 'Dutch'. It was a nickname that stuck. Many years later even Diana's future sister-in-law, Sarah Ferguson, who became a real duchess when she married Andrew, called Princess Diana 'Dutch'.

But 'Gladys' and 'Fred' were the private pseudonyms Camilla Parker-Bowles and the Prince of Wales used to identify each other in secret messages, phone calls and other communication. Diana had learned about the nicknames shortly before her marriage to Charles:

"Somebody in his office told me that my husband had had a bracelet made for her which she wears to this day. It's a gold chain bracelet with a blue enamel disc. It's got 'G and F' entwined in it, "Gladys' and 'Fred,' they were their nicknames.

"I walked into this man's office one day and said: "Oh, what's in that parcel?"

He said: 'Oh, you shouldn't look at that.'

"I said, 'Well, I'm going to look at it.' I opened it and there was a bracelet and I said: 'I know where this is going.' This was about two weeks before we got married."

He said: 'Well, he's going to give it to her tonight.' "

"Why can't you be honest with me?" Diana asked Charles during the resultant confrontation about the bracelet. "But, no, he cut me absolutely dead. It's as if he had made his decision, and if it wasn't going to work, it wasn't going to work.

"He'd found the virgin, the sacrificial lamb, and in a way he was obsessed with me. But it was hot and cold, hot and cold. You never knew what mood it was going to be, up and down, up and down.

"He took the bracelet, lunchtime on Monday, we got married on the Wednesday. I went to his policeman who was back in the office and said: 'John, where's Prince Charles?' "

"And he said: 'Oh, he's gone out for lunch.' "

"So I said: 'Why are you here? Shouldn't you be with him?"

"Oh, I'm going to collect him later.'

"So I went upstairs, had lunch with my sisters who were there and said: 'I can't marry him. I can't do this. This is absolutely unbelievable.' They were wonderful and said: 'Well, bad luck, Dutch, your face is on the tea-towels so you're too late to chicken out.' So we made light of it."

"I never dealt with that side of things. I just said to him: 'You must always be honest with me.' "

"On our honeymoon, for instance, we were opening our

diaries to discuss various things. Out comes two pictures of Camilla.

"On our honeymoon we have our white tie dinner for President Sadat. Cufflinks arrive on his (Charles) wrists, two 'C's' entwined like the Chanel 'C's'. Got it in one; knew exactly.

"Camilla gave you those, didn't she?"

"He said: 'Yes, so what's wrong? They're a present from a friend.' And, boy, did we have a row."

****

Dutch, Gladys, and Fred. Unlikely nicknames for what was becoming the most publicized lover's triangle of the century.

Sir Warren had been silent throughout lunch. Now, as he savored the last mouthful of salmon and crossed his knife and fork on the gold-rimmed white China plate, he smiled and looked deep into the agent's eyes.

"Howell."

"What?"

"Howell, a junior officer on Nelson's ship . . . When you call just say 'Please have Sir Warren contact Mr. Howell's Office. See the irony? The Nelson connection? It will be an appropriate reminder of your first involvement, and the gravity, of this royal assignment. Don't you think?" Such petty things often gave Sir Warren pleasure.

To the agent it all sounded quite childish.

****

Sir Warren was annoyed that 'the Wilford problem' had not been settled but instead still dragged on. Austin Smythe-Pembrooke had recruited a trusted monarchist MI-5 agent to do the same job after the fiasco in Ireland in which Michael Walling, Pembrooke's son-in-law of hardly a year had been tortured and murdered.

The death of Walling didn't cause Pembrooke to shed any sincere tears. In reality he didn't like the man very much. His daughter's marriage to Walling hadn't been with his paternal blessing. He had reared her properly, he thought, always exposing her to the 'right' class of people in the 'right' circles. He always intended she would marry someone of wealth and position. If such a person also had royal blood or came from a titled family, that would have been perfect. The Queen's third son, Prince Edward, The Earl of Wessex, would have been a right and proper union.

But she had taken up with Walling at university and they continued living together after graduation. When she became pregnant, Pembrooke reluctantly approved of the marriage and shortly thereafter used his 'old-boy' connections to secure a mid-level position for Walling in the Foreign Office. And Pembrooke collected his pound of flesh from Walling whenever he needed something unofficial done.

Despite the morals and current norms in the rest of the world, to Pembrooke and his peers, the scandal of having one's issue parent an illegitimate child was socially unacceptable. It just wouldn't do for Austin Smythe-Pembrooke's son-in-law to be employed as a clerk in some third-rate law firm. There were good people, he mused, who still embraced the traditions and standards of the Victorian era. To Sir Warren, Pembrooke and others on The Committee, 'Dutch, Gladys, and Fred' were not among them. And now Leslie Wilford was on the verge of mucking things up more.

The difficulty wasn't in wiring a vehicle so it could be remote controlled, the rogue agent had told Pembrooke. That was fairly basic. The trick was in obtaining the vehicle and performing the task without the owner ever knowing it had been tampered with. Then, after the planned mishap, and hopefully the successful resolution of the problem, the retrieval of the installed device before it was discovered presented an equally daunting task.

Sir Warren listened attentively as Pembrooke explained these things as they again walked near Westminster Bridge this bright and sunny day. Then, as if they were simply two friends out for a chatty walk, Pembrooke interjected something totally unrelated.

"Oh, I knew there was something I wanted to mention. Megan Price, that MI-6 agent who everyone thinks is tough as nails, you know her. . ."

"Yes, of course I do, get on with it. What about her?"

"Well, she met us at the morgue and comforted my daughter Beatrice when we claimed Michael's body upon its return from Ireland."

"Megan Price? I wasn't aware your family was acquainted with her."

"Oh, yes. Yes, indeed. Megan had often been our baby-sitter when Beatrice was a child, like an older sister. The two of them got along famously. I spoke to her alone and she told me she had arrived there earlier that day to make sure the body had been arranged so that everything was in its proper place, and even brought some cosmetologist with her so his face wouldn't look so ghastly."

"My God, man! Surely you didn't permit your daughter to actually look at him?"

"We strongly advised against it but we couldn't stop her. I was very appreciative of Megan's clear thinking. A remarkable woman, she, to do all that and be there for my daughter. I'll not soon forget it."

The Princess of Wales had comforted the six-month pregnant Sarah Lindsay when Diana and the Duchess of York met the young widow upon returning to Northolt from Klosters, Switzerland, with the body of her husband. Sarah, employed in the Buckingham Palace press office, and her husband were well liked by the royals.

Major Hugh Lindsay, the former equerry to the Queen, was killed after plunging some 1,300 feet in an avalanche accident as part of a royal skiing party, including Prince Charles. Diana and Fergie, who was pregnant, were not on the slopes with the royal party at the time but back at the chalet instead. The rest of the royal party cut their holiday short and returned the following day. Diana remembered the tragedy and recalled her role in the events surrounding it:

"Everyone started shaking. They didn't know what to do next. I said to Fergie: 'Right, we must go upstairs and pack Hugh's suitcase and do it now while we don't know what's hit us. We must take the passport out and give it to the police.'

After it was done, Diana told Prince Charles' bodyguard they had put the suitcase under his bed but she and Fergie wanted Hugh's belongings back, his signet ring, his watch, etc., so they could give them to Sarah.

"I felt terribly in charge of the whole thing. I said to my husband: 'We're going home, to take the body home to Sarah, we owe it to Sarah to take the body home.' Anyway there were tremendous arguments about that. I got my policeman to get Hugh's body out of the hospital.

"Anyway, so we came back from Klosters. We arrived back at Northolt and we had Hugh's coffin in the bottom of the aeroplane and Sarah was waiting. It was a ghastly sight, just chilling. We had to watch the coffin come out and then Sarah came to stay with me at Highgrove when I was on my own and she cried from dawn to dusk, and my sister came over and every time we mentioned the name of Hugh there were tears, tears, but I thought it was good to mention his name because she had to cleanse herself of it, and her grief went long and hard. . ."

****

Sir Warren hadn't interrupted Smythe-Pembrooke's reverie about his daughter, son-in-law, or Megan Price. Finally, when the man ceased talking, Sir Warren waited perhaps a minute and brought the original conversation back on line.

"So when, Austin? When can I expect to hear that this problem is behind us? The clock is ticking. This has to be accomplished before Charles and Diana are divorced! Once that takes place, there'll be no stopping our gabby friend. He'll spill more of the beans or perhaps even hang out the entire basket of dirty laundry."

"Beans, Sir Warren?" Pembrooke gave him an odd look.

"Yes, that's what the tabloids, the *American* tabloids, are now saying about the latest chapter in this royal mess," he replied in a gruff, disgusted voice.

"Give them no heed, Sir Warren. Apparently, they don't have enough scandals on their side of the pond to keep them occupied, so they're piggy-backing on our chaps."

"Enough! Don't side track my question. When should I expect results?" Sir Warren's tone was stern. He had lost his patience. This conversation had dragged on far longer than he expected.

Austin Smythe-Pembrooke gave him a reproachful stare before answering.

"In good time. Certainly before any divorce. When our man is satisfied he has the operation worked out flawlessly and so that there is nary a hint of foul play. We agree it should appear as an accident, and so it will. I have the utmost confidence in this agent."

Sir Warren raised one eyebrow. "Your hubris is admirable, Austin. But, I recall, you had confidence in your son-in-law as well." Sir Warren's parting remark was biting. The words were no sooner uttered when he turned abruptly and began briskly walking toward his car.

****

That Halloween, Bat took turns with his sister answering the door for costumed Trick-or-Treaters in her and her husband's new house, a massive, five-bedroom colonial resale in a 10-year old development. He'd been with them for a week, helping them settle in and assisting with the usual chores one needs, or wants, to do, upon moving into a new place. And they certainly kept him busy.

His brother-in-law was an up-and-coming assistant Federal prosecutor who had recently taken on the investigation of a case involving the so-called Russian Mafia's dealings in the fuel oil business of the United States.

Though neither she nor her husband knew the extent of the undercover work he did, they were aware he was employed by the Central Intelligence Agency. The fact that he was armed gave Bat's sister a feeling of security, inasmuch as there had been a number of odd phone calls with nothing said before a hang-up. Her husband tried to convince her it had nothing to do with his case but instead were just some teenagers 'welcoming' their new neighbors. Nonetheless having Bat with them calmed her far more than her husband's assurances.

By chance, and luck of the draw, it was Bat who was closest to the front door and was confronted by what appeared to be a rather a tall teenager, replete with mask and costumed as 'Death'. But as Bat smiled and started to say, "You're a bit old for this sort of thing, don't you think?" the costumed assailant produced a sawed off shotgun from under his cape.

Fortunately, the weapon jammed or misfired and Bat immediately lunged at the man. They tumbled down the steps and onto the lawn where they scuffled briefly before his would-be killer managed to kick Bat in the groin and escape when he saw Bat's brother-in-law charging through the foyer with a baseball bat.
A car waiting a short distance away sped to a stop and the assailants raced away. But in the scuffle the assailant left the shotgun behind. The assassination attempt was obviously intended for his crime-fighting brother-in-law.

Police responded quickly and armed officers stayed on the premises for the remainder of the night, as did two FBI agents. From the next morning on, the house was under constant FBI protection and surveillance with a deliberately conspicuous unmarked car and its occupant parked in the driveway.

In less than a week, authorities picked up suspects in the incident and were able to connect them with the Russian Mafia case, now page-one news. No further incidents occurred, but his sister pleaded with Bat to remain with them a bit longer. His argument that with the visible FBI presence outside and all the newspaper and TV coverage [in which Bat's brother-in-law, not Bat, was deliberately depicted as having the encounter with the gunman] nothing else was likely to happen, fell on deaf ears. Reluctantly, he agreed to stay a bit longer.

The new house became something of a local tourist attraction with area residents frequently driving by and gawking. Being in the spotlight, even peripherally, is the last thing any undercover agent needs. After another week of living there, Bat began looking for a believable way to terminate his stay when a phone call came which would change his life forever.

Bat was quick to accept an invitation from his longtime friend, Tom Culhane, for a week of SCUBA off the Florida Keys. Bat had considerable unused vacation time, and Culhane's offer was so tempting he jumped at the chance. The trip would not only take him out of the fishbowl he felt he was living in at his sister's, it would clear his head of the nagging unsolved problems of terrorists, drugs and work-related baggage he brought home from work each day.

Now, a week later and on his first visit to Florida's John F. Kennedy Space Center at Cape Canaveral, Bat Lynch watched the President slowly patting a dank handkerchief to the edge of his rapidly wilting shirt collar. The President was waiting with other dignitaries and various celebrities in the VIP viewing stands, some three miles directly in front of Pad 38B, for the momentary launch of Space Shuttle 'Columbia.'

Diagonally across from the VIP grandstands was a duplicate structure to accommodate the ladies and gentlemen of the Fourth Estate. It was from these very stands that the world-wide press corps recorded the lift-off of Apollo 11 in July of 1969, and then some 17 years later, the tragic launch of the space shuttle 'Challenger' on January 28, 1986. Here, too, handkerchiefs were collecting rivulets of sweat from warm necks and foreheads exposed to the relentless Florida sun and humidity of Merrit Island.

In the media grandstand viewing area. "freelance photographer" Bat Lynch, an addendum to his cover role as a travel guide book editor, was idly panning the VIPs through his camera's long lens.

When he put in for vacation at the agency and mentioned he would be meeting an astronaut friend at the Cape and they would be leaving immediately after the shuttle launch to do wreck diving off the Keys, his section director arranged for NASA media credentials as a surprise 'thank you' for his recent hard work.

As others watched the President's attempt at relief, a few did likewise. Bat became aware that rivulets of sweat were coursing their way down his face as well. He lowered his camera and reached for his own handkerchief. His visit to the Cape was under the cover of an assignment for a large, German-based, European newspaper chain for whom Bat had actually shot some photography in the past.

Inasmuch as he was above-average handling a camera, Bat

thought he actually could get to enjoy photo freelancing. It would give him the freedom to include or omit things in his lifestyle.

In the last few decades it had become rare indeed for a U.S. President to attend a manned space launch at the Cape. The public awe and the magic that author Tom Wolfe had so aptly used to describe the Original 7 Project Mercury Astronauts, as 'single combat warriors' in his best-seller *The Right Stuff,* dropped a peg with the two-man Gemini program and three-man Apollo missions which followed. The public was quickly galvanized to space flight, and the bravado and daring that once held people breathless was replaced with a complacent ho-hum, been there, done that, attitude.

The exception was the Apollo 11 moon landing in July, 1969. But two missions later, by the time Apollo 13 went up, none of the television networks covered space launches live. After a decade of space flight that culminated with the first landing on the Moon, launches from the Cape had become old hat to the viewing public.

The low-interest live TV coverage was the rule of the day until the Space Shuttle 'Challenger' disaster belied the widely held public belief that space flight was routine, dull, and boring. It was nothing of the sort. Each launch was a major engineering feat that tested man's ability to conquer the earthly elements around him. Nonetheless, only a very limited public interest remained well into the series of Space Shuttle flights.

But this launch was different. The networks were back, the press stands were crowded with eager reporters, and the VIP area was filled to the brim. This mission would determine the fate of the Hubble Space Telescope. It had been repaired by an earlier shuttle mission in 1993, but this necessary fix was more of an upgrade than a repair. And NASA was eager to have it go off without a hitch.

Even with the benevolent shade afforded by the stands' protective canopy, the humidity made the wait uncomfortable. Bat patted the hanky to his brow again then, noticing the tell-tale red "on" light on a network camera panning the media viewing stands, he bent slightly forward and smiled broadly just in case his sister was watching.

Besides being known as the home of America's space center,

this piece of Titusville, Florida, real estate was also designated as the Merritt Island National Wildlife Refuge as a sanctuary for an estimated 2,500 Florida Scrub Jays, various species of Herons, Boat-tailed Grackles, Caspian Terns, Black Dippers, Bonaparte's Gulls and numerous other things that take flight without the help of manmade rockets.

Some fifty yards forward, and visible to both stands, a large digital-display clock stood at ground level. It was positioned in the no-man's-land that existed between the massive rockets that embraced the shuttle and the fragile humans who awaited their ignition.

As white condensation clouds from the gigantic liquid fuel boosters slowly twirled their way skyward, the clock ominously ticked off the minutes and seconds before launch. Photographers with long-lens cameras mounted on tripods of every description jockeyed for position in front of the press stands in an effort to "frame" the shuttle's lift-off with the precise time being shown on the clock.

Nearly identical in size, including canopy, the press stands were, however, replete with the modern tools of the scribes' trade: hard-wired and cellular telephones, portable fax machines, a plethora of lap-top computers. The electric typewriters and occasional rare, manual models that were the mainstay of these stands as recently as two decades ago, were conspicuous by their absence.

All of these necessities to capture and record the moment for history cluttered the surface of built-in, government-issue, gray counter tops. Metal folding chairs stood shoulder to shoulder. Space was at a premium. The attendant glut of cables and wires snuggly criss-crossed each other below the platform's floorboards.

Actually, it was now one of two press viewing stands. When the United States returned to manned space flight some two years after the 'Challenger' disaster, NASA was inundated with requests for press credentials and forced to expand the media viewing area on a first-come, first-served basis. While the TV interest had waned over the years, there continued to be a strong desire to cover launches by the print media.

Always conscious of the impact positive press could have on pending and future budgets, NASA obliged all bona-fide requests. Credentials were, nonetheless, still issued specific to each launch.

Viewing space for the overflow was provided in this second set of stands, located slightly farther back than the original stands. Humorists in the press corps joked that journalists relegated to the SECOND stands were there to cover the demise of journalists in the FIRST stands... if anything went amuck at lift-off. Some of the old-timers in the front stands remembered too well the several launch pad explosions and disastrous failures to launch in the early days of the space program. They were aware there could be a morbid truth in the humor.

The network anchormen and women, the broadcast superstars of the media, on the other hand, had long ago discovered how to cope with the often unmerciful climate of Merit Island.

Since the bygone days of the Mercury, Gemini and Apollo manned space flight programs, these video darlings viewed the proceedings from the comfort of air-conditioned mobile trailers fitted with mural-size picture windows framing the exterior backdrop behind newscasters. It gave the TV viewer the illusion that Tom Brokaw, Dan Rather, Peter Jennings, and their expert guests, were sitting at desks outside.

Today, as in the past, various broadcasters were joined by current and former astronauts who functioned as expert commentators on everything, from what the flight crew had for breakfast to how they would relax during rest time on the mission, and, in some cases anecdotes about their personal experiences.

Never in the history of broadcasting had any anchor person asked the quintessential question Mr. and Mrs. Average America wanted to know most, namely: *how did the astronauts urinate and move their bowels in weightlessness?*

It was a certain bet that inquiries about this very human biological function would be avoided like the plague again this morning.

On cue, and much to the delight of broadcasters, the expert

astronaut commentators would bend, twist and weave their hands or use table-top scale models to simulate staging and other movements peculiar to the spacecraft and its boosters. It was the obligatory show-and-tell that gave the viewing audience a relatively easy description of what would or was happening once the gargantuan missile and its human cargo left the ground.

Some six miles overhead, astronauts Thomas S. Culhane and Stanley English, both veterans of previous shuttle flights, circled Southern Florida in camera-equipped chase planes as they prepared to record the Flight of Columbia. Their spectacular video would be beamed to a worldwide-TV audience. Bat Lynch looked skyward and wondered which of the two jets was under the controls of Culhane, his childhood friend. Bat Lynch and Culhane, who would begin a 30-day leave after his work was done today, would be heading to the Florida Keys the following morning to get in a week of scuba.

As the countdown relentlessly slipped toward liftoff, all eyes became riveted to 'Columbia' and its centurion-like twin booster rockets. In the VIP stands, idle talk and more serious political conversation first dribbled to a whisper, then evaporated totally.

Across the way, U.S. and Foreign journalists, many of whom had been feeding their offices the usual background and color commentary via cell phone and land-line hookups, hastily paused conversations. Several telephones rested on the counter, lines kept open.

Television cameras in the mobile trailers zoomed between newscasters and their expert guests to produce fantastic tight-shots of 'Columbia.' A sudden breeze at the launch site caused the condensation to resemble twisting clouds that tumbled around the rocket's base and mockingly danced along the shafts of its twin booster rockets.

A lazy seagull, oblivious to the global attention focused at that moment on the tremendous upright flying machine directly behind it, caught the tepid Florida breeze. With the warm current gently bussing its widespread, motionless wings, the gull casually swooped down and filled one network's screen for several seconds before forcing its own momentum and suddenly darting away.

The bird's erratic departure caused a wag in the network's technical trailer to suggest the feathered beast had succumbed to an unbroken litany of profanity emanating from the control room in New York some 1,200 miles away.

It was a tension-filled scenario replayed several times over in the last four-plus decades at the Cape, whether or not the general public still thought so. Hushed onlookers clung to every word as loudspeakers amplified an unseen stentorian voice which methodically recited the final seconds before yet another manned journey into the cosmos.

"Five. Four . . three . . we have ignition . . two, one. And liftoff of the Space Shuttle Columbia!"

Consumed by the enthusiastic din from the crowd, the last syllable was forever lost to audio history. Though only twenty minutes late because of a brief hold in the countdown, 'Columbia's' liftoff, from Pad 38B, was well within the launch window NASA had publicly announced.

The launch had caused problems in the President's schedule. He was obliged, however, to remain in the stands a respectable amount of time, neck arched back, and hand shielding his eyes while following the glowing flame and exhaust trail of 'Columbia' as the spacecraft rose into the heavens. He had to stay, his spin doctors had advised, for a short time beyond 'staging,' that portion of the flight when the spacecraft separates from the boosters. On a pre-arranged cue from an aide, the President, whether or not he could actually see the staging, would break into a wide smile, turn to those nearest him and give an enthusiastic, if effected, 'high five.' It would be a great photo op for the several photographers, who were told in advance it was very likely to happen. So much for spontaneity in the news. Bat decided to pass on the moment.

With the communication exchange between Columbia's crew and Mission Control beaming over the loudspeakers, the shuttle was rapidly being reduced to a mere fire-tailed dot in the sky. From the chase planes, Culhane and English were beaming back extraordinary video footage.

Once staging was accomplished, replete with the Presidential 'high five,' NASA officials began leading a procession of sub-contractors associated with the launch through obligatory introductions with the President and any other key officials, or with celebrities they could corner.

Like busy worker-ants, the President's aides wended their way through the entourage. In diplomatic tones, they discreetly urged members of the Presidential party and other staffers to quietly and immediately head for the motorcade that would take them to Air Force One at nearby Patrick Air Force Base. Any extra time spent at the Cape, they suggested, would have a disastrous effect on the rest of the day's schedule.

Once the last of the stragglers was well on their way, a signal to 'go' would be given to the head of the Secret Service detail. He, in turn, would pass it on to the President. And the formalities would come to a polite, but abrupt, end.

Bat Lynch began to withdraw from the press stands. He had gotten his series of launch shots plus two rolls of other photos for himself, not any faux-European clients, and he was now ready to depart the Cape. He wondered if he should begin the approximately 250 mile drive at this relatively late hour in the day, or sleep over and start fresh and early the following morning. It would be a five hour drive.

Bat slouched in his seat and closed his eyes. He would work out the details for catching up with Tom Culhane in the Keys when the two had dinner that evening. A wide grin creased his face. If the others who had been around him in the press stands only knew what he really did for a living.

****

Austin Smythe-Pembrooke was a creature of habit. The routines of his life rarely changed. He arrived at his office ahead of everyone else in the morning, rotated his lunch engagements between three private clubs in the same order each week and departed for home one hour after everyone else had left.

Except on Fridays, when he left two hours earlier than usual to pick up his wife and get a jump on the traffic heading out of London for the weekend. By the time the crunch came, the Smythe-Pembrookes would be well on their way toward their expansive country estate where they would entertain an ever-changing list of friends as overnight guests.

Cormick O'Connor's confederates in London had observed Smythe-Pembrooke's movements for three consecutive weeks with nary a change. Good weather or bad, each Friday Pembrooke departed early for the festive weekend. The IRA tinkerer smiled and put a match to the single sheet of paper containing the brief but pertinent information.

Some minutes later, right on schedule, a soft musical note foretold that the door on the lift in the basement parking garage was about to open. As he had done countless times in the past, Pembrooke moved out into the garage when it did. He had hardly taken three steps when he felt the unmistakable cold shape of something cylindrical pressed against the back of his neck. He froze in his tracks and raised both arms skyward.

"Do not turn around," he was told. "You won't be harmed, *but do not turn around*. Understood?"

"Yes, yes!" Pembrooke nodded slightly. "I don't carry a lot of money around, but you can have it...and my watch as well, it's rather expensive . . ."

"Put your hands down, I don't want your money. This isn't a robbery. I have some questions and, if I like your answers, I have something for you."

Despite the reassuring words, Pembrooke was terrified and trembling. He suddenly had the uncontrollable urge to urinate where he stood. With every ounce of strength he could muster, he avoided the accident but felt his kidneys were going to explode.

"Now, walk over to the rear of that lorry, slowly." O'Connor indicated a dark panel truck that was unfamiliar to Pembrooke. It wasn't a vehicle he had ever seen in the garage before. Including the truck and Pembrooke's Jaguar, the small garage could accommodate about two dozen cars and was nearly full.

When they reached the back of the truck, O'Connor passed a

small sleeping mask with an elastic band to him and told him to put it on. Pembrooke did exactly as he was told. Only then did O'Connor remove the gun from against the back of his neck.

"I'm opening the rear door and I want you to climb in and stay on all fours facing the front and move up. I'll be getting in behind you. Understood?"

"Certainly, yes. I'll do it. I'll do it." Pembrooke lifted his knees into the truck and using his hands rapidly crawled deep into the truck until O'Connor told him it was far enough.

"Now we're going to have our little talk, totally in private." As he started to climb into the truck, O'Connor noticed a puddle on the concrete and a slight wet trail inside the vehicle leading to Pembrooke. He choose not to mention it and avoided contact with the liquid by remaining in a crouched position as he quietly pulled the truck door closed. Once inside, he seated himself on a wooden box he had placed in the vehicle for that purpose. He glanced at Pembrooke's wet trousers and couldn't resist a broad smile. Then, as if flipping a switch, his mood became serious again.

"Why did you send your man to Ireland to locate Cormick O'Connor?"

"Wha. . .?" A surge of fear rippled through Pembrooke as he realized his captor was from the IRA!

"Don't play stupid or ignorant. We know *YOU* sent Walling to do your dirty work and entice O'Connor to come to London and be ambushed." Actually, O'Connor knew that probably wasn't true, but he wanted Pembrooke to confirm what he believed had been the purpose of Walling's disastrous trip.

"No, I had no part in it, Walling's trip. But it wasn't to ambush O'Connor. He, Walling, wanted to hire O'Connor for something."

"Really? Hire O'Connor? And what would that be for?"

"Michael Walling was my son-in-law," Pembrooke readily admitted. There was no reason not to. Pembrooke had been mentioned in Walling's obituary and he figured this IRA gunman would have already known that anyway. He reasoned Walling had easily been broken under torture and figured they knew much more also. He continued, fabricating as he went.

"Michael was distraught, he'd taken leave of his senses. He was convinced that my daughter, his wife, was carrying on with someone. . ."

"Who would that be?" O'Connor asked.

"I don't know. . .someone in government. . . he didn't tell me. It was all in his mind."

"So why would your son-in-law want to hire Cormick O'Connor? I believe the man is in electronics, not marriage counseling."

"That's why, exactly why. He wanted O'Connor to do something so it would appear the man died in an accident."

"And your-son-in-law thought a fine, upstanding Irish patriot like Cormick O'Connor would stoop to common murder? Where would anyone even get an idea like that?"

"Michael was with the Foreign Office. Perhaps one of the chaps suggested O'Connor. Also, I believe that when Michael worked during the holidays while at university he delivered mail to O'Connor."

There was a ring of truth to some of what Pembrooke was saying, but O'Connor knew that the best lies often do contain just enough truth to make them believable.

"May I prostrate on the floor? My knees are killing me."

"Yes, but face your head to your left side."

Pembrooke was much calmer now. As he lowered himself to the truck's floor, he reasoned the IRA hadn't sent this man to kill him but to get information. Now it would be a game of wits.

"But that's not the story Walling told the people who killed him." O'Connor said it slowly and in conspiratorial tones. "He told them a friend of *yours*, Leslie Wilford was about to 'out' some friends of *ours* here in London, and that *you* had sent him to locate and alert O'Connor so the IRA could terminate Wilford."

"I told you he had taken leave of his senses, but he had a devious mind. He must have used my name to give authority and credence to his silly story."

"Well, now let me tell you what we think happened,"

O'Connor decided it was time to play his trump card. "We think you had a falling out with your former friend Leslie Wilford. You and he belong to some of the same clubs, travel in the same snobby circles, and hate the Irish. . ."

"That's not true! I do. . ."

"Oh stop it! Don't insult my intelligence. We know all about you and your monarchist cronies. Walling wasn't stupid enough to make up a story like that and mention your name in it. You sent him to hire O'Connor to kill somebody who had become a royal pain in the ass to you, didn't you?"

"No!"

"Yes! And hiring an IRA man to do it gave you a perfect patsy if the 'accident' turned out to be murder."

"No, no, no. You've got it all wrong. It was just the impulsiveness of a crazed and jealous husband who wrongfully thought his wife was cheating."

O'Connor didn't reply immediately. His contempt for Pembrooke was nearing the boiling point. But he controlled himself and played out his hand.

"I don't believe you for a minute. You wanted Wilford dead and sent a boy to do a man's job and he mucked it up. But what's more amazing is you made three very serious mistakes. First, you thought you could bluff O'Connor into committing murder for you. You really didn't expect O'Connor or anyone else to accept that rubbish story as fact and not check it out, did you?

"Second, you or whoever briefed your lap dog son-in-law didn't do a good job of it. He apparently ad- libbed himself to death. You see, one of the Irish 'moles' that Wilford was preparing to out had died a month earlier. The two animals who interrogated and murdered your son-in-law knew that and acted totally on their own. They're loose cannons. Michael Walling's senseless death was not at the hands of the IRA.

"And third, Cormick O'Connor is not a killer for hire. He's an Irish patriot."

Pembrooke considered continuing to deny it all, but realized nothing he could say would change the man's mind. "So if you believe those things, what do you want from me then?"

"Nothing more. I got what I came for. Now it's my turn to get you to do something for us."

Pembrooke couldn't believe what he was hearing. He knew this man, and his cohorts, didn't trust him or even like him.

"What could I possibly do for you and your kind?" Pembrooke realized the moment the words left his mouth that there had been a dangerously condescending tone in his voice.

O'Connor tossed a thin #10 envelope at Pembrooke. It landed inches from his face.

"I'll be leaving now. Take that envelope and do with its contents as you wish." He paused, then added, "I suggest you remain exactly where you are for a good five minutes or more and leave the sleep mask on."

Pembrooke heard the truck's rear door quietly open and shut the same way. He never heard his captor's footsteps or any other sounds. He waited closer to ten minutes before removing the mask picking up the envelope and exiting the vehicle. He was alone. As he briskly headed for his Jaguar, he stopped abruptly and remembered the envelope in his hand and was tempted to open it then and there. Instead he continued to his car, got in, placed the envelope on the seat next to him, started the Jaguar and exited the garage faster than he normally did.

Smythe-Pembrooke took a different route than he normally did towards home. Foolish, perhaps, he thought, but, even though his business with the IRA thug appeared to be over, one could never be too cautious. When he reached his destination, he beeped his horn in the usual way to signal his wife, Madge. Despite the unpleasantness of this afternoon, he had resolved to say nothing of it to her, nor to change their plans for the weekend.

As he waited for her, he picked up the envelope and opened it. At first he didn't understand the contents or what they meant. He returned the envelope to the seat.

"There you are, you tardy man! So unlike you," she greeted him in patronizing tones as she slipped into the passenger seat, picking up the envelope he had put there. He hadn't reacted fast enough to stop her.

"What's this?" she asked and removed two passport-type photographs. On the backs of each were the names and addresses of Shamus Boyle and Billy Kelly.

"Scruffy looking types!" Madge exclaimed. "You're not considering hiring them, dear, are you?"

"Heavens no. Nothing like that," he said with an effort to act nonchalant. "They're troublemakers and someone just asked me to find out what I can about them."

She really hadn't heard anything he said after *nothing like that*.

"Oh Austin, look what you've done!" she said in admonishing tones. "You've apparently spilled coffee all over your trousers and ruined them! You know you shouldn't be drinking coffee . . . and while you're driving no less. Go inside and change."

"Not to worry. I just want to leave already. I'll change at the estate."

As his wife gabbed on about what she had done that day, things she purchased at Harrods, gossip about friends and, of course, what she'd read in the tabloids about the latest salacious scandal involving the extra-marital activities of the Prince and Princess of Wales, Pembrooke was considering a plan to deal with the murderous slime who had beaten, tortured, murdered and castrated his son-in-law.

"Excuse me, dear," he interrupted. "Have you received confirmation from everyone who will be attending this weekend?"

"Yes, as a matter of fact everything was tidy and wrapped up yesterday when I heard from the last three. Megan Price will be accompanying Beatrice. I swear, that woman is an angel. She's been with Beatrice almost constantly since Michael was murdered. A great comfort. We're fortunate, and Beatrice is fortunate, that Megan is such a loyal friend. It was good of you to suggest including her."

"Who else?"

"Well, Archie Blair is coming, solo. The Brinkleys have said "yes" as well.

"Oh, and we've had one casualty, Austin. The Wilford's are begging off. Seems Leslie has an awful cold. I wished Leslie well and told Anne perhaps next time." She paused, then added. "If there is a next time. I've never liked him very much. Such a serious and persnickety man!"

"There will be a next time, Madge, you can count on it."

****

Some six miles away on a narrow side street proffering a mix of attached brownstone walkup flats and vacant street level shops, a two-year-old Bentley had come to a stop. Though a run-down, seedy part of the city, expensive cars were not uncommon. Landlords and developers often visited in search of unwanted buildings up for sale.

A tall, lanky man, who for all intents was a mechanic in coveralls, guided the driver from the street onto the hydraulic lift in the small garage. A third colleague, casually dressed, who had been posted at the corner, headed back to join them in the garage.

Had any passersby noticed, the incongruity of the mechanic's wingtip shoes belied his appearance. The driver, meanwhile, wore appropriate casual attire for one driving a $100,000+ automobile. In reality the driver would never have been able to afford a Bentley on his former middle-income civil servant salary. But now, as a rogue, a hired gun, such a fine motor car was within his reach.

In fact, no repair work would be done on this Bentley. It was a rental vehicle legally obtained under a bogus name, strictly for the purpose of examination. The trio were rogue intelligence agents, brought from overseas. The mechanic was exactly that. The driver was responsible for obtaining vehicles and eventually coordinating the overall mission. The third man was the muscle. Ruthless and deadly, he provided protection for the others.

Once the overhead door was closed and the driver exited the vehicle, the mechanic engaged the lift to expose the undercarriage. Both men walked under the car. The mechanic moved toward the front where the firewall separated the engine and transmission from the chassis' mélange of tubes, wires and mechanical parts.

"Beautiful," the mechanic said softly as his eyes carefully traced the steering cable.

"It's good then, ya?" the driver asked.

"Ya, piece of cake. I can make the required alterations and

totally conceal them from detection."

"Do you want to lift the bonnet and inspect things from above?"

"No need. Everything I'm going to do will be done from here. Just the small magnetic box secured right here," He indicated a spot on the chassis. "No wires to cut, no screws, nuts or bolts. It will be a simple one-two operation to remove afterward."

As he continued examining the undercarriage of the car, the mechanic pulled a cloth from his coverall back pocket and began wiping and rubbing his hands as if they were dirty, though he had not touched the car.

"It better be. I've never worked out in the field before and I'm the one who'll have to fetch this toy back. How long will this device take to install and remove?"

"It's nothing, just get under the car and stick it on. Taking it off is the same. We'll spend more time getting into his garage then applying the box. Here, I'll show you."

The mechanic realized the driver needed reinforcement. Though they had worked together on other clandestine jobs, the man had never been put in harm's way to the degree he would be this time. Furthermore, he knew very little about the technology being employed since it was the recent brain child of the mechanic.

The mechanic walked from under the car to a work bench. He opened a large black leather case, similar to the kind airline pilots carry, and removed three items. The first was a black enamel device about the size of the electronic current converters travelers are wont to use abroad. The second was a wand that resembled a somewhat longer than normal fountain pen. The third, and largest, resembled a shorter than normal computer keyboard with a trio of low profile joysticks where the number keypad would normally be. He placed the last item back in the leather case.

When he returned to where he had been under the car, he placed the small black box in close proximity to a cable. As he did, he squeezed the device at its sides, engaging a magnetic field which caused it to jump onto the steel undercarriage metal.

"That's it. It's in place. I'll scout the road for the precise location to activate it, and the job will be done. After the accident, you use this to break the magnetic connection and release it," he handed the wand to the driver. It should be done quickly, before the vehicle is removed from the scene. Once the car is in custody, the authorities will certainly check for a steering failure in an accident like this."

"Precisely why I will be on the road behind him when it's happens. I'll expect your call when you engage the device. I want to rush up to the scene, do what needs to be done and be gone before anyone else gets there."

"If you've removed the box in timely fashion, there'll be nothing to find. Not a trace of anything. It will be ruled 'driver error,' The man simply dozed off at the wheel."

The driver smiled. "Do I need to make contact, the wand and the box?"

"No, it operates in a proximity field. They're on the same frequency. It'll immediately disengage the magnet as long as you are within three feet of the box. If the car lands upright just poke the wand underneath and the thing will drop to the ground. Easy to retrieve. If the car's upside down, better yet. Just reach and grab."

"Okay, then. If that's it, I'll be out of here." Both of them withdrew from under the car.

"I have to return this one to the rental firm tomorrow," the driver said as he raised his arm and affectionately patted the door on the Bentley.

"The hardest part will be getting into subject's garage," the mechanic proffered.

"Yes, it could be dicey, but do-able." He paused, then added. "And it's less risky or complicated than lifting the car, bringing it here, and returning it all in the same night. And far more practical than laboriously setting up a blinding flash of strobe on the highway to achieve the same result. Too much clutter, all that. Too many things needed to happen in concert. This will be much more effective."

The mechanic nodded in agreement.

CHAPTER FIVE

In Lerner and Lowe's romanticized 1960 musical <u>Camelot</u>, set amidst the pageantry and splendor of King Arthur and the Round Table, the reflective monarch mulls *How To Handle A Woman* and concludes the answer is to *love her, love her, simply love her*.

Based on T.H. White's <u>The Once and Future King</u>, Sir Warren wished Prince Charles had followed Arthur's advice in his marriage to Diana. Had the heir apparent to the throne simply loved her, perhaps the future of the monarchy wouldn't be drowning in the adulterous mire now engulfing it.

But then the Princess of Wales herself had repeated the extra-marital assignations of <u>Camelot's</u> fallen queen Guenevere with her own horseback Lancelot, James Hewitt, by aping the tragic Broadway love story.

Things had digressed from bad to worst since Charles and Diana's separation. Revelations which appeared in the media, and which were thought by many to be rumors or sensationalized gossip, were shockingly confirmed in televised confessions of infidelity by both parties themselves. The fairy-tale couple in the most watched wedding in television history would not, and had not, lived happily ever after.

Along with the British security agency, MI-5, The Committee's own telephone and parabolic microphone eavesdropping, plus a handful of informers, had made them privy to the tryst when it began as a flirtation and right through to consummation. Both had begun monitoring The Princess of Wales when the first rumors surfaced about bulimia and suicide attempts by the princess. Suicide in the Royal Family was not acceptable.

Diana had been on holiday on Martha's Vineyard in the U.S. as a guest of Paolo Tarso-Flecha de Lima and his wife, Lucia. He was the Brazilian ambassador in Washington. Diana and Lucia shared a close friendship.

Earlier that day Diana had met with Elizabeth Glaser, the wife of actor Paul Michael Glaser and a well-known activist in the battle against pediatric AIDS. Elizabeth Glaser herself was dying from the illness, contracted as a result of a contaminated blood transfusion.

Casual observers at a luncheon gathering hosted on the beach thought Diana was uncommonly quiet and kept to herself. Some attributed her mood as sullen and reflective, given what was perceived as the heaviness of the Glaser meeting.

But The Committee knew otherwise. On the previous day Diana was devastated to learn her former lover, with whom she had a five-year affair, had betrayed her. James Hewitt had willingly cooperated by giving an extensive interview to author Anna Pasternak and shared 64 of Diana's letters with the author for a book entitled <u>Princess In Love</u>. It was due for publication shortly, and he would be greatly compensated for his contribution and participation.

Among other things, The Committee's spying devices had recorded the intimate details of the couple making love in her four-poster bed and on a bathroom floor.

The then twenty-eight-year-old Hewitt first met the 25-year old Princess of Wales in 1986 at a London party when her marriage was in shambles and she and her husband were in the midst of a 39-day separation. Apparently, Diana enjoyed the dashing and handsome Hewitt's company and they hit it off rather well. Diana hired the cavalry officer in the Life Guards as a riding instructor first for herself and later for her two sons. Hewitt, like Prince Charles, enjoyed Polo and the two men had been rivals in that as well.

To Sir Warren's surprise, it was Leslie Wilford who had reminded The Committee that Hewitt had committed a crime against the crown, punishable by death, in having an adulterous affair with the wife of the heir to the throne.

Shortly, there was speculation, and snickers, among the ill-informed masses that a remarkable resemblance existed between Hewitt and young Prince Harry. When some in the media questioned if the riding instructor could be the boy's father, The Committee pointed out the Palace's official timeline, that Harry was born on September 15, 1984, two years before Diana and Hewitt met.

But Sir Warren hadn't shared all the data he had collected about the royals over the years with The Committee. He had cultivated a trio of MI-5 rogue agents as his exclusive informants.

It was from them, for instance, that he had learned there were suspicions Diana had actually met Hewitt prior to her marriage, nearly four years earlier than popularly believed, at a polo match in Hampshire in 1981. He was 23 and she 19 years old. Hewitt was playing for the Army while Prince Charles was on the opposing Navy team. At stake was the prestigious Rundle Cup. The Army Captain and the Princess spoke briefly after the match, and he was smitten by her.

After that first, casual encounter, Diana initiated further contact, calling Hewitt and asking him to join her for dinner in London with some mutual friends. Charles was away. It initially developed into a platonic friendship. It appeared to Hewitt, and everyone else, that Diana was in love with Charles.

Nonetheless, Hewitt was becoming increasingly involved in her life and both of them enjoyed their special relationship. Diana began spending as much time as she could with Hewitt, including at his mother's home.

Sir Warren's spies informed him that, not long after Diana and Charles' wedding, she was pouring her heart out to Hewitt in frequent phone calls. She was telling Hewitt some of her most private marital and personal problems. He had become a friendly ear, a sounding board for her. Diana confided that she desperately wanted Charles to love her, but was coming to the conclusion his heart still belonged to "The Rottweiler," her uncomplimentary name for Camilla Parker-Bowles.

As time went on, Diana confided to Hewitt that she was bulimic, an eating disorder in which the victim 'binge eats' and then deliberately makes themselves sick. This alarming revelation caused The Committee to question her mental state and resulted in around-the-clock surveillance.

Eventually more and more face to face meetings replaced most of the numerous phone calls. They took long horse rides in the countryside and met at Kensington Palace and elsewhere on an average of twice a week. Such rendezvous were out in the open and often at Kensington Palace.

When Sir Warren was informed that Hewitt was wont to drive

right up to and through the police checkpoint at Kensington, park in clear view and knock on the front door, he was appalled. Were they both aware that their behavior had already raised eyebrows in the Establishment? Were they trying to flaunt their relationship? Did they want it exposed? The situation had become a curious conundrum to Sir Warren and The Committee.

Diana shocked The Establishment when she performed a jazz dance routine with Wayne Sleep at a gala for the friends of the Royal Opera House. She presented Charles with a video of her performance as a birthday surprise. Apparently, she still had strong feelings for Charles even though she didn't think he loved her.

Suggestions were made to Diana by close friends that the frequency of her meetings with Hewitt were cranking up the rumor mills, and such things had a way of getting out of hand. She was advised to be discreet.

When Hewitt was hired as a riding instructor for Princes William and Harry, it provided a professional excuse for him and Diana being seen together publicly. In truth his riding lessons with the boys were relatively infrequent.

Sir Warren was convinced Diana's relationship with Hewitt had crossed the Rubicon when he learned Diana had given Hewitt a gold fob watch inscribed "I will love you always" and a gold cross with the message, "I shall love you for ever".

This was unacceptable conduct for the wife of the Prince of Wales. That Charles had given Camilla a gold chain bracelet with the 'G and F' initials of their 'Gladys' and 'Fred' secret nicknames entwined on it was certainly different. After all, Charles was a man, the future king, and his subjects would accept or *expect* the Prince of Wales to have a mistress.

But romantic liaisons by the wife of the future king? Nay, she should be as honorable and chaste as Caesar's wife.

The love affair was in full bloom when Hewitt left London for duty in the first Gulf War. He called Diana using a journalist's satellite phone and in their conversation expressed fear that he might be killed. If he did return safely, Hewitt asked Diana if she would marry him. Sir Warren's sources reported she had said 'yes.'

Sir Warren was so upset about this and unable to suggest ways to prevent it that he dared not mention any of it to The Committee. He pondered and debated what might be done to resolve the problem and avoid a divorce but couldn't conjure up anything satisfactory.

Sometime during his tour of duty, Hewitt was shown a copy of a Sunday tabloid charging he had an affair with the princess. Then, with Prince Charles away, Diana and Hewitt had an emotional reunion upon his return.

Then, unexpectedly, and much to Sir Warren's relief, the problem suddenly went away. For some unknown reason, Diana ceased seeing Hewitt or even taking his phone calls. It was over. But the media wouldn't let this royal soap opera die. Infidelity and betrayal in high places sold more newspapers and books than canned stories about the charmed and proper lives of the royals.

For Diana, when the story wouldn't go away, she saw a way to get two birds with one stone. It had become payback time: First for Charles betrayal of their marriage vows with 'The Rottweiler' and then James Hewitt, the second man she had loved who betrayed their intimacy.

Diana admitted to adultery with Hewitt during a stunning Panorama television interview with Martin Bashir. When directly asked if she had been unfaithful with Hewitt, Diana replied: "Yes, I adored him. Yes, I was in love with him. But I was very let down."

Even to many who were not part of the British Establishment or Sir Warren's brotherhood in The Committee, Diana's television interview and astonishing admission of adultery was a spectacularly self-destructive act. The London *Daily Mail* called it one which "plunged the monarchy into the greatest crisis since the Abdication." A conservative statement, Sir Warren thought.

Diana's tell-all TV interview was the third bombshell in a series of royal one-upsmanship salvos and was seen by more than 21.5 million people in Britain and at least as many millions more in the U.S. and elsewhere, on ABC-TV News *Turning Point,* less than a week later. Diana had been courted by both Barbara Walters and Oprah Winfrey for just such an interview.

Prince Charles watched the broadcast at Highgrove and

exchanged telephone comments with his *inamorata,* Camilla. The Princess of Wales, dressed in a conservative navy suit, shared her most personal feelings about her marriage with Bashir in November, 1995. Devoid of introductions and the closing 'thank you,' the excerpted transcript Sir Warren received the day of the broadcast was one of the most shocking documents he had ever seen:

Q: What were the expectations that you had for married life?
A: I think like any marriage, specially when you've had divorced parents like myself, you'd want to try even harder to make it work and you don't want to fall back into a pattern that you've seen happen in your own family.

I desperately wanted it to work, I desperately loved my husband and I wanted to share everything together, and I thought that we were a very good team.

As for becoming Queen, it's, it was never at the forefront of my mind when I married my husband: It was a long way off that thought.

The most daunting aspect was the media attention, because my husband and I, we were told when we got engaged that the media would go quietly, and it didn't; and then when we were married they said it would go quietly and it didn't; and then it started to focus very much on me, and I seemed to be on the front of a newspaper every single day, which is an isolating experience, and the higher the media put you, place you, is the bigger the drop. And I was very aware of that.

Q: It's been suggested in some newspapers that you were left largely to cope with your new status on your own. Do you feel that was your experience?
A: Yes I do, on reflection. But then here was a situation which hadn't ever happened before in history, in the sense that the media were everywhere, and here was a fairy story that everybody wanted to work. And so it was, it was isolating, but it was also a situation where you couldn't indulge in feeling sorry for yourself: You had to either sink or swim. And you had to learn that very fast.

Q: And what did you do?

A: I swam. We went to Alice Springs, to Australia, and we went and did a walkabout, and I said to my husband: 'What do I do now?' And he said, 'Go over to the other side and speak to them.' I said, 'I can't, I just can't.' He said, 'Well, you've got to do it.' And he went off and did his bit, and I went off and did my bit. It practically finished me off there and then, and I suddenly realized - I went back to our hotel room and realized the impact that, you know, I had to sort myself out.

We had a six-week tour --four weeks in Australia and two weeks in New Zealand-- and by the end, when we flew back from New Zealand, I was a different person. I realized the sense of duty, the level of intensity of interest, and the demanding role I now found myself in.

Q: At this early stage, would you say that you were happily married?

A: Very much so. But, the pressure on us both as a couple with the media was phenomenal, and misunderstood by a great many people.

We'd be going round Australia, for instance, and all you could hear was, oh, she's on the other side. Now, if you're a man, like my husband, a proud man, you mind about that if you hear it every day for four weeks. And you feel low about it, instead of feeling happy and sharing it.

Q: But were you flattered by the media attention particularly?

A: No, not particularly, because with the media attention came a lot of jealousy. A great deal of complicated situations arose.

Q: It wasn't long after the wedding before you became pregnant. What was your reaction when you learnt that the child was a boy?

A: Enormous relief. I felt the whole country was in labor with me. Enormous relief. But I had actually known William was going to be a boy, because the scan had shown it, so it caused no surprise.

Q: How did the rest of the Royal Family react when they learned that the child that you were to have was going to be a boy?
A: Well, everybody was thrilled to bits. It had been quite a difficult pregnancy, I hadn't been very well throughout it, so by the time William arrived, it was a great relief because it was all peaceful again, and I was well for a time.

Then I was unwell with post-natal depression, which no one ever discusses, post-natal depression, you have to read about it afterwards, and that in itself was a bit of a difficult time. You'd wake up in the morning feeling you didn't want to get out of bed, you felt misunderstood, and just very, very low in yourself.

Q: So what treatment did you actually receive?
A: I received a great deal of treatment, but I knew in myself that actually what I needed was space and time to adapt to all the different roles that had come my way. I knew I could do it, but I needed people to be patient and give me the space to do it.

Q: What was the family's reaction to your post-natal depression?
A: Well, maybe I was the first person ever to be in this family who ever had a depression or was ever openly tearful. And obviously that was daunting, because if you've never seen it before, how do you support it?

Q: What effect did the depression have on your marriage?
A: Well, it gave everybody a wonderful new label, Diana's unstable, Diana's mentally unbalanced.

Q: According to press reports, it was suggested that it was around this time things became so difficult that you actually tried to injure yourself.
A: Mmm. When no one listens to you, or you feel no one's listening to you, all sorts of things start to happen. For instance, you have so much pain inside that you try and hurt yourself on the outside because you want help, but it's the wrong help you're asking for. People see it as crying wolf or attention-seeking, and they think

because you're in the media all the time you've got enough attention.

But I was crying out because I wanted to get better, to go forward and continue my role as wife, mother, Princess of Wales.

Q: What did you actually do?
A: Well, I just hurt my arms and my legs; and I work in environments now where I see women doing similar things and I'm able to understand completely where they're coming from.

Q: What was your husband's reaction to this, when you began to injure yourself in this way?
A: Well, I didn't actually always do it in front of him. But obviously anyone who loves someone would be very concerned about it.

Q: The depression was resolved, but it was subsequently reported that you suffered bulimia. Is that true?
A: Yes, I did. I had bulimia for a number of years. And that's like a secret disease. You inflict it upon yourself because your self-esteem is at a low ebb, and you don't think you're worthy or valuable. You fill your stomach up four or five times a day, some do it more, and it gives you a feeling of comfort.

It's like having a pair of arms around you, but it's temporarily, temporary. Then, you're disgusted at the bloatedness of your stomach, and then you bring it all up again. And it's a repetitive pattern which is very destructive to yourself.

Q: How often would you do that on a daily basis?
A: Depends on the pressures going on. If I'd been on what I call an 'away day,' or I'd been up part of the country all day, I'd come home feeling pretty empty, because my engagements at that time would be to do with people dying, people very sick, people's marriage problems, and I'd come home and it would be very difficult to know how to comfort myself having been comforting lots of other people, so it would be a regular pattern to jump into the fridge.

It was a symptom of what was going on in my marriage. I was crying out for help, but giving the wrong signals, and people were using my bulimia as a coat on a hanger. They decided that was the problem, Diana was unstable.

Q: Instead of looking behind the symptom. What was the cause?
A: The cause was the situation where my husband and I had to keep everything together because we didn't want to disappoint the public, and yet, obviously, there was a lot of anxiety going on within our four walls.

Q: Did you seek help from any other members of the Royal Family?
A: No. You, you have to know that when you have bulimia you're very ashamed of yourself and you hate yourself, so, and people think you're wasting food, so you don't discuss it with people.

And the thing about bulimia is your weight always stays the same, whereas with anorexia you visibly shrink. So you can pretend the whole way through. There's no proof.

Q: When you say people would think you were wasting food, did anybody suggest that to you?
A: Oh yes, a number of times.

Q: How long did this bulimia go on for? Two years, three years?
A: Mmm. A little bit more than that.

Q: According to reports in the national press, it was at around this time that you began to experience difficulties in your marriage, in your relationship to the Prince of Wales. Is that true?
A: Well, we were a newly-married couple, so obviously we had those pressures too, and we had the media, who were completely fascinated by everything we did.

And it was difficult to share that load, because I was the one who was always pitched out front, whether it was my clothes, what I said, what my hair was doing, everything -- which was a pretty dull subject, actually, and it's been exhausted over the years -- when actually what we wanted to be, what we wanted supported was our work, and as a team.

Q: What effect did the press interest in you have on your marriage?
A: It made it very difficult, because for a situation where it was a couple working in the same job - we got out the same car, we shook the same hand, my husband did the speeches, I did the handshaking, so basically we were a married couple doing the same job, which is very difficult for anyone, and more so if you've got all the attention on you.

We struggled with it, it was very difficult; and then my husband decided that we do separate engagements, which was a bit sad for me, because I quite liked the company. But I didn't have the choice.

Q: So it wasn't at your request that you did that on your own?
A: Not at all, no.

Q: The biography of the Prince of Wales written by Jonathan Dimbleby, which as you know was published last year, suggested that you and your husband had very different outlooks, very different interests. Would you agree with that?
A: No. I think we had a great deal of common interest, we both liked people, both liked country life, both loved children, work in the cancer field, work in hospices.

But I was portrayed in the media at that time, if I remember rightly, as someone, because I hadn't passed any O-levels and taken any A-levels, I was stupid.

And I made the mistake once of saying to a child I was thick as a plank, in order to ease the child's nervousness, which it did. But that headline went all round the world, and I rather regret saying it.

Q: The Prince of Wales, in the biography, is described as a great thinker, a man with a tremendous range of interests. What did he think of your interests?
A: Well, I don't think I was allowed to have any. I think that I've always been the 18-year-old girl he got engaged to, so I don't think I've been given any credit for growth. And, my goodness, I've had to grow.

Q: How did you cope with that?
A: Well obviously there were lots of tears, and one could dive into the bulimia, into escape.

Q: Around 1986, according to the biography by Jonathan Dimbleby about your husband, he says your husband renewed his relationship with Mrs. Camilla Parker-Bowles. Were you aware of that?
A: Yes I was, but I wasn't in a position to do anything about it.

Q: What evidence did you have that their relationship was continuing even though you were married?
A: Oh, a woman's instinct is a very good one.

Q: Is that all?
A: Well, I had, obviously I had knowledge of it.

Q: From staff?
A: From people who minded and cared about our marriage, yes.

Q: What effect did that have on you?
A: Pretty devastating. Rampant bulimia, if you can have rampant bulimia, and just a feeling of being no good at anything and being useless and hopeless and failed in every direction.

Q: You really thought that?
A: Uh,uh. I didn't think that, I knew it.

Q: How did you know it?
A: By the change of behavioral pattern in my husband; for all sorts of reasons that a woman's instinct produces; you just know. It was already difficult, but it became increasingly difficult.

Q: In the practical sense, how did it become difficult?
A: Well, people, friends on my husband's side, were indicating that I was again unstable, sick, and should be put in a home of some sort in order to get better. I was almost an embarrassment.

Q: Do you think he really thought that?
A: Well, there's no better way to dismantle a personality than to isolate it.

Q: Do you think Mrs. Parker-Bowles was a factor in the breakdown of your marriage?
A: Well, there were three of us in this marriage, so it was a bit crowded.

Q: Do you think it was accepted that one could live effectively two lives, one in private and one in public?
A: No, because, again, the media was very interested about our set-up. When we went abroad we had separate apartments, albeit we were on the same floor, so of course that was leaked, and that caused complications.

But Charles and I had our duty to perform, and that was paramount.

Q: The Queen described 1992 as her ´annus horribilis,' and it was in that year that Andrew Morton's book about you was published. Did you ever meet Andrew Morton or personally help him with the book?
A: I never met him, no.

Q: Did you ever personally assist him with the writing of his book?
A: A lot of people saw the distress that my life was in, and they felt it was a supportive thing to help in the way that they did.

Q: Did you allow your friends, your close friends, to speak to Andrew Morton?
A: Yes, I did. Yes, I did.

Q: Why?
A: I was at the end of my tether. I was desperate.
I think I was so fed up with being seen as someone who was a

basket-case, because I am a very strong person and I know that causes complications in the system that I live in.

Q: What effect do you think the book had on your husband and the Royal Family?
A: I think they were shocked and horrified and very disappointed.

Q: What effect did Andrew Morton's book have on your relationship with the Prince of Wales?
A: Well, what had been hidden -- or rather what we thought had been hidden -- then became out in the open and was spoken about on a daily basis, and the pressure was for us to sort ourselves out in some way.
    Were we going to stay together or were we going to separate? And the word separation and divorce kept coming up in the media on a daily basis.

Q: Did things come to a head?
A: Yes, slowly, yes. My husband and I, we discussed it very calmly. We could see what the public were requiring. They wanted clarity of a situation that was obviously becoming intolerable.

Q: By the December of that year, as you say, you'd agreed to a legal separation. What were your feelings at the time?
A: Deep, deep, profound sadness. Because we had struggled to keep it going, but obviously we'd both run out of steam.
    And in a way I suppose it could have been a relief for us both that we'd finally made our minds up. But my husband asked for the separation and I supported it.

Q: It was not your idea?
A: No. Not at all. I come from a divorced background, and I didn't want to go into that one again.

Q: Did you tell your children that you were going to separate?
A: Yes. I went down (to school) a week beforehand, and explained

to them what was happening.

Q: What effect do you think the announcement had on them?

A: I think the announcement had a huge effect on me and Charles, really, and the children were very much out of it, in the sense that they were tucked away at school.

Q: Once the separation had occurred, moving to 1993, what happened during that period?

A: People's agendas changed overnight. I was now separated wife of the Prince of Wales, I was a problem, I was a liability (seen as), and how are we going to deal with her? This hasn't happened before.

Q: Who was asking those questions? The royal household?

A: People in my environment, yes, yes.

Q: How did that show itself?

A: By visits abroad being blocked, by things that had come naturally my way being stopped, letters going, that got lost, and various things.

Q: So despite the fact that your interest was always to continue with your duties, you found that your duties were being held from you?

A: Yes. Everything changed after we separated, and life became very difficult then for me.

Q: Who was behind that change?

A: Well, my husband's side were very busy stopping me.

Q: What was your reaction when news broke of a telephone conversation between you and James Gilbey having been recorded?

A: I felt very protective about James because he'd been a very good friend to me and was a very good friend to me, and I couldn't bear that his life was going to be messed up because he had the connection with me.

And that worried me. I'm very protective about my friends.

Q: Did you have the alleged telephone conversation?
A: Yes we did, absolutely we did. Yup, we did.

Q: On that tape, Mr. Gilbey expresses his affection for you. Was that transcript accurate?
A: Yes. I mean, he is a very affectionate person. But the implications of that conversation were that we'd had an adulterous relationship, which was not true.

Q: Have you any idea how that conversation came to be published in the national press?
A: No, but it was done to harm me in a serious manner, and that was the first time I'd experienced what it was like to be outside the net, so to speak, and not be in the family.

Q: What do you think the purpose was behind it?
A: To make the public change their attitude towards me. It was, you know, if we are going to divorce, my husband would hold more cards than I would. It was very much a poker game, chess game.

Q: There were also a series of telephone calls which allegedly were made by you to a Mr. Oliver Hoare. Did you make what were described as nuisance phone calls?
A: I was reputed to have made 300 telephone calls in a very short space of time which, bearing in mind my lifestyle at that time, made me a very busy lady. No, I didn't, I didn't.
   But that again was a huge move to discredit me, and very nearly did me in, the injustice of it, because I did my own homework and consequently found out that a young boy had done most of them.
   But I read that I'd done them all. Mr. Hoare told me that his lines were being tapped by the local police station. He said, you know, don't ring. So I didn't, but somebody clearly did.

Q: Had you made any of those calls at all?
A: I used to, yes. Over a period of six to nine months, a few times, but certainly not in an obsessive manner, no.

Q: Do you really believe that a campaign was being waged against you?
A: Yes I did, absolutely, yeah.

Q: By the end of 1993, you had suffered persistent difficulties with the press, these phone conversations were made public, and you decided to withdraw from public life. Why did you do that?
A: The pressure was intolerable then, and my job, my work was being affected. I wanted to give 110% to my work, and I could only give 50. I was constantly tired, exhausted, because the pressure was just, it was so cruel.

It was my decision to make that speech because I owed it to the public to say that, you know, ´thank you. I'm disappearing for a bit, but I'll come back.'

Q: It wasn't very long before you did come back, of course.
A: Well, I don't know. I mean, I did a lot of work, well, underground, without any media attention, so I never really stopped doing it. I just didn't do every day out and about, I just couldn't do it.

You know, the campaign at that point was being successful, but it did surprise the people who were causing the grief. It did surprise them when I took myself out of the game. They hadn't expected that. And I'm a great believer that you should always confuse the enemy.

Q: Who was the enemy?
A: Well, the enemy was my husband's department, because I always got more publicity. My work was more, was discussed much more than him.

And, you know, from that point of view I understand it. But I was doing good things, and I wanted to do good things. I was never going to hurt anyone, I was never going to let anyone down.

Q: What was your reaction to your husband's disclosure to Jonathan Dimbleby that he had, in fact, committed adultery?
A: Well, I was totally unaware of the content of the book, and

180

actually saw it on the news that night that it had come out, and my first concern was to the children, because they were able to understand what was coming out, and I wanted to protect them.

But I was pretty devastated myself. But then I admired the honesty, because it takes a lot to do that.

Q: How did you handle this with the children?
A: I went to the school and put it to William that, if you find someone you love in life you must hang on to it and look after it, and if you were lucky enough to find someone who loved you then one must protect it. William asked what had been going on, and could I answer his questions, which I did.

He said, was that the reason why our marriage had broken up?

And I said, well, there were three of us in this marriage, and the pressure of the media was another factor, so the two together were very difficult. But although I still loved Papa I couldn't live under the same roof as him, and likewise with him.

Q: Looking back now, do you feel at all responsible for the difficulties in your marriage?
A: Mmm. I take full responsibility, I take some responsibility that our marriage went the way it did. I'll take half of it, but I won't take any more than that, because it takes two to get in this situation.

Q: Another book that was published recently concerned a Mr. James Hewitt, in which he claimed to have had a very close relationship with you, from about 1989 I think. What was the nature of your relationship?
A: He was a great friend at a very difficult, yet another difficult time, and he was always there to support me, and I was absolutely devastated when this book appeared, because I trusted him, and because, again, I worried about the reaction on my children.

Q: Did your relationship go beyond a close friendship?
A: Yes, it did, yes.

Q: Were you unfaithful?
A: Yes, I adored him. Yes, I was in love with him. But I was very let down.

Q: How would you describe your life now? You do live very much on your own, don't you?
A: Yes, I don't mind that, actually. You know, people think that at the end of the day a man is the only answer. Actually, a fulfilling job is better for me (she laughs).

Q: How do you feel about the way the press behaves now?
A: I still to this day find the interest daunting and phenomenal, because I actually don't like being the centre of attention.

When I have public duties, I understand when I get out of the car I'm being photographed, but it's now when I go out my front door, I'm being photographed. I never know where a lens is going to be.

A normal day would be followed by four cars; a normal day would come back to my car and find six freelance photographers jumping around me.

Some people would say, 'Well, if you had a policeman it would make it easier.' It doesn't at all.

They've decided that I'm still a product, after 15, 16 years, that sells well, and they all shout at me, telling me that: 'Oh, come on, Di, look up. If you give us a picture I can get my children to a better school.' And, you know, you can laugh it off. But you get that the whole time. It's quite difficult.

Q: What role do you see for yourself in the future?
A: I'd like to be an ambassador for this country. I'd like to represent this country abroad.

As I have all this media interest, let's not just sit in this country and be battered by it. Let's take them, these people, out to represent this country and the good qualities of it abroad.

When I go abroad we've got 60 to 90 photographers, just from this country, coming with me, so let's use it in a productive way, to help this country.

182

Q: Do you think that the British people are happy with you in your role?

A: I think the British people need someone in public life to give affection, to make them feel important, to support them, to give them light in their dark tunnels.

I see it as a possibly unique role, and yes, I've had difficulties, as everybody has witnessed over the years, but let's now use the knowledge I've gathered to help other people in distress.

Q: Do you think you can?

A: I know I can, I know I can, yes.

Q: Up until you came into this family, the monarchy seemed to enjoy an unquestioned position at the heart of British life. Do you feel that you're at all to blame for the fact that survival of the monarchy is now a question that people are asking?

A: No, I don't feel blame. I mean, once or twice I've heard people say to me that, you know, 'Diana's out to destroy the monarchy', which has bewildered me, because why would I want to destroy something that is my children's future.

I will fight for my children on any level in order for them to be happy and have peace of mind and carry out their duties.

But I think what concerns me most of all about how people discuss the monarchy is they become indifferent, and I think that is a problem, and I think that should be sorted out, yes.

Q: When you say indifferent, what do you mean?

A: They don't care. People don't care any more. They've been so force-fed with marital problems, whatever, whatever, whatever, that they're fed up. I'm fed up of reading about it. I'm in it, so God knows what people out there must think.

Q: Do you think the monarchy needs to adapt and to change in order to survive?

A: Change is frightening for people, especially if there's nothing to go to. It's best to stay where you are. I understand that.

But I do think that there are a few things that could change, that would alleviate this doubt, and sometimes complicated relationship between monarchy and public. I think they could walk hand in hand, as opposed to being so distant.

Q: What are you doing to try and effect some kind of change?
A: Well, with William and Harry, for instance, I take them round homelessness projects; I've taken William and Harry to people dying of Aids -- albeit I told them it was cancer – I've taken the children to all sorts of areas where I'm not sure anyone of that age in this family has been before.
    And they have a knowledge - they may never use it, but the seed is there, and I hope it will grow because knowledge is power.

Q: What are you hoping that that experience for your children - what impact that experience will have on your children?
A: I want them to have an understanding of people's emotions, people's insecurities, people's distress, and people's hopes and dreams.

Q: What kind of monarchy do you anticipate?
A: I would like a monarchy that has more contact with its people, and I don't mean by riding round bicycles and things like that, but just having a more in-depth understanding.
    And I don't say that as a criticism to the present monarchy: I just say that as what I see and hear and feel on a daily basis in the role I have chosen for myself.

Q: There's a lot of discussion about how matters between yourself and the Prince of Wales will be resolved. There's even the suggestion of a divorce. What are your thoughts about that?
A: I don't want a divorce, but obviously we need clarity on a situation that has been of enormous discussion over the last three years in particular.
    So all I say to that is that I await my husband's decision of which way we are all going to go.

Q: If he wished a divorce to go through, would you accept that?
A: I would obviously discuss it with him, but up to date neither of us has discussed this subject, though the rest of the world seems to have.

Q: Would it be your wish to divorce?
A: No, it's not my wish.

Q: Do you think you will ever be Queen?
A: No, I don't, no.

Q: Why do you think that?
A: I'd like to be a queen of people's hearts, in people's hearts, but I don't see myself being Queen of this country. I don't think many people will want me to be Queen.

Actually, when I say many people I mean the establishment that I married into, because they have decided that I'm a non-starter.

Q: Why do you think they've decided that?
A: Because I do things differently, because I don't go by a rule book, because I lead from the heart, not the head, and albeit that's got me into trouble in my work, I understand that. But someone's got to go out there and love people and show it.

Q: Do you think the Prince of Wales will ever be King?
A: I don't think any of us know the answer to that. And obviously it's a question that's in everybody's head. But who knows, who knows what fate will produce, who knows what circumstances will provoke?

Q: But you would know him better than most people. Do you think he would wish to be King?
A: There was always conflict on that subject with him when we discussed it, and I understood that conflict, because it's a very demanding role, being Prince of Wales, but it's an equally more demanding role being King.

And being Prince of Wales produces more freedom now, and being King would be a little bit more suffocating. And because I know the character, I would think that the top job, as I call it, would bring enormous limitations to him, and I don't know whether he could adapt to that.

Q: Do you think it would make more sense in the light of the marital difficulties that you and the Prince of Wales have had if the position of monarch passed directly to your son Prince William?
A: Well, then you have to see that William's very young at the moment, so do you want a burden like that to be put on his shoulders at such an age? So I can't answer that question.

Q: Would it be your wish that when Prince William comes of age that he were to succeed the Queen rather than the current Prince of Wales?
A: My wish is that my husband finds peace of mind, and from that follows others things, yes.

When it was over, Bashir thanked the princess and the historic and unprecedented 55-minute television show, which had been edited down from a four hour long taped interview, was over.

The British audience was larger for Diana than Charles had for his television appearance with journalist Jonathan Dimbleby on ITN and came three years after cooperating and permitting Andrew Morton to record her personal misery in his best seller.

Perhaps to show she was quite able to play hard ball the BBC announced the interview on Prince Charles' 47th birthday and, if that wasn't enough, it was broadcast in Britain on the Queen's 48th wedding anniversary. Diana's 'fifty-five minutes of infamy' was considered an overtly hostile gesture, not just against Prince Charles but the monarchy itself.

It was equally as hurtful as Diana's blatantly crude reference *"After all I've done for this fucking family"* in a recorded phone call with James Gilbey, of 'Squidgygate' fame.

If Sir Warren and The Committee found itself blindsided by it all, they could take solace in the fact that neither Diana's staff, nor the Queen's, knew about the taping in the dining room of the princess' Kensington Palace quarters until Nov. 14.

At that time Diana reportedly phoned her sister Jane's husband, (Sir Robert Fellowes), who was the Queen's private secretary. She told her brother-in-law that she had spoken to the BBC. A poll by the *Sunday Times on November 16* found that most Britons, would be happy to see the Waleses divorce.

****

"Excuse me, Sir Warren, it's Mr. Smythe-Pembrooke for you," the butler announced and retreated from the study.

Sir Warren, reclining on an overstuffed leather couch, placed a bookmarker in the tome and set it down on the floor before lifting the phone from the side table.

"Austin, I trust you are fine?"

"Perfectly, Warren," he got right to the point.

"Intelligence has come my way identifying the scoundrels who butchered my son-in-law, and I intend to take them to account for it. I wanted you to know, on behalf of the Committee. I'm preparing to approach and dispatch someone very soon."

"Really? Intelligence? From our usual sources?" The thought that Pembrooke would have been made aware of such information without Warren first hearing of it bruised his ego.

"No. This is from an unlikely source, but it's reliable."

"Well, are you certain you can take matters into your own hands without ramifications? Perhaps you should have these chaps turned over to the authorities instead?"

"Absolutely not. I'll take care of this, and it will be untraceable. I have an agent in mind, someone I understand is very good at this sort of thing. . ."

"No names, please. I'm sure you know what you are doing and will handle matters properly."

As much as Sir Warren wanted to know which agent Pembrooke intended to use, he was a firm believer in 'plausible deniability.' Nothing he had said, nor heard from Pembrooke, could implicate him if things went amuck.

Bat Lynch and Tom Culhane were having dinner at a restaurant in Titusville, famous as a favorite eatery and watering hole for several of the Original 7 Project Mercury Astronauts in the early 1960s. They were making plans for tomorrow's diving adventure.

Culhane, thinking out loud, wondered if he could wrangle a plane so they could fly rather than drive down.

"I should be able to get something, NASA is always keen about astronauts keeping their flying skills sharp. I'll check with the flight officer at Patrick first thing in the morning."

The reference was to Patrick Air Force Base, part of the Cape Canaveral Air Force Station complex and the primary landing site for Air Force One and aircraft transporting Washington politicians and military personnel to the Cape. It was also the site that astronauts flew from to chalk up required flying time.

"Diving and flying? Are you forgetting the rule that says you can fly and dive, but you can't dive and then fly immediately."

"Okay, if we have to, we'll kill a half a day after the last dive. Make you happy?"

"Yes, and I'll hold you to it."

Most experts recommend waiting 24 hours before flying after any diving, although some say 12 hours is OK unless you do multiple dives in one day. Absorbed nitrogen is directly related to both the length and depth of dives. The deeper you dive and the more time you spend at depth, the more nitrogen you have to "off-gas" before it's safe to fly.

"No problem having me aboard as a passenger?"

"I didn't say that, but let me handle the details. And by the way, you're not going to get off easy as a passenger. I'll fly going and you'll take the stick on the return, when my ass will be dragging from diving anyway."

Bat truly enjoyed flying, perhaps because he was so good at it. Culhane believed Bat was a natural, one of those rare individuals who could instinctively fly. Before moving into intelligence work he had briefly flown helicopters in the Army. Even before he was out of his teens, Bat had been certified for single wing and instrument flying.

Jorge Martinez, owner of the Orlando Air Taxi Service, chanced by while they were eating.

"Christ-on-a-crutch, they'll let anybody in this joint!" Culhane exclaimed joyfully as he stood and embraced the man, "Even Cuban air force deserters."

"Anybody with money gets in here, gringo." Martinez looked at Bat and continued the banter.

"Who's this? Another one of your half-assed astronaut amigos who thinks he can fly?"

"Nope. He's not crazy enough to sit on a rocket and get blasted into space, but he's one damn good flyer."

Culhane did the introductions amid more bravado and happy talk. Bat gave as good as he got. It quickly became obvious Jorge and Bat hit it off and they convinced Jorge to join their table. It didn't hurt that Culhane had stage-whispered at his ear that Bat was a better flyer than some of his fellow astronauts. After several minutes of 'pilot talk,' Jorge agreed that Bat was indeed a knowledgeable and experienced pilot.

Then just as Jorge's meal arrived Bat's cell phone rang.

"Hello?" he listened for an instant then paused. He frowned when he recognized the voice of Charlie Stone, his control agent in The Company.

"Excuse me guys. I have to take this, some bullshit from work. I'll be right back." He rose and headed for the restaurant's back patio, which was empty because of an earlier drizzle that had wet all the tables and chairs and hadn't been wiped dry yet. As he paced around the patio, far enough away from the doors leading inside, Bat resumed the phone conversation.

As Bat listened, Stone filled him in on the background. The Agency had been able to connect the drugs found in the car of the Saudi arrested in Texas to a Mafia guy with a list of aliases as long as your arm. One such was Mario Luca. Cross-referencing the Codex files resulted in 23 individuals named Mario Luca, either legally or by fictitious use.

One Mario Luca was believed to be operating out of Belize. Furthermore, a 'Mario Luca' had previously used St. Kitts as his base of operations and had been associated with Bat's dead informer found roasted in his car in the sugar cane fields. Were they one in the same?

"The pieces are fitting together. The drugs going through Luca in St. Kitts, your dead informer, now a Luca in Belize whom we suspect is the same one with a connection to the Saudi, who probably has terrorist connections," he paused then added. "But get this: We can match the packaging paper Scotland Yard found in your dead St. Kitts guy's house to packaging paper found in a Mexican border tunnel into the U.S. And guess what country shares a border with Mexico at the other end of the country? Belize!"

This information peaked Bat's attention. "Tell me about the paper," he asked.

"A Border Patrol vehicle noticed they'd been hitting a depression on a piece of dirt road our side of the Mexican border whenever they went over it. The other day it became a good size sink hole."

"A friggin tunnel," Bat cut in.

"Not just a 'tunnel,' the biggest damn tunnel ever. It's the longest, most sophisticated tunnel yet discovered down there, 60 feet below ground at some points, five feet high, and nearly half a mile long, extending from a warehouse near the international airport in Tijuana, Mexico, to a vacant industrial building in Otay Mesa, Calif., about 20 miles southeast of downtown San Diego. It has a concrete floor, electricity, lights and ventilation and groundwater pumping systems."

"Not your typical passageway for smuggling in illegal aliens," Bat commented.

"That's the truth. Anyone who would build this had to have access to money and people with a strong construction and engineering backgrounds. It's almost like a mineshaft. Only big-time drug money could afford this kind of effort."

"So what's the connection with the Mario Luca in Belize?" Bat asked.

"On the California side, agents found about 200 pounds of cocaine in the Otay Mesa building. The place had several bays for tractor-trailers. The packaging paper matches the St. Kitts paper. On the Mexican side, drug agents found cell phones, two trucks, and a pulley system at the entrance to an 85-foot-deep shaft. Inside the shaft they found some spilt cocaine, probably from damaged bags. Apparently they were too busy to bother to clean it up. But here's the kicker: A trace on one of the cell phones shows a regular stream of calls to Belize."

"That's great, Charlie. Now all you have to do is go nail Luca," Bat replied

"We don't have an i. d. on the Luca in Belize, or any idea what he looks like. You've seen him. . ."

"Once, Charlie, once, five years ago. And it was fleeting. He was pointed out to me in an airport."

"Bat, that's more than we have. All you have to do is pop in, get some photos of him, places he frequents, where he lives, and that's it. We'll send in a squad to keep an eye on him and if it's the right guy, nail the bastard when he's selling more drugs to terrorists."

"You've got to be kidding me! No way, nada, nyet. They broke up the team, remember? It's a dead end, a dead issue. If you're hell bent on chasing ghosts, get somebody else to go. I'm on vacation."

"No, actually you're on *leave* and subject to immediate call-back in an emergency. And this, Agent Lynch, is an emergency. The associate director thinks this is the real McCoy and has reassembled the team."

"Who else is aboard."

"You're the first. I just got the word a half-hour ago. You're an unseen face down there and as a guide book editor you have the perfect cover. I'm flying down tomorrow and will meet you there."

Stone gave him the name of a hotel in Belize City where his secretary is at this same moment booking rooms for both of them.

"But I don't know shit about Belize . . ." Bat protested

"Read the chapter in the guidebook you allegedly work for. It's no big deal. There won't be a quiz."

"This really sucks, Charlie! Are you sure this is the real deal or just a fishing expedition."

"It's as real as it gets. Trust me, Bat, we haven't had anything this good to go on since this thing became operative. I'm sorry it's messing up your private life, but you know about priorities."

Bat's pleas had fallen on deaf ears. The Company needed him to go on an unexpected mission first thing in the morning and that was that. Had this not held the strong likelihood of being connected to the murdered informer he was supposed to meet in St. Kitts, he knew he probably wouldn't have been tapped for the assignment.

Then, as he began returning to the inside of the restaurant he realized Belize had been the place Bill Higgins had tried to get him to go to also to photograph a Jade head!

When he returned to the table he broke the bad news to Culhane, and Jorge.

"That was the publisher, Bill Higgins" he lied, figuring Culhane had already told Jorge he was a travel editor. He used Higgins name as he fabricated the excuse.

"I have to postpone our diving trip a day or two, Tom. They want me to haul my ass down to Belize. Seems the local guy who was writing that chapter for the book dropped dead last night, and his notes, pages, whatever, are incomplete. The copy deadline is already past due. I've got to get there and make sense out of it and turn it in as fast as I can."

"Belize?" Jorge interjected. "Amigo, you are going to spend one frustrating day trying to do that. You can't get there from here without making connections in Miami or Orlando, and then maybe to someplace else again . . ."

Bat exhaled a large sigh and shook his head from side to side in disappointment

"And after you're finished making flights from Belize over to the Keys, it will not be a piece of cake either," Culhane put in.

"There goes the friggin diving trip," Bat muttered. "If I lose a day each way coming and going and then two days down there, that's it. We've shot the hell out of our five days of diving!"

"Unless," Jorge raised an index finger skyward and smiled.

"Unless what?" Culhane asked.

"Unless, I rent Bat one of my magnificent flying machines as a charter. Would your publisher pay for that?" he queried.

"In a heartbeat, as long as it didn't break the bank."

"Oh, it will be more to charter than a commercial flight, that I guarantee. But you could leave tomorrow and be there the same day. No hassles."

"It's do-able," Culhane nodded enthusiastically. "Whatta ya think, Bat?"

"Yeah, sure. But even if I finished up and did a one-day turnaround, Jorge's plane is going to end up sitting on the tarmac in Key West doing nothing. Don't tell me *that* won't be expensive."

"I can price this for you just figuring the charges on the engine instead of a multiple-day rate. I've flown to Belize from here a few times, ferrying archaeologists and their equipment down there. I have the charts and a rough idea of the engine miles. All you have to do when you get to the Keys is put a 'For Sale' sign with my phone number on the plane, I'll give you one."

Bat and Culhane gave each other skeptical glances.

"What's wrong with it? Why are you selling the plane?"

"Nothing is wrong with it, most of the time," he laughed at his own joke. Culhane smiled. Bat didn't. Jorge continued:

"I own seven aircraft. Actually, three are amphibians and that's really one more flying boat than I need. I've been trying to sell it up here for a few months, but few takers. Leaving it parked at an airport in the Keys for a few days would give me good exposure."

"How many engine hours since the last overhaul?" Bat asked.

"Maybe 30. Maybe less. It's a solid plane, but I don't need two backups of this type. It's really excess baggage now. I got it at a good price about five years ago when we were very busy and couldn't pass up the deal. But maybe my eyes were bigger than my wallet. I never really needed it. I've got to sell it. You can help me."

Bat's eyes brightened. Perhaps Jorge could salvage the trip.

"Let me call the publisher and convince him the only way for me to get to Belize tomorrow is by chartering a plane. I think he'll sign off on it. Give me a ballpark number I can throw at him."

Jorge did. Bat was surprised the price was as high as it was. Nonetheless, he called Stone and got approval without any problem.

The next morning, Culhane and Bat went to Jorge's hangar at the airport. He already had one of the three amphibians fueled, prepped and ready to go. After two practice take-offs and landings, one on the runway with the plane's retractable wheels, and the other in the Gulf, had satisfied Jorge and brought an ear-to-ear grin to Culhane's face, Jorge would have let Bat fly anything he had.

Bat liked the feeling of putting the big, lumbering bird down on water. When Jorge repeated to Bat that he had made this run several times and Belize City had more than adequate facilities for an amphibious landing, Bat was determined to put this bird down on the water when he got there. Jorge even provided the charts, replete with hand written comments written in the margins.

Once they filled out the required paperwork, it was already well into the afternoon.

"Okay, Captain Bat Lynch, you're cleared for takeoff!" Culhane gave him a smart salute as they walked to the runway. "And now I commence my journey to Key West."

"Hold it, Tom," Bat paused. "Why don't I fly you to the Keys? Who the hell wants to be starting a long trip like that this late in the day? That's got to be a 300 mile trip."

"Actually, 277 miles. I figure just over five hours," Culhane looked at his watch. "If I leave right now I can be there by nineish."

"What for? I can have you there, from here, in under two hours."

"And what do I do about the rental car? Just leave it here, unused for a week?"

"No, cancel it. They have a station here at the airport. C'mon, whatta ya say?" Bat punched him lightly on the arm. "I'll even let you take the controls of the bird."

"But that's going to put extra time onto your trip and slow you down. If you leave here now, you can land in Belize before dark."

"Nothing to it. Take a look at the charts. It's really not much of a diversion from flying a straight line," he laughed.

"I'll drop you off and go on a bearing due west and make a

slight left turn when I see Mexico and presto! It's a straight run to Belize."

Culhane smiled and nodded. "Let's load the plane."

It wasn't a difficult sell job. On the flight to the Keys, they agreed Culhane would get a lay of the land and do some research beyond what they already knew about wrecks in the area and perhaps do some exploratory dives until Bat joined him.

But dropping Culhane off at Key West wasn't a simple taxi stop followed by an immediate take off as both Bat and Culhane had expected. Manhandling their diving gear from the float plane to a dinghy, then renting another car, loading it up, topping off the plane's fuel tank and more conversation estimating how long it would take Bat to get back to Key West the next day, all consumed precious daylight.

Another factor which could slow him down was the weather report of increasing south to north winds in the Gulf, the remnants of a wannabe hurricane that turned out to get no stronger than a mid-level tropical storm south of Cuba. The wind was not expected to be a problem, but nonetheless, it would cause him to be especially alert to course drifting.

It was 8:45 p.m. when Bat Lynch pulled the stick back and the twin-engine aluminum skinned amphibian lifted off the relatively placid waters of Key West and turned the aircraft to a heading which would take him to Belize.

Hardly fifteen minutes later the undercover Central Intelligence Agency operative was heading toward the amber, and rapidly darkening, Western horizon when he noticed the running lights of what he correctly determined was a cruise ship slightly ahead and starboard. After several seconds, he banked to port, making a wide turn and dropped to a safe altitude to check it out. Nonetheless, the several passengers strolling around deck or star gazing aboard the *Windrush* appeared as insects.

The ship's resident physician, known as 'Doc' by crew and passengers alike, was performing a duty noted in his job description, namely mingling and pleasantly chatting with passengers when not occupied in sick bay.

The ship's manifest revealed there were no less than 23 women traveling without husbands or male companions. On this first day out of Key West, Doc had already met four of them, including a set of identical twins. Now, at the rail on Promenade Deck, he chanced upon one of them.

"Good evening . . .Jennifer. It is Jennifer, isn't it?" he presumed as he joined her.

She turned her head sideways and broke into an instant smile. Her long chestnut brown hair swaying almost in slow motion.

"Yes! Good evening Doc. How do you do that?" She replied softly. "It takes most people quite a while to tell me and Kimberly apart."

"Ah, a medical secret. We physicians know such things." He joked.

Jennifer Carson and her twin sister, Kimberly, were both divorced. Though identical, Jennifer was soft spoken, friendlier and easier to talk to, while Doc got the feeling Kimberly was a 'party girl,' a blithe spirit for a good time before she dropped you like a hot potato.

Jennifer, on the other hand, appeared more refined and lady like. The kind of girl young men always took home to meet momma. But even though Doc didn't feel his age, he wasn't a young man. In fact three years hence he would be a septuagenarian. His cruise ship flirtations were never more than platonic.

High above, Bat Lynch completed the turn and made a direct line for the ship, staying high enough for close observation without getting reported for "buzzing."

Bat felt a strong push as he picked up a tailwind. It wasn't enough to cause concern or forego his plans to inspect the ship below. He would be arriving in Belize too late to accomplish anything much this night anyway, he figured, so a little sightseeing wouldn't be a problem.

Jennifer's attractiveness was accentuated by shoulder length chestnut-brown hair framing deeply set hazel eyes, a delicately sculpted nose, and high fine cheek bones. A diminutive dimple and a radiant complexion complemented her countenance. Strangers wouldn't be surprised to learn that Jennifer had been a first runner-up in the Miss America Pageant, and then, briefly, a model with some of the leading salons in Europe. Today, she was hardly five pounds heavier than her last strut down a Paris runway a decade ago.

Doc continued making chatty small talk with Jennifer. Just as he was about to ask her if the boys were enjoying the cruise so far he heard the sound of an aircraft engine coughing as it passed high overhead and looked up. He immediately caught sight of the plane. Even in the dim twilight he saw what looked like a belch of dark smoke, which quickly turned into an unbroken stream, from the portside engine. *That fellow should get back to land as soon as he can,* Doc thought.

What the hell was that? Bat wondered. He had planned to make another wide circle and do a second fly by of the ship. Instead, instinct and training caused him to pull back on the stick and climb for altitude as his eyes darted to the gauges and dials in front of him. *There it is again!* This time it was a longer sputter, a familiar sound all pilots recognize before an engine dies. He put the plane in a less severe climb to avoid stalling outright, but deliberately continued gaining altitude.

As the aircraft struggled in its effort skyward, Bat noticed the fuel gauge had dropped in the few seconds since he last looked at it. Another sputter, this time from the starboard engine, galvanized him into action. He grabbed the microphone.

"Mayday, Mayday." He worked the dial to several frequencies. "Mayday, can you hear me on the cruise ship below?"

"Bridge! This is the radio room. We've picked up a 'Mayday' from an aircraft..."

"We see it, Sparks, it's off to our starboard side and appeared to be smoking like a chimney as it passed," the officer of the deck advised. "He's definitely loosing altitude. Pipe it through, we'll talk to him." The officer added, "Sparks, SOP to the Coast Guard."

Standard Operating Procedure is to immediately alert the U.S. Coast Guard when an S.O.S. or "Mayday" call was received at sea and relate a precise heading.

Bat was relieved that they had heard him. After a short exchange with the ship, during which Bat spelled out what seemed to be his only obvious option, he banked the plane slightly to port and put it into the widest turn possible.

Doc had politely excused himself and made his way to the bridge where he joined the others squinting to make out the aircraft's lights in the growing darkness. Within seconds after arriving Doc and the other ship officers became aware that they could no longer hear the drone of the engines. The plane was powerless. It had become a glider. Next stop, the Atlantic Ocean. *Poor sod*, Doc thought. *He'll need to do some heavy praying to get out of this in one piece.*

There's an old military adage that Bat Lynch and his wartime buddies would have found quite appropriate for this situation: There are no atheists in foxholes. To that Bat Lynch would have added: O*r in planes that lose power in their engines.* Bat watched the altimeter unwind like the hands on a manual clock someone was resetting after crossing several time zones in October. *Spring forward, Fall back* kept intruding on his thoughts as he did his best to keep the plane's nose up. Without power, the plane had no alternative but to fall into the sea.

If Bat could keep the nose up and continue the wide spiral course he was holding, he had a chance to cushion the impact. Best case scenario would be a landing no more severe than normal. But that was a very long shot, especially in the near darkness which distorted nearness and distance of the ocean below.

Save for Jennifer and the handful of those who remained at the rail on Sports Deck, passengers inside the *Windrush* were totally unaware of the drama unfolding in the sky just ahead of them. At first she had only given the plane a passing glance. Even the engine sputtering had not caused concern or alerted her. It had been the alarmed look in Doc's eyes and his abrupt departure that made her question if something was seriously wrong.

As others near her speculated on what the matter was, and proffered various scenarios for how it would end, Jennifer found herself straining to follow the distant, dim lights of the plane. It was now nearly at eye level, whereas hardly two minutes earlier it was well above them. She shivered and shook of a chill at the thought of being a witness to a plane crash at sea.

On the bridge of *Windrush* the order had been given to make a fast life boat ready. Below decks three SCUBA certified crew members hurriedly donned wetsuits. They would be joined by two other crewmen in the rubber Zodiac that would be launched. Even as they readied themselves their long seagoing experience told them that the ship had reduced speed, a necessary safety procedure for launching their boat.

The ship's captain, who had been alerted to the emergency while doing an interview with a journalist, was now on the bridge. Rapid, but calm questions, recommendations, agreements, and orders belied the life-threatening situation he and his fellow officers found themselves witnessing. Reckoning the distance and angle from the ship where the plane would hit the sea, he had slowed the ship and turned it into the slight wind. If anything was going to help this pilot keep his nose up, he thought, the buffeting wind would.

The sea, growing closer with each passing second, now filled Bat's complete field of vision. Suddenly the plane's nose rose and he caught a glimpse of the *Windrush* nearly parallel to his port side. If only the wind would continue Bat believed he had a good chance of setting the aircraft down. Despite the wind, the sea was relatively calm. The wind was racing along in a current that hardly skimmed the water beneath it.

"Launch now, he's in the drink! Starboard side, about two miles. Three o'clock, in a straight line from amidship." The loud and clear order from the bridge was accompanied by the disengaging and idling of *Windrush's* electric propulsion system's six diesel engines.

Jennifer, and the others on Sports Deck, had moved and taken positions on the starboard side rail. They had seen a trail of white foam along the surface and concluded the plane was in the water. But from this distance, and now a fully dark night, they could see nothing more.

"Why aren't we stopping?" a passenger next to Jennifer asked out loud. "We're going right past it! Hey! Didn't they see the plane on the bridge, or on radar?" he asked no one in particular. He and the others hadn't taken into account that the size, weight and momentum of the ship would continue to move the *Windrush* on the course she was heading for perhaps another mile before a complete stop.

"Look, below, I think that's a life boat moving away from us," someone else observed.

Jennifer watched the little boat as it grew smaller. The forward movement of the large ship made the life boat appear to be traveling sideways. Suddenly, there was a bright light illuminating the sky. The unexpected event created a murmur among those watching.

"That's a flare," someone said. "The pilot must have shot a flare."

In the umbrella of light both the life boat and the floating plane, still some distance away, were now visible. By now though, as the *Windrush* continued moving forward, both objects in the water were aft of the ship and it was becoming increasingly difficult to see them.

As most passengers left the area to take up positions further back to try to follow the drama, Jennifer decided it was time to go inside and left the open deck. If the pilot was able to shoot a flare, she thought, that was a good sign. It all could have turned out worse. As she headed for the bank of elevators, Jennifer wondered if there were any other people in the plane, and if any of them were injured. About this time she became aware that the ship was under power again and correctly concluded the captain had given orders to turn the leviathan toward the rescue area.

A half-hour later, Bat Lynch sipped a cup of coffee and nibbled at the corned beef sandwich he was given as he chatted with the two officers who waited in the small but comfortable room near the bridge. Both were athletic looking and he suspected one or both were part of the security staff, or whatever you call the cops on a cruise ship. He understood and accepted the reason they were spending time with him.

He had told his travel editor cover story to the crewmen who had plucked him and his duffel bag off the sinking plane, the captain and two officers who met him when he was brought aboard the ship, the ship's doctor, who upon seeing he was in perfect condition, gave him a perfunctory physical, and now the two officers he assumed were 'guards.' The door suddenly opened and one of the senior officers who had been with the captain entered. He was accompanied by Doc Bailey.

"Hello again, Mr. Bat Lynch, you check out. Everything is in order. You pass muster both physically and credentially," the doctor declared with a satisfying grin. "Your passport and other photo i.d., the references you provided, the information about chartering the plane, the lot of it. Welcome aboard the *Windrush.*"

Bat picked up the slight remnants of a cultured English accent, which he hadn't noticed previously. It certainly went with the bearing and appearance of the officer before him.

The doctor smiled and added, "Here are your things." The other officer placed the duffel bag on the floor next to where Bat was seated. "We trust you will find everything in its proper place."

The officer who had accompanied the doctor cut in. "Excuse me, Mr. Lynch, but since Doc has everything under control, I must be returning to the bridge. And there is no longer need for your baby sitters either." He nodded to the other two men in the room. They proffered slight waves and nods to Bat and the trio departed.

"Thank you," Bat replied, then turned his attention to Doc. "Is it possible to make a few phone calls from the ship? I've got to tell some people they won't be seeing me tomorrow."

"But they will!" the doctor smiled. "Well, actually, the morning after tomorrow. Monday is a glorious day at sea. But, just as you were, the *Windrush* is headed for Belize and we'll have you there fit as a fiddle early Tuesday morning, minus one aircraft, of course. You can tell your friends about this hair raising experience yourself. No need to disturb anyone tonight."

"To be accurate, one is in Belize, Higgins, the publisher I mentioned. Or he will be by tomorrow. And the other guy is Culhane, the astronaut, the one I was supposed to go diving with in Key West."

"Mr. Culhane was one of the people our Miami office checked

some of your details with, after confirming with NASA that he was indeed an astronaut. He was relieved that you were not injured and said to tell you to call him when you had a chance.

"You are certainly free to call him tonight if you wish, or send an email from the ship's internet café up in the Nobel Library on Atlantic deck, amidship. They also reached a Jorge somebody at Orlando Air Taxi Service who confirmed your plane charter. Unfortunately, our Miami people were unable to reach Mr. Higgins on his cell phone or via the email address you gave."

Bat had deliberately given a bogus telephone number the Company sometimes used in situations such as this and one of the email addresses only he had access to at the publishing house. Bat thought for an instant before answering.

"Well, Higgins is going to be pissed, super pissed. He expected me in Belize today, tonight at the latest. But it took forever to get the plane." *Which was probably now settled on the bottom of the Gulf of Mexico,* he thought.

Then he wondered for an instant what Jorge Martinez's reaction had been upon being told the Orlando Air Taxi Service didn't have the problem of trying to sell the plane anymore. Bat didn't bother asking the officer.

"I know where Higgins will be staying in Belize. I guess I'll try to reach him or leave a message now. What else can I do?"

"Excellent! You can phone him from your cabin or send an email from the Internet Café."

"You said they had trouble reaching him by phone? I'd better send an email."

"Let's go then, follow me. It's some distance from here. You'll be seeing all sorts of nooks and crannies as we make our way. Consider it a Cook's Tour!" Bat grabbed the duffle bag and slung it on his shoulder.

When they reached the café it was empty. Bat put the duffle bag on the floor and sat in front of the screen on one of the computers and immediately began the process of going on line. Doc immediately realized Bat was familiar with such away from home operations and opted to give him privacy.

"I think I'll catch a quick smoke right out here on deck."

"I won't be long. Probably finish sending this before your cigarette is done."

Doc smiled, nodded and departed the room.

Very shortly Bat was composing an email.:

> Dear Charlie,
>
> I'm okay. Had a problem with the plane I chartered and put it into the drink about two hours ago. A total loss.
>
> Fortunately, a passing cruise ship plucked me out of the water. Cover, camera, gear all okay also. The ship is *Windrush*. Reaches Belize Tuesday A.M. Find where she docks and meet me. If you want to reply, do it to my regular address (as above) and I can come back on as a guest later and check for it.
>
> Regards, Bat

Bat reread the email and decided what he said was sufficient and to the point. He was standing at the entrance of the Internet Café when Doc appeared through one of the nearby doors leading to and from the outside deck.

"Finished already? My, my, you are a man of few words. Or should I say an editor of few words?"

"Brief and to the point: Crashed plane, rescued by fabulous cruise ship. May never get off at Belize."

"Well now that that's done, enjoy the rest of the evening and count your lucky stars. That was a remarkable water landing with no power. Not a scratch on you. You must be some super pilot."

"The strong headwinds helped" Bat replied, somewhat self depreciatingly.

"And good for you they did! And also good you had your mishap where you did. The weather outside right now is as calm and quiet as an empty room. Nothing blowing at all. Just the way we like it." Doc was trying his best to be cheery and upbeat.

"Am I free to go then?"

"Absolutely. You have the run of the ship, as do the rest of our passengers. We've swiped your credit card through the scanner for billing and issued you a proper SignAboard Card, which also permits you to enter your cabin, which by the way, is one of the entertainers' cabins." He handed the card to Bat.

"Entertainers' cabins?" Bat didn't understand the term or its significance.

The doctor realized his confusion. "All of our Excalibur Cruise Lines' ships sail full just about every cruise, especially *Windrush*. The proverbial 100% occupancy isn't some lofty goal or dream. For us, it is a way of life. Fortunately, we keep a few cabins open for the various entertainers who come on board do their shows, then, when we get to a new port, they move on to another ship. Along the way, we pick up another entertainer, and so it goes. It is a sort of musical cabins, so to speak. Your arrived at the right time, so you get a cabin!"

"And the SignAboard Card?" Bat queried.

"Yes, as I said, that's your ticket to everything onboard. The card expires on Tuesday when we reach Belize. But then you'll be on your way anyway. For now, though, I'll escort you to your cabin if you are ready to retire."

"Actually, I'm still a bit keyed up from all the excitement. The adrenaline is still pumping. I want to stay awake for a while and key down. Is there a show going on somewhere? A lounge, a café? Someplace with music where I could just go and let my mind adjust to these unexpected surroundings?"

Doc looked at his watch. "If you put a move on we can deposit your gear to the cabin and you should be able to make it in time for the Late Seating show in the Taj Mahal lounge. It is very good. There's an upper level entrance two decks below where we are now. But we'll reach your cabin first, just one deck down, on Upper Deck. We can use the same elevator bank to reach both. But we've got to get a move on."

Bat walked in pace with the officer. As luck would have it, one of the six elevators was open and waiting when they reached the foyer. As they made their way down, the officer produced a small blue *Windrush* Deck Plan and briefly explained its navigation usefulness as he handed it to Bat.

Bat hardly glanced at the cabin as he put his bag on the couch and then, in a few quick steps, pulled the door shut behind him. Despite the doctor's offer to take him to the Taj Mahal lounge, Bat insisted he would be able to find the place one deck down, practically below where they were standing. Nonetheless, the officer insisted. But instead of using the elevator this time they went down the ornate stairs. As predicted, there was a sign and a wide doorway leading into the lounge a short distance away.

They approached it and paused next to an attractive woman about his age who had opened the lounge door a crack and was also looking in. The show had not yet begun.

"Good evening, Jennifer," Doc smiled, his eyes lingering on her briefly before concentrating on Bat.

"This is the top level. If you prefer something lower, either first or second level, I recommend you go in here and work your way down or until you find a seat you like," the physician advised.

"I think it'll get pretty full the lower you get," Jennifer volunteered.

"Yes, that's true," Doc replied. "But I think you'll both be able to find some excellent seats yet, as long as you don't want to be front row, center." He smiled. Both Bat and Jennifer did likewise.

"No, I don't need to be that close, but I'd also like to be a bit lower than up here in the rafters," Bat joked.

"Quite understandable, considering your unexpected fall from the sky earlier tonight. Well, once again Mr. Bat Lynch, welcome aboard the *Windrush*. Enjoy your evening." They shook hands, and with a slight touch to his cap he turned to Jennifer adding, "Ma'am" then turned and left.

"Well, no time like the present," Bat mumbled aloud, but more to himself than to the woman. "Let's find seats before the curtain goes up."

Instead of moving immediately, she half turned and looked at him, actually stared at him, before he could step away.

"Are you one of the people they rescued from the plane?" she asked, somewhat in disbelief. "I was up on deck and saw it all, well most of it.

"The one and only person aboard," Bat burlesqued a deep bow from the waist, replete with an outstretched arm. "Now, for my next trick...," he joked and let the words hang for a pregnant instant before introducing himself with a broad smile.

"Bat Lynch, excellent travel editor, photographer, and pilot. The events of earlier this evening notwithstanding."

She smiled back. "Pleased to see that you are all in one piece, Mr. Lynch, pilot *extraordinaire*. . . and a comedian as well."

He looked at her for the first time face to face and immediately felt a sincere warmth and pleasantness about her. Besides her physical attractiveness, there was something gentle and honest in her voice.

"Actually, I was en route to, of all places, Belize."

"Oh, what good fortune! The ship is going there too." She smiled as she pushed open the door and entered the lounge. Bat was at her side. Neither had mentioned anything but it was obvious they would sit together. This level of the Taj Mahal Lounge was not quite half full. They had several seating options.

After some small talk about how far down or up they should sit, they agreed on a pair of seats in an empty row about midway down.

"Well, now you know who I am but all I know, thanks to Doc, is that your first name is Jennifer and that you attend lounge shows with pilots picked out of the drink!"

"I'm sorry," she said. Bat thought she seemed to blush.

"I'm Jennifer Carson. I'm a writer also."

"Really?" Bat didn't know if he should be happy or alarmed. If the conversation turned very technical about publishing, he wondered if he would be unmasked as a phony. "What do you write?" *Please, please, don't say travel guide books!* He thought.

"Promise you won't laugh?" she queried with an impish grin.

"Cross my heart." Bat's right index finger traced a line on his chest the way he and his younger sister did as children.

"Okay, then, I'll tell you: I write fiction. Romantic fiction, those scandalous trashy paperback novels in which the heroine is always in peril and is saved by the hero, a shining knight who rides in to save her at the last minute. My sister calls them 'bodice rippers' because, in a number of my books, at the predictable mad moment of passion, the hero nearly tears the clothes off the always-willing heroine. Absolutely nothing a man would read, strictly fantasy romances for women."

"Nonetheless, you're a published novelist! I'm impressed. How many books have you written?"

"With the one I'm working on now will be number 16. They're all historical dramas." She paused and another impish grin creased her lips. Bat found it attractive and appealing.

"But in this one, I think I'll work in some scenes about a fair-to-middling pilot who crashes at sea and is rescued by a cruise ship." She covered her mouth with both hands to suppress a giggle."

Bat liked her. She had a sense of humor and didn't take herself seriously. Big plusses to go along with her good looks. He figured he'd better get to the nitty-gritty before his instant infatuation blossomed into something more, even in the very short time they'd be together on the ship.

"And as a woman who constantly writes about romance there is most likely a *Mr. Carson*?" It was blunt and to the point.

"No, there is no Mr. Carson. There was, but 'happily ever after' didn't even last two years. We're divorced. He's history. That was a long time ago, in a previous life."

The house lights dimmed and the orchestra began playing a familiar overture. The stage show was going to be a somewhat abridged ship production of various scenes from Andrew Lloyd Weber's *Phantom of The Opera*.

CHAPTER SIX

"Sir Warren, Sir Warren!" The butler was unusually excited.

"What is it Edward?" Sir Warren looked up from his desk in the library and put down the magnifying glass and tweezers he was using to inspect the new additions to his stamp collection.

"There's been a terrible accident. I just heard it on the tele. Mr. Wilford is dead."

The *de facto* head of The Committee looked at the butler and tried very hard to muster an expression of sadness. But he was barely successful. "How, Edward? Where?"

"They said he must have lost control of his vehicle or fallen asleep at the wheel and gone off one of those sharp turns up on the road towards Mr. Smythe-Pembrooke's country estate."

"Pity." Sir Warren uttered. It was devoid of emotion, then added "I can very well see how that could happen. A treacherous drive, that. It's a wonder Austin himself has done it all these years." He looked at the butler who was still standing there, apparently waiting for further comment or conversation.

"Thank you, Edward," he said, dismissing the man.

Once alone again, Sir Warren scanned the several still unmounted stamps on his blotter. It had seemed like ages since he had spent any quality time with his collection and the backlog of new acquisitions was considerable.

Then he spotted what he'd been looking for: An old 1981 St. Kitts and Nevis booklet of eight stamps issued to commemorate the marriage of the HRH The Prince of Wales and Lady Diana Spencer some 15 years ago but still available in the local philatelic bureau. *I wonder if Diana saw these when she visited?* he mused.

****

Bat carried his plate of food through the automatic glass doors of the Mermaids Grille and out to the Poseidon Pool and Bar area. He took several paces before pausing to decide upon a table to sit at. And then he spotted Jennifer Carson seated at a window along the starboard side. There were two young boys with her.

"Hello," she said in a cheerful voice as he reached the table.

"And hello to you. Are these two young men your sons?" he asked. The boys were busy eating hot dogs and attacking a plate heaped with French Fries. Both appeared to be under ten years old.

"No, they're my sister Kimberly's. She's under the weather this morning so I'm playing Mommy." She paused and smiled.

"Blake and Marshall, this is Mr, Lynch. The pilot the ship rescued from the sea last night."

They both stopped eating and looked at Bat.

"Wow! That's cool. I wish we had seen you crash your plane." Marshall blurted.

"Our dad has a plane, but he never crashed it," Blake added as if failing to crash signified some breach of heroic etiquette.

"Boys!" Jennifer mildly scolded. "Mr. Lynch could have been killed. That was a very serious crash."

They ignored her and resumed eating while all the while keeping their eyes on Bat.

"Will your brother-in-law be joining you for lunch?"

"No again. It's just me, Kim, and her boys on this trip." She was unintentionally evasive.

"Our parents are divorced," Blake, the five year old, interjected.

"But it's a friendly divorce," Marshall, the eight year old, added.

"Won't you join us?" she offered in an effort to cut off the personal chatter of her nephews.

"Don't mind if I do," Bat replied without hesitation. He had enjoyed meeting her last evening, and though their conversations during the show were quick, small talk things of a few words each, he got the feeling she would be an interesting woman and shipboard companion for the now less than 24 hours he would have aboard the *Windrush.* He immediately began eating his omelet.

"You're having eggs? That's for breakfast," Marshall noted. "It's lunchtime."

"Well, it may be a lunchtime for you, but I slept like a log and only got up a little while ago. It's breakfast for me. I hit the sack after the show last night," he glanced at Jennifer as he spoke, "...and went out like a light."

209

"That's really not at all surprising," she replied. "Considering the harrowing experience you went through. After the adrenaline rush and all the excitement, your body crashed. . . no pun intended."

"Yeah, I guess going to the show really helped me wind down. I apologize if I was boring company."

"No apology necessary. We went in to see a show, not chat away. Besides, we didn't know each other, *don't* know each other. What could we have possibly talked about?"

Bat grunted in agreement. She was right. Though under different circumstances he wouldn't mind getting to know her better. He found Jennifer Carson easy to be with. In both of their meetings over the last several hours, she made him feel comfortable.

Jennifer didn't like being at a disadvantage, which is what she felt like now since Bat knew she was divorced while she knew nothing about him other than how he got onboard. She slowly forked a piece of lettuce and a radish from the salad before her.

"So, writer *cum* pilot Bat Lynch, based on your solo appearance last evening, I guess it's safe to say a *Mrs.* Bat Lynch won't be joining us for lunch...but is there a Mrs. Bat Lynch searching the sky for you?" That should level the playing field, she thought.

"No ma'am. No wife, present or former, and no fiancée. I think the only person searching the sky for me is a very rotund magazine editor named Bill Higgins in Belize. That is, unless he's read the email I sent this morning telling him what happened." *Damn, why do I have to keep lying to protect my job?* He thought.

"Were you headed for a business meeting in Belize?" Jennifer began to dig.

"In a sense, you could say that. Besides working on the travel guide book, I do a little freelance photography. Going to Belize was killing two birds with one stone: guide book copy for the book and some photos of a large, ancient Jade head for Higgins' magazine." Bat had used the old telephone conversation with Higgins at the Cape to fabricate an ever growing, more elaborate, cover story.

He felt himself digging deeper and deeper into an abyss of deception to an attractive woman, with no connection whatsoever to his work, whom he believed that under different circumstances he

210

would like to see more of. He realized, or at least admitted to himself for the first time, that he had reached that intangible marker in his career that old timers in the agency call burnout.

'When you start wondering what the hell you are doing this or that for,' his mentor had once said, *'and start considering all the real things in life you are giving up, then it's time to get out.'*

"Really? A Jade head in Belize?" Jennifer asked.

"Yes, he said it is about four feet high and three feet in diameter. Nothing like it has ever been found at a Mayan site. The magazine wants to put out a special issue. This is apparently a big deal if you're into Jade heads, Mayan artifacts, and such."

"Isn't jade green?" Blake asked.

"Yes," both Jennifer and Bat answered together.

"But it's all hush-hush at the moment because the magazine doesn't want the archaeological site crawling with newspaper reporters and TV crews." He looked at the boys.

Even though he believed that Higgins probably already had the photos he wanted, embellishing the story served his cover.

"Can I trust you guys to keep this a secret?" Bat continued. "I wouldn't want anybody else knowing about the Jade head."

"Sure. We can keep a secret," Blake said. Marshall nodded.

"Are you going to Altun Ha when we get to Belize? That's a famous archaeological site." Marshall said.

"That's where *we're* going, lots of people on the ship are going there. It's one of the tours," Blake added.

Stunned, Bat exhaled a sigh. "Actually I'm going a little past it, but close enough. We'll be heading in the same direction. That's the area where the head was discovered and where I'm supposed to photograph it, in its 'natural' surroundings."

"Why did you put an ironic inflection on the word 'natural' " Jennifer asked.

"Because the professor who discovered the head moved it from the site to a nearby shack he lives in so nobody would see it. The government and the locals don't even know about it." Bat was digging himself deeper and deeper into the lie.

"A three-foot round piece of Jade four feet tall must be pretty heavy, don't you think?" Jennifer queried.

"I suppose," Bat said. Then, mentally picturing the object, added. "Yeah, darn heavy I'll bet." Then, before things really got out of hand, he added:

"But when we get to Belize I'll meet with Higgins first and get an update about what's going on. Who knows? With the delay my crash caused, he may have already gotten somebody else to photograph the head, and I'll be off the hook."

"Hey mister," Marshall queried, "Will you take a picture of me and Blake with the big green head? That would be cool!"

"So much for 'hush-hush,' " Bat commented with a weak grin.

Unbeknownst to Bat, the fictional shack past Altun Ha where the Jade head of his story was supposed to be hidden was in the general direction where he would face death.

****

Mario Luca was a big man with a big problem. Two problems actually. The first was that the Mexican tunnel he had his Saudi Arabian 'client' build had been discovered. Loss of the tunnel not only hurt his regular business between the drug cartel and the American mob, it also slowed down as well his lucrative personal freelancing with the Arabs.

His second problem was much more troublesome. He had a gut feeling the Columbians and the mob suspected he was skimming some of their drugs for his private deal with the Arabs.

Almost three months to the day before the *Windrush* would hoist anchor and effortlessly slip away from the dock in Port Canaveral, Florida, on the 7-night Western Caribbean cruise Jennifer Carson and just over 2,100 other souls would be on, Mario Luca was sitting in a popular beachfront bar in Belize City, Belize, nursing a rum and coke and casually eating strips of raw bacon while waiting for Bruce Willow, a near-do-well artist who augmented his income moonlighting as a local real estate rental agent. Luca had only very recently cultivated a taste for raw bacon and paid no heed to medical advice saying that eating uncooked pork was not healthy. And now, at forty-three years old, he had already consumed enough of it to kill or at least make a normal person very ill. But Luca wasn't anything close to what one would call normal. Overweight, often unshaven and unkempt in appearance, clothes hung on him like an unmade bed.

Both Mario Luca and Bruce Willow were Americans living in this Central American country that fronted the Caribbean Sea. Yet, by all appearances this would be an unlikely meeting between two absolute opposites. Willow was a handsome, clean cut and natty dresser in his thirties, who projected all the bearing of a refined upper middleclass education and background. With his thick blond hair, he still gave the appearance the perennial college jock most women dreamed of bring home to meet their parents. Few ever realized his romantic inclinations leaned decidedly to other men.

Mario Luca, on the other hand, was a thug. A feared thug. He was the kind of vicious-looking ape that people instinctively crossed the street to avoid passing. His wanton disregard for hurting, maiming, or killing other people stereotyped him as a psychopath. He liked to think of himself as a collection agent for a wholesale agricultural distribution business. In reality that was a somewhat colorful and accurate euphemism for what he did. Mario was a go-between, and effective enforcer, for a combine of drug traffickers moving shipments from Columbia, via St. Kitts, into Belize.

After Mario would allegedly make what was supposed to be a detailed and accurate accounting of each shipment, it was then moved via truck into Mexico. There, the cellophane-wrapped bags of 'agricultural' product were lowered down a shaft, stacked on a train of rubber-wheeled skids, and made their way through an elaborate tunnel that crossed the border into the United States.

But now, instead of instilling fear in others, it was Mario Luca who was looking over his shoulder. He had done a bad thing. A very bad thing. He had regularly been skimming a share of the combine's product, and now was unable to shake a gut feeling that they were wise to him. He couldn't put his finger on it. He didn't know exactly why he had this feeling, but he did, and it caused concern. He had survived in the mob world's dangerous and deadly drug business for many years by heeding such feelings in his gut. And once again, he feared that his gut would prove to be right.

Other than his criminal mind's innate ability to concoct a workable plan to rob from both ends of each transaction, Mario Luca could not be described as the brightest bulb on the tree. His evil, cunning mind as a thief had served him well. And, as life in the underworld would have it, he chanced into a very lucrative position that paid extremely well.

His bosses were a half-dozen representatives of various Mafia families in the United States, which made up the mob's reigning "Commission," the ruling, overseeing and governing body which determined and approved which mob families did what and where they did it. In many respects, it was the underworld's equivalent of what OPEC was for oil producing nations.

Luca was the Commission's direct link to the two major cartels and several independent drug lords in South and Central America that exported vast quantities of controlled substances bound for the U.S. For all intents and purposes, some 40% of the drugs that moved into California, and then elsewhere, passed through the greedy fingers of Mario Luca.

With so many available sources of drug sellers at one end and his organized crime buyers at the other end, it was probably inevitable that even Mario Luca would stumble on a way to steal drugs and cash from both sides. Mario had been working in this trusted job for the mob for nearly 15 years. Unbeknownst to either side, he had been their silent partner for the last decade.

But he realized early on he couldn't sell the drugs he stole from the U.S. mob back to anyone associated with the mob. So for quite some time he simply stashed away the kilos of cocaine he regularly purloined. It didn't take long, however, for the enterprising expatriate American to find others in the drug trade who clamored for his business. Because of his low overhead, meaning a total lack of personal investment, he was able to keep his prices below the going market rate. He restricted his sales to buyers in Europe and the Middle East. Chief among them was a Saudi Arabian businessman who would take all the drugs Mario could provide.

At first his regular work for the mob kept him tremendously busy, often seven days a week, and caused him to move and travel around South and Central America and much of the Caribbean, both the East and West Indies. Eventually Mario settled into a routine and conducted most of his business from the safe haven of St. Kitts. The two-island Federation of St. Kitts and Nevis received the so-called "Golden Handshake" and independence from Great Britain in 1983. As part of the British Commonwealth, however, it still enjoyed British protection for international defense and security.

Even as late as the early-1990s, the sister islands of St. Kitts and Nevis were reported to still have the same look, charm, and easy lifestyle common elsewhere in the West Indies in the years prior to World War II. Mario Luca was quite happy operating there. In addition to everything else, English was the mother tongue on St. Kitts and Nevis, something that made Mario feel safer than he did in other places where English was the second language to Spanish. He confined his operations mostly to the larger island, St. Kitts. When he did infrequently cross the two-mile channel and go to little Nevis, it was purely recreational.

Geographically, St. Kitts was a perfect way-station drop-off point, as it was midway between the U.S. mainland and Columbia. But the freedom to operate that Luca enjoyed on St. Kitts also attracted other drug dealers, and, after a few years, the increased drug activity and violence between competing factions attracted attention from the U.S. Justice Department. Scotland Yard became involved when a local police official was gunned down amid a growing number of drug-related murders.

Then, when Mario discovered one of his people on St. Kitts had become a copy-cat and ripped a page from his book by skimming 'agricultural product,' Luca was not a happy camper at all. No thief likes other thieves stealing from them. Consequently, Mario took matters into his own hands and permanently removed the individual from the operation.

Luca's intense 'questioning' of the local thief had revealed the man had previously been discovered by U.S. law enforcement authorities and was on the verge of becoming a full-fledged informer. He had a second meeting scheduled with an undercover agent just after Christmas. The charred remains of Luca's would-be informer were discovered in an old, no longer worked, sugar cane field after Bat Lynch aborted the meeting and returned to the States.

Mario knew it was time to move his base of operations elsewhere. He settled on Belize for the same reasons that first brought him to St. Kitts: It was small, they spoke English there, and hardly anybody even knew the place was on the map.

Belize was truly a late bloomer in the world of tourism. It had been mostly bypassed as other tropical sun and sand destinations grew and prospered. Not until the tiny destination became a cruise ship port-of-call did Americans in significant numbers even became aware of its existence.

Yet even now it was still a very low-profile paradise for Mario Luca. He had, some time ago, confined and conducted much of his business aboard boats and small ships anchored off a handful of Belize's several hundred islands.

Mario motioned to the bartender for a refill. The rum and cokes he was drinking were predictably weak but he didn't mind that. It was something to do as he passed the time. Before the drink reached him the real estate agent arrived.

"Good morning, Mr. Luca. Sorry I'm late, please forgive me," Bruce Willow declared as he watched Luca swat several flies away from the open package of raw bacon on the bar.

"Some last minute business walked into my office and. try as I did, I was unable to break away. I hope you haven't been waiting long," the man said rapidly, nearly gagging as Luca put two strips of bacon in his mouth and chewed them in earnest.

Luca reflected on how easy it would be to snap this toothpick in half. Instead he grunted and shot him a cold, dangerous stare, which wasn't lost on the agent.

Nervously, Willow continued: "I have my car outside. If you're ready we can go see the property now," he hoped Luca wouldn't attempt to bring the few remaining slices of bacon with him. "It's slightly more than a half-hour from here, quite rural and remote."

If Luca had a sense of humor, the remark would have made him laugh. Once a person got beyond the city limits of Belize City, just about everything in the country was rural and remote.

"Let's go," Luca mumbled and shifted his massive hulk from the bar stool. Before departing he tossed a $10 bill on the bar. "Keep the change," he said, as the bartender delivered the last drink he had ordered. To Willow's relief, Luca left the untouched bacon behind.

Early on when he commenced stealing from his partners-in-crime, Mario Luca made the decision to convert the money his double-crossing thievery earned into gold. As a result, Mario's ill-gotten fortune was in the bullion gold coinage of South African Krugerands, Canadian Maple Leafs, Chinese Pandas, U.S. Eagles and small Swiss 5 oz. Bars. All of these were easily obtained in small quantities from tourist traps and jewelry shops in Belize and elsewhere throughout Central America.

At first Luca tried to be careful about attracting attention even to the point of limiting the amount of gold he bought from any single location. But, after a few years, he became tired of the long hours of driving and necessary extra trips he was taking to convert cash to gold. He continued buying gold locally, but began making the bulk of his purchases in Mexico City, some 700 miles north.

Though the individual pieces were light and easy to handle, the vast amount Luca had accumulated over the years represented considerable weight. He estimated his treasure had a retail value of more than $40-million. If his gut feeling was again correct he needed to move the hoard to a hiding place from the basement and garage of his mob-owned estate in the swank area of Belize.

If found, the gold would sound Luca's death knell. And if the mob got curious and visited the place, they'd find it. They couldn't miss it. Though it was available for Mario Luca's unconditional use, the secluded, high walled estate had been originally built as a vacation retreat for the former, late, head of an American mob family, and was owned by the Commission. Relatively modest by American mob architectural standards, the large ranch-style house was several notches above most private dwellings in Belize.

But to move the gold Luca would need help. Over the years Luca had foolishly begun stashing the gold coins into kegs which were now too heavy even for him to move. In this regard Luca was a creature of habit. Once he began something he continued doing it, *ad infinitum.*

The kegs became the second Achilles' heel of Luca's obsessive-compulsive behavior in continuing to fill wooden kegs with the gold coins, as was his penchant for continuing to steal from the mob. Luca had long ago put together enough money to retire and spend the rest of his life in total luxury without ever being suspected or caught. But he just kept stealing.

He initially filled two kegs and hid them in the basement. Upon discovering how heavy they were when full he realized he would never be able to move them up to ground level. Thereafter, the remainder of the kegs were filled and kept in the estate's separate garage next to the house, covered by several tarps. Anyone snooping under the tarps would see innocent looking rows of kegs, nearly filling two sides of the rare, three-car garage the property boasted. To a casual observer they could contain wine, perhaps even grain. But there were never any casual observers, or anyone else, permitted in the estate's garage.

As the number of kegs increased, Luca became so paranoid he fired the three former full-time, live-in servants he had employed. Now he always remained on-site when the maid/cleaning lady came twice a week and for the scheduled weekly visits of the gardener. The routine had become somewhat confining and he often thought of himself as a prisoner in self-made confinement.

Each keg contained approximately 144 pounds of gold coins. And Luca had 65 kegs, valued at $630,000 each. He definitely needed help moving what he correctly estimated as 9,400 lbs. of gold, some 4.5 tons. And he needed a safe place to hide it. This was the reason for the trip into Belize City today and the meeting with the real estate agent.

He also needed a truck for transporting the kegs and a backhoe for digging a large hole. He would promise to pay well whomever he hired to help him. Naturally, when the job was done he'd make sure the individual would never be able to mention it to anyone. Luca figured that even if the mob harbored suspicions, if they didn't find the gold, they couldn't accuse him or prove anything. Moving the kegs would keep him alive.

"So where's this place you're takin' me?" Luca asked Willow as he forced his rotund frame into the somewhat weathered Jeep Cherokee.

"Oh, you'll love it. Ever hear of Altun Ha? The archaeological site about an hour out of town? It's not far from there. Easy to reach, perfect for you." Willow's tone reflected the sometimes bubbly and encouraging banter of a real estate agent desperate to close a deal.

Luca hated 'bubbly,' from Willow or anyone else. He snapped his head toward Willow and from between clenched teeth uttered: "Altun Ha? Down here it's the local Disney World. All the tourists go there. . . I said I wanted a place where nobody went!" Mario Luca's rage grew with each word.

"Trust me, Mr. Luca, I paid *very* good attention to what you said your needs were...are. The property is a few miles past the turn off for Altun Ha. No crowds on the road. Tourists never go that far. It's convenient to reach, secluded and perfect. It's a large very, very wooded lot. You could pass right by and never know it was there."

"What kind of condition is it in? The building for sleeping, I mean." Luca asked the question though the accommodations did not matter in the least to him, but he thought a prospective renter should ask such a thing.

"Well, since you said you weren't fussy to have anything as nice as your home, I figured you wanted something akin to a lodge or campsite. Something outdoors-ish, and rugged, right?"

Luca nodded and grunted, though he was having a difficult time picturing such a place.

"Naturally, I assumed that you'd still want some civilized conveniences, such as running water and electricity. It even has a good size window air-conditioner in the living area. I did understand you correctly, didn't I?"

"Yeah, you got it right. This place just better be private. I don't need no busy-body neighbors or people poking their noses around."

"Well then, this property will certainly fit the bill. It's just over 75 undisturbed wooded acres. Nobody near you for almost a mile on either side. It's a virtual private reservation." Willow couldn't think of anything else positive to say about the property so he changed gears.

"You said you wanted a long-term rental or lease, not a purchase. The good news is once you get comfortable there and if you change your mind it is for sale. I think you can practically get it for a song and a dance," Willow lied.

Much to Luca's consternation, Willow was being bubbly again. But he forced himself to ignore it.

"Actually you could own it outright for about what you'd pay in eight years of leasing."

Willow was confident that Luca wouldn't find out that the real estate agent already had a handshake deal to purchase the land for an even better bargain price than he had suggested. His aim was to lock Luca into a five year lease that would more than cover the purchase price.

"I never plan that far ahead. I may need it for only a year, maybe less. Now shut up. I wanna' think."

Luca also could have added that he avoided, like the plague, signing anything which left a paper trail. That was one reason why living in Third World countries was attractive. It was something of a credo with him: *When you paid cold cash for anything, nobody worried about paperwork. And nobody could trace what you did.*

The real estate agent's enthusiasm quickly deflated. He considered Mario Luca to be a rude, uncouth, Neanderthal and hated every minute he had to spend with the big lug. But if even half of the whispered gossip he heard about Mario Luca regularly buying large quantities of gold coins from local shops was true, this gorilla sitting next to him was an extremely wealthy man indeed. Willow stood to make a nice piece of change if he could pull off this deal the way he wanted to.

He believed he was smarter than Luca and would eventually be able to convince him to take a long-term lease or buy the place outright. Either way, Willow could come out a winner.

Several miles of lush greenery passed as they drove deeper into the countryside. Finally, and in a casual tone, Luca asked:

"Say, Bruce, if I like this place and we shake on it, do you know where I can rent a heavy duty truck and a fork lift? I have some things at my city house that I'm thinking about bringing out here. You know, the kind of necessary stuff to make the place cozy, like a refrigerator. . . And maybe a backhoe. You got any contacts in construction? Maybe I could even put in a swimming pool. I got some friends in Mexico who do real good custom work, but I gotta have the hole dug first. Know somebody I can talk to?"

The questions were as friendly, casual and chatty as Luca could make them. He realized that by asking Willow, and no matter what answer was, he would have to kill him. Telling Bruce Willow what he just did meant the man now knew too much.

Willow was encouraged. Perhaps this was all more promising than Luca's earlier remark about only wanting a the place for a year had suggested. You don't put in a swimming pool unless you intend to be there a while. He actually didn't have to think about whom to recommend, but Willow delayed giving an immediate answer in order to make it appear he had been mentally culling names. After a brief pause he recommended someone to Luca.

Luca filed it in his head even though he had been only half listening. The intense heat of Belize had made his throat dry and he thought how nice it would be to be sitting in front of a cold beer right about now.

****

An ocean away another killer was, in fact, sitting in front of a cold beer. Shamus Boyle was enjoying the last of several pints he'd consumed that night in one of the pubs to which he frequently made the rounds. He had broadened his choice of watering holes since Cormick O'Connor had warned him and Billy Kelly to stay away from the IRA's meeting place, *The Pig & Whistle*, after they brutally murdered Smythe-Pembrooke's son-in-law, Michael Walling.

As usual, the loud mouthed, bragging thug was telling a tall tale of beating two 'coppers' to a pulp. In truth, Boyle himself was usually on the receiving end of a police beating for resisting arrest for any number of reasons. But this night his audience would not listen quietly.

"C'mon, Shamus, you're so full of shit your eyes are brown!" the comment from a heckler brought a round of hearty laughter from the bartender and quartet of regulars.

"Last time you told that story it was only one cop!" The added remark from another patron was a cue for more laughter.

"Piss on you. . ." Boyle tried to remember the man's name but, in his drunken stupor, couldn't. ". . .both of you! Piss on all of you!" he added. But this simply brought on continued laughter.

"Where's your sidekick and crony, Billy Kelly? He's the *real* fighter, not you," the bartender put in, egging him on and anticipating that anything Boyle said would be amusing. But Boyle didn't bite. Instead, he grew as serious as he was able.

"Poor Billy. He's home flat on his back sick as a dog. He thinks it's just 'the bug,' but I think it's pneumonia, I do. Sometimes he goes delirious and flails his arms wildly. I fear he isn't going to make it."

The gravity of what he said, even in his drunken voice, was evident to the others present. They listened in silence.

"He's so sick that his sister won't even come over to tidy up his place. She's worried about bringing whatever Billy has home to her children." The man closest to him was sure Shamus' eyes were suddenly watery and glazed. The bartender noticed it as well, and tried to cheer him up.

"Ah, don't go hanging a crepe on his door so soon. Before you know it he'll be off his ass and the two of you will be out raising hell again." Nods of somber agreement followed.

Shamus didn't reply. He was sitting hunched over his nearly empty glass staring into it as if he expected to find a solution.

"Here, Shamus, have another, on me." The bartender began drawing a fresh pint when Shamus held up his hand.

"No. No more. I've got to go over and see him. He's my best friend in the world and I haven't been by his place since this morning."

No one tried to stop him. The man was *three sheets to the*

wind, and now obviously melancholy. As he got off the bar stool, with some degree of difficulty, the others resumed talking softly among themselves.

Once outside Shamus paused to suck in a lung full of fresh air then wobbled around to the side of the building where he usually parked his bike. It wasn't there. It took him several seconds of thinking before he remembered he had come to the pub in Billy's car.

After all, he remembered thinking, what with Billy being so sick, there was no need to peddle a bike around when Billy Kelly's perfectly good automobile was just sitting there doing nothing. Now the question was where the hell had he parked the car.

While he was pondering this difficult question a lone figure emerged from the shadows and spoke his name.

"Shamus Boyle, isn't it?"

"Oh, bejesus, you scared the life out of me!" he replied in a startled voice. "Yes, Shamus Boyle Himself, if you please. And who might you be?" He squinted to no avail. The darkness of the alley prevented seeing the person's features.

"You don't know me. . .but I know of you and your friend, the late Mr. William Kelly."

"Well, if you don't know me. . .what did you say about Billy? Late for what? He's home near death's door, sick in bed!"

"No he isn't, I assure you. He's here. In my car. And he is quite dead already. Want to see him"

Shamus found what the stranger was saying very confusing and he became defensive. He raised two fists in a fighting stance and asked:

"Who the hell are you?"

The stranger ignored the question but asked again, "Don't you want to see your dear friend? He's in my car, right here."

For the first time Shamus realized there was a car parked a few feet away in the alley. He moved forward as the stranger backed towards the vehicle.

"That's better. I'm sure you and Billy Kelly will have a lot to reminisce about," the stranger said while opening the trunk and shining a flashlight into it.

There stuffed haphazardly into the trunk was indeed the late Mr. William Kelly, but he somehow looked different. His cheeks were puffed and extended. Shamus leaned forward for a closer look and realized what he was seeing.

"Jesus, Mary and Jos. . ." he never completed the sentence. The stranger snapped his neck in a powerful single motion.

At dawn the following morning, the first patrol of the day on the road leading to the British military garrison discovered the mutilated bodies of Billy Kelly and Shamus Boyle. And, like the corpse of Michael Walling, they had been castrated and their genitals stuffed in their mouths.

Megan Price was back in her London flat in time for breakfast.

****

While his chauffeur/bodyguard leaned on the car's fender a discreet 20 yards behind, Sir Warren sat on a park bench, hunched over, his elbows resting on his knees. He was melancholy and fighting depression as he slowly went through motions of dropping bread crumbs for the phalanx of pigeons which had gathered around him. He thought little of the advancing birds for whom such regular feedings had once brought him satisfaction and amusement.

How had it all come to this? He mused. When did the public's devotion and respect for the monarchy begin its degenerating slide to shocking headlines and television sound bites?

Had more than a decade and a half really fallen from the calendar since the great feelings of joy and celebration that filled St. Paul's Cathedral? The pomp and splendor of the wedding had been a magnificent show, to be sure. And, quite properly, the media handled coverage of it all with proper decorum and good taste. Nothing less would have been acceptable, or expected.

But the essence of the thing, the reason for the celebration was the great expectation that this union between The Prince of Wales and Lady Diana Spencer would beget an heir to the throne after Charles' eventual succession.

His fingers moved around the bottom of the empty bag for several seconds as Sir Warren stared blankly at a passing barge mid-river on the Thames. He finally realized he had expired the brown paper bag's contents.

"Sorry, my little friends, all gone. . . look," Sir Warren said softly as he turned the bag upside down. The miniscule residue of the stale bread dropped to the pavement and was quickly collected by the closest birds. He neatly folded the bag and rose from the bench to deposit it in a public receptacle some distance away.

As he walked, his remembrances drifted back to earlier, happier times, before the current state of affairs.

Since the invention of the motion picture camera, the practice of filming the Royal family had been traditionally permitted for public appearances on special and state occasions. The unique exception, unfortunately, had been the worldwide media coverage of Edward VIII's scandalous romance and subsequent abdication to 'marry the woman I love,' the twice-divorced American, Wallis Simpson.

With the outbreak of World War II in 1939, Elizabeth's father, George VI, thought it would be helpful for morale if the royals were regularly seen in newsreels and permitted carefully-monitored footage of Princess Elizabeth. Interviews or cameos of the Royal family had to be submitted to the Royal Press Officer.

Upon her father's sudden death at 52 years of age in 1952, the BBC approached Prime Minister Winston Churchill for permission to broadcast live television coverage of the 25-year-old Elizabeth's coronation as Queen. Churchill was against it and the palace declined, saying it would put an added strain on the Queen. But Elizabeth herself disagreed and the media had a foot in the door. Thereafter, every major Royal event would be televised.

On Elizabeth's Coronation Day, a reporter for the Daily Mirror noticed Princess Margaret, the Queen's younger sister, with a divorced man, Group Captain Peter Townsend. However, the paper's editor refused to print the story.

"We can't upset the ladies' day . . ." was his gallant, and very proper, comment.

But such Victorian attitudes couldn't survive against growing media interest in Princess Margaret and Townsend's romance. Newspapers began reporting every instance when they were seen together. Photographers began following him.

When the editor of *The Times*, Sir William Hayley, wrote that the Royal Family was a national symbol of family life and that if the Queen's sister married a divorced man it would damage the institution of the Monarchy, the couple was viewed as doomed lovers. The competitor, *Daily Mirror,* condemned the Palace for adopting Hayley's advice and forcing Margaret to choose between love and her royal status.

But propriety, albeit with nudge, won out and in 1955 Princess Margaret publicly terminated the relationship, ending the crisis:

"Mindful of the church's teaching that Christian marriage is indissoluble and conscious of my duty to the Commonwealth, I have resolved to put these considerations before any others. I have reached this decision entirely alone. And in doing so I have been strengthened by the unfailing support and devotion of Group Captain Townsend. . . I am deeply grateful for the concern of all those who have constantly prayed for my happiness. . ."

In 1957, Queen Elizabeth's Christmas message to the nation was televised for the first time. Hardly three years later, Princess Margaret's romance with photographer Anthony Armstrong Jones, and their subsequent marriage, hiked newspaper circulations throughout the Commonwealth to new heights.

Margaret was the first of the royals to be described in print as 'glamorous,' 'attractive,' 'shapely,' and 'cool.' She was without question the paparazzi's first Royal target. Nothing about the Royal family would ever be private, or ignored by a restrained media, again.

The incursions into the private lives of the monarchy, and the reporting of every detail to satiate the growing appetite of 'royal watchers,' evolved from what they wore at such and such event to include such extemporania as: 'Princess Anne Stopped for Speeding' or 'Prince Charles Collects Toilet Seats.' The invisible wall around The Firm had been penetrated so often it no longer existed.

Sir Warren casually watched the afternoon sun retreat below the tall trees as his chauffer kept pace in the car inching ahead on the road parallel to the path. He reflected that there had been high-spirited media interest in a half dozen or so women over the years whom Prince Charles had seen more than once.

But it was the appearance on the royal stage of Lady Diana Spencer and her anticipated engagement to The Prince of Wales that opened, nay, crashed through, the flood gates. The camera loved her, and she instantly became the photo every newspaper and magazine editor wanted. She was a phenomenon unlike any other seen in England in a millennium.

The surveillance of the royals had taken place in the natural course of things. With greater public awareness of them and their outside interests, it was first employed as a protective measure for their benefit. Even the taping of telephone conversations had its genesis in the need for keeping a few steps ahead of, for security reasons, where the Queen's closest relatives might be off to and whom they would be seeing.

Sir Warren shook his head sideways. In his wildest dreams he wouldn't have thought he would become privy to incidents of near suicide, marital infidelity, separation, and talk of divorce! Granted, it wouldn't be the first divorce in the Royal Family, he thought. But it would be only the second since Henry VIII in the 1500s.

The Queen's own sister, Princess Margaret, and the Earl of Snowden ended their failed marriage in 1978, by which time the media had tired of following her and hinting at her numerous affairs. But Margaret and Antony were not as close to the throne, no pun intended, as The Prince and Princess of Wales. Diana's husband and her first-born son were both expected to be future Kings of England.

Even as the divorced mother of the heir to the throne, Diana wielded a kind of threatening power to the security of the crown that her also divorced sister-in-law, Sarah, the Duchess of York, did not. Sir Warren and The Committee had long ago dismissed any interest in what Sarah Ferguson was doing.

The media had been teasing the general public for some time about a rift in Diana and Charles marriage. But to a populace which had heard such unfounded tales an average of twice a year during the first 25 years of married life between the Queen and Prince Philip, it all seemed like tommyrot. Sir Warren knew it wasn't.

Returning to the car, he announced to his chauffeur that he wanted to go to the club instead of directly home. he wanted to share his thoughts with Smythe-Pembrooke. He believed he had put his finger on where everything had truly begun to spiral out of control: *It was those God-damned Squidgygate tapes*!

Gilbey's unwitting use of his pet name for Diana during a taped telephone call guaranteed that their private conversation would have one of the most remembered names in British royal history. In their sexually suggestive exchange, the Princess of Wales and the Lotus automobile salesman sounded very much like intimate lovers. Diana, however, would flatly deny that in the later television interview in which she did admit to adultery with James Hewitt. Transcripts of the titillating conversation were eagerly read the world over:

Diana: "I don't want to get pregnant."
Gilbey: "Darling, that's not going to happen, all right?"
Diana: "Yeah."
Gilbey: "Don't look at it like that. It's not going to happen. You won't get pregnant."
Diana: "I watched EastEnders today. One of the main characters had a baby. They thought it was by her husband. It was by another man."
Gilbey: "Squidgy, kiss me (sounds of kissing). Oh, God, it's wonderful, isn't it? This sort of feeling."
Diana: "I love it."

Further on, the conversation digressed into what sounded like 'phone sex.'

Gilbey: "I know. Darling, umm, more. It's just like sort of . . .
Diana: "Playing with yourself?"

'Squidgygate,' it had been reported, was picked up by an amateur radio enthusiast. But Diana's defenders insisted that the Princess had been the target of a dirty-tricks campaign put into motion by elements of the British intelligence community in order to publicly discredit her.

When, a few weeks later, another amateur radio enthusiast was credited with picking up a telephone conversation between Camilla and Charles, which became known as the infamous 'Camillagate,' the roles were reversed. Now Charles' loyalists charged that Diana had someone in British intelligence providing her with ammunition to shoot back.

Even at the time, people with a limited knowledge of electronic surveillance scoffed at the suggestion that amateurs had recorded mobile phone conversations. It would have been technically impossible for amateur equipment to intercept mobile phone calls since mobiles continually shift frequencies, undetectable to the user. A thorough investigation by British and American experts eventually determined both these tapes were professionally produced, officially or unofficially, by the British intelligence services.

The amateurs who picked up the calls had been duped. The Squidgygate tape was recorded by SIS from it's tap on Diana's phone line. It had been electronically enhanced to improve quality and then broadcast on the public airwaves until it was picked up by an amateur radio enthusiast 4 days later.

Sir Warren had been aware of the Squidgy tape and agreed with the reason for releasing it to the media.

But he had been caught completely off guard by Camillagate.

And, as difficult as it was to accept, he had also been duped by an amateur: Diana herself.

The princess desperately wanted something of value to negotiate with when she and Charles sat down with their solicitors to frame out the legal separation she wanted. She believed solid, undeniable evidence of Charles' dalliance with Camilla would be dynamite. She approached members of the Security Services with whom she was friendly and trusted, explained what her needs were and convinced them to make her a copy of any tape that would be damaging to Charles.

She arranged to have it sent to her anonymously so she'd have the bargaining chip when the time came. It was a good plan but it backfired. A copy of the Camillagate tape found it's way into public hands.

Instead of a bargaining chip for herself, she had brought embarrassment to The Firm.

****

Mario Luca could feel the blood throbbing in his temples as he listened to the answering machine message Bruce Willow had left him. Everything had gone perfectly well up till now; actually, better than Luca could have imagined. But now he would have to wait for Willow to return from an unexpected business trip to Mexico to sell some of his art before cleaning up the last piece of unfinished business. To Mario Luca, Bruce Willow was definitely a piece of unfinished business, a dangerous piece of unfinished business.

The 75-acre wooded property Willow had shown Luca was good, very good. It was perfect for his intended use and it was as secluded as Willow had said. The interior of the old cement block building had been crudely divided with two-thirds left as a storage area and one-third serving as a dwelling. It had obviously all been a storage complex of some sort at one time. Despite the obvious storage area, hiding the kegs of gold coins there was never a consideration. They would be buried on the property.

The partitioned interior walls had all the unskilled earmarks of amateur work. But it was functional if one needed a roof over one's head. Luca had never given a second thought to spending an overnight in the place. What pleased Luca the most was the dense, closely knit cluster of trees, providing an impenetrable shield from curious eyes on the road. The building wasn't even slightly visible until a person ventured some twenty feet onto the property. Willow had been truthful when he said a person driving by would never know habitation existed just beyond the thick, jungle-like forest.

Luca wanted the site. But when Willow reached into his

attaché case and produced a boiler plate lease contract Luca balked. He was adamant about not wanting to sign anything. This impasse continued for a few minutes until Luca finally offered Willow a full six months of the agreed to lease fees in advance. Reluctantly, Willow took it. He'd worry later about what to tell the relatives of the late former owner, if anything.

After shaking hands on the oral lease, the real estate rental agent again reminded Luca about Geoffrey Hindel, the American who was the local manager for a construction company based in neighboring Guatemala.

Willow told Luca that, for a very attractive price, his friend Hindel would probably do the work for Luca 'on the side' without the construction company owners' knowing about it. It was exactly the kind of arrangement Luca wanted. As a crook, Luca found comfort in doing business with other crooks.

Luca and Hindel, who had the muscular physique of a body builder, spent more than two hours on an extremely hot and humid Tuesday loading the kegs of 'metric nuts and bolts' at his estate onto the truck, then driving and unloading them into the storage portion of the building at the site. "I'm an exporter," Luca had told Hindel.

Luca slept that night. Though the air-conditioner Willow had mentioned did, in fact work, the big man had been uncomfortable.

The following morning, Hindel returned pulling a flatbed trailer with the back hoe on it. He also had the several dozen long planks and gallons of tar Luca requested for reasons unknown.

By lunchtime the young American had dug the huge hole, at Luca's instructions, to have an expansive 20x20 foot deep rectangular section at the extreme right, where the usual 6.5 foot depth would normally be in an 25m x 50m Olympic size pool. It was the oddest looking swimming pool excavation Hindel had ever seen.

"Deeper, over there," Luca grunted in monotone after Hindel called him outside to inspect the ditch when the job was done.

"*What?*" Hindel's high-pitched reply was in direct volume to the surprise he felt. "This is *already* way beyond the typical grade and depth for an Olympic swimming pool. I've dug dozens of them. If you make this any deeper your expert pool guys are going to kill you with extras and add-ons for custom-custom work!" Hindel protested.

"Deeper in that end over there," Mario pulled another limp strip of bacon from the now warm package he was holding. "I want the header end deeper, another ten feet more, at least. And extend that whole side back there by another 10 feet too."

He turned and faced Hindel. Feigning a weak, insincere smile added. "I got a lotta' friends who like to dive deep, real deep, like off the cliffs in Acapulco. The pool's gotta be deeper and longer at that end." He extended his arm and pointed. His greasy fingers still holding a piece of bacon.

"Jesus H. Christ, Mr. Luca, what do you want to do, float a small yacht in there? I could put my truck, trailer and back hoe in the size hole you'll end up with!" It was a prophetic comparative analogy.

"This is going to be a BIG hole. You must have money to burn. I'll have to cut a graded ramp into one side to get the back hoe down there. You're going to end up with at least 20% more dirt. "

Luca simply shrugged as he chewed the last handful of bacon from the package. He slowly rubbed his greasy hands on his thighs and locked his stare on Hindel.

"That's what I want. Do it my way." Missing, but understood, were the last two words: *or else*.

"But don't bother to refill that ramp gut you make. The pool guys will need to drive into it."

Hindel looked at the wristwatch on his dirty, sweaty arm as he returned to the back hoe cab. "You could have saved yourself a lot of money by just hiring somebody down here to do this job instead of bringing in an outfit from Mexico," he called after Luca, who was already walking back to the building.

"Don't worry about it," Luca stopped, turned and gave Hindel another menacing stare before he resumed walking. Then, as an afterthought, added:

"You better get going and finish up, they're gonna' get here on Monday," Luca lied. There was no Mexican pool company arriving Monday or any other day. Indeed, there would never be a swimming pool, Olympic or otherwise, on the site.

Inside the building, Mario passed from the 'living quarters' into the storage area. He stood there silently for some time trying to decide exactly how he would arrange the kegs in the hole. Should they be on their side, or standing straight, row after row? Fortunately Hindel had left the fork lift on the property after the first trip, preferring to take everything back at one time when the job was done. *"Moving them kegs without the fork lift I'd be busting my balls big time,"* Luca reflected.

There really was no choice. He would have to roll the kegs onto the fork lift four at a time from the storage area and back the machine down into the hole, using planks as ramps. He would then manhandle them around into tight rows. There would be more than enough room, even with the extra items going into the hole.

Almost an hour later, Hindel was finally finished and again called his employer out for an inspection. When Luca appeared Hindel noticed he was carrying a long cardboard box, the kind florists use when delivering very long stem flowers.

Luca walked to the ditch and was quickly satisfied that Hindel was indeed finished. Satisfied that the extra depth in the header area was, as he figured, more than ample to serve the intended purpose, Luca looked around approvingly for several seconds then suddenly stopped and stared intently into the deepest end of the hole while silently gesturing Hindel to his side with a slow hand motion. Curious, the man came beside him and looked into the hole himself, as if expecting to see whatever was holding Luca's attention.

"What the hell are you looking at?" Hindel's eyes rapidly searched the bottom of the hole and then turned to face Luca.

"Your grave," Mario said as he caught Hindel off balance and pushed him into the ditch. In an effortless smooth move he produced the shotgun from the box and fired a blast into Hindel's back the same instant his body bounced in the bottom of the hole. The second shot, to the head, was overkill.

Luca had deliberately observed the procedures Hindel had gone through starting and moving the back hoe and the fork lift. He climbed into the larger machine, engaged it, and drove it back into the ditch. He did the same thing with the truck and trailer.

With some difficulty he made his way back up the ramp and from the top took in the overall site. As he had planned there was at least five feet from the top of the vehicles and the grade level surface where he stood.

Luca then began loading the kegs onto the fork lift and taking them down into the hole. When that task was done, Mario placed several planks atop the kegs then laid the tarp that had covered them in his garage and most recently in the storage area of the building on top of them. He nailed the tarp to the planks at the four corners and in the center and poured several 5 gallon drums of tar he had previously purchased over it all as a crude seal. He put the fork lift into the building and covered it with the tarps he had used on the kegs.

He worked late into the night that Saturday and most of Sunday shoveling the huge mounds of excavated dirt back in. He was physically spent. The final step of his improvised camouflage effort was raking dry dirt, loose ground cover, leaves, branches and dead chunks of dry, fallen trees over the entire area. When he was finished there was hardly a trace that the large area of land behind the building had ever been disturbed. He collapsed in the overstuffed chair in the building, too tired even to get a package of bacon out of the refrigerator or even to lean forward and try to reach the television remote on the table. He was exhausted. Mario Luca slept the next twelve hours straight.

It was now midday on Monday. Luca figured by now people at the construction company knew Hindel was absent from work. Ditto the missing backhoe, truck and fork lift. The combination of these things would cause a search. What excuse should he prepare if, by chance that *pussy* Willow (he couldn't help breaking into a fit of laughter at his unintentional pun) said something about Hindel doing work for him.

Of course, he would deny ever seeing Hindel, but planning exactly how to convey it as believable required a lot more thinking and planning. Luca decided to return to the comfort of his estate. He needed to take a shower then lie down again and think. Plus, he was out of bacon here. But there was more in the refrigerator at home.

So now, as he replayed and listened to Willow's message advising callers he'd be in Mexico City between Friday and Wednesday selling paintings, Luca considered it might be possible to just play dumb and get away with the whole thing if Willow told the authorities he had recommended his missing friend to Luca. But that was a gamble he wasn't willing to risk. He would stick to his original plan and dispose of Willow, the only person who could link him to Hindel, the missing truck and back hoe. Mario Luca planned to meet Willow the day the real estate agent returned. It was never too soon to tie-up loose ends.

At least he was now back in the comfort of his estate, not the cement block hovel, and there wasn't a trace of the gold anywhere to be found here. He went to the refrigerator and removed another pound of bacon and headed for the shower. All this work and thinking made him hungry.

That Wednesday Luca laboriously climbed the stairs to the second floor of Willow's art studio/real estate office on Prince Street.

The overweight man was only slightly winded when he walked into Willow's studio, but he made a deliberate effort to catch his breath and look exhausted before attempting to kill him with his bare hands. Instead, he found his intended victim hunched over his desk and quite distraught.

"What's amatta, Bruce, you got a problem?" It was as good an opening and distracting comment as any when you show up unexpectedly at somebody's place, especially when you plan to strangle them.

"Hello, Mr. Luca. What a pleasant surprise," he lied, "on such a dreadful day. I'm at my wits end."

"What's wrong?" Luca said in as close to a compassionate tone as he could muster. He wondered if it had anything to do with Hindel being missing. But never expected to hear what followed.

With such little encouragement Willow blurted out that he had just been paid a visit by the police who were looking for

Geoffrey in connection with the disappearance of one of the construction company's vehicles and other equipment.

Luca decided to let the man talk and provide more information while at the same time Mario continued to recover from climbing the stairs. And Willow obliged.

"He's gone. Vanished. Not even a goodbye note!" Willow shook his head from side to side in disbelief. "I thought we. . . had become close friends. How could I have been so foolish?" The question was more introspective to himself than for Luca.

"Gee, whatta shame. Yous guys was tight friends, huh?"

"Friends? Yes. Good friends. . . But I had to tell the police about Geoffrey's gambling. He owed money all over the place. Including a small fortune, by my standards, to me. Some of the people he was in debt to are real shady types, Mr. Luca, the criminal kind. I'm sure you know what I mean. They would even send a shudder through a big man like yourself. They can be frightening people."

Mario doubted it. He hadn't seen anyone in Belize, or most places for that matter, who frightened him. But he let Willow continue.

"I loaned him money, several times. Actually sold some of my best paintings. Now I can stick my fingers up my . . ." he paused and amended the crude comment he was about to make, then continued, ". . . now I can just whistle Dixie."

"I suspected Geoffrey was trouble the first time I met him. He could be cruel and mean, and especially nasty when he was drunk." Willow appeared more angry than hurt at losing his friend.

"Now the stupid sonofabitch steals a truck and high tails it out of here, probably to Mexico and some tramp whore waiting for him. He leaves a steady job and a good life here with me for what? Some slut? Talk about burning your bridges."

Luca listened intently. This story was turning into a perfect cover.

"You mean he scrammed outta here for some dame?"

"Probably. He never lost his eye for a tight skirt or great knockers." Willow's last few words sounded spiteful.

Mario Luca had cautiously inched closer to the desk Willow was sitting at for a better position from which to strike from behind. But instead of moving behind him, he paused and let Willow continue talking.

Willow half turned and quickly looked at Luca.

"The ungrateful sonofabitch! I thought getting him that little side job with you for extra income would finally give him some money to begin paying off his debts and make a clean start.

"Yeah, gee, I never saw him. He never showed up," Luca tested the lie.

"I'll bet the bastard never intended to do your job, Mr. Luca. When I told him I was going out of town for a few days he took the opportunity to vanish."

Then, as if suddenly realizing that he was babbling on about more of his personal life than Mario Luca needed to know, Willow abruptly changed the mood.

"I'm sorry, Mr. Luca, I shouldn't be burdening you with all this. I'm just annoyed, pissed off really. What is it they say: *No good deed goes unpunished?* Ain't that the truth! Try to help somebody and they kick you in the rump."

"Rump? What the hell's a rump?" Luca wondered, never having previously heard the usage. *"Balls maybe?"*

"Do you still need somebody to move your boxes, or whatever?" Willow asked. "I think I can probably find someone reputable. It's the least I can do."

Luca's leathered face masked the utter surprise in what he was hearing but, nonetheless, he couldn't avoid blinking at Willow.

"No, no, Bruce. Thank you. Everything's fine. I changed my mind about that, and forgot to tell you." Luca quickly improvised, "I just took a few things I needed up to the place in my car." There was a pregnant pause as neither man spoke. Then Luca continued.

"I decided I really didn't like the place that much after all, so no need to fill it with stuff better left at home, know what I mean?" Then in what was nearly overkill he added, "I probably won't be going up there as much as I thought. Maybe every now and then. That living in the country stuff is just not what I expected. Those damn biting red ants are all over the place and, boy oh boy, the mosquitoes out there are as big as pigeons," he exaggerated. "Real nasty fuckers" he added in profane emphasis.

Willow, suddenly fearing that Luca had stopped by to try to get out of the lease, and now expected his money back, replied boldly.

"But Mr. Luca, a lease is a lease. A legal document." Suddenly his anger at Hindel was put on hold. Business was business. Willow had resumed the persona of the hard-sell real estate agent.

"Though you paid for the first six months in advance. We agreed to a two year lease. I don't think the owner will be at all keen to...."

"No, no Bruce, you got me all wrong!" He interrupted, holding up the palm sides of both hands. "A deal is a deal. I ain't no welcher, I didn't come here to try to break no lease," *I came to break your silly neck you twit, but you must have stepped in shit and got lucky,* Luca thought to himself.

Willow's chest heaved slightly as he let out a sigh of relief. "That's a relief. Sorry if I misunderstood your intentions. I would have been hard pressed explaining to the owner why I failed to get a signed lease." Now it was Willow's turn to lie.

"It's okay. I'll find some use for the place in the future. Maybe even sub-lease it if somebody wants to do something with it. I don't know. That's okay, ain't it?" Luca asked, sounding as naïve and innocent as he could.

Assured by Willow that there would be no problem sub-letting the property, Luca smiled and vigorously pumped Willow's hand before making a quick departure.

Even before the big man's footfalls had stopped creaking the flight of stairs, Bruce Willow had retrieved a handkerchief and was vigorously engaged in wiping bacon grease residue from his hand. As he did, it occurred to him that Luca hadn't actually mentioned the reason for the unexpected visit. Then, he realized, it must have been the thing about the sub-letting.

CHAPTER SEVEN

Sir Warren's hands were loosely clasped behind his back as he rocked from front to back before the floor-to-ceiling glass window in his London office. The extensive vista overlooked a broad expanse of the city below. In the foreground busy pedestrians, moving cars and lorries below appeared to br so many Matchbox toys and ants scampering about.

But the retired former deputy director of SIS, now a civilian septuagenarian, was melancholy and reflective and such observations held no interest for him this day. Even the comforting and imposing sight of St. Paul's dome in the distance failed to bolster his mood.

Whenever he had first-time visitors to his office, Sir Warren would unfailingly usher them to the window and, with the enthusiasm of a child showing off new toys, point out the city's landmarks. St. Paul's was always saved for his closing remarks. He never failed to relate how the cathedral with its magnificent dome had survived unscathed from Luftwaffe bombing during the Battle of Britain in World War II.

Then, the stage set, he would gently turn them to their left where a matted 10" x 14" photo of St Paul's hung. The Cathedral is seen illuminated in a cocoon-like bright and clear sky while neighboring areas are surrounded by dark, tumbling, cordite clouds and flames. It is one of the most famous British wartime photos ever taken. If the guest happened to be an American, Sir Warren would proudly point out that the first American to join the Royal Air Force, Robert M. Fiske III, was the *only* American buried in St. Paul's.

St. Paul's, he mused, where the Prince and Princess of Wales took the sacred vows neither of them tried very hard to keep.

Sir Warren turned from the window and sat behind his desk.

As he had done in the park during his recent visit, he was again considering the ominous implications and consequences of the royal marriage gone wrong. He had often predicted to The Committee that the Prince and Princess of Wales would divorce. And it had come to pass. The public disclosures of their libertine ways made resolving their differences out of the question.

The surveillance on the Princess of Wales by MI-5 had been thorough for several years. It was considerably increased after her suicide attempts more as a precaution and security measure to protect the newly born Prince William from harm by an 'unbalanced' mother.

But things have a way of drifting and developing a broader base. He was still deputy director of SIS when the service's monitoring revealed the Princess of Wales had developed relationships that were more than platonic with various men. Sir Warren had his agents increase their efforts to total, ultimate spying. Her every move, her every phone conversation were dutifully recorded. And the royal households, Kensington Palace and Highgrove, were bugged with sophisticated audio and video systems, beyond anything previously used.

He was able to justify the extraordinary intrusions under the guise that it was to protect the government, not for any palace interest in her romances or private life. Using the excuse that as the wife of The Prince of Wales, a woman whose mental state was questionable, she might inadvertently utter something and violate national security to her string of male admirers or celebrity friends. Consequently, virtually every aspect of the troubled princess' life was under surveillance, including monitored telephone conversations in which her two sons, Princes William and Harry, were the only topics.

Although many such innocuous tapes were transcribed then deleted and cleaned for reuse by the British, their American spy agency counterparts kept and transcribed every single word they snatched during Diana's visits to the United States. As per a long-standing relationship with their overseas spying counterparts, the actual tapes were provided to the monitoring authorities in London. The Americans simply kept transcriptions, in Diana's case, in an ever growing file.

Informed observers from other nations' cloak-and-dagger types had long believed that the British and U.S. intelligence agencies were 'joined at the hip' and, besides information about

Diana, shared information on just about everything.

Though retired, Sir Warren remained the silent player in the game. His loyal minions in the ranks of SIS faithfully provided Sir Warren with access copies of everything they monitored and everything turned over by the Americans.

After the shocking 'Squidgygate' tape, closely followed by the unbelievable 'Camillagate' tape scandal, Sir Warren ordered his spies to pay closer attention to Prince Charles as well. Consequently the reports from SIS, and Sir Warren's even greater rogue agents' surveillance, provided him, and The Committee with more information about the private lives of the royal couple than anyone had a right to know.

Sir Warren removed the Manila folder labeled <u>Executive Summary: *Affairs of the Heart*</u> from his locked deep desk drawer and gazed at the real and wannabe lovers in Diana's life. This was the brief 'quick read' containing information from the lengthier reports and transcripts locked in his vault.

In centuries past, the information in the folder would have been more than enough to have the wife of the Prince of Wales hung and her lovers drawn and quartered. Under British law, Diana's sexual affairs with other men constituted high treason for both parties. But the arrest, let alone a trial, of the popular princess would never be accepted by the public.

He laid the file open flat on his desk, lifted and stared at the page marked 'Gilbey' containing the 'Squidgygate' transcript. He returned it to the left side of the folder, face down. No more time need be spent regurgitating that, he thought.

Next was the oldest one in the file. It was marked 'Sgt. Mannakee.' As Sir Warren began reading it, he tried in vain to visualize the man's face, but couldn't.

The earliest sign that the princess felt neglected by her philandering husband was the unusually close relationship Diana enjoyed with Barry Mannakee, one of the Special Branch detectives who protected her. It was first noticed by staffers loyal to Charles in the royal household just before the couple's fourth wedding anniversary.

"I tell you one of the biggest crutches of my life," she would later say during the first of 20 videos she made with voice coach Peter Settelen in 1992, "which I don't find easy to discuss, was when I was 24, 25, I fell deeply in love with somebody who worked in this environment. And he was the greatest fellow I have ever had." The relationship may have taken the breath of Settelen, but it was 'old news' to the listening spies of the SIS.

In the video, which was made to help Diana improve her public speaking, she said with candor: "I was always waiting around trying to see him. Um, I just, you know, wore my heart on my sleeve. I was only happy when he was around. When asked if her bodyguard gave her the intimacy missing in her relationship with Charles she simply replied, "Yeah."

With Mannakee, Diana had found a male companion who let her just act and express her feelings about things other women of her age were interested in. He represented a comfort level missing in her life since that walk down the aisle of St. Paul's.

At first, even with the knowledge of Charles" infidelity, Diana had desperately hoped her husband would have treated her with the affection, respect and loving care she was getting from a stranger after the birth of her two sons. He didn't. But Mannakee did.

"He was the greatest fellow I have ever had. I was only happy when he was around." Diana admitted she "fell deeply in love" with Mannakee and said of her marriage to Prince Charles: "I was quite happy to give it all up . . . just to go off and live with him (Mannakee).

"Can you believe it? And he kept saying he thought it was a good idea too."

Not surprisingly, the relationship was brought to Charles' attention by staffers loyal to The Prince of Wales. They correctly assumed he hadn't the faintest clue to what was going on. Once aware of the situation he looked for the telltale signs and quickly concluded his wife and the policeman, the hired help, were much too cozy.

"Charles thought he knew but he never, never had any proof," she said confidently.

"It got so difficult and eventually he (Mannakee) had to go," Diana said as the tape rolled on, "And, um, it was all found out and he was chucked out." She had been completely devastated when the affair ended. Mannakee was transferred to other police duties that kept him out of total contact with the royals.

"I should never have played with fire," she said. "But I did. And I got burned."

The man who had given her such great joy died in a motorcycle accident in 1987. In a comment that many at the time would have considered paranoia, Diana said she was certain Mannakee was "bumped off." Diana thought Mannakee had been killed to hide a royal scandal.

"I think he was bumped off, but I will never know." The princess relied on a clairvoyant to help her cope with his death.

Diana also related on the tape that she felt Charles had deliberately been cruel when he broke the news to her. They were together in a limousine en route to the Cannes Film Festival when Charles announced that he had been killed.

"And that was the biggest blow of my life, I must say. That was a real killer. And he just jumped it on me like that and I wasn't able to do anything. Of course, it wasn't supposed to mean as much as it did."

When they arrived at the festival she had to switch on her public persona and was not permitted to show pain or distress.

"I sat there all day going through this huge high-profile visit to Cannes. Thousands of press. Just devastated."

That was the first instance, Sir Warren recalled, in which the marriage, and The Firm, dodged a serious bullet. Others followed and some were impossible to contain from the prying eyes and ears of the press, who also had the princess under their own limited electronic surveillance.

In the years following her separation, Diana appeared to be foot loose and fancy free for the first time in her adult life. She almost seemed to be making up for lost time, being seen with and dating a number of other men. A relationship with a medical student said to be more than 10 years younger lasted for nearly two years.

But, as had happened with James Hewitt, she suddenly ended the affair.

Even before the details of Diana's illicit romance with Hewitt caused another feeding frenzy in the media, the press had romantically linked Diana and international rugby star Will Carling.

The muscular captain of England's most successful rugby team ever, Carling and Diana met at the gym where they reportedly enjoyed coffee and intimate conversations. As with Hewitt, Carling impressed Diana with his quick-witted sense of humor and ability to get on with her boys, both big rugby fans. He gave William and Harry rugby shirts, and made Diana laugh.

Much to Sir Warren's frustration, his surveillance teams could never prove beyond a doubt that the couple's relationship was physical rather than platonic. But the tabloid press didn't need a smoking gun. They knew how to use suggestive innuendoes.

Eventually the press coverage linking Diana and her husband put a severe strain on Carling's home life, resulting in his television celebrity wife Julia showing him the door. And when she did the scorned Julia didn't mince words when expressing her thoughts about the Princess of Wales. The media gobbled it up. Some even labeled Diana a 'home wrecker,' the infamous mantle bestowed on Camilla Parker-Bowles only a few years earlier. Not long after the Carling marriage broke up things also cooled between Diana and Will.

When she confirmed her affair with James Hewitt in a television confession, the Princess of Wales felt something akin to being liberated. The charades were over. Added to the separation, the guessing games of whether the fairy tale royal couple's marriage could or would survive were almost meaningless. She no longer had to worry about the media ambushing her with rapidly flashing light bulbs and blunt, intrusive questions about her private life. It was all out there. An open book.

But the flashing bulbs continued wherever she went, and only the names of the male players changed. The personal questions about her life that she detested so much still intruded on her privacy.

Sir Warren lifted another page he hadn't reviewed in some

time. Merchant banker Philip Dunne, the well-to-do godson of Princess Alexandra, had a warm relationship with Diana on the ski slopes at Klosters. At the Marquis of Worcester's wedding party, Diana ran her fingertips through his hair and kissed him on the cheek before the couple danced together much of the night. When Dunne invited her to stay overnight at his family home while his parents were away, she accepted. The rendezvous was fodder in the mill for gossip columnists.

Next was Captain David Waterhouse of the Household Cavalry, who went with Diana on a ski trip to Klosters in 1987. The couple was seen doing the London night life scene on occasions. Considered tight-lipped and loyal to Diana throughout her troubled years, he remained a favorite of the Princess even as others came and went Waterhouse was spotted out on the town with Diana on occasions. The Princess often told friends how charming and witty he was. In 1992, Diana was on the verge of inviting Waterhouse to join her on another ski holiday in Austria, but, fearing the ever-present eyes of the media, she opted against it.

As with so many of her relationships with men, the companionship Diana enjoyed with Waterhouse was doomed by annoying press intrusion. Sir Warren put the page face down and went to the next one.

"Ah, the art dealer, Oliver Hoare, a strange fling indeed," Sir Warren thought. And as if to underline that the lonely Princess of Wales was on the prowl for male companionship, this romance began at Chelsea Harbour Gym, where they were both members. Hoare appeared debonair and sophisticated as one might expect of the purveyor of expensive artworks. However, besides being physically fit, he was also charming. Diana was smitten with him. The pair was often seen working out together shortly after seven in the morning, then lunches and eventually quiet candlelit dinners.

But then, Sir Warren recalled even before reading the footnote, as his interest in the princess cooled and their once promising relationship seemed to rip a page from the movie *Fatal Attraction*. Hoare reported to police that he was constantly receiving nuisance phone calls. He'd answer and when whoever was at the other end heard his voice, they would hang up. Diana was suspected of being the mystery caller. It all stopped by the time she set her eyes on a new heart throb. Another page turned over face down.

Her next romantic interest caused serious concern in The Firm. The man was a Muslim. By virtue of his work, the only one of her male companions who publicly shared Diana's well-intentioned concern and compassion for the infirmed was heart surgeon Doctor Hasnar Khan. They met in 1996 at the Royal Brompton Hospital during one of her frequent visits. This mutual interest, coupled with his charm and, when they were together, his ability to elevate her above her whirlwind life in a media circus, Khan made him welcome in her world and a desirable companion. She soon added Pakistani silk dresses to her enormous wardrobe.

Far from the echoing footfalls in antiseptic hospital corridors, the Pakistani surgeon entertained Diana on his yacht. Though such cozy moments and surroundings were a far cry from her honeymoon cruise aboard the royal yacht *Britannia*, replete with 300 male crew and staff present, Diana told friends it was enjoyable. She and the good doctor also talked softly and smiled at each other on dinner dates. The media, and even some of her close associates, believed there was more to the relationship than a mutual desire to heal and comfort the infirm. But the page Sir Warren was reading did not confirm anything of a positive sexual nature.

Again, though, the media shared the blame for the end the budding romance, Khan abhorred the sudden press meddling into his private life and their relationship even more than Diana, who had lived with such intrusions for more than 15 years. Their togetherness ended under the strain.

Sir Warren couldn't resist grinning as he picked up and perused the page about Bryan Adams, the popular, gruff-voiced British singer. *"Oh here, indeed, was a romantic departure for the princess,"* he thought.

Though he had written a song named for Diana in 1985, years before they ever met, Adams' biggest hit, <u>Everything I Do, I Do It For You,</u> was from the movie *Prince of Thieves*. Curiously, the romantic ballad briefly portrayed the otherwise rough looking singer as having a tender, romantic persona. He did his best to erase that as soon as he could.

Reports in the file suggest that Adams went out of his way to endear himself to Diana's various friends. After the split from Charles the two finally met. The singer's former girlfriend, Cecilie Thomsen reportedly said Bryan and the princess became intimate in 1996. But the dalliance appeared more of a lustful physical attraction than romantic for both of them. Diana was moving around, seeing several men and Adams had a long-term relationship in progress with someone else.

The penultimate profile in the folder was from a joint effort in conjunction with SIS' American cousins after one of the princess' visits to those former colonies. Though it appeared to be just another meaningless caprice with no future involvement, Sir Warren considered it further proof of the loose morals of the mother of a future king.

According to the rumor and gossip mill, there were hints that Diana enjoyed a brief romance with the young American prince John F. Kennedy, Jr. And although Sir Warren's rogue's did acquire suggestive audio, no video or stills have ever surfaced.

John-John, as Sir Warren's people teasingly refered to him, had contacted Diana during a New York visit to give him a personal interview for George, the magazine he founded and published.

Diana initially declined the request. But Kennedy, the man a majority of Americans believed would one day pick up the torch of *Camelot* and become President of The United States, wouldn't accept 'no' for an answer. Not only did he have his late father's handsome looks, he also had his share of the Kennedy persuasive persistence.

Eventually Diana agreed to meet him in her suite at the Carlyle Hotel. Instead of word play, it became foreplay, with America's uncrowned prince and Britain's real princess spending the night together. But the story ends there without any follow-up or future rendezvous. The irony here is that the Carlyle was allegedly the same New York hotel where John F. Kennedy and Marilyn Monroe once frolicked between the sheets.

Finally, Sir Warren came to the last page, simply marked 'Dodi.' He didn't have to read the previously gathered information, inasmuch as everything in the file had been gathered in the last several months. This romance was current and had all the earmarks of being the most dangerous affair yet. And with another Muslim.

Emad El-Din Mohamed Abdel Moneim Fayed, born April 15, 1955, in Alexandria, Egypt, was known by the nickname 'Dodi.' He was heir to a fortune which included his billionaire father's ownership of the world famous Harrods department store in London and the equally famous Ritz Hotel in Paris. His mother was Samira Kashoggi, sister of the feared and notorious arms dealer Adnan Kashoggi, known to intelligence services the world over.

When Dodi was fifteen his father presented him with a chauffeured Rolls-Royce and a Mayfair apartment in London. He was a graduate of the British Army's elite Sandhurst Military Academy, their equivalent of West Point, and for some time served as a junior officer in London for the United Arab Emirates.

He enjoyed a wealthy lifestyle beyond what most people could imagine in their wildest dreams, with access to private jets, yachts and a fleet of luxury cars. He had homes in London, New York, Los Angeles Switzerland plus a love-nest apartment in Paris.

Dodi was considered an international playboy because he had romanced several well-known and beautiful actresses such as, Julia Roberts, Brooke Shields, Cathy Lee Crosby, and Britt Ekland. In fact, when he wasn't racing around in his expensive toys or wooing some beauty who had captured his fleeting attention, Dodi Fayed seriously dabbled in producing movies. His Hollywood credits include the 1981 Oscar-winner *Chariots of Fire*; *The World According to Garp*; *F/X* and *Hook*.

Dodi's father, Mohamed Al Fayed, was a friend of Diana's father, the late Lord Spencer and his wife, Raine. The elder Fayed had been at the center of a corruption scandal that helped lead Britain's Conservative Party to defeat in the recent election. Sir Warren was also aware that Dodi's uncle, Adnan Khashoggi, was a widely-known Saudi arms dealer.

Diana first met Fayed almost 10 years earlier when he and

Prince Charles played polo on opposing teams. But Fayed and Princess Diana's close friendship became clear to the outside world after the couple took a series of holidays together in the Mediterranean.

Such high profile jet-set sojourns weren't simply the casual resurrection of an old acquaintanceship. The elder Fayed had played the role of an Egyptian *yenta* for his son, plotting and planning to bring the star-crossed lovers together.

In this regard, despite his business acumen and great wealth, Mohamed Al Fayed was the ultimate 'royal watcher.' His fascination with the Royal family included the purchase of Villa Windsor in Paris' Bois de Boulogne district. The property had been the former residence of the abdicated Edward VIII and his American bride, Wallis Simpson, who once lived there as the Duke and Duchess of Windsor.

In his seemingly obsessive quest to associate the Fayed name with British royalty, he wasted little time setting a lavish trap for the newly divorced Princess of Wales. When Diana accepted his invitation, with her sons, for the first Mediterranean holiday that summer, Fayed quickly purchased the *Jonikal*, a 208-foot yacht, half as long as the 412-ft. Royal Yacht *Britannia*.

In much the same way as James Hewitt and Will Carling, Dodi aped them by getting on the good side of William and Harry. But Dodi had limitless funds. He provided the young boys with jet-skis, discos and amusement arcades on holiday in San Tropez.

Once Diana entered his life, Dodi seemed to be a changed man. His interest waned in the several and pleasurable distractions his wealthy lifestyle could provide.

"I will never have another girlfriend," Dodi announced. Diana had captured his heart.

Diana herself described their days and nights on their two holidays together as "bliss." Some of the pictures taken illicitly of the couple during their all too brief romance make it abundantly clear that they were extremely comfortable with each others bodies.

In the first week of August, *The Sunday Mirror* speculated Dodi and Diana were in love. On Aug. 10, pictures of the couple kissing in the Mediterranean aboard the *Jonikal* were published. The paper reportedly outbid other papers and paid 250,000 pounds (about $400,000) for the romantically suggestive photos.

Dodi's ex-wife, model Suzanne Gregard, told the paper Fayed had telephoned her and said the romance was "serious." His 1994 marriage to Gregard lasted just eight months.

And hardly a week later, Diana was quoted in the French newspaper *Le Monde* saying she would have left Britain were it not for her children:

"Any sane person would have left long ago, but I cannot. I have my sons," she was quoted as saying.

Despite that public pronouncement, *The Mirror* speculated that Diana and Fayed would announce their engagement next month and a winter wedding would follow. It further said the newlyweds would make their home not in Britain, but in the United States.

Sir Warren didn't bother to turn the page over as he dropped it into the file. He closed the folder firmly, actually slamming the flat of his hand on his desk.

The situation had become dangerously critical. Her admitted adultery with Hewitt, the near confessional pillow talk with Gilbey, the carrying on with the singer Adams, and her other affairs had been bad enough, but somehow the monarchy remained untouched. However, this current jet-set love with Fayed was the straw to break the proverbial camel's back!

It didn't take an army of intelligence operatives to know what people in the street were speculating about and already saying: *"What if she gets pregnant?"* The thought of Prince William, the future King of England, having a brown Muslim half-brother or sister was the worst possible scenario Sir Warren could think of.

"What if Diana actually married Dodi and then she turned Muslim?" He thought, with a bone-chilling shudder.

Prince Philip, the Queen's husband, reportedly exploded in rage over the speculation, and saw the liaison as a serious threat to dynasty if it endured: "Such an affair is racially and morally repugnant and no son of a Bedouin camel trader is fit for the mother of a future king," the often politically incorrect Duke bellowed.

In the eyes of The Firm, the British Establishment, and the population in general, there was grievous concern that Diana was single-handedly destroying the fabric of the nation and monarchy which Sir Warren had pledged to defend. All members of the MI-5 and MI-6 intelligence agencies, members of Parliament, and military officers swear an oath of loyalty to the monarchy, not to the United Kingdom. In the U.K., the monarchy is the state.

The time for continuing the game of 'wait-and-see' what the princess would do next was over. Drastic action now appeared to be the only solution which could change the disastrous course ahead.

Sir Warren shook his head in dispair and slowly returned the folder to the desk drawer.

****

The intelligence services of most countries will, from time to time, engage so-called rogue agents to carry out sensitive 'Black Ops' (Operations) in foreign countries. Often these missions are undertaken without the expressed approval of the nation's leaders. The use of non-nationals to do a country's covert and clandestine work has supposedly provided a long line of presidents, prime ministers, and heads of state to have 'plausible deniability'--- meaning they could honestly say their government did not plan or execute the dirty deed. It's a very gray area and one which more than a few such world leaders have been comfortable with, and thankful for.

On the other hand, the majority of regular intelligence agents, no matter which country we are talking about, are traditionally loyal, patriotic, and true believers in the ideology of the incumbent regime. These agents may, from time to time, bend the rules in executing their assigned tasks, but they can justify any moral queasiness they have by convincing themselves what they are doing is in the interest of their country.

Not true with rogue agents. They do what they do strictly for money. Rogues can be former agents from the soliciting country who have been separated from the agency for one reason or another, but more often than not they are former operatives of other countries who have long ago abandoned any national loyalty or ideology and now are totally dedicated to taking care of *Number One*, themselves.

The useful 'shelf life' of an active undercover agent varies from service to service, but it is rare to find any agents still functioning after more than 10 years at the same level of activity, with the resolve, vigor, and unflinching dedication they possessed when they entered the service. This malady is known as burn-out. Often, when such symptoms surface, such an agent's days with the service are numbered, and separation for a more pastoral, average life follows. Those who can adjust to normalcy live uneventful and hopefully happy lives in second careers far from any connection with the spy business.

Sometimes the reason an agent leaves a service is the result of disillusionment with the system they once embraced or the world political scene in general. Such people can't, or don't want to, adjust to what they consider the hum-drum existence of an 'average Joe' life. These are the rogues, the former trained field agents who now make a living as hired guns, soldiers of fortune, freelance killers. They have a high value to any potential employer because of their talents, abilities, contacts and know-how to get a job done.

In the mid-1990s, a *nom de plume* bylined article in the intelligence community magazine, *Covert*, speculated that if all the rogues worldwide banded together there are enough of them in the world at any given time to overthrow most Third World countries with relative ease. The difficulty in employing them has always been locating and approaching them, the article pointed out.

During his years as a deputy director in SIS, Sir Warren Wormsley was considered by the Americans, Israelis, Germans, Soviets, and other agencies as having the resources to reach out to more first-rate rogues than anyone else in intelligence. As his reputation grew, it further increased his access to new blood. The fact that he always paid well, and in advance, also didn't hurt his recruiting efforts.

Now, as his chauffeur guided Sir Warren's classic Rolls Royce Silver Cloud past Marble Arch, the limousine was suddenly reduced to creeping in heavy traffic. His eyes drifted to the magnificent structure which had once been the primary entrance to Buckingham Palace. When the Palace was extended in 1851, the Arch was moved to its current site at Hyde Park.

His thoughts, however, were not of the Arch. Instead, they were of the incredibly fortuitous, just completed, lunch meeting in the Dorchester Hotel's Promenade restaurant. The man who hosted him was a trusted rogue whom Sir Warren had worked with some years ago. He had impeccable Middle East credentials and contacts. In recent years the man worked as a consultant for the Libyans.

Sir Warren agreed to the lunch because in the last year the ex-agent's name had been linked to Ashraf Marwan, a powerful and dangerous individual if ever there was one. Sir Warren was aware that many foreign services, including the U.S. Central Intelligence agency, had Marwan red flagged for international arms dealing and terrorism activities.

But most interesting to Sir Warren, and the reason he would meet the man, was the widely known fact in intelligence circles that neither the Libyans nor Marwan had any great love for the Fayed family, particularly Dodi's father, Mohamed. There had even been unconfirmed reports of failed assassination attempts over the years. Consequently, Fayed employed a staff of 40 security personnel, mostly bodyguards.

Sir Warren's professional intuition told him the invitation to lunch wasn't a coincidence. The anti-Fayed faction in Europe and the Middle East would certainly be aware that The Firm and the British Establishment in general were not pleased about the romance between the mother of a future king and Dodi Fayed, a non-Christian foreigner.

****

"Stop by the club," Sir Warren told his driver. "Austin should be waiting under the awning." The heavier rain which began as the Rolls pulled away from the Dorchester was now just a light drizzle.

The elder Fayed, usually photographed smiling and waving to people spending money in Harrods, had made some dangerous enemies en route to buying Harrods and becoming a billionaire. He had crossed the kind of people who would think absolutely nothing of assassinating him or, for revenge, killing or harming his only son.

There was solid intelligence that all the Fayeds were safety conscious and lived in something akin to a mild state of paranoia. It was known by employees that all the telephones in Harrods were bugged and anything of a sensitive, suspicious, or threatening nature was reported to Mohamed Fayed. In Paris, it was the same at the Ritz.

In 1972, when Dodi turned 17 years old his father gave him a Mini-Moke, along with a personal bodyguard. That was increased to two protectors by the time he was in his twenties. Their presence amused Dodi's fellow party-goers at fashionable London night spots such as *Tramps*. One bodyguard always remained close to Dodi while the other moved around assessing possible threats.

At times, such as when his father was in the much-publicized and nasty battle for control of Harrods, Dodi's bodyguard army was six strong. Ashraf Marwan had been a key player on the losing side of that little war.

SIS agents reported that if Dodi lost sight of his table at a night club, he would have all the drinks removed and replaced with fresh rounds. He was keenly aware someone could spike his drink.

Old habits, and fears, die hard and he continued the wasteful practice as he became older and worked on films in Hollywood. He would dismiss the curious behavior by telling new friends, "My father is involved with some very dangerous things." He once admitted there had been a "kidnap attempt in Egypt when I was young."

****

"I see him," Sir Warren said even as the driver was about to pull the long black Rolls Royce to the curb.

"Sir Warren" The acknowledgement was all Smythe-Pembrooke said as he entered the spacious back of the car and seated himself next to its owner.

"An interesting lunch," the retired deputy director said without being asked. "Let me tell you about it."

"Yes, please do. I'm all ears, as they say."

Before he began, Sir Warren engaged the button in his arm rest and the opaque, sound-proof barrier rose from the back of the front seats, providing absolute audio and visual privacy.

"You said you suspected the meeting might have something to do with Diana's latest boyfriend, Fayed's playboy son, Dodi?"

"Indirectly. More like the Fayed family. It was just a hunch, but now I'm sure of it."

"For God's sake, man, out with it!" Smythe-Pembrooke's deep voice filled the compartment, but Sir Warren was certain the sound-proofing would have prevented the chauffeur from hearing a gun being discharged.

"You realize I will not reveal the name of the rogue. He's quite high-level, and specifically asked his identity be protected."

"Yes, of course. . . And here's the file on Marwan you wanted to review," Smythe-Pembrooke said as he produced the document from his attaché case. "Young Blair sent it immediately, via courier." He thought for a moment and added: "But it doesn't take much to figure out that whomever you met with was there at the behest of Marwan."

"Don't rush to conclusions," Sir Warren raised a hand for emphasis. "I'm not certain of that. He could have been on an errand for someone else. The Fayeds have made dangerous enemies."

****

Who exactly was Ashraf Marwan? And, if he did, why would he have a confederate approach the retired deputy director of SIS? And what did Mohamed Fayed have to do with all this?

Analysts in the CIA thought Ashraf Marwan worked both sides of the street as double agent for a number of Middle East security and espionage services and some in the West as well, especially Britain. Despite widely held beliefs to the contrary some things obviously were *not* shared with the U.S.

The reasoning behind such beliefs was that Marwan could not otherwise run some of his arms deals and other nefarious operations in London or Paris without immunity or protection. The Americans and the Mossad, Israel's intelligence and national security agency, were sure that Britain's SIS was aware of whatever enterprises Marwan was involved in.

The conjecture was that if they apprehended Marwan for any of his illegal activities they would have blown one of their most valuable double agents. Naturally, the British denied this to the Americans and Israelis. But the Mossad pointed out that Britain had a history of letting innocent people die in the interest of keeping a valuable secret:

British intelligence knew more than 48 hours in advance that the Luftwaffe intended to bomb the city of Coventry in World War II because cryptologists at Bletchley Park were reading the German 'Ultra' code, which the Nazis considered unbreakable. If Coventry's population had been warned, Germany would have realized Ultra had been compromised and immediately replaced it. The ability to read the Wehrmacht's military communications was simply too valuable to divulge.

The raid lasted more than 10 hours. Casualties were close to 1,000 and much of the city, including the 14th century cathedral, was destroyed.

In May 1985 the Chief of Libyan Intelligence, Ahmed Gaddaf Dam (sic) and Ashraf Marwan were passengers on a private Lear jet going to Cairo. Dam was a cousin of Libyan President Colonel Muammar Gaddafi. Both passengers were murderers. Marwan was known in Egypt as "Dr. Death."

Their Cairo trip was to blackmail Egyptian President Husni Mubarak into renouncing the 1977 Camp David Accord which Mubarak's predecessor, Anwar Sadat, had signed with Israeli Prime Minister Menachem Begin after the two were Jimmy Carter's guests at the Presidential retreat in the Catoctin Mountains of Maryland, some 70 miles from The White House. In December, 1978, Begin and Sadat were jointly awarded the Nobel Peace Prize.

Sadat was assassinated in 1981 and Mubarak was elected president in one week later. It was widely suspected that Marwan had organized or at the least been a key player in the assassination. Menachem Begin died in 1982.

Now, with neither of the signers alive to protest, if Mubarak did not renounce the Accord, Marwan and Dam threatened to blow up Tahir Square, where Sadat had been killed. How the blackmail attempt was resolved is not known. But the two murderers withdrew their threat.

Years earlier Marwan had been appointed a "roving ambassador" for Egypt under then-President Abdul Gamel Nasser. His assignment was to roam the world as a playboy-diplomat. Though evil, Marwan had charm and intelligence. His job, mainly in the Arab world, was to probe governments' attitudes towards Nasser and to lobby in his behalf. He was adept at showing he was "close to the throne" and other Arabs were convinced that what Marwan said, was the voice of Nasser himself. Marwan forged invaluable links through the Middle East. Purely for himself.

Marwan also began organizing arms deals. By the time Nasser died, Marwan had stashed several million dollars into various European and off-shore banks. Marwan rose to Minister-Without-Portfolio, keeping all his diplomatic privileges, which permitted him to get into arms dealing in a very big way. He added to that the roles of Chief of Staff for Information and Chairman of the Arab Corporation for War Industries, Head of the Security Forces. This made him not only the head of the army and air force, but also the civil and secret police as well. In his roles as head of the armed forces and Chairman of the Arab Corporation for War Industries, he was able to award his paper-front companies all the arms contracts, and the millions rolled in like clockwork.

This was one of the powerful men who would become principal players against the Fayed family.

Between 1974 and 1978 Marwan ordered mass arrests and created sophisticated torture chambers for Egyptians who he felt were a threat to him. He became known as "Dr. Death." While Sadat was in office, Marwan's personal fortune grew to a mind-boggling $500-million. He invested heavily in choice real estate, mainly in London, and an apartment on the 'most expensive street in the world,' Avenue Foch in Paris.

Along the way, Marwan had invested more than $7-million in

the House of Fraser, the 58-store chain which included Harrods. The parent company of the House of Fraser was Lonrho, Inc., and Marwan was aligned with R. W. Rowland, chief executive of Lonrho. Nicknamed 'Tiny,' Rowland had fought bitterly with all his resources for seven years to keep Harrods.

However, in 1985 Mohamed Fayed bought controlling stock interest in the House of Fraser using money borrowed from his friend, the Sultan of Brunei -- considered the richest man in the world. Fayed then used the company's properties as collateral to raise loans to repay the Sultan!

The Fayed take-over had been acrimonious and profane, with life-threatening epithets exchanged. Fayed had been considered an outsider, a spoiler, the other major player in the fight. In a one-on-one fight the opposition, led by Rowland, was more powerful than Fayed. Many of them resented Fayed greatly because they knew he had used OPM, other people's money, to steal Harrods from them. The bitter loss had earned Fayed a number of revenge-minded enemies.

The campaign Rowland launched to destroy Mohamed Al Fayed was massive, expensive, and hateful. Marwan was Rowland's associate and employee for intelligence matters and the source of all the negative information on the Fayeds. Rowland passed Marwan's findings to the Lonrho-owned newspaper, *The Observer*, and instructed the editor to produce a special 16-page edition under the title <u>Exposed: The Phony Pharaoh</u>. Other than smear Fayed's reputation, it did nothing to satisfy the hatred Tiny Rowland's associates had for Mohamed Fayed and his family.

"So, Sir Warren, what did your mystery man want from you at lunch?"

"Curiously, just some technology which, by the way, I'm certain SIS doesn't have."

"Really?. . . technology you say? Is it something we could acquire from outside sources?"

"Perhaps, but I didn't let him know we didn't have it. I led him on to find out how and on whom they intended to use it."

"What is 'it'?"

"He said they were interested in purchasing some automotive computer chips that could be activated by remote control."

"Perhaps our German friends?" Smythe-Pembrooke queried.

"Exactly whom I thought of as well."

"So, then, we're simply playing 'middlemen' in this affair.'

"Well. . . not quite. I boldly told him that if we provided what he wanted, at a price yet to be determined, there would be some rules that were not negotiable."

"Rules? You have some balls! You don't even know if you can get what he wants yet you make rules."

"He doesn't know that. I needed to know what their plan was and who the target was."

"And did you?"

"Absolutely. But first let me tell you what I got him to agree to. I said we would need to have our people do the necessary mechanical work on the automobile. We'd also need one of our agents to consult with them on how, where, and when they intended to execute the mission, and finally, that the target could not be taken out on British soil."

"Amazing! And this fellow didn't tell you to take your computer chips and shove them up your bloody ass?"

"He didn't even blink. Actually, he said London was never an option. They were, of course familiar with the Milosevic Plan and had their own enhanced variation of that and were considering one of the traffic tunnels in Paris. That suited me because then it would be a problem for the Frogs."

[*According to a sworn public statement by former MI-6 agent Richard Tomlinson, the secret service had a 1992 plan to assassinate Slobodan Milosevic, the President of the Yugoslav Republic of Serbia, by staging an auto accident.*

The scenario was to take place during one of Milosevic's visits to the International Conference on the Former Yugoslavia (ICFY) in Geneva, Switzerland. An extremely powerful strobe light would be flashed to disorient Milosevic's driver as the car passed through one of Geneva's motorway tunnels. It was believed that a high speed tunnel crash greatly increased the chance of killing the subject.]

More recently another former MI-6 agent, David Shayler, told the BBC that MI-6 had channeled US $160,000 to an underground, Islamic fundamentalist group in Libya to finance the assassination of Libya's Gaddafi. Shayler had been attached to the MI-5/MI-6 joint Libyan task force. A large road bomb was planted in February, 1996, but as the Libyan leader's motorcade passed, it detonated under the wrong vehicle. Six bystanders, government officials, and security personnel were killed. Gaddafi escaped unharmed.

"Exactly how do they propose to enhance it?" Smythe-Pembrooke asked.

"The computer chips they want are related to the vehicle airbags and can be remotely discharged prematurely. But they have one more surprise: tampering with the car's seat belts so they appear closed but open easily when a given level of body weight is thrust against them."

"They've done their homework. We should keep this all in mind if we ever get our hands on such computer chips. One never knows when they could be needed. Now all you have to do is contact this man and tell him 'Sorry, my good fellow, apparently the chips have proved unreliable for this or that reason and they are no longer available in our inventory.' You could explain that, therefore, in good faith, you couldn't accept his money . . ."

"But we _will_ accept his money if you find out our German friends have such chips."

Really? You seem hell bent in having our hand in this without knowing who their target is.

"No, he didn't mention the target by name, but I'm certain it's Mohamed Fayed!"

Smythe-Pembrooke blinked in slight confusion.

"Mohamed? Dodi's father? What good would that do? It's his son who has become a royal pain in the ass to the Monarchy, pardon the pun. Let the Palace handle, or do what they will, with that social-climber. Our concern is his son's relationship with Diana."

"But when they can't get to the father that's exactly who they'll go for. Dodi bounces in and out of Paris regularly. They hate the Fayeds, especially Mohamed. Killing his only son would be the ultimate revenge."

"Am I to take it, then, that we will hereafter remove, with extreme prejudice, any lovers the princess takes whom we don't approve of?" The edginess of Smythe-Pembrooke's question made it appear reproachful.

"That may not be necessary."

"Forgive me, I don't understand."

"Suppose the princess is in the car with Dodi at the time?" Sir Warren queried.

"Already considered: Diana absolutely always uses her seat belt. Dodi only does sometimes, but more often not. However, he has a penchant for always sitting directly behind the driver. Never fails. So the solution is, we have the back driver's side seat belt modified, just in case he uses it.

"That way even a sudden stop crash at 60mph would most likely prove fatal for him. Diana, on the other hand would be badly shaken up, perhaps even injured somewhat. The result would be the sad ending of the love affair and we could have Diana taken care of in the hospital so that she can never become pregnant."

"How can you be sure of that?" Smythe-Pembrooke asked.

"Don't be ridiculous! Don't you think we have French friends in the medical profession? It's not hard for the seemingly unhurt victim of an accident to suddenly go into convulsions or otherwise exhibit dire medical problems."

"This must all be expensive, and take a lot of personnel to carry out, but worth it, I think" Smythe-Pembrooke nodded.

"The Arabs get the revenge they want and our problem is solved as well. Diana is no longer a welcome member of the Royal Family. We owe no allegiance to her, just her sons, one of whom is the future king. If she's seriously injured or crippled, we wouldn't be hearing and reading about her bed-hopping with every Tom, Dick, and Harry for some time, perhaps ever, would we? And we wouldn't have to worry about her having any little bastard brothers or sisters for the future king."

"Then we must impress on Megan that only the one seat belt be tampered with," Smythe-Pembrooke said gravely.

"Most certainly," Sir Warren agreed insincerely.

****

A month had slipped off the calendar since Mario Luca buried the 65 kegs of gold coins on the property he leased from Bruce Willow. In the weeks that had passed he noticed a small story on one of the advertising cluttered inside pages in the local English language newspaper mentioning that no new clues had turned up in the theft of the construction company truck and backhoe, but a former employee of the company, American Geoffrey Hindel, who reportedly was in severe debt, was the prime suspect. The last paragraph noted that the Belize authorities had alerted the Mexican police to be on the lookout for Hindel and the stolen vehicles.

Case closed, Luca thought. Willow had earned a free pass. No need to eliminate him now. The man had provided the police with a generous amount of information leaving Luca in the clear. He figured he was home free.

Mario Luca figured wrong.

It was one of the Colombian cartels, not the American Mafia, that was Mario Luca's undoing. During one of the regular cycles of drug lord gang wars South of the border, a relatively small time operator who had been providing a goodly amount of illegal substance to Luca for years had the misfortune of being captured. Under the unspeakable persuasive methods used during such interrogations, the man blurted out that he had regularly been selling his supply to "the thief, Mario Luca, in Belize".

The revelation surprised his captors, not for what the man said, but for what it implied. They held no silly notion that they were the only source of supply for the American gangster, but hearing this peon call Luca a "crook" raised questions. So they pressed their captive for details with all the finesse such people could muster. Their methods made the Spanish Inquisition's dreaded Rack seem like child's play.

In short order, the man sang like a bird. Once they were certain he had made his last tweet of any consequence, he was promptly dispatched to songbird heaven. He had told them how

Luca would regularly short change him by as much as 5% per transaction, claiming the purity of the product was less than the dealer knew it was. Nonetheless, he continued to do business with Luca because the no hassle safety factor of delivering the goods to Luca at an island off the coast of Belize.

If Luca was indeed cheating this low-life they wondered if he could also somehow be cheating them? After much talk they concluded that whatever Luca was doing was most likely a private thing. If he was stealing then he was stealing for himself, not his bosses in the U.S. Greedy as they were, the Mafia had enough sense not to try to short-change the cartel. But Luca, on the other hand, was probably dumb enough to try to rob both sides. What he was doing to the peon was common, everyday, small time stuff. The peon didn't have enough muscle to question or challenge Luca, so he happily accepted the crumbs.

The reason made sense. Dealing with Luca had given this dealer a very low profile and thus kept him below the radar of the cartel, which had a zero tolerance for private enterprise. But even if Luca was ripping off this small time supplier, how could he possibly be doing the same thing to them? A review of the previous year's transactions revealed nothing that sounded an alarm. Yet, they believed, if Luca had found a way of stealing from a small timer, he may have, by now, found a way to skim off profit from their transactions as well.

Armed with suspicion, the cartel positioned a man in Belize City to track and follow Luca's every movement. It took hardly two months for their spy to find a rhythm and routine in certain things Luca did. For one thing, he left the Belize City marina on his private boat on a fairly regular schedule. The cartel ascertained that his boat trips coincided with meeting incoming deliveries from the cartel and other suppliers. But more revealing, Luca made frequent visits to several jewelry shops in Belize and as far north as Mexico City.

All it took was some well-placed bribes to discover that Mr. Mario Luca had an unending penchant for buying large quantities of gold bullion coins. In certain cases, he had ongoing standing orders with large shopkeepers to purchase dozens of coins at a time.

The cartel was convinced he was double-dealing and that the money for the coins was what he was skimming, probably from both sides of the drug deals he was the overseer for. It wasn't a long stretch to figure that if the man who controlled the distribution of several million dollars of other people's money each month was also spending several thousand dollars every *week* on gold coins, the guy must have his hand in the till.

Mario Luca was obviously stealing from the cartel, and just about everybody sending drugs to him. But they didn't have a clue how. Nor could they figure out how he stole from the Mafia. But they had an idea.

It didn't take the Colombians long to bring their suspicions to the attention of the American mob. Some wanted to send a hit man up to Belize immediately and take Luca out. But cooler heads rationalized that might piss off the Americans and that could be bad for business. Instead, if Mario Luca were to be removed, and the Colombians believed that really wasn't even debatable now, then all that needed to be done was alert them that they had a thief in their house. Let the Americans do it. It was their mess to clean up.

An overnight International FedEx letter from the Colombians to their Mafia contact in Miami was used to get the ball rolling. The FedEx was safer than using telephones and permitted a printed detailed report that was an easy to follow paper trail. The Colombians correctly concluded that the people reading this information in Miami would undoubtedly reach the same conclusion they had. And they did.

To the Miami mob it made no difference if Luca was stealing from the Colombians or from the Commission. He was a thief who couldn't be trusted. If word got out that he was getting away with this, it would be bad for morale and might encourage others to do such a dumb thing. Mario Luca would soon be dead meat.

The previous evening Professor John Longacre was slouched on a bar stool in a local, dark and dingy Belize bar so far off the beaten tourist track that the place didn't even have a sign with its name on it. To anyone passing it simply looked like another dilapidated store front in the poor section of town.

Longacre had been drinking regularly for several hours and for some time was entertaining two newly made friends, telling them tall tales and risqué stories about women he seduced, real and imagined, during his salad days on archaeology digs he had participated in over the years.

In recent years, anybody who picked up Longacre's bar bill automatically became his friend. At this point in the evening the pair had plied him with so much free booze that Longacre felt his new companions had earned the right to almost qualify as family. To put it mildly, he was drunk as a skunk.

"John, this bar is starting to feel mighty hard on my elbows. Let's move over to a table, over there in the corner," the man who called himself Jake Paterson suggested.

"Yeah, me too," his companion, known to Longacre as Bobby Benz, added. Benz feigned pain in his arm and rubbed it vigorously. Patterson smiled and winked at him.

"Okay. Fine with me. If that's what you guys want." Longacre punctuated his remarks with a low belch and made a serious effort to focus on the floor and lift himself off the stool. Paterson and Benz assisted him and the trio made their way past several empty tables till they reached one far off in the corner. It was about as far away from the bar, and the few local customers in the place, as they could get.

"Hey, did I tell you guys why I drink single malt Scotch?" Longacre asked as they guided him into a chair.

"Yes, John, you did." Paterson said in a kind voice as Benz went back to the bar to order another round of drinks. Though Longacre was consuming Scotch on the rocks, Paterson and Benz had been changed over to just cola in their rum and cokes some time ago, and Longacre was none the wiser.

"It's cause you never get a hangover drinkin' Scotch! Did you know that? And single malt is the best!" Longacre made the statement and answered his own question as he tried to hold Paterson in his gaze. Slowly, very slowly, his brain processed Paterson's previous answer and he added. "Sure you know that. I told you before. Remember?" he giggled, then swung his head at the empty chair. To his alcohol-soaked vision the chair appeared to be several chairs, all swirling past as if horses on a merry-go-round.

"Where's Bobby?"

"He went to get another round. Here he comes now, see?"

Bobby Benz deposited the three drinks on the table and slid onto the chair across from Paterson. Longacre was ensconced between them.

"John, let's drink another toast to your success," Paterson declared as he hoisted his cola drink. Benz did likewise and the two held their glasses together as they waited for Longacre to join in.

Longacre appeared to look first at one, then the other before wrapping his hand around his drink and squinting as he slowly lifted it into position with the others. Actually, he really hadn't seen them clearly, he was reacting to the spoken word.

"To me, and to my archaeological success!" he said rather loudly and broke into a fit of laughter.

"Shhhh! John, you're causing a scene. People are looking over at us," Benz proffered. In truth nobody was paying any attention to the trio. Paterson turned to observe the few other patrons in the place and noticed two locals involved in an animated conversation at the far end of the bar and a couple huddled up in a booth in the dark corner opposite them. The man was all over the woman like a cheap suit. Paterson was satisfied nobody was paying attention to the cozy little trio he was part of. It was time to get down to business.

After several seconds Longacre's laughing stopped and he calmed down.

"John, we've been drinking to your success all night and we're good friends, right?" Paterson asked.

"Right, Good friends. I really like you fellas," Longacre slobbered, gagging. Benz thought the man was about to cry or throw up.

"So if we're all good friends, and we keep celebrating your success, don't you think you should tell us what that success is?" Paterson asked in a tone that sounded hurt.

Longacre looked at Paterson, or tried to. Even when he tried to, his vision was now so blurred it was capturing several images of Paterson and all of them seemed to be moving, drifting, to the left. Every so often he would catch a glimpse of Benz as well. He wondered how they were able to do that, gliding around in so many places in front of him.

"John? Tell us. Tell us what you found and why we are celebrating," Benz asked.

Longacre giggled again. "They think I found some big old Jade head. A friggin' Mayan artifact. But I didn't. I found something more better!"

"Oh, you did? So who are 'they' and why did you tell them you found a Jade head?" Paterson asked. It was a painfully slow process but now, finally they were getting to the information they wanted.

"*They* are the magazine dummies who financed this trip for me. I really believed the big Jade head was real! I was sure that it existed. I even had a beat-up, crummy map I bought from an old fart con man in Mexico. An 'honest' man. It was a real good, genuine map, I thought." Longacre briefly fumbled in his pockets to no avail for several seconds then gave up, adding: "I must lave left it back with my stuff."

"But if you didn't find the Jade head, why did you tell them you did?" Paterson was dying to get right to the point but knew that even in this drunk condition Longacre had to be coaxed, played.

"I had to tell them *something* because my permit to do the dig was expiring." He belched, then continued. "No permit, no visa, and zip!" He threw up his arms, "...you get thrown out of the country like that." He let his left arm come crashing to the table but with his right arm still in the air Longacre attempted to snap his fingers for emphasis, but found the task was impossible to do. This time he brought his arm down much slower, but nearly knocked over his drink doing it. Longacre was completely oblivious to a quick move by Benz to push it aside.

"I had to tell them I found a friggin' head," Longacre continued, ". . .so they would get the permit extended for 90 days. Just 90 lousy days, can you believe that?" he asked. Neither Paterson nor Benz understood, or cared about, the significance of the extension.

"These are important people at the magazine. Big guys with big bucks and influence. I'm a nobody. They can do that, get the extension. I couldn't do that from here. All it cost them was $100. Chump change!"

Longacre stopped talking and his eyelids seemed to be closing. Paterson reached for his arm and shook him gently at first. Then vigorously. "So you found something better than a Jade head and the magazine got your permit extended?"

"What?" the professor acted as if he was hearing Paterson's voice for the first time.

"The extension! The magazine got you the extension to continue the dig?" Benz put in.

"Yes sir-re-bob, they did, just like that," Longacre was reasonably awake again. He made another unsuccessful attempt to snap his fingers.

Both Paterson and Benz could tell Longacre was about to say something else but was having difficulty forming his thoughts. But at least he was awake again. Longacre had finally loosened his tongue and Paterson believed he would go on now with little encouragement. Paterson gave Benz a cautious, squinty look which the man correctly understood to mean *let him talk*. And Longacre did.

"So what happens next?" Patterson made the question sound as innocent as possible.

"Then the feces hit the overhead cooling device," Longacre said, again being giddy.

Puzzled, it took Paterson and Benz a few seconds to realize that Longacre was politely saying *the shit hit the fan*. But they continued to listen without interrupting.

"The friggin magazine sent some photographer here to take pictures of this wonderful, big, Jade head I didn't find. Can you believe that? A photographer came here to take pictures of the head I didn't find. And there is no friggin head. I made it up!"

"But you found something else, didn't you?"

268

Longacre tried to look at both of his out-of-focus friends. "You know why we are celebrating? Because I'm gonna' be a very rich man from what I found!" he smiled.

"But John, you still haven't told us what you *did* find, and where it is." Paterson said, adding, "Maybe we should help you hide somewhere safe. Longacre closed his eyes and, slowly his lips began turning upward.

"Gold coins. A friggin shitload of gold coins! Barrels of 'em. So many I'm gonna' need a truck to carry them away." As he finished talking, Longacre's head fell forward and hit the table with a loud thump.

Paterson looked at Benz and both men exhaled a silent sigh of relief. As suspected, the old drunk archaeologist had stumbled upon the cache of gold coins hidden by the thief, Mario Luca. They didn't know exactly how many coins were involved, but based on what the Colombians and the Miami mob suspected the coins probably represented millions of dollars Luca had siphoned off over several years of stealing drug money as a trusted go-between.

Longacre, who lived in a small village about 35 miles from Belize City, often hiked in the countryside during his fleeting encounters with sobriety, and had by chance come upon the large, rectangular shaped, depressed area of soil in the clearing behind Luca's building one morning.

****

Luca's gut told him to stay away from the site until this uneasy feeling of being watched left him. It had been nearly two months since he buried the coins there, and he instinctively still avoided the place.

Ever the archaeologist, Longacre loosened the strap, swung his metal detector off his shoulder and clicked it on.

The buzzer immediately went wild, rapidly chirping a loud staccato. He was standing on a large amount of metal. When he tuned the discriminator, his heart sank to see the gauge swing deeply into the 'ferrous metal' zone. *"Junk!"* He thought in disgust. Probably a large deposit of iron ore. But as he began walking away, and before he had turned the device off, he had hardly taken more than a few steps when the needle jumped again replete with a tonal change. He looked down at the gauge.

Longacre's eyes widened to their maximum extreme. The discriminator was now smack in the center of the 'gold' area and no matter if he moved several steps to the right, or the left, or forward, it remained there.

Sans shovel, pick or any other useful tools, other than his Swiss Army knife, Longacre was unequipped to dig. Though in an otherwise thick jungle-like forest surrounding the old building and the clearing with the depression, the spot was only some 100 feet or so off the road known as the New Northern Highway. His walk had been parallel to it. He made his way to the highway.

Longacre intended to walk back the approximately two miles to the village where he lived, counting his paces, and return with shovels and tools in his pick-up truck. But he quickly realized counting paces would be useless if when he returned he would be riding in a truck! He'd have to mark the almost unperceivable, nearly fully grown over dirt trail that ran from the main road to the building hidden further back and the clearing behind it. This far away from Belize City, one stretch of trees looked like the last and the next. And even going slowly in a vehicle one could easily miss the trail onto the property.

He walked back and made his way to the concrete building that apparently served as a house for someone at the site. He recalled seeing a few pieces of old rusty construction rebar in the pile of rubble near the building. When he found them, he selected a piece about four feet long and, when out at the road again, he used a large rock to sink it into the dirt just in front of some low palm fronds.

That had been several weeks ago and since then he had made daily trips to the site. After a lot of hard work and digging, Longacre finally discovered, and recovered, several pounds gold coins from one of the kegs his shovel had penetrated. Spending as little time there each trip as necessary for fear of being discovered, he would stuff as many coins in his backpack as he could then quickly cover the hole with dead branches and palm fronds. But he dared not show or try to sell any of them.

Now the only person besides Luca who knew where the kegs of gold coins were hidden was passed out drunk in a bar in Belize.

∗∗∗∗∗∗∗∗∗∗∗∗∗∗∗∗∗∗∗∗

Bat had packed his gear, turned in his cabin key and been outside on the Observation Deck searching the pier for any sign of Charlie Stone by the time the *Windrush* tied up. He was still there, leaning on the rail and straining to see if his supervising agent was in one of the handful of private vehicles scattered among the several taxis and busses passengers would use for their day tour of Belize.

"Well, Mr. Lynch, you look fit as a fiddle and no worse from your unpleasant ordeal," Doc, immaculately dressed in shipboard whites, said as he came up alongside Bat.

"And see? We're depositing you right in your destination as promised."

"Thank you, Doc." He half turned and smiled at the ship's physician before resuming his search. Suddenly, to his lower left, he saw movement on the gangplank as passengers began debarking the vessel.

"But you know, you really should get down below. Did you hear the captain's message that we've been cleared by customs and now it's a mad rush for the gangway."

"Yes, I just noticed. I've been up here looking for someone I expected would be here to meet me. . ."

"Oh, you're not doing it the right way. If someone is down there they'll have their eyes locked on that queue of passengers going ashore," Doc gestured at the gangplank. "If they're there, they'll find you before you ever see them."

Three decks below, Jennifer and Kimberly and the two boys stood as close to the wall near the purser's desk as they could to avoid being trampled or pushed along by the crowd advancing toward the gangway a few feet away.

"So where's your mysterious pilot?" Kimberly asked with a slightly patronizing tone. "Maybe we missed him?"

"I don't think so. I've been here for some time. I saw the first people go off. He wasn't among them."

"Jen, if the guy is here to work and take pictures, the last thing he needs is two women and two kids he doesn't know tagging along."

"I mentioned to him last night that we would probably hire a cab instead of taking the tour bus out to Altun Ha and he said, 'That would be nice' and the way he said it sounded like he meant it. Had you been there, you would have heard it yourself."

"But that's not a *'Gee, lady, since I'm going that way too could I hitch a ride with you?'* You're dreaming, Sis."

"I know, you're probably right. He's got other things to do."

"Well, look, you can stay here and wait for your Mr. Wonderful, or you can take the boys, go ashore, grab a taxi before they're all gone and wait for me. I'll be down in a jiffy. Right now I have to go back and visit that little room in the cabin. . . in a hurry." With that, Kimberly began pushing her way through the crowd.

Jennifer had a sour pout on her face, but only for an instant. She had no sooner lost sight of her sister when she saw Bat in the middle of the masses coming down the wide double stairway some 30 feet directly across from her.

"Bat!" she waved, but got no reaction. He hadn't seen her.

"Bat Lynch!" she said louder this time

He heard her and saw her two arms over her head waving back and forth. Realizing it would be like swimming up stream to get to her through the tightly-knit and plodding human herd, he motioned toward the gangway and mouthed *"I'll see you outside."*

"Hold my hands, boys. Each of you take one and let's go," she told her nephews. Then in a low, mock prison convict voice added "Okay, you mugs, we're going to make a break for it!" The boys giggled at making an imaginary escape.

As the human movement inched its way ahead, Jennifer and the boys' forward progress was at an angle pushing to the right. Bat realized what she was doing and pressed on pushing to the left. They reached the gangway at almost the same time. He deliberately let a few people glide past him and they were together when Jennifer flashed her and the boys' photo i.d. boarding passes at the gangway officer. Bat didn't have a boarding pass and didn't need one. He smiled at the man, who had been one of the security officers with him in the holding room when he was rescued and brought aboard.

"Good luck," the officer said as Bat passed.

"How wonderful to see you again before you leave us . . . I mean leave the ship," Jennifer said with a broad and warm, but somewhat awkward, smile. He let her go first, down the somewhat steep, single-person wide ramp, and brought up the rear behind the boys.

"Yes, I was hoping our paths would cross one final time," he half lied. True, he wouldn't mind seeing her again but this, of all places, wasn't what he would have picked. He had to meet Charlie Stone, come up to speed on the latest information about Luca and then try to locate the man. Though having a woman and two boys with him might certainly provide a good cover, it would also prevent him from asking the kind of questions he needed to ask.

Nothing else was said by either as they concentrated on their footing. As they reached the bottom and stepped aside out of the traffic flow, Jennifer was on the verge of saying *"We're hiring a taxi to Altun Ha, and since you're going that way also, perhaps we could drop you off?"* But before the words could come out she heard Bat's name being called.

"Hi. . .Bill," he caught himself from almost saying Charlie.

"I'd like you to meet some nice new friends I've made. This is Jennifer Carson and her two nephews, now let's see if I get this right," he patted both boys on the head in turn saying "Blake and. . . Marshall"

"No! I'm Marshall. He's Blake"

Bat gave the child a weak smile and continued, "And this is Bill Higgins," Bat said quickly, "The editor I'm down here for to photograph *the you-know-what*" he raised an index finger to his lips to remind the boys of the secrecy of it all.

"Pleased to meet you, Mr. Higgins," Jennifer gave him a broad smile, but she was thinking, *"Why did you have to be here? You're ruining everything!"*

"Likewise, ma'am, boys," Stone said with a tepid smile and slight nod. Then added, "I hate to be a kill-joy and break up this party by taking Bat from you all, but there is work to be done and we really must be going, right now." As he was talking, Stone moved his hand up and took Bat's arm near the bicep. He squeezed it ever so slightly, but enough that Bat got the message.

Regardless, Bat stood his ground and made a proper goodbye.

"I really enjoyed meeting you all on the ship." He looked directly into Jennifer's eyes. "It was the bright spot of my abbreviated flight. Perhaps we'll meet again," then he realized he had no idea where she was from. She realized it also.

"Well, you said you're from the New York-New Jersey area," Jennifer reminded him. I'm in Alexandria Virginia, under 'J. Carson' in the phone book. If you're ever in our neighborhood, please give me a call. I'd like that."

"Wow, was that a veiled, or not so veiled invitation or what?" Bat thought. Even as Stone squeezed his arm again, he couldn't let it pass without showing her he would be inclined to follow up.

"Yes, yes, indeed, I most certainly will," he added for emphasis. "I often do freelance assignments for publications in D.C., which practically puts me in your back yard! I'll track you down."

"Goodbye, again." This time Stone's tone was less pleasant. He turned Bat away from Jennifer and, after pointing him in the direction of a black SUV, released his arm. Jennifer watched as they walked briskly towards it, got in and drove off. *"Rather fast,"* she thought.

"Hi Sis!" Kimberly said as she joined her sons and sister. "I see you took my advice and gave up looking for your *Wrong-Way Corrigan.*"

"Who's Wrong gay Culligan?" Blake asked.

"Yeah, who?" Marshall echoed.

Jennifer twisted her lips in annoyance and rolled her eyes without looking at her sister.

"Boys, sometimes you just have to ignore your mother. She says silly things," Jennifer said in a patronizing tone more for Kimberly's benefit than for the boys.

"It's Corrigan, not Culligan," she continued. He was a pilot a long time ago who thought he was traveling to Europe, but instead he ended up in California. Because of the mistake people started calling him 'Wrong Way' Corrigan." She shot a spiteful smile at her sister, then added: "Your mother was being funny. She was really talking about Mr. Lynch."

"We found him, mommy. We didn't give up," Blake replied excitedly as he turned to face his mother.

"He was just here," Marshall put in.

"Actually you missed him by a minute," Jennifer added, and continued, "If some people knew when to call it a night and leave some libation for the rest of the passengers, then 'some' people wouldn't have to hurry off to the bathroom so often. They'd be around to meet new people." She stuck her tongue out at her sister, mocking their childhood habit of indicating that was the final word on a topic.

Undaunted, and ignoring the remark, Kimberly pressed on.

"Sure, sure, and now he's run off to photograph The Great Giant Green Grape!"

"No, silly," Marshall admonished his mother. "It's a giant Jade head" he stage whispered.

"Okay, okay, I give up!" Kimberly threw her arms up in defeat. "Let's go see these old ruins."

****

As the agency driver wended his way through the streets of Belize City, Stone told Bat he and the four-man team had been pretty much laying low for the last day and a half waiting for Bat to arrive and finger Luca. They've spent much of their time familiarizing themselves with the small city, getting the lay of the land, which roads, alleys side streets and shortcuts were best to use, especially in a 'situation.'

"Four man team? What's with the small army? When you called me you said you just wanted me to see if this was the same Luca connected to St. Kitts, take some pictures, and you'd send a team down to tail him till he cut another drug deal with the terrorists."

"Yeah, I know. But the deputy director decided we should

have our guys in place to begin working the case the moment you make him."

"A hell of a lot of effort and expense on what could be a wild goose chase," Bat remarked with a hint of annoyance.

"If he's in this sweatbox, you'll find him. It's not that big and we haven't seen many Americans who don't look like tourists. We've discretely asked some general questions about the size of the American expatriate community, but it doesn't appear they do much of anything together."

"How many are there?"

"Pick a number from a half dozen to 50. Everybody has a different opinion," Stone shrugged. "But there is one guy from the States, a little light in the loafers I hear, who sells real estate and does villa rentals. He should be a good place to start. We went by his office twice yesterday but he wasn't there. Here's his address," Stone handed Bat a small piece of paper. "It's right off the main street, on the second floor. He's got a sign hanging on the building. You can't miss it." Stone reached into his jacket pocket.

"Here, it looks like a regular cell phone, but no matter what you dial on it I'll be on the other end."

"Thanks," Bat answered and put it in his shirt pocket instead of with his gear.

"As soon as you spot Luca call me with your location. We have three cars. Two of them will be out cruising. They can reach me the same way you can."

"What about a car for me?" Bat asked.

"No, you're a travel writer who just came off a cruise ship. It's more natural if you go up and down the main drag and talk to shopkeepers, bartenders, anyone who might give you a lead on Luca.

"Where will you be?" Bat asked.

"Probably in the hotel room, near the computer, GPS, other phones, the usual stuff."

When they reached the front of their hotel Stone and Bat got out of the SUV and the driver proceeded to the car park area with the vehicle.

"Anything you want me to take upstairs? You don't want to lug this thing around with you," Stone said touching Bat's large bag.

"Yes. You're right. Just let me take my camera bag out and you can have the rest." Bat removed the bag and slung it on his shoulder.

"Good hunting," Stone said as he hoisted Bat's bag and entered the lobby.

While appearing to be casually strolling down the street without a care in the world, Bat was reading shop and store signs and observing the people he passed. Before he reached the real estate agent's location he went into a small bar took a stool, and ordered a beer.

"American or local?"

"Local, please," Bat responded and put a U.S. five dollar bill on the bar.

It was still morning and the bartender was busy setting and arranging things for the business he was certain would come in time for lunch. He quickly brought a glass and a short stubby bottle of *Beliken*, the national brew and poured it in front of Bat, who wasted no time quaffing two large gulps.

"Nice," Bat remarked. "Reminds me a lot of the beers in Germany."

"The brewery uses the same methods and processes here. All of the ingredients except the sugar and water are imported," the bartender offered. He picked up the five and when he came back from the register he placed three U.S. singles down near Bat's glass.

"This is good," Bat said. This time he had taken a smaller sip. "Do most of the Americans who live here drink this, or do they stick to American beers?" he asked with a friendly smile.

The bartender shrugged. "I don't know. Only a few of them come in a place like this. Maybe I don't keep it fancy enough." The man spoke as he continued refilling near empty liquor bottles with the contents from other open bottles of the same brands.

"Are there a lot of Americans living in Belize City?"

"In the City? No. In the country, maybe." He shrugged again while continuing to work, without looking at Bat.

Bat emptied his glass in two more swallows and removed two of the three singles from the bar. As he was about to slide off the stool and say 'goodbye,' the bartender made his day.

"There's this one American, a big man, heavy, he comes in once in a while. The barber told me he lives in an expensive house outside town. His name is Marlo, Marco . . ."

"Mario, is it Mario?" Bat asked.

The bartender thought for an instant. "That could be it. . .yes, I think it is Mario. I don't really know him, he doesn't talk a lot, but you could ask the real estate man, Willow. He's an American too. They probably know each other. His office is just down the street."

Hardly three minutes later Bat found Bruce Willow busy packing his large Jeep Cherokee parked on the side alley of the building next to his office.

"Excuse me, Mr. Willow?"

"Yes," he said as he moved around Bat from the rear of the vehicle to pull something more forward via the open side door. "If you're here about buying something or a rental you're too late. I've sold the business to our prosperous local travel agency here in town and you should go talk to them. Good luck! I'm leaving."

"Leaving Belize City?"

"No. If you must know, I'm leaving Belize, the country. I'm returning to the United States, something I should have done a year ago. I can't stand to live here and get eaten alive any more. The mosquitoes can be the size of pigeons," he found appropriating Luca's exaggeration a useful way to avoid the truth. ". . . so just go down the street. You'll see the travel agency."

"No, I'm not here about real estate. Actually I'm trying to locate someone who may be a former client of yours, an American. I believe his name is Mario Luca?"

Willow stopped what he was doing and finally turned to face Bat, looking him over from head to toe.

"What in the world could someone like you want with a character like Luca?"

"So you do know him, then." Bat ignored the question for the moment

"Yes, he lives on the outskirts about seven miles *thata-way*." Willow gestured to his left, then added, "And I rented him a piece of the local jungle out *thata-way* and pointed in the opposite direction.

"Could you be more specific with regard to addresses?" Bat said as he removed a small notepad and pen from his canvas camera case.

"Mr. . . . .?" Willow dragged the word out waiting for Bat's name.

"Bartholomew, John Bartholomew. I'm with the U.N. World Health Organization's Contagious Disease Center." Bat fumbled in the case to produce the appropriate photo I.D. credentials.

"Oh, stop. Don't bother. Who would make up something as preposterous as *that*?" Willow asked. "What in heaven's name do you want Luca for? Is he dying from something?"

Before Bat could go into his standard 'ominous blood count' routine, Willow spoke again:

"I'll bet it's Trichinosis. That's it, isn't it? He devours packages of raw bacon all the time! You could get very sick from that if the pork has a parasite. Who but a madman would risk that?"

Bat caught himself before he made a disgusted face. *Raw bacon???*

"No, quite frankly, that's not what his blood work revealed. . ."

"Blood work? Luca? He doesn't strike me as someone who takes time for medical attention."

"Well, I have no idea what precipitated it, but he recently had some blood drawn and the testing lab contacted our agency immediately. He may be carrying an acutely infectious disease that could kill him and others he's been close to. We have to locate him immediately."

"You're shitting me! Luca's a big, uncouth lug and all, but it gives me the shivers to think about what you're saying." Willow seemed genuinely concerned.

Bat decided to play his trump card.

"Could you possibly spare a few minutes and take me by his house?"

"Me? Go there with you?" Willow flattened the palm of his

hand against his chest as he laughed, "Pa-leeese. You can't be serious! You just said he had an infectious . . ."

"No. I said *may* have," Bat corrected. "A simple oral saliva test, which I'm licensed to administer on the spot, can resolve this. There will be no need for you to enter the house, or even go on the property. Just drop me off and remain in your vehicle."

"But suppose he is infected, and you come out and then get in my car?"

"I've had the immunization shot, I can't get infected or be a carrier. You won't be at the slightest risk. I wouldn't ask you to do this if it weren't extremely important. Time is of the essence. You'll be providing a fellow American with a much needed medical test and possibly saving the lives of hundreds of people, if he is infected." Bat had delivered various versions this spiel perhaps a half dozen other times in his agency career and by now had fine-tuned the tempo, pace and emphasis.

Willow propped his hands on his hips in a macho stance, looked up at his office window, then at the car, and finally at the ground deep in thought for a few seconds before answering.

"Alright, I guess," he shrugged. "Hop in. I've packed everything I want from here."

Bat was tempted to call Stone and bring him up to speed but he decided he'd better wait until he made an i.d. on Luca, if indeed that was the man they were looking for.

Bruce Willow was a fast driver and endless talker during the trip. Early on, he asked several questions, which Bat artfully fudged. As they drove, Willow frequently removed his hands from the steering wheel to punch or stab thin air as he emphasized various points he didn't like about aspects of life in a foreign country.

In the time it took before they approached Luca's walled estate, Bat heard more than he ever wanted to know about living and surviving in Belize.

Finally, Willow said the words Bat had been waiting for: "Here we are. This garish stone wall runs the length of the frontage and all around the property. Ugh!"

"Okay. Stop here. We're close enough, this will be just fine. I can see the gate up ahead," Bat pointed toward it, "Right there."

"They're solid double panels. Press the intercom on the side. If Luca wants to let you in they'll automatically swing open."

"Thanks. Stay here. I'll be back as soon as I can." He opened the door and began making his way along the high stone wall to the tall gate. Nothing on the other side could be seen from the outside.

Willow had simply nodded but said nothing when he left.

As Bat approached the gate, he noticed a closed circuit camera staring down in his direction from one of the several overhead tree branches. He also heard the unmistakable hum of a lawn mower. Then he noticed a three foot long thick piece of wood was keeping the two sections of the gate ajar. He went in and replaced the wood as he had found it.

Even passing through the gate and walking along the paved driveway, he was unable to see the house for some 20 yards. The dense foliage on both sides provided a solid green wall as protective as the stone wall and opaque gate behind him. Finally he came to a clearing and saw a poorly dressed youth driving the mower in rows across the front lawn.

Bat nodded to the boy as he proceeded up the pathway leading to the front door, flanked on both sides by thick, lush plantings and dominated by thick tall hedges at both sides of the entrance. As he did he reviewed his excuse for being there one final time. Just as he was about to lift and slam the knocker against the solid brass plate, he heard the lawn mower shut down.

"Mister! He not home." The boy was standing next to the machine and crisscrossing his arms in a waving motion much like a baseball umpire would ruling a runner safe.

"Away. Away. He no here."

Bat acknowledged the information. "Do you know when he is coming back?" The boy stared at him blankly.

"Perhaps I can help you? My son doesn't speak English well."

Startled, Bat jerked his head to the right and saw an elderly man holding a manual trimmer emerge from behind one of the hedges.

"Yes, I hope you can. I'm looking for Mr. Luca. I'm from . . ."

"Oh, he's not here. He let us in about an hour or so ago and left. He asked me to slam the gate when we were finished so it would lock. We take care of the grounds."

"You wouldn't happen to know *where* he is, would you? At his country house, maybe?"

"No, I'm sorry," the old man smiled warmly. "I didn't know he had another house. He never talks much. Only about our work. But I don't think he will be back today, or tomorrow even."

"Why's that?"

"Because when he goes away on Sundays he doesn't return the same day, ever. Where he goes he must stay overnight."

Bat thanked him and was off the property and back in the seat next to Willow very quickly.

"He's not there. Mr. Willow, could I impose on your generosity to take me to that piece of property you rented to Mr. Luca?"

"Yeah, why not. I figured this could happen. But as I said, it's in the opposite direction." Willow did not seem overly excited.

"Thank you. I can't say it enough: it's really important to locate him."

"I know, I understand. I should be able to find it."

Bat gave the man a surprised glance. "Should?"

"Let me explain. The last time I spoke to Luca, I told him it hadn't been a good idea to remove an old mailbox that had hung on a tree near the road for eons. It was an easy reference point to find the place. Most of the countryside terrain looks very, very, similar, even to me. I actually passed the property, twice, looking for him the day I came to say the owner wanted to sell it outright."

"Really," Bat only said something to keep the talkative Willow happy.

"Yes. He told me he nailed a beer bottle cap on the tree and he knew the mileage distance from a specific point in the city. So when I left, by the way he's not interested in buying the place, I measured my mileage on the way back by using a familiar reference point of my own. So we're in luck! As we near the mile marker I'll slow down enough so we can both look for the tree with the bottle cap.

From your window it will be eye level at the edge of the road."

"Sounds like a plan to me," Bat said.

"Yes, *A man, a plan, a canal. Panama*," Willow said softly, almost to himself. Bat smiled at the familiar palindrome and recalled how amazed he was when he first heard it as a child.

"By the way we'll be heading that way through Belize City proper, and I'll want to stop for gas," Willow blurted.

"By all means do," Bat replied. "And, please, let me express my appreciation for all this chauffeuring around by buying the gas. Top off your tank."

What a sport! Willow thought sarcastically.

****

The archaeological site of Altun Ha is the most extensively-excavated one of its kind in Belize and practically an obligatory stop for foreign tourists. On days when cruise ships are in port, Altun Ha is a very busy place, much to the chagrin of the working archaeologists in residence. The core site includes 13 clustered ancient Mayan structures covering two Classic Period plazas.

The drive there from Belize City was 28 miles on the New Northern Highway and then a right turn onto the old Northern Highway for some 11 more miles.

With so many bus tours today, some groups had roamed the site while waiting their turn at orientation. Jennifer and company were in this lot. Now their self-guided tour completed, they stood in the shade of the welcome pavilion and half listened as a guide went through the introduction and orientation they had missed earlier.

"Upon entering the grounds your first stop will be Plaza A, which is enclosed by large temples on all four sides. Here a magnificent tomb was discovered beneath *The Temple of the Green Tomb*. Dating from 550 AD, this find yielded a total of thee hundred pieces, including jade, jewelry, stingray spines, skins, flints and the remains of a Maya book. . ." she went on calling attention to the various things Jennifer, Kimberly and the boys had already seen.

Marshall and Blake had quickly become bored with the imposing ruins, which all looked similar to them. And the reflective heat didn't help any either. Now having to listen to the guide ramble on was almost like a punishment. They had already asked their mother several times when they were leaving.

Both boys perked up, however, when they heard reference to a Jade head found at the site. But although it was described as the largest Jade head ever found, it was no larger than a basketball.

"Oh boy, wait till they see the pictures of Mr. Lynch's head!" Blake said loudly.

Kimberly gently pressed a hand over his mouth and pulled him against her as several nearby adults laughed at the remark. She gave them a weak smile. They assumed the child was talking about some person he saw with a large head. Jennifer bowed her head and seemed very interested in looking at the ground. Blake looked around nonplused, unable to comprehend what the sudden attention was about.

The guide's oratory lasted for another five minutes before the crowd dispersed. Marshall looked from his mother to Jennifer as he asked if they could go now and find Bat and the Jade head.

"But we really don't know where he is, or if he is even there," Jennifer replied sympathetically.

"Yes we do!" Blake said with childhood innocence. "He said the head was near here. We can find him."

"It's on the long road we were on, before we turned to get here, our taxi driver will know."

"Excuse me, guys," Kimberly interrupted. "We're not going *anywhere* before mommy finds the modern Mayan 'throne room.' Jen, I suggest you stay in the shade with them. I'll be back as soon as I can." She was off in an instant in search of the lavatory.

"Aunt Jen, when mommy comes back can we go find Mr. Lynch, please? He said he would take a picture of us with the giant head," Marshall said in his best please-pity-me voice.

"He said no such thing. YOU were the one talking about him taking a photograph," she answered, unsuccessfully trying to sound authoritative. But the boys didn't buy it. They knew Jennifer was a doting aunt and a soft touch they could manipulate far easier than their mother.

What they didn't know was Jennifer's heart was telling her she wouldn't mind seeing Bat Lynch again either. He was the first man since long before her divorce that stirred a spark of romantic interest in her.

"We should ask the driver. I'll bet he'll know," Blake added, nodding his head up and down vigorously.

"Okay, okay. Here's the deal: When your mother returns, if she's ready to leave here also, we'll ask the taxi driver if he has any ideas or if there is anything further down the road worth seeing. If he says anything encouraging, then we'll go."

"YES!" Marshall exclaimed. He and his brother exchanged 'high fives.'

When Kimberly returned to where they were, and Jennifer asked if there was anything else she wanted to see at the site, or go back and revisit, her sister's reply was as expected.

"Thank you very much for asking, but no thanks, my dogs are killing me," she raised and bent one foot across her other knee and massaged it through her thin tennis sneaker.

". . . and it's hot as hell out here. Besides I've had enough temple and tomb gawking to last me for a long while. All I want to do is get back into that air-conditioned van and relax. Let's go."

Jennifer and Kimberly made light conversation on the walk to the car park and their waiting transportation. The boys, several paces ahead of them, could hardly contain their excitement.

Once they were all seated in the vehicle and the driver began moving along the dirt road, Jennifer spoke:

"Excuse me, driver. That main road we drove here on . . ."

"The New Northern Highway. This road is the Old Northern Highway."

"Yes, the new one," she continued. "If you continued on it, instead of turning toward here, does it pass anything of interest?"

He caught her image via the rear view mirror for a few seconds but returned his eyes to the road as he answered. "Not really. A lot of trees, bushes. Some houses. Nothing tourists want to see for a long time. There is a small village where the archaeologists live, but the buildings are modern, not old Colonial."

Jennifer half turned in her seat to look at her nephews in the row of seats behind her and Kimberly. She expected to see total dejection on their faces. Instead they both had their hands locked together as if in devout prayer and were looking at her silently mouthing *"please, please, please."*

She glanced at Kimberly as she resettled in her seat. Her sister had removed both sneakers and was slowly massaging her feet again.

"How far away is that village?" she asked the driver.

"Maybe seven miles, maybe eight, when we get back on the new highway," he casually replied.

"Okay then. Would you mind doing that little detour, just as far as the village? I'll pay you extra."

She didn't have to see what the boys were doing. She could hear the vinyl squeaking as they bounced on the seat.

"What village? Why are we going to some village instead of back to the ship where I can soak my feet in the tub?"

"Kim, the boys are very interested in having Bat . . . Mr. Lynch. . . photograph them with the big Jade head. And since this is a vacation trip for them, I thought it would be nice to do it if we could. You don't mind, do you?" She was sure her sister wouldn't want to be the loser in a game of bad-cop, good-cop.

"The *boys* want to do this, see this Lynch again?" Kimberly said staring at Jennifer. Her sister nodded in the affirmative.

"Not you." To this Jennifer replied with a sheepish shrug and a weak, coyish smile. Kimberly took it as a definite 'yes.' Kimberly was actually delighted her sister was showing interest in a man again. Even if this mysterious guy was a half-assed pilot who took photographs.

"Okay, I give up. Let's see if we can find your hunk."

****

Mario Luca's gut was telling him it was time to visit his 'country place.' For the last two days he hadn't had the feeling that he was being watched and it had been several weeks since he checked to make sure things were as he had left them. But as he went through Belize City, he stopped at the outdoor Sunday market for some freshly cut pork. If he couldn't get packaged bacon from the supermarket which was closed on Sunday, it became a matter of any-port-in-a-storm to him.

Next, he pulled into a service station for gas and while he was there got into a discussion with the mechanic about mechanical questions he was experiencing with his car. When finished he resumed his trip.

As he always did, Luca had reset the TRIP MILES indicator in his Lincoln when he started the trip after letting the gardeners in at his estate. The market and fuel stops were both along the way and had no effect on the distance. Without doing that, he would have a difficult time knowing where to stop along the highway. To Luca, all the trees along the route looked remarkably the same, as if they were devilish clones some mean Mayan god had planted there to confuse him.

By never having pulled off the highway onto the property's unpaved access road since the late contractor Hindel had trampled it with his vehicle, the rapid, natural course of tropical plants had again pretty much overgrown it. Taking the property's mailbox down didn't help matters either.

When the indicator reached the appropriate mark, he pulled the car onto a small clearing just off the shoulder of the road some fifty feet beyond his property and began walking back along the road. On foot, going slowly, he would recognize a specific tree he had nailed a beer bottle cap onto.

But even before he located the tree, Luca saw a green van backed in, off the road on his property! Several palm fronds had been thrown on it and propped up against it in a feeble attempt at camouflage. He debated whether he should push on or return to the Lincoln and retrieve the old double-barrel shotgun from the trunk. He decided on the latter and checked to make sure both barrels were loaded.

A few minutes later, he had carefully made his way onto the site without being detected. Staying close to the side wall, he reached the building's back corner and peeked around. The first thing he saw about 50 feet away was obviously a body on the ground. Then, to their left and another 15 feet or so ahead he saw a man squatting down and apparently talking to someone else in a hole.

"The bastards had found my kegs, and they're robbing me!' He screamed inwardly.

As Luca made his way up behind the body he paused for a second to see if it was Willow. It wasn't, and he had never met Longacre. Finally, he had gotten to within five feet of the man now standing above the recently dug eight foot deep hole. The man wore a brightly colored short sleeve shirt hanging outside his long pants. People hiding a gun and not wearing a jacket always wore their shirts outside their pants.

The last thing Jake Paterson ever heard was the distinctive clicking sound as Luca pulled back one of the hammer's on the shotgun. When he instinctively turned around Luca pulled the trigger and the man went airborne almost completely across the large open hole. He bounced off the far end before slowly sliding down the side.

Even before Paterson's body finished its macabre ballet to the bottom, Luca had pulled the other hammer back and sent the other shot into the face of the other mob hitman, the frantically moving Bobby Benz. Chunks of bloody tissue and bone fell into the open keg he had been removing gold coins from.

Luca was sweating profusely. He used their aluminum folding ladder to climb down and check their pockets for identification, but their wallets told him nothing. Finding a 9mm tucked under Paterson's shirt gut suggested to Luca they were the mob muscle, the hit men his gut had been warning him about. He climbed out of the hole and dragged Longacre's body back to it and tossed it in, along with a metal detector laying nearby.

His first thought was to refill the hole with its dirt and restore the surface to resemble the rest of the area. *"Maybe there were more hit men on their way?"* he wondered. If not, others would surely be sent to finish the job. Perhaps he should go into the hole and at least empty all the gold coins out of the already open kegs? That would probably be all he would get a chance to recover. He knew he had to leave the country as quickly as possible, if he wanted to stay alive.

He had to think. Dangerous as remaining there now was, Luca lumbered back to the building and took a cold beer from the amply stocked refrigerator. He was going to drop into his favorite chair and decide exactly what he should do next. Then he remembered the parked van backed in at the front of the property. He figured he should check it out. He took the double barrel shotgun with him.

As he finished peeking through the van's rear windows he made his way toward the driver's side front. He first heard, then noticed a large silver Jeep, Willow's Jeep, slowing down and stopping a few feet past the tree Luca had nailed the cap into. *"That wimpy sonofabitch must have tipped them off,"* he reasoned, while quickly crouching down behind the van.

"What's this? Did Luca finally get rid of his Lincoln and buy a van?" Willow asked as he saw the vehicle only a few feet into the property. "No. . . . he must have company. He never parks on the property, he drives up and parks on a small clearing up ahead then walks back. Ridiculous, don't you think? Like people passing wouldn't put two and two together and know someone is in the woods nearby?"

"Not if he doesn't want anyone to know where he is," Bat said. "I can faintly see part of a structure back there from here." Bat took the cell phone Stone gave him out of his camera case and placed it on Willow's dashboard. If Stone decided to call him, Bat couldn't risk having it ring if he was sneaking around the property. He didn't even know if it would ring, or just vibrate, but he dare not take such an unnecessary chance.

"I'd appreciate it if you didn't use this, not even for a local call. They're tough as hell about non-business calls." He smiled as he got out of the vehicle.

"No problem. I'm going to get out and stretch a bit," Willow replied cheerfully.

Bat stuck his head through the camera case's shoulder strap so it crossed his body. That served the purpose of not having to worry about it sliding off his shoulder while at the same time freeing up his hands. He also thought it gave him a proper 'nerdy' look which people didn't find threatening.

"If that bottle cap gets any rustier it will be harder to see and useless," Willow said as he came around the front of the vehicle and immediately assumed the posture of an athletic warm up stretch.

"I'll just wait outside again," he called to Bat who had walked ahead and was already approaching the van. Willow turned away and stretched his body fully, extending his hands high above his head, did a few jumping jacks and jogged in place for a few seconds. He didn't see what happened next.

Luca lunged out from behind the side of the van holding the shotgun's stock and swinging the double barrels like a weapon as Bat reached the front fender. The heavy steel smashed into the right side of his head and part of his face. Bat was thrown against the vehicle and Luca caught him with another vicious blow on the other side as Bat began to crumble to the ground, face first.

The man who had just murdered the two mob hit men would have emptied a blast into Bat if he had remembered to reload the double barrel. Instead, he turned the gun around and, like a lumberjack standing over a log, he intended to bury the wooden stock in CIA agent's skull. But, as he rapidly hoisted his arms back over his head, the sweat on his hands mixed with traces of pork grease to catapult the gun into the air behind him.

"Shit!" he screamed. And used his feet to repeatedly kick Bat in the stomach and chest. Then turned Bat onto his back.

Willow recognized the voice and heard the thud sounds as the shotgun collided and bounced off three trees before hitting the ground. When he turned he was about to wave and call out a cheery *"Hello Mr. Luca,"* but instead saw the giant jumping and coming down on one foot, only to repeat the move again and again. Willow rushed forward and saw that what Luca was stomping on was Mr. Bartholomew's kneecaps.

"Stop!" he screamed. "Stop. He's here to warn you about a health problem! What are you doing?"

Luca turned and saw Willow rushing towards him and getting closer with every word. But when he was about six feet away the real estate agent stopped dead in his tracks. He looked at Bat's motionless body, bloody face and head and began slowly stepping backward.

"You've killed him! Why? What kind of crazy wild animal are you?" he asked as Luca's forward motion matched each step Willow took backward. Since he was taller than Willow, Luca's strides were somewhat longer. Soon they would be off the property and on the highway itself.

"Who is he?" Luca queried. "Another one of the mob's goons sent here to get me?" he kept inching closer.

Willow had no interest in asking what that meant. He realized Luca had gotten closer and Willow wondered if he could make a dash and get back to the Jeep before the ugly gorilla caught him.

His other choice was to turn and run down the road, which seemed the wiser option since he was sure he could out run the older, much fatter man. He'd have to decide fast, the heel of his shoe had just come down on pavement. They were at the front of the property parallel to the fronds where the old mailbox had once been.

Luca made a surprisingly quick advancing move, hands outstretched to grab Willow by the throat. He was seconds away from dying. But before moving to Belize, three solid years of chorus line dancing in San Francisco's off-Broadway shows blessed Willow with very strong, muscular legs.

Willow let loose with a powerful kick to Luca's groin which immediately halted the mobster's forward motion and doubled him up. For an instant Luca groaned, obviously in great pain, then, still hunched over, he slowly turned around trying to shake the breath-taking feeling away.

In an effort to knock Luca off his feet so he could run to his Jeep and escape, Willow charged at him from behind and threw his full body weight into the heavier man.

It worked. The contact thrust Luca forward. He staggered and wobbled a few steps before dropping face first into the palm fronds.

Mario Luca was impaled clear through the throat and out the back of his neck on the rebar stake Longacre had hammered into the ground as a marker. Arching squirts of blood, like some colorful fountain show in Las Vegas, immediately began pumping out of

Luca's artery as his body shook convulsively.

When he saw what he had done, Willow stood there mesmerized for several seconds not believing the horrible sight before him. He didn't budge till he realized there was no more movement, no more motion, no more life in the repulsive man he had rented the property to. Then he looked over at the other unmoving body a bit further back on the ground, Mr. Bartholomew, John Bartholomew who claimed to be with the U.N. World Health Organization's Contagious Disease Center.

Luca had asked if Bartholomew was 'another one,' a goon sent to kill him. Willow wondered who he was as he slowly walked over to take a last look at the handsome man he'd just driven to this awful place. As he gazed down at Bat's swollen face he noticed one eyelid flutter slightly. *"My God! Could he still be alive?"*

The former chorus dancer who had lifted a kick to Luca's groin which most professional football punters would be proud of, reached down and felt for a pulse. He found one. *"He is alive, maybe only barely. But Alive! Health worker or gangster, no one deserved to die out here alone,"* Willow thought.

Without hesitation, and with total disregard for the universally known medical advice not to move an injured person before professional help arrives, Willow sat him up and from behind was barely able to lock his arms around Bat's chest. As he laboriously dragged him toward the road and as he got abreast of the dead Luca, Willow was fatigued. He slowly and easily lowered Bat to the ground, moving the camera case off his chest and to the road side of his body.

He sucked in several deep breaths and reconsidered his situation: *"If I put him in my car and head back to the hospital in the city, what happens if he is dead by the time I get there? Who would believe my story if I told them what happened? Worse, when they came here and found Luca I could be blamed for his murder . . . or at best manslaughter, even if I swore on a stack of Bibles that it was self-defense."*

Willow looked down at the body he had dragged out to the road. Bartholomew, or whatever his real name was, still seemed to be alive. Suddenly what to do struck him. He once again struggled to move Bat's body, but this time only so it was totally on the road's shoulder where anyone passing would see it. After it was done he quickly returned to his Jeep and drove off. As he did he opened the driver's side window and reached for the cell phone Bat had left on the dashboard and dialed the local police number from memory.

"Hello", the voice on the other end said.

"Hello, I'm just a concerned tourist who just passed an almost dead man laying on the shoulder of the New Northern Highway, going north, about twenty-five miles out of Belize City."

"Who is this?. . . Is Bat Lynch with you?"

"I don't know any Bat Lynch. I don't want to get involved. I've reported what I saw. Goodbye!" Willow ended the call and threw the phone out the window. He was on his way back to the United States.

****

Willow's Jeep was well out of sight when the taxi driver looked down at his odometer and announced to Jennifer and Kimberly that the village where they would turn around was about two miles ahead.

"Well, it's now or never, sister. If we don't find your hunk soon he's history," Kimberly sitting behind the driver said. Jennifer, to her far right, was about to agree with her when she saw something that shocked her.

"Oh my goodness! Is that a body on the side of the road right there?" the driver had seen it also and was already slowing the vehicle down. It came to a full stop hardly ten yards past Bat.

"Please wait here. I'll go and inspect," the driver said as he rushed back to where Bat was. As he trotted away Jennifer closed her eyes and said a silent prayer for the poor soul prostrate on the side of the road.

"Yeah, right, mister," Jennifer said though she was out of his earshot. "I'm going to have a look."

Hardly a half minute later, both the driver and Kimberly were reentering the vehicle.

"We've got to go ahead to the village and phone for help. That man is dying. And there is another one there who is already dead," the driver said in a trembling voice.

"Wait a minute!" Kimberly said loudly halting the man's efforts to drive away. She looked at Jennifer.

"What color shirt did your pilot, or photographer, or whatever he is, have on today?"

"A blue denim, short sleeve. They gave it to him on the ship. Why?"

"Did he have a camera case?"

"Yes . . . he did. Canvas, one of those canvas colored . . . KIMBERLY! *Oh my God!*"

****

One month before her relationship with Dodi Fayed took flight, Diana sat at her desk in October, 1996, and wrote a long, confidential letter that she addressed and gave to her loyal butler, Paul Burrell, who had worked for Diana and Charles since 1987. The princess retained Burrell's services after the couple split and brought him to Kensington Palace, where she lived after her separation. Her divorce from The Prince of Wales had been finalized less than two months earlier. As future events would transpire, the handwritten letter would be considered one of the most eerily prophetic documents ever written.

"I tell you, Austin, something is bothering me about that blasted letter." Sir Warren and Smythe-Pembrooke were taking a brisk walk in St. James Park on a chilly November morning.

"Who ever heard of a royal writing, and addressing what is obviously a personal and confidential letter, to a servant and saying *'just in case'*? What the hell does that mean, eh?"

Smythe-Pembrooke couldn't rattle off any names of royals who had become particularly close with members of their staffs and could very well have done such a thing, but that didn't mean it hadn't been done. Anyway, he thought, the letter could be about anything. He didn't share Sir Warren's concern.

Earlier that morning, over a typically light breakfast in Sir

Warren's office, the pair watched a PAL format copy of video and audio generated by one of the few strategically placed FOTT dots in Kensington Palace. The VCR in the meeting room accepted both the European PAL and North American VHS format tape to accommodate video sent by the cooperating intelligence services 'across the pond.'

"I'm going to date this and want you to keep it… just in case," Diana said to her butler, as she sat at her desk in Kensington Palace.

The video had been captured by a FOTT on the wall across from Diana's desk. Sir Warren mused that if there had been a FOTT behind her, or perhaps on the ceiling above where she sat, it might have been possible to read what she was writing. But that's hindsight, he admitted to himself. They were fortunate to have placed the few that they did.

After their separation Prince Charles lived primarily in Highgrove, only a few miles from Camilla Parker-Bowles, while Diana and her sons remained at Kensington Palace. The Committee's spies were forced to overcome the difficulties which in the past had limited surveillance to Highgrove. In a surprisingly short time, they had compromised the security of the London residence.

"We need to know what she wrote," Sir Warren persisted. "Who knows what goes on in her unbalanced mind? She may have fantasized and concocted all sorts of nefarious things about the Royal Family and written them down. . . And given such a letter to a butler 'just in case'???" His voice raised a half an octave with the last phrase.

"Suppose the tabloids get hold of it?" Sir Warren continued. "We don't know what's in the letter, we'd be blindsided if they ever published such trash! We need to know what she wrote so we can be prepared to combat whatever it contains by planting contrary information. . . . in advance if possible."

"And just how do you propose we do that?" Smythe-Pembrooke asked. "She gave the letter to the butler and he tucked it away somewhere off camera, unfortunately."

"Well, that's obvious . . . Get young Blair to send in one of his chaps to search the butler's quarters, find and photograph the letter and return it so there is no trace that it was ever disturbed."

When the pair finished their walk, they returned to Sir Warren's offices where several members of The Committee had already gathered. Minutes after their arrival, they adjourned to the meeting room where Sir Warren opened the bar. It was show time, and his somber mood had changed.

They watched the usual fare of boiled down and edited video surveillance, as they routinely did, and mildly debated issues and options. These meetings, Sir Warren thought, had returned to being orderly sessions since the sudden and 'unexpected' demise of Leslie Wilford.

But today's gathering would end with something different. At Miles Blair's urging, his son Archie had SIS technicians put together a short, amusing composite video. It was one of the lighter moments the royal ordeal had provided. The tape took scenes from various FOTT videos and edited them together using fades, dissolves, wipes and other first generation special effects of yesteryear.

The audio had deliberately been replaced with the kind of piano music used as background in the silent movie era and appropriately rose to suspenseful crescendos at various times. The entire tape, in black and white, was re-recorded to appear as if it had been shot in the 16mm speed used when motion pictures were in their infancy at the turn of the century. The old fashioned title frame simply read: DIRTY WORK AFOOT?

With interruptions by their own laughter, The Committee saw Princes Diana and Paul Burrell push furniture in her sitting room to one side and roll up an Aztec Indian looking rug and the larger carpet and backing under it. Next they were seen using screwdrivers to pry and raise floorboards. The film continued in its jerky motion as Diana checked electric sockets, lamps and light switches, looked behind picture frames, and in other possible places of concealment.

The final scenario shows Diana talking on the phone to someone then fading into the on camera appearance of a former SIS intelligence officer she was known to trust. Sir Warren and a few members of The Committee recognized the ex-agent who was seen doing an extensive sweep for electronic listening devices. Nothing was discovered. *"The FOTT dots were worth their weight ten thousand times in gold, nay . . . priceless!"* Miles Blair thought.

The film ended with a classic shot of Charlie Chaplin, in costume as *The Tramp,* raising his arms chest high, turning his palms up and shrugging in despair. As he waddled away, twirling his cane, the screen filled with THE END to a courteous, but reserved, round of applause. Sir Warren didn't think the effort was that funny at all. He thought it had been a waste of good money and time, but he kept such feelings to himself.

"Perhaps," Sir Warren rose and, with a broad, sweeping motion of his arms, continued, "The princess' concerns about spying on royals, espionage, skull-drudgery and other such fantasies about what our intelligence chaps are capable of doing is in part fed by Diana's interest in James Bond!" His remarks brought a laugh from those assembled.

"We have it from very high authority," he feigned a cough, ". . .that she was keen about the whole spy thing when she visited the movie set of *The Living Daylights* and asked actor Timothy Dalton all the usual James Bond gadget questions." He paused for effect, then, in a mock questioning tone queried:

"I wonder what she said to Sean Connery at the premiere of *The Hunt for Red October?* Oh, silly me. He wasn't playing Bond in that film, was he?" More laughter. Sir Warren enjoyed the attention.

"No, he wasn't. His last role as Bond was in *Never Say Never Again,* in 1983," Miles Blair said enthusiastically. The comment was useless trivia and earned by a blank stare from Sir Warren, and puzzled silence from the rest of the group. It had been an unnecessary correction, and intruded on Sir Warren's spotlight.

"But, Sir Warren, James Bond saved Princess Diana and her sons from a tragic fate at EuroDisney in John Gardner's novel, _Never Send Flowers_," Smythe-Pembrooke, always the loyal Ed McMahon to Sir Warren's Johnny Carson, added to light laughter.

"Yes, he did, didn't he? Well, I guess that should prove to her that SIS isn't staffed with lowly scoundrels who listen in on people's private phone conversations!"

CHAPTER EIGHT

The two agents Stone contacted after receiving Willow's call brought their speeding vehicles to screeching halts. With guns drawn they approached Jennifer who was obviously in great distress as she knelt on the highway crying and talking to the unresponsive body on the pavement before her. The doctor, whom Kimberly and the taxi driver had returned with from the nearby village, was attempting to ascertain Bat's injuries. Determining that the distraught woman and the man administering to Bat, obviously a physician, were not threats, Stone's men holstered their weapons.

The doctor ignored the agents' obvious questions about Bat's condition as he strained to hear a faint heartbeat. Kimberly had remained in the van with her two sons, who desperately wanted to be out in the thick of things on the road. The taxi driver, meanwhile, fidgeted nervously as he stood behind Jennifer.

One of the agents shot a cold stare at him.

"You're the driver?" and before the startled man could respond, added, "How fast were you going when you hit him, you sonofabitch?"

"Oh, my God! No. I didn't hit him. Ask the misses. We found him and the other one here as we were driving." He pointed a few feet away to the impaled Luca, whom they hadn't yet noticed.

"He's dead, yes. Very dead I think."

While one agent moved to inspect the grotesque carcass Stone pulled up at the site in the third vehicle.

"I'm afraid this man will be dead also if he doesn't receive immediate intensive care," the doctor said, adjusting the stethoscope now hanging around his neck.

Jennifer momentarily took her eyes off Bat and looked up at the small crowd now hovering above her. She immediately recognized Stone from their brief meeting at the ship.

"Mr. Higgins? How could this have happened?" she said through her tears. "He left with YOU to take pictures of your Jade head! Why weren't you with him? Who would do such a horrible thing to him and that other man?"

Stone's eyebrows both raised in surprise and his eyes quickly darted around the area.

"It could be Luca," the agent nearest him said softly, indicating the dead drug dealer with a penchant for raw bacon.

But Stone's first concern wasn't Luca.

"Where's the nearest hospital?" He practically shouted.

"In Belize City. We only have a small clinic in the village. This man needs serious surgery. I've already called for an ambulance," the doctor said.

Jennifer, Kimberly and the boys were in the taxi following the ambulance as best they could. They were the fourth vehicle. Ahead of the ambulance was a police car, siren screaming, hardly able to stay in front of Stone in the SUV.

Seeing how upset her sister was over the condition of this man Jennifer hardly knew, Kimberly tried to keep a conversation going. The boys, listening intently, took it all in.

"So did Higgins, or Stone, or *whatever* his real name is, tell you if Bat Lynch was your 'photographer's' real name?" she asked.

"Yes. That's his real name."

"But he's not really a travel book photographer, he works for our government?"

"He *is* a travel editor, and a real photographer, and a pilot. But he was working undercover for the CIA." Jennifer said, clutching and twisting the handkerchief Stone had given her.

"I don't think I should be telling you that," she added, giving her sister a weak smile.

"C'mon, Sis, if we didn't stop, your new friend would have died before anyone found him! What's the big secret?"

Jennifer shrugged. "Stone, that's his real name, not Higgins, is Bat's superior, and he said they believe the dead man is the person Bat was sent here to find." Even as she spoke Jennifer couldn't help recalling the vision of Luca's upper torso partially suspended above the ground with the steel rod through his neck.

"So, see what I mean? Your undercover agent's mission is obviously over, no need for all the secrecy."

"Oh Kim, it's all so confusing and horrible. . ." Jennifer

choked up, ". . .He's seems so nice, and normal. I can't picture him as one of those spies in the movies."

"Fact is, that's exactly what he is. And he *lied* to you about it," Kimberly said softly.

"He was undercover!" Jennifer and Marshall said in unison. Blake looked at his brother then his aunt and finally at his mother who was giving Marshall one of those *keep-your-mouth-shut* looks.

"Was he cold? I didn't see any covers," the child wondered.

Usually, the return trip from anywhere always seems faster but Jennifer felt this journey back to Belize City seemed like it would never end. Kimberly continued chatting to keep Jennifer's mind occupied, but she made small talk carefully avoiding anything about Bat or related to their recent shocking experience.

"I'm going to have to spring for some film when we get back to the ship. I shot more than I expected at Altun Ha-*ha*," she joked.

Marshall laughed first, quickly followed by Blake, who wasn't sure why he was laughing.

"It'll be more expensive than back home, but I don't know if I should trust buying film from any of the shops in town. I'll bet that stuff cooks in the heat down here, don't you?" she asked Jennifer.

But it was Marshall who answered. "We should get a digital camera like Mr. Lynch has . . ." Even as the words trailed out of his mouth he could feel his mother's piercing eyes.

Jennifer's lips curled downward and it was obvious she was on the verge of bawling again, but instead she spoke:

"When we get to the hospital, eventually, you should go back to the ship with the boys. I'm going to stay there."

"And catch a cab later?" Kimberly asked. "Remember we pull out at 8 PM and. . ." Kimberly glanced at her watch, ". . .it's almost five already. Don't dilly-dally or you'll be late for dinner."

"No, I don't care about dinner, or the rest of the cruise for that matter. I'll stay at the hospital until they let me talk to Bat."

"Jen, you can't be serious! If it helps, we'll all wait at the hospital with you, but we'll all be back on the ship together tonight. And if we miss dinner we can order something to the suite."

"Kim, you don't understand. I want to stay there and comfort him. I want to be there when he wakes up."

Kimberly's jaw dropped. She snapped her head from side to side, but before she could form a protest Jennifer spoke.

"I know I just met him the night before last and you probably think this is all crazy." She looked at her sister with pleading eyes and continued. "But something inside tells me he's the one: the man I was destined to meet."

"Jennifer, you're not the heroine in some soapy plot from one of those bodice rippers you write. This is the real world. Snap out of it, kid. This guy moves in a different world than we do. He plays with guns and nasty secrets." Kimberly was being firm. "He's not for you. . . And don't give me any of that 'love at first sight crap.' That's in books and movies, not in real life. Ask me."

Jennifer ignored her sister's comments and simply stared out the vehicle's window at the fast moving scenery.

When the taxi pulled up to the hospital emergency entrance parking area, the driver noticed it was already over crowded with the police car and Stone's SUV.

"I think I should let you all out here if you're going inside. I'll find a place to park on the street if you want me to wait.

"Yes. Wait," Kimberly said, digging a ten dollar bill out of her shorts and handing it to the man.

"But you'll only have three passengers going back to the ship," Jennifer added firmly.

"Jenni. . ." Kimberly tried to protest.

"That's it, Kim. You heard me. I'm staying till I can talk to him," Jennifer said as she made her way out of the vehicle.

Once inside the small waiting area, Jennifer saw Stone.

"How is he? Did he say anything on the way?"

Stone shook his head. "He was unconscious all the way. The doctor said it's a concussion, maybe a fractured skull. And his jaw is broken, both sides. They're doing x-rays right now. His legs, the knees, are really messed up too. Bat took one hell of a beating."

"Oh God . . . Do they expect him to make it?"

"The doctor couldn't say. They don't know yet if he has internal injuries to his stomach, or organs, or if there's massive internal bleeding. That could mean big trouble. I've got a feeling it will be a bit longer before they can tell us anything for certain."

"I'm going to wait," Jennifer said to no one in particular as she dropped into an empty chair and exhaled.

Stone looked from her to the two boys, then Kimberly. Obviously sisters, and very attractive. Lynch couldn't have gone wrong picking either. *"But the one sitting in the chair seemed softer, more caring,"* he thought.

A short time later, after Kimberly was again unsuccessful in convincing Jennifer to return to the ship. She kissed her sister before leaving with the boys in the taxi heading back to the *Windrush*.

****

Diana loathed the feeling of constantly being listened to and watched. She suspected listening devices had been planted in her living quarters. She lived in a fishbowl. The government-issued bodyguards were there to protect her sons, especially William, the future king, but she suspected most were The Firm's spies. To alleviate this somewhat, she declined police protection for herself.

Even with the end of her private protection, Diana believed she was being observed by electronic surveillance. Her critics and allies of Charles pointed to such concerns as her paranoia. But she had good reason to suspect that. As the title of Miles Blair's little film suggested, there indeed was *dirty work afoot*.

Though the former SIS man whom she trusted had been unable to detect any surveillance devices when he swept her living quarters in Kensington Palace, the FOTT dots were in fact there and functioning beyond Sir Warren's best expectations. He, and The Committee were aghast, for instance to discover that a member of the Royal Family actually warned Diana: "You need to be discreet, even in your own home, because `they' are listening all the time."

Diana's trusted ex-SIS confident was seen showing and explaining hi-tech surveillance techniques and advising her that SIS was capable of monitoring her movements with equipment and technology that could be employed off premises as well. Using state-of-the-art parabolic microphones conversations in her home could be listened to or recorded from a lorry or van parked outside. The common way to deliver a signal into a building was to direct it at a mirror to bounce it back.

Diana found that information so eye-opening that she went around the rooms she most frequented in the palace looking for suspect mirrors. A round convex mirror above the marble fireplace in her sitting room was opposite a window. It was removed.

Besides the unwelcome eavesdropping, the princess had grown increasingly concerned about her personal safety as her marriage to Charles deteriorated over the years. A close friend would recall she had joked more than once, "Just because you're paranoid it doesn't mean they're *not* out to get you!"

It was exactly that kind of information Sir Warren expected to be contained in the letter Diana had written and given to Paul Burrell eight months ago. It had taken three different violations of the trusted butler's living quarters to finally discover the letter. On the chance Diana had said or revealed something damaging to the monarchy, Sir Warren had asked Archie Blair to have his man persist searching for and photographing it.

But the former deputy director of SIS could never have imagined what The Princess of Wales had written when the aforesaid photos of the letter finally arrived. He kept reading the stunning revelation over and over:

"I am sitting here at my desk today in October, longing for someone to hug me and encourage me to keep strong and hold my head high. This particular phase in my life is the most dangerous. My husband is planning 'an accident' in my car, brake failure and serious head injury in order to make the path clear for Charles to marry."

Sir Warren saw the words in Diana's own hand, but nonetheless couldn't believe what he was reading. He quickly skipped through the entire letter, using a red marker to highlight various things in this unprecedented royal document. The envelope that contained the letter was simply addressed by Diana to "Paul."

"I have been battered, bruised and abused mentally by a system for years now, but I feel no resentment, I carry no hatred. I

am weary of the battles, but I will never surrender. I am strong inside and maybe that is a problem for my enemies. . . I have become strong, and they don't like it when I am able to do good and stand on my own two feet without them. . . Thank you, Charles, for putting me through such hell and for giving me the opportunity to learn from the cruel things you have done to me. . . I have gone forward fast and have cried more than anyone will ever know. . . The anguish nearly killed me, but my inner strength has never let me down, and my guides have taken such good care of me up there. . . Aren't I fortunate to have had their wings to protect me. . . I just long to hug my mother-in-law, and tell her how deeply I understand what goes on inside her . . .I understand the isolation, misconception and lies that surround her. . . I so want the monarchy to survive and realize the changes that it will take to put 'the show' on a new and healthy track. I, too, understand the fear the family have about change but we must, in order to reassure the public, as their indifference concerns me and should not be. . . I will fight for justice, for my children and the monarchy..."

But it was the ominous words in the second paragraph that shocked Sir Warren *"My husband is planning 'an accident' in my car."* All the rest was the kind of outpouring one would expect from an equal player in a wrecked marriage, he thought.

What could have possibly given her such an idea? Could she have overheard something Charles foolishly said in jest on the phone to Camilla? Had The Committee's own operations appeared so threatening that Diana assumed SIS was in cahoots with Charles to do away with her?

In her unstable condition, Sir Warren wondered, could Diana have interpreted a joke to mean something sinister? The telephone interrupted his concentration. He touched the button to put it on speaker phone.

"Hello?"

"Hello dear, I just got off the phone with Madge and was wondering when you were coming home and if you'd care to join her and Austin for dinner this evening?" his wife asked in her typically cheerful voice.

"Dinner?. . .Tonight with the Smythe-Pembrookes?. . .No . . .I don't think so. Not tonight. I've had a terrible, terrible day."

"Oh, dear," she pouted. "A fine retirement you're having. You should be enjoying these golden years instead of still keeping yourself so busy at that silly office."

"It's been the family business for nearly 200 years. My brothers tended to it while I was in government service. Now they're gone and it's my time, my duty, retired or not."

"And look what it does to you. You sound positively miserable. Well, when you come home we'll have a quiet dinner together and you can tell me all about your day. Good bye, dear."

He pushed the button to end the call and realized he hadn't said good bye to her. He would have to fabricate something as the reason he had been depressed and upset when she called. He wouldn't tell her, couldn't tell her, or anyone, about the princess' letter. Not even Smythe-Pembrooke.

****

Four days had passed since Bat had been nearly beaten and stomped to death. Jennifer had remained at his bedside every moment since the doctors permitted her to do so almost three days ago. Stone had used the agency's influence to secure a private room for his bloody and broken agent, and didn't mind at all that Jennifer wanted to stay there too. Having 24-hour supervision was a bonus in the otherwise short-staffed hospital. He arranged for a cot to be brought in and she took her meals there as well. The medical consensus was that he could wake at any time. Staff nurses brought her English language magazines from the reception area and she selected books from the hospital's lending-library cart.

At Stone's request, the agency flew in specialists from the States to consult with the attending local physicians who determined after examining Bat, viewing his myriad the x-rays and various test results, that he was a man very lucky to be alive. As near-fatal as his head injuries were, the doctors were very hopeful there didn't appear to be permanent damage. Cuts on both sides of his face and back of the head all required stitches, and the extensive bruising and facial swelling had reduced his eyes to appear as tight slits.

His most severe injury was his shattered right knee cap, which would need reconstructive surgery back in the States. His left knee had miraculously escaped the same fate, though both showed extreme pressure trauma as did his badly bruised mid-torso, from what were assumed to be powerful kicks.

Jennifer was seated on a chair next to Bat and holding his right hand in hers. She looked at the immobile puffy-faced man in the bed and wondered what powers had drawn her so forcefully to him. Kimberly was, of course, right. Jennifer hardly knew this man who had fallen from the sky and into her life. Yet, in her heart, she couldn't deny her attraction to him or dismiss the feeling that they were soul mates.

If there really was such a thing as reincarnation, she thought, then perhaps her life and Bat's life had previously been entwined many times in the past. Jennifer no sooner completed the thought when she remembered she had written nearly those exact words as character dialog in one of her books! *"Maybe Kimberly is right,"* she thought, *"I'm confusing reality with the make-believe romantic world I create."*

She reached to the table and picked up the old hardcover book. It was one of many she had always promised herself she would read, but never found the time. Now, reading out loud to Bat, helped pass the time. To better grip the book she gently slipped her right hand from his and began reading softly, almost in a whisper:

"Last night I dreamed I went to Manderley again. It seemed to me I stood by the iron gate leading to the drive, and for a while I could not enter. . ."

"Why are you reading *Rebecca* to me?" Bat managed to ask, almost in a whisper. "Don't you have any of your books with you?"

"Oh, my God! Oh Bat!!!" She let the book fall to the floor and quickly rose then leaned forward to embrace him, then hesitated.

"I want to hug you and kiss you, but your face is swollen so bad I'm afraid of hurting you!"

306

"Try the tip of my nose. That's the only part that feels normal."

She did indeed kiss the tip of his nose, then very gently his lips, several times. No words were needed or necessary between them, for each realized how deeply the other cared. Soon, too soon, this private romantic interlude was broken when a nurse, followed quickly by a doctor, came in to see why Bat's monitoring device was showing several spikes.

Hardly twenty-four hours later, the flight back to the United States carrying Bat and Jennifer touched down at Andrews Air Force Base, Maryland, and not long afterward his bed had been raised to a sitting position in Bethesda Naval Hospital, also in Maryland.

Since Bat awakened from his comatose state the previous day, Jennifer's face had been locked in a grin from ear to ear. Though it was somewhat uncomfortable for him to talk, he had been told the more facial exercise and movement he did, then the quicker the circulating blood would help with the healing process.

"Well, Bartholomew, you were certainly a sight for sore eyes the last time I saw you," Stone said lightly as he entered the room, adding "Hello Jennifer Nightingale," and smiled warmly at her. She returned the greeting as she rose from the chair.

"Fellas, I promised my sister I'd call her once we were settled in here. I'm going outside to use my cell phone." She blew a kiss to Bat as she crossed to the door.

"Here," Stone handed her his topcoat. "You're not in Belize any more. It's cold out there."

She put the coat on. It hung almost as loosely as her father's suit jackets when she and Kimberly played 'dress up' as children. Jennifer extended her arms straight out as she made a complete revolution. "How do I look, gentlemen?" she said jokingly.

"Get outta here, go," Stone laughed, as Bat tried desperately not to. He knew his face would hurt.

Jennifer was out of the room in an instant with a long "Byeeee!"

"Thanks for everything you've done, Charlie. Jennifer said

you practically took over the hospital, but I don't remember any of it." Bat answered through his still bandaged jaws.

"Not surprised. You were out like a light for three days in Belize."

"Yeah, so Jennifer tells me. I woke to find her sitting next to my bed softly reading to me." Bat paused, then continued. "She actually gave up the rest of the cruise to stay behind and be with me."

"Sounds like a 'keeper,' Bat, I've spoken with her quite a bit, and I get the impression she's in love with you, crazy woman!"

"Ouch, it hurts!" Pleased at Stone's observation, Bat had tried to smile but it caused him discomfort.

"Did you ever find out what the hell hit me? The last thing I remember was walking toward a parked van and then everything went dark. I don't even remember feeling pain till I woke up.

"Probably a good thing. Luca whacked you a number of times with the barrel end of a shotgun. Your DNA was all over the gun in copious amounts."

"Luca? Did you get him?"

"Didn't they bring you up to speed during the debriefing?"

"No, I don't have a clue. All your merciless henchmen did was take a statement and then take off like bats out of hell. . . So, was it the right Luca, the same one from St. Kitts?"

"Oh yeah, that was him, alright, the forensic boys nailed a match. But we don't have him in custody."

"What???"

"Nope. He's in the morgue in Belize City." Stone thought for a second, then added. "Check that, maybe by now he's just ashes in a numbered jar or pushing up daisies."

"What happened to the real estate agent, Willow, the man who drove me out there?"

"Well, we think he's the one who killed Luca then used the two-way phone to call in the report that got us out to you, before he high-tailed it out of there. We haven't found him."

Bat played the just heard information around in his mind and tried, with little success, to picture the effeminate, talkative, Bruce

Willow actually killing someone. It was hard to believe.

"Oh, and get this, we found four more bodies in the yard. Two were definitely mob guys that Luca took out with a blast apiece from the double-barrel. You're lucky he didn't have a pump action with more rounds in it or you wouldn't be here, *amigo*."

Bat grunted a sound that Stone took as being in agreement.

"The third guy was an archaeologist with no previous criminal record We don't know how he plays into al this, but we found his prints on a metal detector near the hole."

"What hole?"

"The hole loaded with barrels full of modern gold coins, millions of dollars worth. The more they dug, the more barrels they found. Oh, and the fourth body was an employee of a construction company who vanished a couple of months back with a truck and backhoe. He had been in the excavation longer than the others."

****

It was with anticipation of a very good payday that the three German 'tourists' waited on park benches and loitered in the *Jardin des Tuileries*, the spacious, beautiful, and profusely planted garden in front of the Louvre for his appearance. At a few minutes before the specified time, a well dressed young boy of about 13 years of age entered the garden from the Rue de Rivoli side. He panned the visible esplanade before him row by row. Taking great care to explore both sides of the long pathways, he appeared to be distraught and looking for someone. Each of the three Germans had noticed the animated boy, but none made any sudden moves or outward signs of recognition.

The individual they were expecting always sent an intermediary to advise a second location. One couldn't be too careful in the spy business. This boy seemed to be just such a messenger.

After approaching a passing couple and a fast walking young woman, stopping both to ask questions, the boy reached one of the seated agents who seemed to be casually reading a newspaper. The approach to the seated agent all but confirmed to the other two that

this was indeed the contact they were waiting for. The two slowly
began heading for different, prearranged, exits from Tuileries.

"Excuse me sir," the lad asked. I'm looking for someone. Have
you seen a little girl about ten years old wandering around here
alone?"

"No, but I'm wearing a German wrist watch," he replied."

"The gentleman says to please cross the Rue de Rivoli and go
to Place Vendome. Take some photos and then read the plaque on
the monument." The boy bolted away, without waiting for a reply,
with the same urgency he had exhibited upon arrival. Some distance
away he continued his performance and asked another couple the
same question.

The rogue German agent slowly folded his paper and
deliberately extended his right arm, bent at the elbow, to chest level
to examine the time. The others picked up the sign. Hardly fifteen
minutes later, the trio was in Place Vendome. Only one of them
stood by the monument taking his time to line up angles for several
photos. The other two played the roles of window-shopping tourists
slowly moving around at distant extremes.

After a few minutes, an elderly looking woman customer
emerged from one of the shops and began crossing from one side of
the square to the other.

"Follow me into the hotel," she said as she passed the Rogue
who was now reading the plaque on the monument. He let her
almost reach the door of The Ritz before casually walking toward it
himself. Equal time intervals would be repeated by his two
colleagues.

Once inside, she said only two words to each of them as they
arrived individually: "Hemmingway Bar," and with her eyes
motioned to the proper corridor, sending them on their way.

Arguably the best known bar in any hotel anywhere in the
world, the Hemmingway Bar drips with a rich history and lore. It
was already an internationally 'in spot' when 'Papa' Hemingway
was a regular at the   world famous hotel before the Second World
War. The Ritz is so lavish that, decades earlier, it had become a
synonym for elegance and luxury and was the source of the phrase

for things being *"Ritzy"* and the popular song *"Putting on the Ritz."*

When the American writer returned to Paris during World War II as a correspondent for Collier's magazine, his arrival at The Ritz was the stuff of which legends are made.

Though all German occupation decisions were made by the Commanding General of Greater Paris at his headquarters in the Hotel Meurice on the Rue de Rivoli, the Ritz had served since 1940 as the official residence for Nazi dignitaries, including Reichsfuhrer Hermann Göring. The rotund head of the Luftwaffe reputedly spent a lot of time in his lavish Ritz suite high on morphine and, reportedly, dressed as a woman.

Hitler had demanded that General Dietrich von Choltitz destroy the city so that all the advancing Allies would liberate was a pile of rubble. Explosives had been planted at all of the City of Light's major monuments and the 20 bridges that cross the Seine from the Right to the Left Bank.

As the Allies approached the city's outskirts on August 25, 1944, Hitler, in Germany, screamed over the phone at his Paris commander: *"Brent Paris?'* (Is Paris Burning?).

"No, not yet," the general lied to the leader of the Third Reich, "But it would be, shortly," he promised Hitler. But von Choltitz couldn't give the order. A day later the city was liberated, intact.

Fortunately Von Choltitz who realized his own capture was eminent, didn't want to be remembered in history as the man who destroyed what many consider the most beautiful city in the world. The general ordered the occupation troops to withdraw while he and some staff officers remained behind to face the inevitable.

When Hemingway's jeep pulled up in front of The Ritz the Germans had already pulled out and a relieved Von Choltitz was surrendering to American and Free French troops. Paris was no longer his problem.

Hemmingway, who once said "When I dream of life after death, the action always takes place at the Ritz," gave the hotel's lobby a cursory look, and immediately headed for his favorite watering hole, ostensibly 'just in case' some German stragglers found it difficult to leave and were still hanging around the place.

Yet all that was left for the hard-drinking writer to do was belly up to the bar and celebrate the Wehrmacht's departure with a round of dry martinis. Magnanimous in victory, the self-declared 'liberator' of The Ritz even offered a round of drinks for the German troops he and his cohorts had taken prisoner on their drive into the city.

Upon meeting Hemingway for the first time, Robert Capa, the famous combat photographer thought the *prima dona* writer was a general. Hemingway's entourage included a public relations officer, a lieutenant as an aide, a cook, a driver, a photographer. . . and a special liquor ration. When Capa himself arrived in Paris, via a jeep, he was certain he was miles ahead of anyone else. But when he pulled up at the Ritz, Capa saw Hemingway's driver standing guard with a carbine slung over his shoulder, while Hemingway held court at the bar. In short order, other troops entered the place. The bar bill for the event, courtesy of Hemingway, included 51 martinis.

Eventually the small and cozy bar/lounge, which resembles an oak-paneled upscale English-club setting, was named in Hemingway's honor and is akin to being a mini shrine to him. While The Ritz is ritzy, the Hemingway Bar is clubby and cozy. The décor includes a piano, several photos of the hunter-fisherman-writer, plus shark jaws, bookish memorabilia and rows of newspapers, and homage to other writers lining the walls. It is still located on the main floor, close to the hotel's Rue Cambon entrance.

It took almost five more minutes before the three German rogue agents were all seated at a corner table with Smythe-Pembrooke. As was his preference, he had his back to the wall and could see whoever entered or looked into the bar.

"I've ordered just water for all of us," was the first thing he said to the group. He motioned for the waiter and nodded. The man had been tipped well in advance not to disturb them, nor seat anyone else in the area. The latter wasn't expected to be a problem since their meeting was taking place at a day of the week and time which was usually slow for the otherwise popular bar.

312

When the drinks arrived the waiter retreated promptly.

"I must tell you, I'm very impressed with your choice of a meeting location," the agent on the left said in fluent English. He glanced around with appreciation at the furnishings. "The famous Ritz Hotel itself. I could get used to this." The other two joined him in voicing their approvals as well.

"My grandfather was on Göring's staff during the war and always talked of this place as if it was heaven," the seated agent on the right volunteered. "The *fieldmarshall* was a frequent guest during the occupation of the city," he added, nodding.

"Now on to business, Smythe-Pembrooke said in a no-nonsense tone, bringing what he considered useless conversation to an abrupt halt.

"We need to have three vehicles prepared in a special way so their forward motion can be altered at our discretion."

"Like we did with that Bentley some months back." Though it sounded like a question it was in fact a statement from the first agent.

"Not exactly," Smythe-Pembrooke commented dryly. "You'll be told shortly what needs to be done."

"*What needs to be done?* Isn't that a bit condescending?" the leader asked. "We know what to do to make a car crash using remote control," he added. He removed and began fiddling with the plastic drink stirrer which The Ritz put in all beverages it served, even water.

"Yes, I know you do. You've proven that in the past. But the method used for this 'accident' can not be the same as the recent one. We're thinking of something with more than one coordinated element. The failed attempt against Milosevic was basically sound, but we'd like to add some backups to it. The perpetrators will most likely not have the ability to remove any device you attach before the car is impounded and taken away. And I assure you the vehicle will be meticulously inspected for any foul play. A method virtually impossible to detect needs to be employed."

Smythe-Pembrooke's mention of Slobodan Milosevic, the then President of the Yugoslav Republic of Serbia, refered to MI-6's

313

failed 1992 attempt to assassinate the Serbian leader by using a blinding strobe light to disorient his chauffeur as his car sped through one of Geneva, Switzerland's, road tunnels.

"Yes, you could use a military strobe flashed from the rear of a passing car or van," the leader said casually. "But it should be coupled with some calibrated filing of the seat belts in all of the vehicles so they release at the moment of impact.

"Then, to be sure" he continued confidently, "one of us will need to return to Germany to get some special equipment if you're thinking of a device to, say, make the driver's airbag go off at a precise moment."

Smythe-Pembrooke couldn't conceal his surprise at the remark. "What made you come to that conclusion???" he asked, still in shock and amazed that the man would have said something touching on the truth.

"Please. . . give us a little credit, we're not just automated mechanics whom you can call to prepare your dirty work. We've worked in the intelligence business for years. There are very, very few ways to take over control and crash a vehicle which we haven't used."

Smythe-Pembrooke stared blankly at the man. If this former German intelligence agent knew how to replace a computer chip to cause an air bag to prematurely inflate, would the French authorities also know this, and look for it? He had to know.

"Would the French know this as well? Would their people inspect the vehicle's computer system?"

Smythe-Pembrooke's mention of a car's computer system set off an alarm in the German's head.

"Highly unlikely, if the accident takes place in a tight, confined area," the third man answered. "That's why we didn't suggest anything like this for the last job. The Bentley was on a lonely winding road, going down a steep grade at night. The driver misses a curve and goes ass over teakettle off the hill. Conclusion: he lost control. Totally believable."

"But suppose the French know about such air bag *chips*, wouldn't they check?" Smythe-Pembrooke asked.

Now Smythe-Pembrooke recognized surprise in the faces of the other three.

"First of all, I never mentioned computer chips." The leader was furious that this man knew the secret technology, but since he obviously did, the German decided to play out the conversation, and find out how he knew.

"But Rolf here," the leader indicated the third man, "designed it and wrote the program himself." Rolf couldn't believe what he was hearing. He wondered if they would kill the Brit right here in the bar.

"But then have you tested it? Used it on a job? Are you *positive* it will work?" Smythe-Pembrooke asked.

"There is no question about that. Yes, we've used it, and always we not only installed the chips but we operated the remote control ourselves. Our clients have no idea how we did it. As a matter of fact, no one else in the world has or even knows such chips exist. So, tell me, how do you know about it?"

"I'm not so sure of *that*, that nobody knows. I'm not psychic. I've heard about it," Smythe-Pembrooke replied smugly dismissing the comment.

"Apparently you do. But what do you mean? How do you know?" the leader's eyes narrowed. He had initially thought the Brit was truly surprised at the alternative technology he had mentioned. Now he realized this very large piece of British shit actually knew about the chip. *But how?*

"I've already said more about all this than I should have," Smythe-Pembrooke answered, obviously uncomfortable about not being the one holding all the cards.

"Listen to me, old man," The leader's tone was menacing. "You'll tell us what you think you know or you'll never again see those beloved White Cliffs of Dover you English sing about in your chummy little pubs."

Smythe-Pembrooke had no doubt the German was serious. He changed his focus downward and withdrew a handkerchief as if to wipe his brow, but didn't use it. He again looked into the man's stern face and concluded that he had better respond properly.

"Alright, I'll tell you. . . But only because we all have to know if this chip thing will work and not be discovered afterward."

"Go on!" the leader ordered. He unconsciously snapped the plastic drink stirrer he was holding.

"One of our operatives was approached last week by a foreign gentleman he has worked with before on other such delicate matters. The chap wanted to buy the kind of chip we are talking about. No one in our organization had ever heard of, or thought of, such a chip to prematurely activate a car's air bags. My colleague. . ." he was talking about Sir Warren but he didn't know they knew that, ". . .suggested you might be acquainted with such a thing."

"Where was this 'gentleman' from?" the first man asked.

"The Middle East. He works for an arms dealer with whom we have an uneasy acquaintance," Smythe-Pembrooke realized he had spoken much too candidly without meaning to. He misspoke because he was physically and mentally terrified by the German.

"Describe him. How tall, his dress, manner. You know what I'm talking about."

Smythe-Pembrooke did as he was told. When he finished his heart sank. He had totally lost control of the meeting. This would not sit well with Sir Warren.

"The God damn Egyptian!" The third man blurted out and stopped himself before smashing his fist onto the table. The leader snapped toward him with a menacing look as intimidating as the one he had shot at Smythe-Pembrooke.

After a pregnant pause, he turned back to look at Smythe-Pembrooke, and the corners of his mouth were turned up in an evil grin.

"Well, my English friend, it appears that we are indeed talking about the same man. The reason he knew about the chip is because we've had a profitable, on-going, relationship with his employer and he previously paid us very well to use a chip on a job for them. It was unfortunate and unavoidable that he learned about it. We foolishly believed he would consider it privileged information. But we were obviously wrong. Perhaps he paid us too well. He came to us again, recently, but we turned him down."

"May I ask why?" Smythe-Pembrooke asked. He needed to know if there was a problem that could backfire or involve The Committee and himself personally.

"Let's just say his politics had become too high profile. We don't do business directly with people who could be arrested any moment."

"I can assure you we've looked at that as well, and we are confident there is no danger of anything like that happening before this job is done, or ever happening."

"Is that so? Then perhaps what we've heard, that the Egyptian and his employer are protected by your SIS people, is true?"

"I wouldn't know anything about that. I'm not affiliated with SIS. Even if I did know anything about what you are saying, I certainly couldn't blab about it."

"I understand," the leader gave him a sly smile. "But since he's now shopping with you for the same thing that only we have. I guess that would make you a middleman."

"Yes," Smythe-Pembrooke nodded. "It would appear that would be the case. We want to provide what he needs because, in some respects, it could serve our needs as well. . . but I wonder who else he has approached?"

"That, my English friend, is our problem, not yours. We'll go ahead with this job without his being any wiser. Once it's over we'll see to it he never again forgets which cow he gets milk from."

Smythe-Pembrooke couldn't resist grinning at the colloquial Germanic bromide. He noticed that the three men facing him appeared more relaxed now. The conversation immediately turned again to the business at hand.

"Three cars you say? Sounds like you and the Egyptian big-mouth suddenly have a lot of enemies," the leader offered. He was Smythe-Pembrooke's primary contact and responsible for recruiting the other two whenever mechanical expertise was required. He was the one who configured and placed the magnetic device under Leslie Wilford's car.

"Not really. The individual who is causing problems for both of us travels frequently and often comes here when he is in Paris. He always goes to and from the airport in one of the hotel's vehicles. I don't even know if our Egyptian friend will ever have the opportunity to use your handiwork. Then again, things could suddenly change, but unless they do, we need to have several options available as well. Your role in preparing the cars is simply one option."

"So, tell me again. Will we be working for you or the Egyptian?" the leader asked, adding "I'd prefer if he didn't know you employed us."

"Certainly. Not a word will be mentioned. Actually, we are only providing a solitary senior agent for technical and logistic assistance. It's their show, really. Perhaps our agent will recommend appropriate locations for implementing the deed. The same agent who liaisons with you will be with them throughout the preparation stages. Once the vehicles are prepared, you're gone. And our agent is withdrawn also. Your part in all this shall remain undisclosed."

"But so many cars! Three will require triple the preparation and effort changing the chips and preparing the seat belts. Plus the work on the strobe car. All this extra work increases our risk. And these chips are all made one at a time. They come at a price considerably higher than the other option," the leader said. "It's a damn tall order whether the one chip is ever engaged or not!"

"We've taken that into consideration," Smythe-Pembrooke interrupted. "You'll all be appropriately compensated."

A sudden silence, which lasted several seconds, engulfed the table. Smythe-Pembrooke removed three envelopes from the inside breast pocket of his jacket and slid them across the small table. One envelope bore a small corner mark. He tapped it and, saying nothing pointed to the leader. The three men each picked up an envelope and opened the unglued flap to examine the contents. After a few seconds, during which each slowly counted his envelope's contents, Smythe-Pembrooke spoke.

"I'm sure that can be doubled, before you do the job," he only said that upon realizing his table guests didn't appear ecstatic with their payments. As if on cue, they quickly finished counting and focused three sets of eyes at him. They responded from left to right:

"Fine with me" . . . "Satisfactory, with more to come" . . . "I'm okay too, with double what's here."

"Good, if we are in basic agreement, I'll acquaint you with the particulars."

"The vehicles in question are not owned by the Ritz, but rather leased from and maintained by the livery service Etoile Limousine. Your most likely opportunity to alter them will be in rotation when they are there, not here."

"That could take quite a while without knowing how regularly they are serviced," The leader groaned, shaking his head side to side

"Not really. Our man in the Ritz says the vehicles are sent to the garage several times a week to be washed, cleaned and detailed. Mostly cosmetics, plus minor this, minor that. The hotel absolutely demands these automobiles always be presented in first-rate appearance at their very best," Smythe-Pembrooke replied.

"Rolls, or Bentleys, again? I hope they're not 'Frog' cars. They're not easy to work on."

Smythe-Pembrooke let the derogatory term for the French pass without comment, partially because he was inclined to use it frequently himself.

"No, none of them. You should be pleased to know The Ritz only uses your fine German Mercedes automobiles."

"Another reason to like this place. They have excellent taste in motor cars also!" the grandson of Göring's aide quipped with a sly grin."

His comment passed without the slightest hint that Smythe-Pembrooke or his companions heard it.

"Would you happen to know the years and which models we will be working on?" the leader asked.

"As a matter of fact I do," As Smythe-Pembrooke busied himself fumbling to remove a sheaf of paper from the inside breast pocket of his jacket, the leader gave a slight smile and sideways glance to the agent on his left. The man was regularly employed as a technician for Mercedes in Germany. The chips he would alter, therefore, would be perfect matches to the ones he removed, making detection absolutely impossible.

"Here we are. You'll also find on this page a telephone number to call on the morrow. An associate at the other end will be the liaison and only contact for the duration of this matter. She will set up a reporting schedule and all other necessary details. Her decisions are final with me. "

As the leader read the page his companions leaned in for the same purpose. None of them commented on Smythe-Pembrooke's 'she will' unexpected revelation that they'd be working with a woman.

"Call her on the morrow and let her know when you will have your necessary things and be able to commence operations. We'd like you to get underway with this as soon as possible."

"Of course, you're no different than anybody else. Everyone always wants the job done yesterday. But such things can't be rushed if they are to be done properly," the leader said, then added: "It will take us three, perhaps four weeks to obtain the chips and prepare what else we need. We will need to return to Germany to get the proper tools and actual chips before modifying them."

"That is the outside limit. Your end of this job must be done quickly," Smythe-Pembrooke said in a firm but low voice. He spoke again.

"At the bottom of the page is information about the hotel you'll be staying at. . ."

"You mean we're not staying here?" The first German joked."

"Certainly not," Smythe-Pembrooke answered in a patronizing tone, adding, "Our agent needs to know a bit in advance when you are coming in order to firm up rooms for you and alert the people who will carry out the mission after you've finished your part in this. This is Paris, in case you've forgotten, and it is the summer. The city is full of foreign tourists, including some of your countrymen on nostalgic visits." He rose to leave.

"And a bit of friendly advice: Don't hang around here for the rest of the day running up a bar bill. If you do, you'll be returning to the *Fatherland* penniless. The drinks here cost a small fortune."

CHAPTER NINE

On September 7, 1980, James Whitaker and Ken Lennox of *The Daily Star,* caught Prince Charles kissing an unnamed girl at the river Dee on the royal estate of Balmoral. It would soon be learned that the young woman was 19-year old Diana Spencer an assistant at the Young England kindergarten in Pimlico who had also supported herself as a maid and nanny. At the end of her teens, she dropped out of Swiss finishing school to live with friends in London. Diana had a younger brother, Charles, and two older sisters, Sarah and Jane.

Prince Charles had once dated her beautiful sister, Sarah, whom Diana felt intimidated by. Diana once asked Sarah for a lift back to London after a weekend in the country, but Sarah refused telling Diana the extra weight of another person in the vehicle would cost too much in gas. Feeling lonely and constantly the 'odd-man-out' because of other such rejections, the shy and lonely young woman spent a lot of time reading the romance novels of her best-selling step-grandmother, Barbara Cartland.

Even as this first known kiss was witnessed, the magazine *Private Eye* was reporting on Charles' relationship with Camilla Parker-Bowles. By the end of the month the media began speculating that this unknown woman might be the future Princess of Wales. In October, *The Sun* carried the headline: "Charles Set to Make Lady Di His Bride Next Year." Diana was under siege by British tabloids for the rest of her life.

Diana had been a shy and attractive, relatively carefree young woman, free as a bird with her whole adult life ahead of her prior to that fateful kiss. Her family had been close to the British Royal Family for decades. Her maternal grandmother, Lady Ruth Fermoy, was a longtime friend of, and a lady-in-waiting to Elizabeth, the Queen Mother. As a child, she had played with Charles' younger brothers Andrew and Edward. And Charles had even briefly courted Diana's other sister, Jane.

By tradition, the woman whom the Prince of Wales and heir to the throne would marry had to have an aristocratic background, could not have been previously married, should be Protestant and, preferably, a virgin. Lady Diana Spencer fulfilled all of these qualifications.

But even before an engagement could be anounced Charles had to gain the approval of his family and their closest advisors. At one time that panel also included Charles' great-uncle, the late Lord Mountbatten of Burma. Some years earlier, Lord Louis firmly ruled out Camilla Shand because she was 16 months the Prince's senior, had previous sexual experience, and supposedly lacked suitable aristocratic lineage.

Yet it was Camilla who helped Charles select Lady Diana Spencer as a potential bride. Nonetheless, Charles and Camilla continued their then star-crossed relationship even after she married Parker-Bowles, a godson of the Queen Mother, and had two children.

Buckingham Palace announced the engagement on February 24, 1981, and Charles and Diana exchanged vows five months later on Wednesday, July 29, 1981, before 3,500 invited guests and an estimated 1 billion television viewers around the world.

Diana became the first Englishwoman to marry an heir-apparent to the throne since 1659, when Lady Anne Hyde married the Duke of York and Albany, the future King James II.

Upon her marriage, Diana became *Her Royal Highness The Princess of Wales* and was ranked as the most senior royal woman in the United Kingdom after the Queen and the Queen Mother.

However, after marriage, this woman just out of her teens was under constant and increasing pressure. She was obliged to observe the protocol and strict traditions of being part of Britain's Royal Family. Whatever her own personal demons were, following such a strict code without understanding or support from her husband and in-laws was too difficult and, perhaps, too much for the young new princess.

Her now well-known problems with bulimia and suicide attempts, her and her husband's infidelities had all become common knowledge by the time the fairy-tale marriage ended in August, 1996.

After the divorce, Diana started leading an active life with increased emphasis on charitable work. She crusaded against AIDS, breast cancer, and publicly worked for the betterment of the needy and underprivileged children. The Princess of Wales then truly became the 'Princess of the People,' as the media had dubbed her.

Perhaps her most widely publicised appearance for social causes was her January 1997 visit to Angola as an International Red Cross VIP volunteer. She visited landmine amputee victims in hospitals, toured de-mining projects run by the HALO Trust, and attended mine awareness education classes about the dangers of mines immediately surrounding homes and villages.

Photographs of Diana heroically touring a minefield, replete with a flak jacket and helmet, were on television and published in newspapers and magazines worldwide. It called tremendous attention to the horrors and dangers these weapons of war left behind. Her interest in landmines focused on the injuries caused, often to children, long after the conflict was over.

Actually, mine-clearance experts had previously taken great pains to clear the exact pre-planned path that the princess would take, wearing the protective equipment. It was a marvelously staged 'photo op' that worked beyond the planners wildest expectations. But her devotion to changing public opinion about these killing and maiming devices went on as she visited Bosnia and other areas with the Landmine Survivors Network.

In her personal life, the 35-year-old Diana received a $26 million settlement from the divorce, making her one of the wealthiest women in Britain. Her total fortune was over $65 million in U.S. dollars. Nonetheless, other than on her wardrobe, she was very frugal about spending her money. Some media reports said she spent over $4,000 a week on clothes and accessories.

Diana remained a member of the royal family, albeit at arm's length, shared equal custody of her children, and was permitted to keep the considerable amount of jewelry received over the 15 years of marriage.

She also retained the title 'Princess of Wales', but lost the style 'Your Royal Highness,' all previously awarded military honors, and the opportunity ever to become the queen consort to the presumed future king, Charles.

Over the years, *People* magazine had featured her on a staggering 51 covers. Her exposure in British publications equaled or surpassed that. A majority of the general public in the British Commonwealth was outraged. Opinions in the U.S. ranged from the Queen being 'petty' to 'titles mean nothing.'

The Princess, much like many of the people who worshipped her, was addicted to reading the tabloids. Often, over breakfast at Kensington Palace, she would read the British scandal sheets, namely: *The Sun, The Daily Mirror, The Daily Mail* and *The Express,* to not only find out what was being written about her but for other juicy tidbits as well. During her years as Princess of Wales she had met numerous celebrities from both sides of the Atlantic and considered a number of them her friends. Occasionally, she would laugh out loud upon seeing something outrageously false about someone she knew and made a mental note to remember to tease them about it. After reading such gossip, she would turn to the supposedly 'dignified' newspapers for hard news. Frequently U.S. magazines were also perused.

The people obviously sided with and loved Diana, despite her known failings and flaws, which many blamed Charles for causing, and wanted Diana to retain the HRH style. There was a rash of opinion in Britain suggesting that Charles should renounce the throne and pass it on to his son. Most expressed the opinion that even if Diana should remarry they'd continue to support and love her. But all of that had happened, and had been said, before Diana's doomed romance with Dodi Fayed took root.

Would the adoring English Protestant masses be so acceptable if their beloved princess married a Muslim?

****

The evening before she was scheduled to leave London for Paris, Megan Price joined Austin and Madge Smythe-Pembrooke and their widowed daughter, Beatrice Walling, for dinner at the elder couple's home. Her father had told Beatrice to invite Megan.

He also made it clear to Megan that she should to be sure to accept.

As was often the case when those loyal to The Firm got together, the early part of the dinner conversation rehashed the most recent rumors, gossip, and tabloid headlines concerning the Princess of Wales and what a shame it was that one 'mentally unstable' woman could cause such havoc in the House of Windsor.

"What do you make of Diana's latest dalliance with that Fayed character?" Madge asked Megan, "Is there anything to it, or is she just being spiteful and trying to embarrass the Royal Family?"

"Oh, I have little to say on that subject and no personal opinion of consequence," the MI-6 agent lied. "As a civil servant, I try to remain removed and uncommitted from sensitive political issues and happenings. I just do my job as best I can and rely on my superiors, and a few trusted advisors, for guidance." She nodded slightly at Austin. A slight, approving smile creased his lips.

"Smart girl indeed," Smythe-Pembrooke thought, *"skillfully dodging Madge's question like that."*

"Well, I wouldn't even be asking if *my husband* shared some of the secrets that he, Sir Warren, and the others on their 'Committee,' get all worked up about."

Megan stole a fast glance at both Austin and Beatrice. He didn't seem in the least concerned and Beatrice was busy enjoying her last mouthful of the Beef Wellington.

"Madge, I've told you a number of times, some of the people in that group are tremendously influential and have a pipeline to Buckingham Palace. When we discuss such matters, it's merely to gain a consensus among ourselves, so we are all on the same page, in the event there is a need to pass on our thoughts, advice, or recommendations."

He sounded so convincing that if Megan didn't know otherwise she would have believed him herself.

"Enough about the royals," Beatrice put in. "I respect and love them dearly, as all good English subjects do, but our own Megan here will be off on the morrow to God-knows-where on some secret mission. She won't say where, Daddy, but do you know?"

"Me? Why in heaven's name would I be privy to something

like that? SIS doesn't consult or advise me when posting an agent."

"Because you and Sir Warren are like two peas in a pod, Frick and Frack. Michael used to say. . ." Beatrice nearly choked up at the thought of her murdered husband, ". . .that you two were joined at the hip. Even though Sir Warren is retired, it is believed by some people, that he is still consulted by SIS on many things." She fought to avoid locking eyes with her mother, the source of the comment.

"Well, *some people* are wrong, my dear," Unlike his daughter, Smythe-Pembrooke didn't hesitate to direct a glance, almost a menacing glare, at his wife.

"We share many mutual interests including philately and our concerns for the public image of the Crown," he continued, in serious tones, "but if Sir Warren is knowledgeable about the current workings of SIS, it's news to me. That part of his life has been over with for several years and very rarely comes up in conversation."

There were several seconds of silence at the table as the three women all busied themselves with arranging their utensils, sipping wine, or fiddling with their napkins.

"I hope you all understand that I'm not at liberty to divulge or even suggest anything about my assignment. I assure you that it's all proper and very safe. Frankly, I see no reason why these restrictions are imposed across the board, even on the simplest and most mundane of things," Megan lied with a shrug.

"And your reticence in such matters is a credit to you and your training. You are to be applauded," Smythe-Pembrooke said in near theatrical oratory. Beatrice and Madge, knowing when to throw in the towel, both smiled weakly and nodded in agreement.

"Now, Special Agent Price, if you have some free moments—wherever it is you're going—I have something for you to take along to read. I'll only be a moment." He left the table, causing puzzled looks from his wife and daughter. Megan responded to their stares with a surprised shrug.

When Smythe-Pembrooke returned less than a half minute later, he handed her a wrapped package about the size of three magazines.

"It's from Archie," he lied. His father gave it to me at the club earlier today and said to make sure you got it."

"There's another one who goes off on mysterious trips," Madge huffed. Then in a kinder voice, added:

"Megan, dear, I think young Blair still fancies you a bit!"

"I doubt it." Megan always felt uncomfortable whenever people rehashed the almost-romantic relationship she and Archie had briefly when she first joined MI-6. She had encouraged Blair's advances to stem questions about her sexual preferences. Such gossip could get one drummed out of the service in a heartbeat.

"That was several years ago, ancient history. Dear Archie and I are still friends, of course but its strictly platonic, like siblings. Actually I'm still looking for 'Mr. Right' and it *won't* be anyone in the service!" Megan casually smiled and glanced across the table at Beatrice, who smiled back. Madge and Austin both laughed lightly.

"This package is probably just brochures and information about cars. Archie's been talking about replacing his old Morgan lately, getting something newer, and for some reason has gotten it into his head that my opinion matters. I'm sure he's put hand written notes in appropriate places on what's in here." She had fabricated the scenario when Sir Warren had called her just before she left for dinner and said Smythe-Pembrooke would be giving her some documents she'd find interesting on her mission.

Smythe-Pembrooke smiled. Megan was a born equivocator, he mused. By God, she would do very well in Parliament!

"Ah, Archie's Morgan. . . I love that car," he said, lost in reverie. "It's a classic 1964, you know."

****

The following day in Paris, Megan Price sat in a comfortable chair in the hotel room she had rented some months ago for the rogue agents. As she waited for them to return, Megan nursed a bottle of water that had become tepid in the August heat. She was reading the information in the package Smythe-Pembrooke had given her, allegedly from Archie. In truth, Blair wasn't aware of the contents.

The first page she lifted was a single sheet someone in the

home office spent considerable time putting together for no apparent reason other than its 'gee-whiz' value. It pointed out the coincidence in names between Diana's mother, Frances Shand Kydd, and Camilla Shand, the maiden name of Mrs. Parker-Bowles. It reported there was no evidence that the two were related. *"Who care about such useless trivias?"* Megan wondered disapprovingly.

It also noted that The Prince of Wales had considered marrying Lady Diana Spencer but changed his mind and married Princess Augusta of Saxe-Gotha instead. However, the Prince of Wales, in this instance was the son of George II, who died in 1751 before becoming king. The last piece of earth-shattering news on the page reported that the first husband of Wallis Warfield Simpson, for whom Edward VIII abdicated after being king for 325 days, was Earl Spencer. The same name as Diana's father. *Mildly interesting, but of no intelligence value and equally useless,* Megan shook her head in annoyance.

The page ended with a comment from whoever compiled the trivial information that all these things were 'coincidences.' Even Megan, who believed there were no coincidences in life, had to concede that in these instances, perhaps it was possible.

Among the various intelligence reports on the Princess of Wales were several related pages with the markings of pass-along reports gathered by the U.S. Central Intelligence Agency. Collectively they comprised an extraordinary document written in typical intelligence report style littered with codes and abbreviations. The first page was titled DOMESTIC COLLECTION DIVISION Foreign Intelligence Information Report Directorate of Intelligence and carried a typical boilerplate security box: WARNING NOTICE - INTELLIGENCE SOURCES AND METHODS INVOLVED FURTHER DISSEMINATION AND USE OF THE INFORMATION SUBJECT TO CONTROLS STATED AT BEGINNING AND END OF REPORT.

The secondary deck, containing the name of the subject the report was about, piqued her interest: REPORT CLASS: TOP SECRET REPORT NO: 00.D 831/173466-97 COUNTRY: France DATE DISTR: 17 June 1997 SUBJECT: File overview: Diana

Princess Of Wales-Dodi REFERENCES DCI Case 64376 SOURCE: CASParis/CASLondon/COSGeneva/CASKingston/UK citizen Ken Etheridge

Even before she read it *in toto,* certain things seemed to jump off the page to her.

"Such an affair is racially and morally repugnant and no son of a Bedouin camel trader is fit for the mother of a future king." The quote was attributed to Prince Philip and appeared to reflect his personal displeasure of Diana's carrying on with Dodi Fayed, calling it a 'threat to the dynasty.'

Long before Diana Spencer joined the family, and then Sarah Ferguson, Megan remembered that the media had labeled Prince Philip as The Firm's original 'loose cannon.' The Queen's husband was quite capable of putting his royal foot in his aristocratic mouth, and often did. The man's public utterances were often outrageous. Yet he was the same seemingly caring father-in-law who had written a letter to Diana saying: "I cannot imagine anyone in their right mind leaving you for Camilla." *Did he mean it"* Megan wondered.

The report mentioned a request to a "U.S. liaison" from MI-6 Director David Spedding *"for assistance in providing a permanent solution to Dodi problem. Blessing of Palace secured."* Megan hadn't been aware SIS had approached the CIA for help and found that interesting. Equally important, it was the first time she had ever seen anything in print suggesting The Firm was aware of the plans and preparations.

Another item referred to the sabotage of an Al Fayed Mercedes and, incredibly, reported that one had been *"stolen and returned with electronics missing."* It said nothing of what might have been added to the car.

Megan couldn't believe that such information was being freely exchanged between the two English speaking services. There apparently were more people aware of the problem and impending solution than she felt comfortable with. And with the mention of the Mercedes having been stolen she speed-read through every page to see if *she* had been mentioned by name. She hadn't. But she had no doubt the report was current.

When they were unable to do what they wanted at the limousine garage, the rogue Germans had stolen the Mercedes S280 from outside the fashionable Taillevent restaurant in Paris. The vehicle was discovered stripped and abandoned outside the city two weeks later. Missing parts were replaced, the car was cleaned and returned to its primary service for the Ritz Hotel.

During the time the car was missing, the agents Smythe-Pembrooke hired had installed GPS tracking devices as well as a sound-activated voice transmitter. Including a FOTT dot was briefly considered, but its usefulness was thought to be minimal and, more importantly, that would have revealed the technology to the German rogue agents. Sir Warren rejected the idea. The seatbelt latches were computer calibrated and filed to just enough tolerance so they would open under the amount of pressure caused by a sudden, full stop. Passengers would not know the seatbelt buckles had been doctored because the latches would still click shut. And finally, the very important computer chip to activate the air bags by remote control was installed.

A biographical page provided information on some of the support players. At least two had high-level experience in international espionage. The first, Oswald Le Winter, was an Austrian-born American whom, she had previously heard, was a high-ranking CIA officer. The other was Karl Koecher, a notorious and daring Czech agent during the cold war.

Koecher had once been captured by the US as a Czech spy. In one of the more notable cold war exchanges Koecher walked across the Potsdam Bridge into East Berlin at the same time Soviet dissident Natan Scharansky walked west. Such exchanges were always appreciated by spies on both sides.

Le Winter was known to have claimed he had been a high-ranking CIA agent. He was actually hired as an intelligence consultant for the movie *The Double Maltese Cross* which proffered the theory that the December 21, 1988, explosion of Pan Am Flight 103 over Lockerbie, Scotland, killing 270 people was the work of Syria, not Libya. The film had been financed by Mohamed Fayed's nemeses in the 'Harrods Wars,' Tiny Rowland.

And, Megan knew, Sir Warren and Smythe-Pembrooke believed that one of Rowland's long time associates, Ashraf Marwan, the multi-millionaire double agent, was behind the request to assassinate Dodi Fayed.

But a reference to *"a squad from the Israeli secret service Mossad"* based in Switzerland made Megan wonder who she was actually turning the mission over to. Was the so-called team from Libya and Egypt really Israelis posing as Arabs? *Were Sir Warren and Smythe-Pembrooke being played? Or were they playing her?* She wondered.

There were other reports in the file, basically confirming information she already knew. But the last two were incredible. One was an older report she had never seen, but she suspected the information it contained had come from her own observations. Now, as she read it, her suspicions were confirmed and all the pieces fit.

The short executive summary noted that while they were separated, but prior to her divorce from Charles, the Princess of Wales had a secret abortion in 1994 as a result of an adulterous affair. The validity of the event was contained in a statement from Lady Victoria Waymouth, daughter of the 9th Earl of Hardwicke.

SIS knew about Diana's relationship with wealthy art dealer Oliver Hoare from the outset, as did the press, which had a field day speculating about it. Megan recalled an earlier surveillance report saying that Diana snuck out of Kensington Palace, at least once, wearing just a fur coat and high-heels, and otherwise stark naked. Though Hoare was not mentioned as the father, in fact no one was, the MI-5 agent who wrote the document pointed out that Lady Victoria and the Hoares were "very" friendly.

The copy of Lady Victoria's statement in the file noted that, early on in the pregnancy, the princess reportedly vacillated between wanting to keep the baby and telling her sisters and her tight circle of friends that she hoped it was a girl, to the other extreme: knowing she had to abort it. If she didn't, she feared, Charles would certainly use the pregnancy against her in the now expected divorce proceedings to gain total custody of her sons.

'The truth will out!' Megan recalled her own mother saying

about the dark secrets people kept. Though some of the other agents who worked on royal surveillance shared Megan's suspicions at the time, none of them ever discussed it the way Camillagate and the Squidgygate phone conversations were.

Lady Victoria's comments explained Diana's strange behavior during this period in her life. Unlike other relationships which the princess herself cooled off, when the romantic involvement with Hoare was over, it appeared he had dumped her. Simultaneous to that, Hoare and his wife began receiving a confusing rash of anonymous nuisance calls at all hours of the day and night for quite some time. Often, they reported, as many as 30-40 calls in a single day.

When they could no longer stand it, the Hoares went to the police. The calls were traced to Diana;s private lines at Kensington Palace, and she was made aware that she had been discovered. However, the Hoares declined to file a complaint. Reported in the media, the incident was thought to be Diana's inability to cope with rejection. She was a woman accustomed to getting her own way in everything for years, they said, and found it difficult to believe someone could refuse her.

Now her strange behavior made sense. Diana hadn't been a spoiled royal filled with fury that some man would reject her. Instead, she was a frantic, abandoned married woman living the nightmare of being pregnant by someone other than her estranged husband. *No wonder she acted crazy*, Megan thought. It was one of the few times in her life that the MI-6 agent actually felt sympathy for the Princess of Wales.

The bottom of the page described how Diana made the abortion arrangements and fabricated a cover story including an appointment with close friend and financial adviser Joseph Sanders.

Megan scoured the page again to see if she had missed the identity of the lover who made Diana pregnant in 1994. But there was nothing there.

But if that incident caused Megan to feel a rare flush of sympathy for Diana, the next item she read negated it: A medical document confirmed Diana was pregnant again.

It had been Sir Warren's obsessive fear ever since Diana and Dodi were being mentioned in the press as a 'romantic couple.'

Unlike the report about the abortion, this was limited to a half-page medical form with boxes checked off and lines filled in with the patient's vitals, i.e.: age, weight, blood type, medical history and, circled in heavy red marker, the word POSITIVE on the line for pregnancy test results. The patient's name was left blank. But a handwritten memo across the bottom told the tale: "POW, confirmed, Aug. 10, 1997. Megan recognized the standard abbreviation POW for the Princess of Wales.

"Paternity DNA sample: EEDMAMF." To casual observers they were just initials. But Megan knew they were the initials of the father's full name: *Emad El-Din Mohamed Abdel Moneim Fayed,* The document indicated that this time the mother of a future king of England was pregnant with the child of a Muslim!

The red imprint of a 'CLASSIFIED' stamp appeared at the top, bottom, and in the left margin. But something about this piece of paper made Megan feel uneasy. She couldn't put her finger on it, but of all the thousands of surveillance pages and reports she had read about Diana, this one raised an annoying concern. She forced herself to shake off the strange feeling.

"That explained why Smythe-Pembrooke was so insistent that only the one seat belt be altered," she thought. *He and Sir Warren expect Diana will be IN THE CAR with Dodi when the accident happens,* she reasoned. *"A bit risky, to be sure, but certainly survivable if one is properly buckled."* Megan knew from all the time she had spent observing the Princess of Wales that Diana *always* buckled up. *"And in a good high-speed accident she'd probably lose the little Arab bastard growing in her stomach. Perhaps there IS a God,"* she thought.

Megan reckoned correctly that Sir Warren had arranged that in the event Diana's injuries weren't sufficient enough to miscarry from the accident, steps had been taken to make sure she wouldn't be pregnant, or ever again be able to have children, once she left the hospital. This would have been a natural backup in such a situation.

Her head was still spinning and trying to cope with what she had just read when she heard the rogue German agent come into the room.

"Knock, knock," he said as he closed the door behind him. He was alone. His cohorts had already left Paris.

"Not very professional of you leaving the door unlocked."

"I wasn't expecting anyone but you," she closed the file and washed her mind's screen of her recent reading and feelings and got right to the point.

"We are not pleased with how things have turned out," she said sternly. "You were paid to alter the three cars used by the Ritz. You only did one, and to do that you had to steal the bloody car!" She returned the file to her attaché case on the floor next to her chair as she looked directly at him.

"You're beating a dead horse, give it up already!" he responded, obviously very annoyed the subject was still coming up.

"I already explained what happened to your pot-belly limey friend who hired us. The damn fool actually called me! Some pair of balls he has."

"He was, he is concerned. We are all concerned. You were paid good money and you've failed to produce the desired results," Megan said with the demeanor of a teacher scolding a student.

"We watched the routine and timed everything!" the German said in defense. "There was no way we would be able to get close enough and have even the minimum amount of the time we needed to work on the vehicles at the Etoile Limousine garage. Plus, with only short notice of when each car would be back in for any length of time. . ."

"We told you these cars were returned at some point every day for cleaning. . ."

"That's cosmetics! Washing, vacuuming, polishing, that's all. They're in, made to look spic and span, and back out again. They don't make money when those cars are sitting around in a garage. The cars weren't left alone for any amount of time. It sounded like a good idea when we heard it, but in reality it just doesn't work."

"Really? What if I told you that well before this present operation, DST bugged the three Ritz cars to eavesdrop on occasional high-profile politicians and influential guests who frequented the hotel?" Her reference was to the *Direction de la Surveillance du Territoire*, the French domestic security service. "DST found a way to gain access and plant voice activated audio transmitters in all three vehicles. What have you got to say about that?"

"I'd say you're full of shit," he had lost patience with her and his rude comment showed it. He clinched both fists.

But Megan was in no mood to suffer his abuse. She sprang out of the chair and went eyeball to eyeball with him.

"Listen to me, you Nazi bastard, you screwed up and now I have to make things right . . . and you're going to stick around to help me when the Arabs get here." Megan's eyes were ablaze. He could tell she was one wrong word away from physical contact.

Fifteen years ago, he wouldn't have hesitated to make a preemptive strike and put her down. But she was younger and obviously confident in her own abilities. Furthermore, he knew MI-6 would not send an administrative clerk on a field mission of any consequence. This British bitch, he felt, could most likely be lethal. There was no need to find out.

"Okay, okay, back off," he raised his arms in front of his chest, the palms of his hands facing her and pumping. "I'm willing to help, to make things as right as we can. If we think it over together, we can still work things out before your Arabs get here."

"They arrive on the morrow, and I'll have a lot of prep work to do with them. And I don't want them to know about you, so let's get to it." He would soon realize she had already given considerable thought to the preparations.

"Fine with me. You start first, tell me everything you know about how they intend to do it," he turned and walked over to the bed and sat completely on it with his back against the headboard. He crossed his legs and extending his right arm lengthwise across the cheap-looking chrome riser. Megan slowly lowered herself back into her chair. As she did the fury drained from her face and she furrowed her brow in thought.

"We told the client that if they expected cooperation from us the hit had to be done outside of London, outside of the U.K. for that matter. They immediately suggested Paris because the principal frequently travels between both cities."

"Has MI-6 involved the DST?" he asked.

"That's not my area, but I personally doubt that we'd say anything to the Frogs. Too many people are already involved in all this. No need for more."

"Well, I'd appreciate it if you could check with your home office. If this thing falls apart we could be arrested as spies. I don't want to spend my last years eating stale croissants in some dank dungeon." He paused, waiting for a response from her. But there was none.

"For you," he added, ". . .of course, it would be different: Your proper Englishmen would simply latch onto some poor Frenchman at the embassy and hit him with trumped-up espionage charges, then offer an exchange, him for you. You'd both ride past each other on trains in the Chunnel while I was cooling my ass off and crushing roaches in a piss-stinking French jail."

Completed in 1994, the $15 billion Channel Tunnel made the dream of a ground link between Great Britain and continental Europe a reality for the first time since the Ice Ages. The crossing from Cheriton in Kent, England, and Sangatte in northern France, takes about a half hour.

Megan didn't reply. She couldn't reveal that her role in this mission was at the behest of The Committee, not MI-6.

"If it makes you feel better I'll discreetly look into that this evening," she lied.

"Okay. Be sure you do." This time it was he who was menacing. "And let's back up a minute. How do you know DST put bugs in the limos?" he added.

"The usual way. We have a paid informer on the Ritz security staff. And he plays an important role in communicating the principal's movements."

She told him that the Arabs had easily agreed that a car crash would be the method for eliminating the principal, which he already knew had obviously been settled before he and his companions were hired. There was no doubt that a bombing or sniper shot would be easier to carry out but that would also leave the undeniable imprint of murder.

What she saw no need to explain was that these Middle East killers wanted to avoid something so obvious less it start a blood feud. As much as they disliked the Fayeds, they didn't underestimate his wealth nor his reach.

A properly arranged vehicular accident, on the other hand, would be dismissed as an unfortunate occurrence. With at least 100 people killed on European roads every day, another accident would just be part of the statistics.

But when she mentioned that besides the security man inside the Ritz she would also have an agent posing as one of the paparazzi hounding the principal, the German was startled. The agent who routinely followed Diana was a member of Megan's rogue team of part-time MI-6 agents who provide miscellaneous services to MI-6 such as surveillance and photography expertise.

"Hold on! Who *is* the principal? Some big shot politician or celebrity? Some half-wit rock star who pissed the Muslims off by saying something blasphemous against Mohamed? We didn't sign on to be part of anything that will be splashed across the newspapers." His remark was more in an effort to underline the significance of his continued cooperation and bolster the chances for future work from MI-6.

"You were hired to do a job. The names are not important. I may or may not need further assistance from you once this is turned over to the Arabs. Consider anything you do from here on out as 'good will' make up points for the way you mucked up the original task." She read and understood what he had said, and what his intentions were. And she wanted him to know it.

"But who *is* the principal you want so dearly to remove?"

Inasmuch as he was likely to find out shortly anyway, she told him.

"Our Arab friends want to take out Mohamed Fayed, the owner of Harrods in London and The Ritz Hotel here in Paris. But they have been unable to get to him. . . so his son Dodi is the revenge target. That's who you've prepared the Mercedes for. "

Another reason the Middle East assassins had been so quick to settle on eliminating Mohamed Fayed, or his son Dodi, in Paris, rather than London, was that it would have been impossible to prepare all of the vehicles either one had access to in London where they had a fleet of more than 60 Rolls Royce's at their disposal.

Fayed, the father, bought the cars partly because he could afford them and partly because he liked them. But his ownership of things British was all part of the public persona for acceptance. In addition to Harrods, he owned several expensive apartment buildings on Park Lane, the 40,000-acre Balnagown Castle in Scotland, the Fulham Football Club, and *Punch*, the legendary satirical magazine. He wanted very much to acquire British citizenship, but it had been denied. He was truly excited that his only son was romantically involved with the Princess of Wales.

"Phew. . . the old man is certainly a high visibility target. But the son? Why would MI-6 help the Arabs murder him? He's probably just a rich playboy." Why would paparazzi be chasing him?"

"They don't exactly chase him. It's who he's now often seen with. . .the Princess of Wales."

"The Princess??? Diana? The Arabs want to knock her off too?"

"No, that's not the plan. They are not concerned with her. To them she's just an English whore. But my superiors wouldn't mind at all if she is badly shaken up, even gets injured." *A few ugly scars on that pretty little face would quickly take her out of the public eye*, she thought but didn't say.

Megan just looked at him, totally non-committal.

The German thought for several seconds. "I understand. The Arabs want . . ."

"They're not Arabs, they're probably Egyptians." Megan corrected. "Why does everyone want to call them Arabs? There's a difference."

"A fine line. They pray to Allah, they're all dirty sand-niggers to me," He thought for several seconds, then continued.

"These Muslims want one of the two Fayeds dead and your people want to end the princess's romance with the Arab. . .oh, don't look at me with those big pussycat eyes, everybody knows the Palace is shaking as if it was hit by an earthquake, even your newspapers are talking about it. . . so you let the Arabs think you're doing *them* a favor, but actually you're getting the perfect solution to ending any chance of Diana becoming a desert princess." He nodded in satisfaction. "Only one problem," he added.

"And what's that?" she asked.

"Suppose they change seats this time and she's the one sitting behind the driver? He lives, she dies, and you've pissed off the Arabs in a big way."

"Our man at the Ritz will make sure he is sitting where he should be before the flag drops for the mission. And if you've done your job properly--on the *only* car you managed to work on-- then everything else should go as planned."

The German didn't bother asking where they intended to do it or how they planned to make certain the car would take the precise route they wanted. From his years of professional experience, he knew how easy it was to 'guide' a vehicle to the exact place you wanted it to be. And he was also aware of their failed effort to eliminate Serbian President Milosevic in 1992 by causing a crash in a tunnel. *It'll be a tunnel again*, he thought. *The British are creatures of habit. They'll keep doing something till they get it right.*

"I trust you'll have sufficient vehicles to make it work." It was a statement, not a question. "You'll need several."

"That's been taken care of," she concluded.

****

According to close friends and former palace staffers, Princess Diana feared she was being watched, overheard, and spied on. It wasn't paranoia. These things were actually being done.

Besides the extensive MI-5 and MI-6 SIS files, and the almost as voluminous files collected by Sir Warren's faithful agents, and, when necessary, trusted rogue agents, information about the Princess of Wales was also routinely gathered by American security and spy agencies whenever she visited the United States.

For instance, the National Security Agency (NSA), basically monitors everything it considers related to U.S. national security outside the United States using sophisticated satellite technology listening devices and computers to intercept telephone calls, faxes, e-mail and other messages. The agency is insatiably curious and was eventually forced to admit having 39 'Top Secret' documents, totaling 124 pages, involving and about Princess Diana.

The NSA's ECHELON global spy system coordinates and shares intelligence gathering with and by fellow spy agencies in Britain, Canada, Australia and New Zealand. These agencies also share intercepted information about each other's nationals. The significance is that they all have 'plausible deniability' if concerns are raised about spying on their own citizens. The British services once got around such limitations by using Canada's Communications Security Establishment (CSE) to collect intelligence on British citizens. Fortunately, Sir Warren thought, such restrictions didn't apply to surveillance of the royals.

Much of the material in the American Central Intelligence Agency's (CIA) secret Diana dossier was the direct result of eavesdropping on her private telephone conversations. A surprisingly large volume of this was between her and her very close friend, Lucia Flecha de Lima, wife of the Brazilian ambassador in Washington, and the couple with whom she was on holiday with in Martha's Vineyard when she learned about the impending publication of former lover James Hewitt's book. All such information was regularly passed on and circulated among the British intelligence community.

Perhaps the American files regarding Diana which even raise eyebrows in British espionage agencies are those collected by the Pentagon's Defense Intelligence Agency (DIA). This super-secret military intelligence resource for the U.S. military policy makers has what is described as classified "information" and "product" mentioning Princess Diana. When questioned why the DIA would have any files on the princess, Lt. Col. James MacNeil, a DIA spokesman, said he had "No idea why. All of our stuff is on military.

Obviously she wasn't in the military."

But Sir Warren, and others, thought the reason was Diana's activity in the movement to ban land mines. Her stance was not something the Pentagon was happy with. Though American military leaders publicly support a reduction in these anti-personnel weapons, they have strongly resisted a total ban. Consequently, the generals in Washington would be interested in keeping abreast of any news Diana was privy to in the campaign against land mines.

So it was that Britain's SIS had received from their acronym cousins across the Atlantic, the CIA, NSA, and DIA, more than 1200 pages of confidential surveillance of Princess Diana. Though when this became publicly known in the States, defenders of the spying policy said U.S. intelligence agencies had been collecting information about Diana as a 'protective measure' from a possible terrorist or IRA attack.

****

It had been six months since Bat's sudden trip to Belize, his plane crash into the sea, meeting Jennifer, and nearly being beaten to death by the bacon-eating killer, Mario Luca. After corrective surgery to his badly injured right knee and attention to his other wounds, he was released from Bethesda. The doctors had advised against any 'field work' for the agency until his next physical.

Though his sister and her husband had offered to have him stay with them, it was Jennifer who won the day. One of the excuses he used was, that with his sister having a new baby, she wouldn't need a big baby to tend to as well. Actually, when Jennifer insisted that she not only had the room and time to look after him while he mended, he jumped at the opportunity to be with her.

Even Kimberly, the twin sister he somehow had missed meeting on the ship and in Belize, urged him to stay with Jennifer. She realized how much Jennifer cared for him by the way she looked at Bat every time Kimberly visited the hospital. And the feelings seemed to be mutual. Bat appeared to care for her as well.

She dearly wanted her sister to find the happiness she and her former husband had in the beginning. But for Jennifer she wanted it to endure. Her logic was that if this romance was 'the real thing,' as Jennifer had told her more than once, the close contact of being under the same roof for an extended time would put it to the test, for both of them.

"Aunt Jen! Aunt Jen! Watch me!" Marshall called from the diving board.

Jennifer was wearing a modest two-piece swimsuit sitting in the shade in a lounge chair by her pool. She leaned the tabloid newspaper she was reading against her chest and gave her nephew her attention. "I'm watching. Go ahead."

Marshall took a running start and leapt off the board. He tucked his knees under his chin, locking his hands around them. The splash was as expected. Younger brother Blake, who was afraid of the diving board, was sitting on the wide pool stairs and busied himself with his small toy boats.

"You're getting better," Jennifer said in encouragement. "That was almost a '10!' " She had intentionally moved the lounge chair closer to the shallow end knowing that at some point in the day Marshall would want to show off his cannonballs.

"Hey, Mister Smarty Pants, I told you to stay in the low end. No more diving board tricks," Kimberly admonished as she came through the double doors of the family room. "Get into the shallow end RIGHT NOW!"

"But Mom. . ."

"No 'but Mom,' you either move immediately or we're going home, young man!"

Marshall made a face and held on to the floating raft as he paddled to the low end.

"You're back fast," Jennifer said as her sister sat in a straight-back chair next to her.

"Yeah, I thought it would be longer too. Sometimes you get lucky. There were only five cars in front of me. Thanks for baby-sitting at the last minute. The thought of having these two Indians cramped up in the motor vehicle inspection line isn't my idea of fun. Oh, by the way, the car passed with flying colors."

"Want something to drink? There's diet soda in the fridge. Or the coffee I offered you before you sped away?"

"No thanks. Nothing right now. Sorry about not coming in, I just wanted to go there and get it over with." She thought about borrowing one of Jennifer's swimsuits and joining her sons.

"Look at them. You wouldn't know they had a pool at home," Kimberly said. "But I guess it's more fun coming to see Aunt Jen who's 'living in sin' with the recovering spy," she teased.

"I hope you don't say things like that in front of the boys," Jennifer frowned as she rested the paper again.

"Don't be ridiculous, of course I don't. Besides, the real reason they get so excited about coming over here is to see 'Batman'. They talk about him all the time. He's some sort of hero-father-figure."

Jennifer smiled. "Bat enjoys them a lot. They ask him all sorts of questions about being a 'spy.' He answers the stuff that he can, but when the questions get too involved he uses a conspiratorial voice and says it's top secret. The boys absolutely love it. He's their real-life James Bond."

"That only polishes his image with them more, I'm sure," Kimberly replied in a friendly tone.

"He's so good with children. I told him some day he's going to make a very good father. He blushed!"

Kimberly smiled, but didn't reply. Instead she glanced at the tabloid Jennifer had closed and set down on the small table between their chairs.

"So! That's where you get those trashy scenes from for your books."

"I've never written trashy scenes in any of my books. Passionately suggestive, I'll admit. But it isn't necessary to tell readers verbatim how consenting adults make love."

"So why the paper? You never read that kind of garbage."

"Bat and I are going to London to visit locations that will be in my next book, *Love's Tender Rage*. It's about the WASPS, the Women's Air Service Pilots who delivered aircraft from the U.S. to bases in England and elsewhere in Europe during World War II."

"And there's a story about them in that rag?"

"No, silly, I want to catch up on the latest gossip about Princess Diana, so I'm informed if I meet someone over there and the topic comes up."

"You're using this scandal sheet as a primer?"

"Oh, I realize much of this stuff is, at best, exaggerated. But you know what they say: where there's smoke. . ." she left the ending off the rest of the cliché.

"Going to London? I guess that answers my next question about how your man's recovery is coming."

"Very well, thank you. He's been using a cane to walk and, up untill today, I've done all the driving, but otherwise he's just about 100% in every way. I suspect now the cane will be history."

"A hundred percent, eh? Then you two better be careful skinny dipping or doing the 'dirty deed' in the pool at night. Any low-flying helicopter's you see might belong to his buddy Stone and have infra red cameras that can film in the dark."

"You're incorrigible. Just because we're living under the same roof that doesn't mean we're being intimate. There's much more to a relationship than just having sex, you know."

"Really?" Kimberly said facetiously, adding, "I wish someone had told that to my ex-husband."

Jennifer half turned in her chair.

"Can I tell you something you absolutely, positively can not repeat to anyone?"

"Oh, sister, how quickly you forget. I was the one who could always keep a secret when we were kids. You were the blabbermouth!

"I'm late this month," Jennifer blurted out with a gleeful twinkle in her eyes.

"Oh, my God! Does Bat know?" Kimberly couldn't conceal the concern in her voice.

"No, I don't want to pressure him. I think he is going to ask me to marry him during our trip."

"Now sis, don't go giving yourself false hopes. Hearing that kind of news could bring on a change in him overnight. Remember this guy's been a bachelor all his life. He might not be the marrying kind."

"Kim, listen. I know what I'm doing. The other day when I came home from shopping, I walked in on him and he was on the phone. He laughed awkwardly and said he'd call the person back the next day. When I asked who it was he said an army buddy from the Gulf War. Something about planning a reunion." Jennifer paused, then added, "I figured it was Bat who had called this 'buddy.' How would the man know to call Bat here?"

"Maybe Bat's sister told him. If he called her she could have given him your number."

"Oh, sometimes you're such a killjoy," Jennifer pouted.

"So that's it? What am I missing here? Where was the part about him wanting to marry you?"

"There's more, Miss Know-It-All. Last night we went into the village for dinner and afterward we were strolling on Main Street looking in the windows of all the closed shops and stores. . . and when we passed the jewelry store he stopped and brought me closer to the window and started commenting and asking questions about rings. He asked me which type was my favorite. The rings he was looking at were engagement rings! Remember, he stopped. I didn't."

"Keep going, there could be a small flame here, not much. It has possibilities. Men *never* stop to look in jewelry stores unless there's a reason." Kimberly added.

"See what I mean? There's more. He let out a whistle as he read the prices on some of the rings. Then he said the family of a guy he was with in the Army with has a jewelry store in New York, in the Diamond District, and Bat said he bet he could save me 'a bundle' if I needed any jewelry."

"Typical man. Looking at romantic things and only thinking about the price."

"But don't you see? He makes a call to his Army buddy. Then yesterday mentions an army buddy's family is in the jewelry business. . ."

"I hope you're right. But, don't forget it all could have been innocent chatter. Don't read more into it than is really there. It could be a coincidence. I'm sure he had more than one 'buddy' when he was in the Army. Speaking of your super-spy, where is he?

"As a matter of fact, he went for what could be his final physical. He's so upbeat about it he insisted on driving himself. After that he said he was going to Langley to tell them he is retiring. . . or is it resigning?"

Technically, the CIA's headquarters is in both Langley and McLean, Virginia. Langley is the name of the McLean neighborhood in which the CIA resides eight miles out of downtown Washington, D.C. The town of McLean was founded in 1910, but prior to that the area where the CIA is was known as Langley. It got the name in 1719 when Thomas Lee purchased a tract of land from the sixth Lord Fairfax, honored by the county name in which McLean is located. Lee named his parcel 'Langley' after his ancestral home in England. The name stuck.

Bat knew the routine as he drove up to the gate and popped the trunk without being asked. He pulled Jennifer's car to the proper position so the guard watching the monitors in the concrete building could have a perfect view of the vehicle's underside. A second guard took Bat's credentials and took his time checking and confirming them as a third one released a sensor to detect any trace of explosives in or around the car.

He parked in one of the 'visitor' spaces and walked past the statue of Nathan Hale, the first American executed for spying for his country, and entered the Original Headquarters Building's main entrance. It was designed in the mid-1950s by Harrison and Abramovitz, designers of the United Nations building in New York.

The OHB, as it is called by those who work for the agency, is pre-cast concrete construction set in a college campus-like atmosphere and covers 1,400,000 square feet. With the steel and glass New Headquarters Building it sits on 258 acres of land. The lobby to the OHB still remains the official main entrance to the Agency.

The new building is joined to the west facade of the original building and includes two six-story office towers built into a hillside behind the OHB and linked in a seamless blend of the two structures. The main entrance to the New Headquarters Building is on the fourth floor. Inside the entrance, one is greeted by a huge skylight ceiling and, at the end of the entry corridor, a spectacular view of the OHB.

Inlaid in the floor of the OHB main lobby of the is a large granite CIA seal measuring 16 feet in diameter. Recognized the world over, the emblem has been the symbol for the Central Intelligence Agency since 1950. Etched into the wall of the original building's main lobby is a biblical verse which also characterizes the intelligence mission in a free society. It reads:

"And ye shall know the truth and the truth shall make you free."
John VIII-XXXII

Bat paused inside the OHB lobby and looked to his right at the north wall with its 83 stars, framed by the American and the Central Intelligence Agency flags. The simple inscription reads "IN HONOR OF THOSE MEMBERS OF THE CENTRAL INTELLIGENCE AGENCY WHO GAVE THEIR LIVES IN THE SERVICE OF THEIR COUNTRY." A glass-encased Book of Honor below the stars lists the names of 48 officers which can be revealed. The remaining names remain secret, even in death.

Except for the first time he saw it, Bat had passed the wall dozens of times during his career but hardly gave it more than a passing glance. Now, he reflected for a moment and realized that but for the grace of God a star could have been added for him as well.

Charlie Stone had been reassigned back to Langley from New York after the Belize mission. Bat announced himself to the officer at the information desk and told the man Stone was expecting him. The appointment was confirmed in short order and instructions given.

As Bat got off the elevator on the 4th floor of the new building, Stone and several people were waiting to greet him.

"Welcome home, Agent Lynch. Your country and the agency owe you a great debt." Stone moved alongside him and placed an arm around Bat's shoulder. On cue, a handful of others, obviously put up to it by Stone, broke into a round of welcoming applause. Embarrassed, Bat smiled and looked around the small group but didn't see any faces he recognized other than Stone's.

Without further fanfare the well-wishers quickly dispersed as Bat and Stone walked down a side corridor.

"Looks like the agency is robbing the cradle. They're all kids," he commented.

"Ah, but these kids are among the best and the brightest. Each exhibits extraordinary talent for their specific job. They're the heart and soul of the 'new' agency, depending more on electronic surveillance than we ever did. You and I are dinosaurs, Bat, the few remaining cloak-and-dagger gunsels from a bygone era."

"And I never fired my weapon on a mission," Bat shrugged. But he knew Stone couldn't say that. Stone's daring and bravado in Eastern Europe and South America was well known in the agency.

"And you may well never have to again," Stone said as they reached his office. Then in a total change of conversation, he added. "You look fit as a fiddle. I take it you're all recovered?"

"Yes. Saw the doctor before I came here. No further visits required." Bat paused and took in the sight.

"Is this your office?" He recognized by its size and location that such accommodations were reserved for deputy directors.

"Yes, thanks to you," he said as they entered the spacious room. Instead of sitting behind his desk, Stone motioned Bat over to the comfortable looking overstuffed leather couch and joined him there. Stone got right to the point.

"I was planning on giving you a call this week anyway but since you reached me first I might as well tell you now." He paused as Bat gave him a questioning look, then continued.

"I need to see a friendly, familiar face around here. Oh, the people I'm working with are all fine, no problems there, but you know what I mean. I'd like to have somebody here that I've known and worked with for a few years. Somebody I could go out after work and hoist a few beers with. And such a person would be moving up a at least a pay grade."

"Me? You're asking me if I want to get out of field work and come here, to headquarters?"

"You always were bright, Bartholomew. Figured that out just from the things I said, did you?" Stone teased.

"Very flattering. I think I'd enjoy working closely with you, and working here. No more disguises, false identities, secret missions. And kicking up the paycheck a notch or two would be good also, but . . ."

"What's the 'but'? You could actually live in the same house or apartment for years, have a social life, settle down, even get married to that great looking woman who adores you, if that whack on the head in Belize loosened some screws. You could have the whole nine yards."

"But. . .to continue . . . I called you because I've decided to resign from the agency. I've thought about all the things you just described, as well as others. I spoke to an old friend in the magazine business and the publishing company that's been my cover these many years, and both said they would hire me in a heartbeat."

"Wow, I didn't see that coming," Stone said, truly surprised. "Are you sure about this, or is it just a delayed reaction after getting all messed up in Belize?"

"Yes, I'm sure. Damn near getting killed didn't help me want to continue in this line of work, but I had actually been thinking about leaving before that trip. Then, meeting Jennifer, I finally realized she was the woman I had always fantasized about marrying, but couldn't, and wouldn't, with all the baggage this job would bring to the marriage."

"How about taking another 30-day extension and giving it some more thought? Come around here as often as you like, look around, get used to the place, meet some of the people. . ."

"Thanks Charlie, but I don't need any more time. I've made my decision, I just want to fill out my papers. Besides, I've been out six months. There's no way I can get another extension."

Before Stone could reply his phone rang.

"I gotta take that. I told the secretary to hold all calls once you got here." He rose from the couch and answered the call. A few seconds later he replaced the receiver in the cradle.

"It's a bullshit quickie briefing about something that has nothing to do with my sections, but they want all of us to be in on it. Shouldn't take more than five minutes." Stone said as he came around the desk.

"I'll be here," Bat smiled.

As Stone reached the door he paused and turned to Bat.

"See that pile of folders on my desk? That's the kind of stuff one of my sections works on. Absolutely nothing critical. Go ahead, take a look at them while I'm away. You'll see what a piece of cake this job is. All we do is review stuff and add our opinion. . .I'll be right back."

Bat just relaxed at first, but then his natural curiosity as an agent got the best of him and he lifted himself from the couch and took Stone's seat behind the desk. As he fingered through the nearly dozen folders reading the heading labels one caught his eye: PRINCESS OF WALES.

"What the hell would the agency be doing with a file on her?" he wondered. He pulled it from the others and opened it as he pushed back the swivel chair to a semi-reclining position to read it. He hoped he would find something innocuous or trivial that he could mention to Jennifer and his sister.

He read parts of pages dealing with Diana's visit to Martha's Vineyard some years earlier as a guest of Paolo and Lucia Tarso-Flecha de Lima. He was the Brazilian ambassador in Washington, and his wife was apparently a close friend of the princess. Next was a photo of Diana and her husband taken in The White House with President and Mrs. Reagan. Bat realized the pages were not in chronological order as he came across a report on Diana's trip to Washington and a meeting with the Clintons, and a photo of her dancing at The White House with actor John Travolta at a White House dinner. It was dated November 9, 1985, on the back.

There was a chatty detailed report, replete with quotes and observations of Diana's 1996 New York and Washington visits. A hand written notation in the margin noted it was her first major international engagement since the royal divorce. The purpose was to raise money for breast-cancer research. Diana was quoted as calling the disease "a great dark enemy stalking women."

A quote from designer Isaac Mizrahi said, *"Charles really blew it when he dumped her"* and Colin Powell, who had been Chairman of the Joint Chiefs when Bat was an intelligence officer during the Gulf War. Powell, ever the charming soldier, had the first dance with the princess and said afterward: *"She's a lot of fun."*

Nothing, it seemed, escaped the agency's prying eyes and ears. *"Earlier that day, Diana shared a fund raising breakfast of egg, tomato and crab Napoleon breakfast with First Lady Hilary Clinton,* The Washington Post's *Katharine Graham and more than 100 others."* Even the simple comment by the First Lady was noted: *"This is one of the nicest British invasions of the White House."*

There was a memo that Clinton's wordsmith, George Stephanopoulos, shared a chatty lunch with Diana. That evening, the wordy report noted, Diana wore an ivory lace, beaded backless gown for the ball. The observing agent thought it was similar to one worn by Elizabeth Dole, but said it looked better on the princess!

More copy about her dancing mentions Oscar de La Renta and Calvin Klein as partners and a comment from Bill Blass: "They decided only married men could dance with the princess, and they had to be taller than she was." The event organizer, Ralph Lauren, didn't make the dance rule cut either, the file noted.

The report ended with the comment that, as the Princess left, the band played *I Will Survive*. Fitting, if dramatic, Bat thought.

But it was the next page that caught his attention. An asterisked notation typed at the top of the page and in a different font than the rest of the report read *Cooperating foreign agent: Megan Price, SIS*. He read it again to make sure he actually saw her name there. Bat shook his head in amazement. He couldn't believe SIS would waste the talents of a fine field agent to collect the kind of silly gossip he had read on the other pages in the folder. This item dealt with a meeting between the princess and John F. Kennedy, Jr., in a New York hotel.

As he skimmed down the page looking for any mention of her, he thought of what Archie had said about Megan. Perhaps her kill-rather-than-capture style was too much for the staid British gentlemen she and Archie worked with.

The report, which he personally thought read more like suggestive pornography, was vague and full of conclusions and innuendos but nothing of verifiable substance. Then, at the very bottom, he finally found a mention that related to Megan.

In his concluding remarks, the CIA operative wrote that when the event was over he thanked the SIS agent, whom he had known previously, for her assistance and remarked it had been a fortunate coincidence for him to have run into her and that she had been so helpful.

"Then she said something I don't quite understand," the agent wrote. *"She smiled and made a witty quip: 'In our business there are no coincidences.' I only mention that in the interest of thoroughness. The British apparently do have a sense of humor."*

Bat fingered through other equally mundane instances in the folder detailing seemingly useless spying on Princess Diana. He closed the folder and returned it to the spot he had marked in the pile. No sooner had he done that than Stone returned.

"Sorry about that. They had a q&a and some people in that room just like to hear themselves talk. You wouldn't believe some of the asshole questions."

"And you want me to come here to work so I can go through that kind of crap, too?" Bat smiled as he rose from the chair.

"Stay there, stay there. You look good in that chair. It could be yours a lot sooner than you would imagine."

"What are you talking about, you just got the promotion. Don't tell me you want to quit now too because you don't like the things people say at meetings . . ." Despite Stone's remark, Bat came around from behind the desk. He and Stone were now standing in the middle of the room.

"Hell, no, I've worked too long for this . . .and it could get considerably better real soon. I just heard, as the meeting broke up, that two of the senior deputy directors may be on their way out. One is as old as the hills, and he is gently being nudged towards the door. The other had a stroke, and the scuttlebutt is he won't be back."

Bat asked their names, he recognized them but didn't know either man personally.

"I heard this from the *big man* himself. Just me, nobody else. He called me over and made some small talk, asking how I had adjusted to the new job and all. But when the room cleared he mentioned it looked like there were going to be two senior level openings." Stone was obviously pleased with the turn of events.

"Bat, I know, I just know, he wouldn't have mentioned that to me if he wasn't testing the waters to see what my reaction would be." He added, "And if I move up, I'll recommend you for my job. You're a natural. We have similar field backgrounds, and that's what they want for deputy directors heading groups and sections."

"No thanks, Charlie. I'd go stir crazy pouring over the kind of stuff in that pile on your desk."

"Oh, so you did read some of the files?"

"Yes, but just enough of them to realize I'm not cut out to be a desk jockey, no matter how much money, perks, or whatever else goes with it. I enjoyed working in the field, but I've been bitten by the old burnout bug. It's time to throw in the towel."

"How about this? Take the 30 days I mentioned, go away on a trip, talk it over with Jennifer and come back here after that. If you're still hell-bent on retiring, I'll get the papers for you myself. Deal?"

"Deal, but only because I want to get back to Jennifer's. Her sister and the boys will probably be staying for dinner, and it's getting late," Bat paused and extended his hand to Stone.

"To be honest, my mind won't change. I'll take the 30 days, but get the papers ready. Ciao, for now, I'm outta here." Despite the pain he still sometimes felt, there was a slight spring in Bat's step as he walked toward the elevator. He felt the familiar gray cloud of the world of intrigue had been lifted from over him. He was about to begin a new life. . .with Jennifer, he hoped.

****

On the morning of July 14, 1997, Dodi Fayed watched the marchers and celebrants in the Bastille Day parade go down the

Champs Elysées from the balcony of his Paris apartment. He was with his current girlfriend, Kelly Fisher, the American model. But as the strands of *The Marseilles* and other anthems echoed and bounced off the canyon walls along the grand avenue, his thoughts were wandering to his father's yacht in the placid waters of the Mediterranean. Before the last marcher had exchanged their uniform for civilian clothes, Dodi would be comfortably seated in the Harrods' Gulfstream jet headed south himself.

Three days earlier the Princess of Wales and her sons William and Harry had arrived at the Fayed family's $18-million cliffside villa estate, Castel Ste-Thérèse, at St-Tropez. The lavish compound included swimming pools, terraces and gardens and proffered privacy and protection, courtesy of on-site police dogs and more than a dozen armed security guards, including Alexander 'Kes' Wingfield, based at the villa.

The previous day, the royals boarded Fayed's new $36-million yacht, the *Jonikal* and sailed off the Cote d'Azure. Immediately after purchasing the yacht, Fayed had the *Jonikal* extravagantly and feverishly refurbished to his own taste, nearly doubling its $20-million purchase price. The Egyptian-born Fayed, who once sold Coca-Cola in the streets of Alexandria, and worked as a sewing machine salesman, had amassed a fortune estimated between $880 million and $3.3 billion.

He made his money after he married the sister of the international arms dealer, Adnan Khashoggi, who employed him in his import business in Saudi Arabia. Eventually, Fayed established his own shipping company in Egypt, before becoming a financial adviser to one of the world's richest men, the Sultan of Brunei, in 1966.

Diana and her young sons joined the owner of Harrods and his former Finnish beauty-queen wife, Heini Wathén, and their four Finnish-British children aboard the yacht. Two Special Branch detectives were with the group for the protection of Princes, William and Harry. The party group would shortly be joined by Dodi, Fayed's son from his first marriage.

Though Diana had politely refused previous invitations to

enjoy his hospitality, with her sons, the princess finally gave in and accepted. It was widely rumored that Diana's acceptance this time was due in part to her awareness that Fayed had accompanied Queen Elizabeth in presenting awards at a recent Windsor horse show sponsored by the Egyptian tycoon.

Fayed's own security people, and some members of the crew, curiously asked the Special Branch detectives how they should address the future king and his brother. They were told to simply call the young boys by their names, William and Harry.

When ashore, the Special Branch detectives and Fayed's security men all dressed casually and similarly to the people they were guarding. And their behavior blended in as well so their subjects didn't stand out either.

This Bastille Day, after leaving his soon-to-be-former girlfriend, Kelly Fisher, Dodi headed for the Battersea heliport and took Harrods' helicopter to Stansted airport, northeast of London. He was accompanied by one of the security men, Trevor Rees-Jones, a former British paratrooper and military policeman, employed by Fayed for the specific task of being a bodyguard for Dodi. Fayed's total security staff was more than 40 people.

From there they flew Fayed's Gulfstream jet to Nice where their baggage and supplies were loaded into a van for the drive to St-Laurent-du-Var, where they boarded Dodi's modernized former torpedo boat, the *Cujo*. Their sea-going journey to Cannes would take approximately 45 minutes. Dodi used the *Cujo's* onboard radio to inform the *Jonikal* of their progress. He also contacted the security people responsible for communications at his father's Castel Ste-Thérèse villa.

Mohamed Fayed, Diana and the rest of the entourage immediately left to meet Dodi when he tied up the *Cujo* at the dock. But he had beaten them there. Nonetheless, the holiday party group was transported by tender out to the *Jonikal*. It was nearing six o'clock in the evening and Diana's sons were excited at the prospect of watching the local Bastille Day fireworks from aboard the yacht.

Once onboard things moved quickly. Diana and her sons followed the family members moving towards the rear deck. The area had been laid out for dinner so the meal could be taken before the celebratory fireworks began.

At the appropriate hour, several close reports signaled the display had commenced. William and Harry gave the coastline's night sky their undivided attention as profusions of spectacular color burst into blossoms that quickly turned to embers falling earthward.

Diana divided her attention between watching her sons' enthusiasm, the fireworks, and the already gathering navy of paparazzi-filled small boats stalking the yacht.

****

Sir Warren never forgot what he had been told in training when he joined SIS a half-century ago: *"With regard to our legal standing, SIS hasn't got one. The Service cannot function properly under the typical restraints of other government departments because our work very often involves transgressing propriety or the law. That's what you signed up for. Live with it, every day, or get out now."* It was blunt, to the point, and he fully subscribed to it.

On his desk Sir Warren had a three-inch long piece of polished brass that he used as a paperweight. He had received it as a gift years earlier, and it was the code he lived by:

> *"Unlike any other crime, espionage leaves no trace,*
> *and proof is virtually impossible*
> *- unless a spy either confesses or is caught in the act."*
> --Peter Wright, Spycatcher

Author Peter Wright had been associated with MI-5 from 1955-1976. Then, as now, incoming agents are immediately told the service lived by the 11th commandment, "thou shalt not get caught". Though Sir Warren couldn't suffer former agents who wrote memoirs, he was in agreement with the man's philosophy.

Even into the Cold War, Britain's Intelligence and Security Services had *carte blanche* in making decisions about removing people they believed should be *terminated with extreme prejudice*. So trusted was SIS by the British Establishment that they did not need authorization from the Government before killing someone they deemed a threat to the monarchy and state. It was his knowledge of such unchallenged authority that caused author Ian Fleming to give his fictional agent James Bond a 'license to kill.'

However, by the late 1960's Prime Minister Harold Wilson changed the rules. He took steps to insure that all such actions had to be presented, justified, and permission sought from the Prime Minister or Home Secretary before anyone was "permanently removed." That has remained the policy of successive British governments.

Nonetheless, a loophole in Wilson's changes permitted the intelligence agencies to retain their right to kill if they believed there was an unmistakable clear and present danger to the security of the state. And not even the Prime Minister needed to be informed till after the fact, if at all.

Most of Sir Warren's civil service career in SIS had been under the old rules. He had seen prime ministers and governments come and go. But he and other loyal monarchists remained faithful at their posts and devoted in their sworn oath to protect the crown. A handful of these spies and spymasters never subscribed to Wilson's changes but instead embraced the loophole. They believed the ends did, indeed, justify the means and carried on business, if not as usual, with proper discretion. They eventually became a viable functioning rogue cell within the greater British intelligence community.

When not involved with royal surveillance, either for MI-6 or The Committee, Archie Blair mostly worked in the Eastern European Controllerate (EEC) division of MI-6. One of this group's major activities was a large and complicated operation to smuggle advanced Soviet weaponry out of the disorganized remnants of the Soviet Union. Rather than meet in the U.K., this group had been holding their update and evaluation meetings outside the country for several years. Most regularly took place at the Ritz hotel in Paris.

Along with Archie, Megan Price was still listed as part of EEC, although she hadn't participated in any of their activities. Sir Warren had arranged with SIS for her almost exclusive services some years earlier after their lunch together at his club when he almost childishly insisted that she use various code names when communicating with him. Neither Archie nor any of Megan's regular colleagues in MI-6 questioned her absence from the group and trips abroad because it was rumored to be the result of sensitive 'deep cover' behind the former Iron Curtain.

Some years after that fateful August night in Paris, it would be learned that Britain's MI-6 had a six-member squad in Paris conducting surveillance operations against Princess Diana. In the U.S., meanwhile, a Freedom of Information Act lawsuit would cause the CIA, NSA, and other American spy agencies to acknowledge they had monitored her movements right up to that last day of August. But there was no one to come forward and ask Sir Warren and The Committee what their role had been.

The job of planting bugs and FOTT dots in Dodi Fayed's London apartment had been carried out by a regular domestic intelligence team from MI-5. Archie Blair, meanwhile, was part of the officially sanctioned regular MI-6 operatives who gained access and planted devices in Dodi's Paris apartment. With the ever decreasing and irreplaceable supply of FOTT dots, which were now being shared with MI-5, their use was not initially approved for the Hotel Ritz. Though re-useable and moveable to other locations as needs would arise, it was discovered that was easier said than done.

Often even the agents who had placed FOTT dots had a difficult time locating the virtually invisible, extraordinarily thin clear 'plastic dots' for retrieval. Though technically they were not plastic at all, that's what they quickly became known as among the very limited number of agents who dealt with them.

Sir Warren, as one might expect, had not given all the dots to the sister security agencies. He held fully a third of them for future use by The Committee.

Megan Price's role in the Paris mission was not officially sanctioned by SIS. Unbeknownst to the regular team which Archie was part of, Megan now ran a small rogue cell under the auspices of, and fanatically loyal to, Sir Warren and Smythe-Pembrooke. She, and they, believed they were operating on behalf of The Committee. It was paramount that Megan and her rogues not be seen by the regular MI-6 team in Paris. They took every precaution.

Once it was learned that Dodi and Diana would be stopping in Paris for an overnight before returning to London from their Mediterranean trip, it was Megan's rogue team that got the job of putting a single FOTT in place at the Ritz. This way, whether the couple stayed at Dodi's apartment or at the hotel, their privacy would be invaded. Since the hotel had an extensive closed circuit television network, which the rogue team had little difficulty tapping into, only one FOTT needed to be employed.

It was known that Dodi favored the hotel's Imperial Suite when he chose to entertain women at the property, rather than his own apartment. The FOTT receiver, monitors, PAL video taping machines and audio equipment were easily walked right through the hotel's front door as luggage and set up in a regular Ritz hotel room.

That evening, Megan organized her thoughts and prepared the logistics of a plan that could be implemented in hours. Because Megan was monitoring the MI-6 team that Archie was part of, she would know the couple had ended their holiday in the Mediterranean and were now on their way to Paris even before the Harrods jet had landed at Le Bourget airport.

The next day, on schedule, the assassins checked into the hotel she had reserved for them. Her contact on the team had wired her a surprisingly large amount of money. She knew that if they were even the slightest bit professional they would arrive with considerably more. They identified themselves as the "K Team." She had no interest knowing why they choose that designation.

When she arrived to meet them she was surprised to see that instead of the five people she expected, there were more than a dozen. But actually that worked out. Based on the primary plan she had sketched out, Megan was afraid they would have to quickly send some additional people. The unexpected additional personnel gave her more drivers to work with.

Megan anticipated and planned various scenarios and the number of support vehicles needed to make sure that once the target car was en route from the Ritz, it would be unable to take the usual route up the Champs Elysées. That would be the logical, most direct way to reach Dodi's apartment on Rue Arsene-Houssaye, close to the Arc de Triomphe. But they needed the Mercedes to go through the Pont de l'Alma tunnel which runs parallel to the Seine.

The vehicle had to be prevented from turning onto the Champs Elysées from the Place de la Concorde. Then it had to be prevented from using the access road along the river so that it had no choice but to go into the tunnel. Cars, motorcycles, even a large, slow lorry might be used.

The tunnel had been selected as the site to terminate the mission because entering it was somewhat difficult at speeds above 50 mph. Though the posted speed limit on the approach was 37 mph, Megan was confident her 'paparazzi,' and K Team support vehicles, which the principal would believe were also press photographers, could goad the Mercedes driver into going faster.

Two individuals from the team would be posted in close proximity to the Ritz so her 'paparazzi' could keep them abreast of the situation and confirm by cell phone when the couple had actually left in the target car. Three days before they arrived, using some of the money provided by the assassins, Megan had put a deposit on an expensive vacant shop on Place Vendome, across from the Ritz hotel but still some distance away. It was a perfect vantage point for observing the comings and goings through the main door during the day. At night it had limitations. But the phone call from their paparazzi-spy would be the final word.

The day before they arrived, she had the German cover the interior windows with drop cloth and brown paper, leaving appropriate panels high up that could be lifted for viewing outside. Curious passersby outside could not see inside.

Two other team members aligned and affixed a mirror to either a tree, post or building. The mirror had to be correctly aligned with the tunnel so a signal to inflate the front airbags could bounce off it and travel into the tunnel. The same signal would engage a powerful military strobe light from a vehicle just in front of the Mercedes. While strobes could be purchased by civilians, those of the military type Megan called for were not for sale. They were capable of blinding anyone in the immediate area for 45 seconds, long enough to disorient a driver and cause a crash. Megan thought the light was unnecessary if the airbag chip worked properly. The K Team drivers in the tunnel would have a three second advance buzzer warning to flip down intensive light-blocking shields over their eyes. The two assassins would work from a parked truck just outside the tunnel.

Much of the electronics and other items Megan recommended as necessary for the job was paid for, promptly and without fuss, by the Arabs even though Megan was certain she could have obtained much of it for free from Sir Warren.

The meeting lasted nearly an hour, and no detail was overlooked. Megan recommended they spend Friday rehearsing in full-blown dress runs using all vehicles and electronic equipment.

If what Megan was aware of from electronic surveillance on Fayed's yacht, Dodi and Diana would be arriving in Paris Saturday afternoon. Perhaps there would even be time for a final run through that morning.

The Arabs were very attentive to the overall plan she had presented and made very few suggestions to the contrary. The only point that met with resistance was her demand that none of the drivers in the chase cars and on motorcycles be carrying weapons. She had concerns about what would happen moments after the crash if they determined Dodi was not dead.

In the plan she proposed, Megan told the assassins she needed three people to get out of their vehicles and immediately rush to the car as if to provide assistance. One would inject Dodi with air to stop his heart. The driver had to receive a large high-proof mixture of alcohol, enough so the findings would provide a reason for the car crash: drunk driver. She understood that in the tension and pressure of the moment somebody on the team might be tempted to empty a clip into Fayed. That would make useless all the work, all the time and effort to create an accident.

The assassins told Megan that all bets were off, as far as they were concerned, if the elder Fayed came to Paris before the mission. Every effort would be made to take him out, instead of his son.

She nodded, indicating she understood, but had already suspected as much and passed her concerns onto Smythe-

Pembrooke. He assured that her appropriate steps would be taken to make sure Mohamed Fayed did not go to Paris before the mission was complete.

****

Tempus Fugit, the Roman sage is often quoted saying, especially when one is having a good time. It was already Saturday. Princess Diana had spent the last week aboard the *Jonikal* and much of August on the French Riviera with Dodi Fayed.

This trip had been the couple's fourth together since mid-July. By now the media was touting them as an 'item.' To all observers, including The Firm, Sir Warren and fellow members of The Committee, each passing get-together Diana had with Dodi seemed more affectionate than previous relationships she had been in. The tabloids had speculated that the pair was already secretly engaged.

Beaming with satisfaction at the way his arranged July meeting in St. Tropez was working out, Mohamed Al-Fayed confided to friends and associates that a close connection did, in fact, exist between his son and the Princess of Wales.

Fueled by tips from 'informed sources,' some newspapers even said a wedding would happen before the end of the year, perhaps in the autumn. The romance rumors had given way to marriage talk. Consequently, everything they did on that last trip together was scrutinized and reported.

Sunday, August 24th: The *Jonikal* lifted its anchor in the harbor at Monaco and sailed towards Portofino. The paparazzi feverously clicked away as they were treated to an appearance on deck by the loving couple.

Monday, August 25th: The *Jonikal* left Portofino and moved south. They dropped anchor at Portovenere, Italy, south of La Spezia, for swimming and lunch. The paparazzi, using helicopters, small boats and any other means possible, kept pace.

Tuesday, August 26th: Diana and Dodi spent the day and evening off Elba, the island Napoleon had been confined to. In wires, faxes, and emails back to their newspapers the couple were called 'lovers.' There were no longer any questions in the minds of the paparazzi about the depth of the relationship.

Wednesday, August 27th: The *Jonikal* 'Love Boat,' as the tabloids were calling it, moved again. This time toward Sardinia.

Thursday, Friday, and Saturday, August 28th, 29th & 30th: Sardinia appeared to be the location they fancied the most. Photographers had numerous opportunities to capture them together on film, including holding hands and laughing in Olbia, in the northeast of Sardinia.

That Saturday morning Diana and Dodi relaxed on deck, appreciating the beauty and the calm waters of Sardinia's Emerald Coast.

Dodi's butler, Rene Delorm, delivered their morning coffee and orange juice with a breakfast selection of assorted fruits including oranges, bananas, grapes, apples, kiwis, croissants and jams. Diana began with a glass of juice and added hot milk to her coffee. Dodi waved off the orange juice and sipped black coffee.

During breakfast Dodi received a cell phone call from Frank Klein, president of Ritz Hotel and the property manager of the Windsor Villa. He was returning Dodi's Friday call.

Windsor Villa in Paris had been the self-imposed exile residence of the Duke and Duchess of Windsor after the former King Edward VIII abdicated the throne in 1936 'for the woman I love.' Before the much-publicized carryings on of Diana and Charles, the romance between Edward VIII and the divorced Wallis Simpson had been the Royal Family's scandal of the century.

After Edward became *persona non grata* to The Firm, he was nonetheless allowed to keep the style HRH in front of his name. Yet, Diana, the Princess of Wales, was not.

More than a decade earlier Mohamed Fayed had obtained a long-term lease on the estate from the Paris governing body. This September he was having the Duke and Duchess's effects auctioned at Sotheby's for charity so the property could be used by the Fayed family. However, Dodi had his own idea as to who should live in the prestigious estate.

Klein told him the villa had been emptied. Everything was out of the house and it would all be sold in less than two weeks. The house stood empty.

"Good," Dodi replied. "I've spoken to my father about moving in. My friend doesn't want to stay in England." He deliberately avoided using the name of his 'friend' since he had long become acquainted with the capabilities of eavesdropping devices. Nonetheless, he just about gave it away when he added:

"We want to move into the villa, Frank, because we are getting married in October or November."

The couple intended finishing this holiday on Sardinia. Now more than ever Dodi was eager to bring it to an end. In Paris, this very day before the sun set, he intended to bring Diana to Windsor Villa and tour what he hoped would be their new home together.

This cruise on the now world-famous yacht had been their second such sea trip in a month. When not plying the waters of the Mediterranean, the twosome had also spent time together at three different Fayed residences: Dodi's apartments in Paris and London, as well as the residence in Surrey.

Today, Saturday, August 30, was departure day. Diana sat on deck enjoying the last vestige of Mediterranean sun, nibbling at breakfast.

Again, this final morning, she was pestered the paparazzi who photographed Diana and Dodi on deck entwined and kissing in romantic embraces, playing loving-teasing games while swimming, and seeming like honeymooners window shopping ashore.

Diana was aware of the long lenses framing her every mouthful of food but tried to ignore them. With the instant transmittal capabilities the media now had, she realized these silly *'Diana Eating'* pictures could appear in newspapers this very day.

Recently, in a playful mood, she went up to them and teased: "I have a huge surprise for you! You just have to wait a little bit."

The previous day, however, may well have been the proverbial straw that broke the camel's back. The media seemed to have gotten out of control. It was just enough of an incident to make Diana feel somewhat relieved that they were heading for Paris in a few hours.

Around lunchtime one of *Jonikal's* tenders tied up by the five-star Hotel Cala di Volpe near Arzachena, along the Costa Smeralda. Diana and Dodi went for a swim in a nearby inlet as *Jonikal* crew members made an effort to prevent photographers from intruding with their little boats and constant clicking. For their efforts they would have had another photo of Diana in a bathing suit, nothing earth-shattering.

Two of the disgruntled photographers approached the yacht, shouting abuse. The *Jonikal's* captain came ashore and told them what he thought of their conduct. Another paparazzi, who had not been one of the trouble makers, also told them to behave.

This didn't sit well with one of the original loud mouths and he pushed the man. The photographer who had agreed with the captain responded by punching the pusher twice.

Perhaps the sudden aggression among the ranks of the paparazzi had something to do with the reaction that bathing suit photos of Diana had caused back in the U.K. earlier in the week.

A copy editor writing photo captions at one of the tabloids wrote that the princess appeared to have gained a bit of weight . . .in the stomach. The picture, and caption, quickly generated speculation, with some people wondering out loud if the Princess of Wales might actually be pregnant. Photos of Diana and Dodi, who was being described as her latest 'love interest' and with leading headlines including such words as 'Wedding Bells For Di?' appeared in newspapers all over the world.

In Los Angeles, Kelly Fisher, the beautiful model whom Dodi had left on Bastille Day to join up with his father's party at the villa and on the *Jonikal*, appeared before television cameras crying and calling Dodi Fayed a cad and heartbreaker.

"He promised to marry me," she said, "He wanted to marry me this year." Ms. Fisher flashed a sapphire set in diamonds, which the TV cameras closed in on. She said it was her engagement ring.

The Fayed family press office said Dodi and Kelly had been together until January. Since then they had remained friends and the ring was an expression of friendship, nothing more. If the media had any interest in pursuing the story such thoughts would vanish in less than 24 hours.

A few days earlier, before Dodi's plans to show Diana the Windsor Villa had crystallized, the couple had decided they would end the trip on Saturday and she would return to London, via Paris, after a last evening together in the City of Light before the Princess could be with her sons.

****

Jennifer read most of the time during the trans-Atlantic flight while Bat slept almost the whole way to Paris. Though they originally planned to visit London first and make Paris the second part of their trip, they were unable to get the kind of convenient airline flights they wanted this last week of August in the summer of 1997. Consequently, they reversed the order and Paris, the 'pleasure' part of the trip would be first, followed by the 'work' part in London and its environs. Bat had previously visited London, Jennifer, meanwhile, had not been to either.

Bat and Jennifer's flight from the U.S. arrived at Orly International Airport shortly before 10 AM local time on Saturday, August 30. Their pre-paid hired limousine followed the customary route to Paris along the A6 highway, exiting at Porte Maillot onto Avenue de la Grande Armee all the way up to the Arc de Triomphe at Place Charles de Gaulle. By the time their car made the half circle around the monument, Bat had already shot more than a dozen photographs.

Next was a right turn onto the Champs Elysées and very shortly the car made another turn right and drove past several well-known designers' shops before pulling to the curb in front of their Paris hotel, the 253-room Plaza Athénée on fashionable Avenue Montaigne. They were hardly ten miles from the airport, but a million miles away in ambiance.

"Oh, Bat, this truly is a beautiful city. Everything I've read, everything people told me, didn't do it justice at all!" Jennifer was more excited than he had ever seen her.

"Honey, that was just the drive from the airport, we haven't even scratched the surface," he smiled, amused by her enthusiasm. As they exited the vehicle, a bellman appeared with a rolling rack cart for their luggage.

"I know, I know. But Bat we're really together in Paris!" She flung her arms around his neck and kissed him long and slow.

"Ahem," the bellman made the polite sound. Bat and Jennifer looked and noticed that he and the driver had loaded their luggage onto the cart. They ended their embrace and Bat dug into his wallet to tip the driver, and while he was at it he tipped the bellman as well.

At the front desk in the lobby, they presented their passports and the copy of their reservation as the cart with their luggage was rolled away from the area. Check in was 3:00 PM, and they were early. The next time they'd see their things would be when they were in their room.

"Boy, you sure can pick 'em. This is some place," Bat said as he took in the tasteful and elegant surroundings.

"Madam Carson, I have good news: your suite is actually ready now," the desk manager announced.

"Suite?" Bat looked at Jennifer.

"Yes, dear. I figured coming to Paris with you meant we should go first class all the way. You like?"

"I like." He was happy she had made all the travel arrangements. He didn't want to think about the endless list of medium-priced hotels he had stayed at over the years and would have been very embarrassed if he had booked them into a Paris hotel along the lines of those he was used to. Then he wondered if there actually were any hotels like that in Paris.

A short while later, after taking a brief tour of the hotel and as they were unpacking luggage in the suite, Jennifer paused.

"What's wrong?" Bat asked.

"Nothing. Absolutely nothing. I'm here in the *City of Light*, everyone's second city, with the man I love! It's so perfect and romantic," she said as she threw her arms around his neck and pulled him towards her. They kissed long, tenderly and slowly for several seconds.

"I have an idea," she suddenly announced as they broke. "Let's leave the rest of this till later and go out and see as much as we can today."

Even though Jennifer thought Bat had been 'out like a light' on the plane, he actually had a broken sleep. He would have preferred sacking out for an hour or two, but he enjoyed Jennifer's exuberance at being in Paris so much that he acquiesced.

They told the taxi driver to take them around to the major sites as if he were showing Paris to visiting members of his family who had never been there.

The smiling driver obliged and in no time they were turning past the Arc de Triomphe and on to the Champs Elysées. In very understandable English, the driver gave them a running tour guide narration. He noticed Bat and Jennifer kept glancing at a large unfolded map.

"Your map may say the Arc is at Place Charles de Gaulle, but older citizens refer to it by the former name, Place d'E-toile. That is very much the same way New Yorkers tell me many still call the Avenue of The Americas Sixth Avenue.

"If you wish I can stop, anytime. Perhaps you would care to stand under the Arc and read the list of Napoleonic conquests etched in its walls and observe the 12 avenues that converge on the square?" the driver asked, adding "One cannot help being mentally pulled back into history. This was the very spot where the fallen Corsican's remains were returned to the city."

Bat had to think for a moment before remembering that Napoleon had been born on Corsica.

"Saying good bye to the Arc, we are now driving down the most beautiful boulevard in the world: the Champs Elysées with its mélange of sidewalk cafes, boutiques and shops that best typify today's cosmopolitan Paris. It is a Paris that is positively French with its well-preserved buildings, but not foreign to visitors such as yourselves." Jennifer wanted to compliment the driver and say that his helpfulness and attitude was a pleasant surprise. She had been told to expect the French to be aloof and condescending. But she decided no matter how she said it he would probably take it as an insult to his countryman.

"Your English is quite good," she said instead.

"Thank you. I was born here but my mother was French, my father American. He was transferred back to the U.S. and I lived there until I was in my teens. When he died my mother and I moved back to France," he casually commented and moved ahead with describing the passing vistas.

"At each intersection I'll go slowly so you can look toward the Left Bank. What you see will gratify your senses. Here, for instance, we are passing Avenue George-V, and looking south you can see the Pont de L'Alma at the far end. It's one of the 20 bridges that span the Seine and collectively reflect more than 2,000 years of history. That's where you catch the glass-topped river cruise boats. You can eat dinner on the Bateaux Mouches, and see how beautiful Paris is at night. They depart from Quai de la Conference, reached from Place de l'Alma."

"Oh, darling, we must do that," Jennifer practically giggled. Bat nodded in agreement.

"Well, then you should make reservations at least a day ahead. It's almost always impossible to get aboard on the spur of the moment..

"Next is the street where your hotel is, Avenue Montaigne. If you look, you can see the Eiffel Tower."

The driver continued this way and, in rapid order, the Grand Palais and Petit Palis on Avenue Winston Churchill came into view. At the far end of the avenue was what many considered the loveliest bridge in Paris, Pont Alexandre III.

"Beyond the bridge, the dome you see belongs to Hotel des Invalides, Napoleon's tomb. See how it juts into the skyline?"

Bat and Jennifer's attention was no longer divided between quickly looking at the passing scenes on the Champs Elysées and the down the avenues to their right. Looming before them was Place de la Concorde as a foreboding monument to revolutionary justice,

"Isn't this where the king. . ." Bat didn't get to finish.

"Yes, where Louis XVI and Marie Antoinette, and many others, were put to the guillotine. The exact spot is right where that 3,000 year old Egyptian obelisk now stands. In one way it's a monument to your American Revolution."

"Why do you say that?" Jennifer asked.

"Well, you set the example in 1776! Your patriots showed the world that people could cast off the yoke of kings and be free.

Waiting to cross this famous square with its seemingly endless traffic were several pedestrians. The driver made one, then a second, revolution around the traffic circle to afford Jennifer and Bat the opportunity to take in everything surrounding the square.

He drove at such a slow speed it visibly annoyed other drivers.

"Driver we're not far from Place Vendome, and The Ritz, are we?" Jennifer asked as a courtesy, but knew from the map that they were relatively close.

"No, ma'am. I can get you there in about two minutes."

"Would you, please?" she asked. Then she turned to Bat.

"Honey, I hope you don't mind. I want to go inside for a few minutes to get the flavor of the place. When you were sleeping on the plane I read that all the important Germans stayed at The Ritz during the war. I would like to see it for a scene in *Love's Tender Rage*. You know, for color, to mention what the Germans were doing as a break between scenes of the WASPS flying planes into Britain?"

Bat nodded. "I'd like to stretch my legs anyway," he said as he gently rubbed his knee.

True to his word, the taxi driver pulled up in front of the four white canopied portals at 15 Place Vendome less than two minutes later. As Jennifer negotiated with him about how much extra it would be to wait for them, Bat spotted someone he recognized heading for the main entrance of The Ritz.

"Deja vu, Blair!" He called out. "Honey, I know that guy," he said as an aside to Jennifer.

Archie stopped in his tracks and turned to his right to see who had called out his name. It took him an instant to put the clean shaven face with his last memory of Bat on Nevis almost five years earlier.

"You again! Captain Lynch, we must stop meeting this way." He joked as he altered his direction and headed for them. He noticed an attractive, smiling woman joining Bat.

"And who's this? Is there finally a Mrs. Lynch?" he asked with a sly grin.

"Jennifer Carson, I'd like to introduce you to Archie Blair, one of those rowdy and randy Brits I met during Desert Storm. Coincidentally, we also ran into each other a few years ago down in the Caribbean." Bat had deliberately ignored the 'M-word' question.

"My pleasure, indeed, Jennifer." He took her hand and, instead of shaking it, made a minor performance of bowing and kissing it, while he continued turning on his charm by giving her a big wink.

"Oh, my goodness, a gentleman! I have a sister that I know would just LOVE to meet you," she laughed. But her heart had sunk when Bat hadn't given a good answer to Archie's *'Mrs. Lynch'* question. *Had Kimberly been right? Had she assumed too much, or jumped to conclusions?* She wondered.

"Hey, what are you doing here? Don't you ever spend time in London?" Bat asked Archie.

"What am I doing here? London and Paris are a hop, skip and a jump from each other across the channel. You're in MY backyard. I should be asking you what you're doing here, in the summer with all these American tourists filling up the better hotels and restaurants."

"We're mixing business and pleasure. Jennifer is an author and we stopped here for three nights before going to London so she can research locations for a novel."

"Ahhh, another writer," Archie said to Jennifer in mild surprise. Then he focused his glance on Bat, "And I take it you are still doing those God-awful travel guides?"

"Yes and no. I resigned from the agency, so it's not a cover anymore. I'm talking to the publisher who wants to actually hire me as a real editor. Then again, I may go into photography full time. I'm still working it out. Nothing is firmed up yet."

Archie stiffened at Bat's remark. *He must be keen on her,* he thought, *for her to know about the CIA.*

"Shall we all go inside where it's air-conditioned? Jennifer asked. "I'm melting in this heat."

"Absolutely," Archie glanced at his watch. "It's just after noon. Sun's the hottest in the middle of the day." They proceeded from the street into the lobby.

"Good," Jennifer said, fanning herself with the map she and Bat had looked at in the taxi.

"Let me buy you two American writers a drink in the most

famous bar in the world. And it happens to be named after another American writer, Hemingway."

"Oh, thank you. But first I'll leave you two to exchange war stories. I need to spend a few minutes taking in the atmosphere and making notes. I'll meet you in the bar. I'd love to see it too!"

"Go have fun. We'll be there when you're done." Bat planted a gentle kiss on her cheek, and she was off.

Archie stepped off in the direction of the bar and Bat kept pace with him.

"Sorry, old man, if I put you on the spot asking if she was your wife. I just assumed. . ."

"No harm done, she probably never even picked up on it," Bat said smugly.

"Oh, do you have a lot to learn about women!" Archie replied, rolling his eyes.

"Well, no matter. I'm going to ask her to marry me before we leave Paris," Bat announced proudly.

"Very good. She seems like a fine lady. I hope she says yes, for your sake."

"She will. Her sister tipped me off, she's kind of expecting it. Jennifer walked in when I was on the phone with a buddy who's family is in the jewelry business. I had to do a fast one-two step on that one." Bat patted the breast pocket of his blazer as they entered the Hemingway Bar, "I've got the ring right here."

"The bar or a table?" Archie asked.

"Table. So I can stretch my leg," he answered. "I had a bad encounter with a gorilla who used me as a trampoline about six months back and my right knee still acts up if I push to much."

"You mentioned 'resigned.' I take it you meant from the agency?"

"Absolutely. Bat Lynch is just going to be plain old 'Joe Civilian' from now on. No more spy crap."

"Well I'm sure you've given it proper thought so I won't serve any sour grapes about how this business we're in is so wonderful. Good luck to you. And in your marriage as well."

A waiter came over and they ordered.

"So how's your love life? Ever rekindle the spark with Megan?"

"No, not on your life. I could easily let myself fall in love with her. And I think the feeling may be mutual. She's attractive, bright, and can be a very fun person to be with outside of work, but there's a dangerous rage just below the surface and I suspect she sometimes can't control it. So, sadly, Megan's not for me. Actually nobody's for me for some time now, I've become a slave to my work, and it's getting very depressing."

"Your life, or your work?"

"Both. They seem to feed off each other. Sometimes I feel as if I no longer have a life of my own. I'm drowning in other people's lives."

"Wow, you sound as if you may be ready to chuck in the towel. Are you working on something tedious or very sensitive?"

"A little of both. SIS has had me back keeping tabs on the royals again almost full time for the last three years."

"Really? That's what you and Megan were doing on Nevis. That was more than three years ago."

"Exactly. Right after Charles and Diana separated. But instead of her simply fading out of the royal picture things got worse." Archie thought for a second then added. "Actually they had been worse for years, but I hadn't been involved or aware of it. I made the mistake of showing what a marvelous Peeping Tom I was and little by little MI-6 assigned me to royal duties."

"See? What does that tell you? You went the extra mile and it bit you in the ass. My rule was: Do the assignment and do it well. But don't do it so good they pigeon-hole you as a friggin 'expert.' "

"Lynch, you're so full of it your eyes are brown. You've always been a Type One personality, an over achiever. You couldn't just do the job if your life depended on it."

"I know," Bat mused, "but I thought it was the right thing to say. You really do seem down."

"Does it actually show that much?" Archie asked.

Bat nodded and added quickly, "But here you are in Paris, sitting in an air-conditioned bar."

"Yes, sounds great. But I'm not on holiday. I'm part of a joint MI-6, MI-5 team hovering around waiting for the Princess and her new boyfriend to get here."

"Here? Princess Diana is coming to Paris?"

"Yes, Paris, but this hotel specifically. We have informers on the staff and knew days in advance our soiled princess will arrive this afternoon before returning to London on the morrow."

"I'm must bemissing something, I think. Why is it so important for you to be here?"

"Because, of late, Diana, our divorced Princess of Wales, has been carrying on with Mohamed Fayed's son, Dodi. And, in case you didn't know it, Dodi's daddy owns the hotel."

"That's been in the papers. Between Jennifer and my sister, I am unfortunately aware of such morsels of gossip by osmosis. They both follow the Diana soap opera. Frankly, I couldn't care less who she's sleeping with, that horse trainer, or whomever."

"Really? Good for you, Yank." There was an obvious edge in Archie's voice. "A lot of concerned people in Great Britain, I among them, would disagree with your sentiments. We certainly do care."

"And just why would that be?" Bat's tone was questioning, not confrontational.

"Diana and Charles eldest son, William, will be monarch one day. It would be bad form for people to be wondering, whispering, and giggling about who his tramp mother is bedded down with."

"Boy, you monarchists are obsessed with controlling every aspect of royal life." Bat shook his head in disapproval. "Get a life, get over it. Diana and your Bonnie Prince Charles are divorced, Kaput! She's free as a bird."

"Not as easily done as said. She and her foreign-born, rich playboy, visited a jewelry store in Monte Carlo a few weeks ago. Repossi's, they also have a shop right here in the Place Vendome. And the reason Diana and Dodi are stopping here in Paris instead of going straight back to London is so he can pick up an engagement ring that Diana herself had selected. One of our people followed them and confirmed it. Now the romantic Muslim intends to pick up the ring tonight and give it to Diana. What do you think of that?"

"Sounds seriously romantic, if anybody cares. Sounds like you're worried your one-time Cinderella could be preparing for another walk down the aisle. Then again it could just be an expensive gift from a rich guy trying to get her in the sack."

Archie twisted his lips in disgust at the thought.

"That's been done already, I assure you . . . we have the evidence," Archie last four words trailed off in an audibly lower tone. Then he continued:

"My man pressed the issue and saw jeweler Alberto Repossi's entry in his consignment book. It's an emerald and diamond encrusted ring recorded there as an 'engagement ring.'

"Let me spell it out in detail: Diana spotted the ring in Repossi's Monte Carlo shop. Dodi had one of his people at the Ritz contact the jeweler's Place Vendome shop to say the couple . . . and I emphasize *couple*, not just Dodi. . . was interested in a ring they'd seen. Repossi met Diana and Dodi in St. Tropez and she selected the ring herself. It was from the shop's *'Say Yes'* engagement ring collection in plain view, right in the shop's window."

"Why didn't the paparazzi jump all over this?" Bat asked the logical question.

"Because they had no idea it was going on. It was all hush-hush, the meeting with Repossi, and a clandestine rendezvous during which Diana was measured for the ring. They were told when the ring would be ready and Dodi made plans to pick it up here in Paris today," Archie told him.

"And not a hint of this was discovered by the press? Pretty good for amateurs constantly being watched," Bat's comment was more akin to thinking out loud.

"It isn't information we care to share with the press. But Diana herself almost blew it, nearly spilled the beans when she teased journalists by telling them she was planning to make an announcement that would 'give everyone a big surprise'. That caused some idle speculation, but that's all it was."

"So your informers told you all this and you knew they would be in Paris this weekend."

"Certainly, and we had plenty of time to install additional

surveillance toys at Dodi's Paris apartment and right here in the hotel." Though Archie knew Bat would be very impressed with the FOTT dots, he couldn't mention or even hint at their existence.

"We know everything that's going on, wherever they are. Our surveillance has really been kicked up an extraordinary few notches since the divorce. Excuse the vulgarity, but Diana can't even fart, and try to blame the Queen's corgis, without our knowing it."

"Archie, tell me something? Why does British intelligence, and my country's services as well, waste so much money and manpower on tracking her like some dangerous master spy? She's just another jet-set celebrity."

"Very long and complicated story. You're certainly aware your CIA and our people work hand-in-hand covering and scratching each other's back. It's a reciprocal thing."

Bat nodded. It was no secret in the intelligence community that the exchange of information between the Americans and Brits was one of the closest relationships ever among spy networks.

"But my understanding is that your country's NSA chaps have other reasons," Archie said. "Diana's outspoken campaign against landmines is a thorn in the eye to America. NSA is keen to be aware of whom she associates with in such matters. They don't very much care for influential foreigners who threaten American policy, and therefore America's national security. It's quite similar to your country's surveillance and files on John Lennon. I understand you have a rather chunky dossier on the former Beatle."

"Archie, give me a break. The FBI files on Lennon are under 300 pages, not even a quarter of what's been gathered on Diana. And Lennon was a different issue entirely. He was an outspoken critic of America's prosecution of the Vietnam War. The Nixon White House gang agreed with the FBI that, with his worldwide popularity, his antagonistic remarks could turn support at home against the war effort. . ."

"Precisely. The same way Diana's vigorous campaign against landmines could turn opinion against America's failure to renounce the use of such things. Is she not a similar threat?"

Bat considered the logic and validity of what Archie had said.

He had no viable argument.

"Touché," he replied. The point had been made.

"Now regarding Britain's concerns over Diana," Archie resumed, "I have it from good sources that everything being done to keep track of the princess is with the blessing of Buckingham Palace. The Queen most probably doesn't know the details of our, or your, country's covert work, or darker practices when necessary, but everyone in The Firm is aware of the power such institutions are capable of wielding.

"In the U.K. we have *carte blanche* to act in whatever way is considered in the best interests of state and monarchy. So it's naive for anyone to think that, from the moment she married Prince Charles, the princess would NOT have had her telephone calls bugged, or that the associations she made were not checked. We're major players in the so-called 'Establishment,' along with that undefined, invisible network of interlocking private sector social circles laboring for the great and the good continued existence of the monarchy."

"But," Bat replied, "besides the royals' safety, and matters of national security, you continue to meddle in Diana's private life as well. And somehow this trashy stuff mysteriously finds its way into the media. Sounds a bit tacky to me. Very un-typically British."

"Bat, it's a matter of routine and policy that members of government and the Royal Family are monitored. Divorce doesn't change a thing in Diana's case. Consequently, The Firm is absolutely shocked, in stunned disbelief, at the prospect of the mother of the future King of England marrying a Muslim! That's the crux of it."

"Very provincial, and somewhat racist, thinking, especially since she's now divorced from your future king. It's really none of the palace's business whom she marries. She *is* a free woman."

"Oh Bat, the anti-monarchist fervor of your Declaration of Independence still beats in your colonial chest! Of course it matters to us, whether you accept that or not. We *are* a monarchy, and it is an institution we will aggressively protect the traditions of."

"Sorry, no sale this time. It's one of the things the national psyches of our two countries do not have in common."

"No? Should I remind you how disapproving and outspoken such a large portion of Americans were when your 'American Queen,' the widowed Jacqueline Kennedy, shocked the country and married Aristotle Onassis? Despite the Greek's vast wealth, people throughout America felt the leather faced old man was beneath her, not the proper equal for *your* version of Diana, your national icon."

"Bullshit. Totally different scenario," Bat groaned. "We've gone way a field of what you were originally saying about the ring. Is there anything more?"

"Yes, as a matter of fact, there is. Apparently, Dodi may want to pop the question in private, not here at the Ritz, where we expect they'll have dinner later. If our information is correct they'll then motor over to Dodi's love nest. He keeps an apartment on Rue Arsene-Houssaye, up near the Arc de Triomphe. Even though Diana knows the ring is coming, her Egyptian lover can't resist trying to bring in an element of surprise. Romantic, isn't it."

"What's romantic?" Jennifer asked as she returned and joined them, planting a kiss on Bat's cheek. "And did I just hear something about a ring?" She asked Archie. She couldn't resist the tell-tale teasing.

"Romantic? You thought you heard me mention the 'R' word in front of Ba Lynch?" Blair decided to change the subject with humor. "Do you know what his mates in the Army called him during Desert Storm? 'Bat The Bachelor,' the bloody man doesn't have a romantic bone in his body! Never did."

"Oh, Archie Blair, you obviously don't know your old wartime buddy as well as you think you do," Jennifer smiled and snuggled up close to Bat who put his arm around her.

"You tell him, babe. These silly Limeys don't know diddly-poo about romance. It wasn't even in their language till they stole it from the French."

Archie feigned some quick footwork and threw a quick combination of punches intended to catch nothing but air. Bat and Jennifer smiled, then she added:

"Well if you two haven't caught up on all your war stories I can take our cab back to our hotel and I'll see you there when you're done. Perhaps after lunch we can go out again?" She asked Bat as she leaned up and went to kiss Bat's cheek again. Instead he deliberately turned so their lips would meet. It was more than a peck.

"No, I'm leaving too," Bat said after the display of affection, looking at her warmly.

"Archie has things he has to do." He gave Blair a smile. "Give me a call tomorrow if you're still here. Maybe we can all get together for lunch, otherwise we'll catch up with you in London." Bat extended his hand and Jennifer said "Nice meeting you."

"Delighted to have met you as well, Jennifer," Archie said as he and Bat shook hands. Then he winked at Bat and said, "Panama."

As they walked down the corridor heading for the front entrance Jennifer asked him.

"What was that 'Panama' thing? One of your military codes?"

"No. It's a Palindrome. Like Madam, I'm Adam." The doorman signaled and their taxi quickly pulled up.

"I have no idea what you're talking about," she said.

"You've a writer and you never heard Palindromes?" Bat teased.

"No, sorry. I led a sheltered childhood. Until I was married, I thought condoms were those multi-family buildings people lived in," she laughed.

"C'mon, you joker, I saw that same Stallone movie," Bat chided.

"Tell me what a Palindrome is," Jennifer demanded.

"Okay. It's a word, phrase, verse, or sentence that reads the same way backward or forward. It works if you just move the spaces and lose the commas: *A man, a plan, a canal, Panama*." He uneasily recalled Bruce Willow saying it in the car in Belize

They got into the cab and Bat simply mentioned the name of their hotel to the driver.

"Wait a minute," Jennifer fumbled in her purse for a pad and pen. "Oh, sorry, I mean him, not you driver. Go on, Bat."

"In Desert Storm a lot of grunts cut it down to 'Panama' to

indicate they liked or agreed with a plan. Archie was being cute, he was agreeing we'll try to touch base in London."

"Okay. Say it again, but slowly, darling. Just a minute I'm writing this down. Marshall and Blake will love it. I'm ready, go ahead. . .A man. . . a plan. . .a. . ."

****

On Wednesday, August 27, as Diana and Dodi were frolicking in the Mediterranean aboard the *Jonikal*, Edward Williams an area resident, went to the Mountain Ash police station in South Wales just after 2 PM to report a disturbing a premonition he had about the Princess of Wales.

Police in the U.K., and everywhere for that matter, were accustomed to people coming in to report incidents of crop circles, UFO sightings, or alien encounters. Such things went with the job.

On the other hand, premonitions or dreams about assassinations, physical harm or great danger to public officials were looked at differently in the event that what was being reported was actually a veiled or unconscious threat from the person dispensing such information.

However, Williams demeanor, and past predictions, put him in a different class than people reporting the usual fantasies. So much so that the interviewing officer filed an 'incident' report that was duly forwarded to Special Branch officers. That report appears in the department's permanent police blotter and reads, verbatim:

> *"On the 27th August at 14:12 hrs, a man by the name of Edward Williams came to Mountain Ash police station. He said he was a psychic and predicted that Princess Diana was going to die.*
>
> *In previous years he has predicted that the Pope and Ronald Reagan were going to be the victims of assassination attempts. On both occasions he was proved to be correct.*
>
> *Mr. Williams appeared to be quite normal.*

Diana herself would have been concerned had she been aware of the dire prediction by Edward Williams. The Princess of Wales had a fascination with the occult and paranormal and had patronized various psychics, astrologers, and fortune tellers since her teens, among them, Penny Thornton, introduced to Diana in 1986 by her sister-in-law, Sarah Ferguson.

Though Thornton was the princesses' personal astrologer for 6 years, Diana also consulted with astrologer Betty Palco for several years into the early 1990s and was replaced by astrologer Debbie Frank. Diana's astrological charts were replete with concerns about untrustworthy people around her, lies, and her husband's adultery.

There was also Simone Simmons, a psychic healer and one of Princess Diana's closest friends and confidantes, psychic Rita Rogers, and another healer, Oonagh Shanley-Toffolo, an Irish nurse who was also an acupuncturist and treated both Diana and Prince William.

The Princess of Wales believed her deceased paternal grandmother, Countess Spencer, watched over her from beyond the grave. The late Countess had been a lady-in-waiting to Elizabeth, the Queen Mother, and Diana believed it was this ghostly influence that often helped her survive life as a member of the Royal Family. She called her "my protector."

Diana was receptive and curious about the whole gamut of so-called 'New Age' beliefs. She believed in the special powers emitted by crystals and often wore one. She dabbled with feng shui and t'ai chi.

In that spring and early summer of 1997, her curiosity about the much-publicized 'Bible Code' found her reading as much information on the phenomenon as she could.

The Bible Code, written by former Wall Street Journal reporter Michael Drosnin, was published in May, 1997. Diana, like millions of other people, was fascinated and initially impressed by the published examples of alleged predictions about historical events. According to the book's premise, when God provided the first five books of the Old Testament, it included prophecies in a skip code, i.e.: every fifth letter in a sentence formed a word.

True believers and Drosnin supporters claimed 'no other book contains these codes" and the inclusion of these messages in the

Bible was unique.

Critics, who from the outset reasoned that, with mathematics being what they are, codes could be found everywhere, in just about anything ever written.

But Drosnin rejected such conjecture and in the June 9, 1997, edition of *Newsweek* is quoted saying: "When my critics find a message about the assassination of a prime minister encrypted in *Moby Dick*, I'll believe them."

So, using computers the critics accepted the challenge, much to Drosnin and Princess Diana's chagrin.

Not only did the skeptics find astonishing 'coded messages' in *Moby Dick*, they repeated the feat by listing messages, and where to find them, in *War and Peace*! Mathematicians explain that such 'codes' are the result of random selection when millions of letters in a text are examined in crossword fashion. It is simply the law of probability.

In *Moby Dick,* the naysayers proved one could find 'codes' predicting famous assassinations. For instance, Soviet leader Leon Trotsky was murdered with an ice pick. The *Moby Dick* code reads: "ice, hammer, executed, the steel head of the lance." Martin Luther King's death code reads "to be killed by them, prepare for death, gun, agents deed." Even the assassination of John F. Kennedy can be found noting, "Kennedy was shot in the head by rifle."

Diana's bubble was burst and her faith in the Bible Code was shattered. She would do no reading about the discredited Bible Code while lounging on the deck of the *Jonikal.*

Yet, just as the Princess of Wales would have been concerned if she had been aware of Edward Williams prediction about her death to the Mountain Ash police, she would probably have been in stunned disbelief hardly a few months later when one of the most complex matrix crossword 'codes' predicting a future event was discovered in the pages of Moby Dick: "Lady... Diana... royal... Dodi...Henri Paul... mortal in these jaws of death."

****

Archie Blair was in his hotel room, legs crossed, comfortably propped up on his bed while working on his laptop. He was keystroking in the surveillance team's daily update when the envelope was delivered by the bellhop. It had arrived at the Ritz by courier hardly two minutes earlier.

As the senior London agent on site, such reports were his responsibility. The SIS resident agent in Paris would also file a daily report. According to protocol, the two were not expected to compare notes. It was a regulation rarely followed.

Megan Price, meanwhile, was under no such obligation to file daily reports to Sir Warren about activities, status or progress of the K Team rogue agents she was advising on this mission. As was always the case in such instances nothing would be put to paper until the mission was concluded and she had returned to London. Compiling a paper trail for a rogue operation in progress was not a good idea.

Instead of returning to the bed, Archie chose instead to sit in the uncomfortable looking Louis XVIII straight back chair in front of the writing table. Upon opening the courier envelope he recognized the large white linen envelope Sir Warren always used.

Inside was a copy of the same medical document that Megan had received suggesting Princess Diana was pregnant with a child fathered by Dodi Fayed. A yellow Post-It note with a handwritten "Call me" was attached to the document. There was nothing else in the package. Archie read the short document twice more and spent a few minutes in thought before placing the call.

Sir Warren picked up the phone before the second ring. He was expecting the call.

"Hello, Wormsley residence," he answered in what he thought was a proper sounding butler's voice just in case the call was from someone other than Archie.

"Sir Warren, is that you?" Blair asked.

"Yes. . .damn it," he replied, mildly frustrated. He had thought the affected accent had been rather good.

"Archie, here, Sir Warren. I've just received the document. . .and I'm calling as instructed.

"Good. Very prompt. Thank you, Archie. I trust you've read it and understand the implications?"

"Well, sir, I've read it. And as for any implications they're quite obvious . . . if indeed this report is authentic."

"What do you mean, *if it's authentic*? Of course it is. We spared no expense or danger getting our hands on it when we became aware it existed." Sir Warren hadn't expected a questioning reaction from Blair.

"I'm sure, Sir Warren, but the ambiguity of it all: no patient name, an unreadable examining physician's scribbled name, and handwritten initials at the bottom that conveniently point to. . .a particular pair of individuals we have an interest in. It's all really rather vague if you consider it." Archie paused for a breath and added "Actually, I have some blokes who could whip up something like this in no time at all. . ."

"Preposterous! I'm surprised at you, Blair. You know my strict penchant for the truth. I wouldn't pass something like this along to you unless I was absolutely satisfied and convinced it was genuine. There's too much at stake, and too much previous evidence to dismiss this report as bogus."

Sir Warren paused and waited for a response from Archie, but none came, so he continued.

"Evidence, I might add, which you yourself helped compile over these last several years. You know very well what's been going on. Why are you suddenly getting cold feet?" Sir Warren demanded.

"It's not 'cold feet' or anything like that. I thought you knew me better." Archie said somewhat annoyed, which surprised the older man.

"I have no doubt you forwarded this to me in good faith because you are convinced it is authentic," Archie lied. He knew too much about Sir Warren's methods and ways to just blindly take anything the man said as gospel. With Sir Warren one always had to consider the possibility of an ulterior motive.

"Well, that's good. That's more like it. Get these questioning fantasies out of your head. I sent this to you because it appears the time has come to take matters into our own hands, in a most grievous way. Something needs to be done. We need to discuss the matter and come up with a plan."

Sir Warren was preparing to drop the proverbial other shoe, and Archie knew it. If the document was authentic then it represented the great fear that Sir Warren had often voiced to The Committee as well as to Archie, Megan, and a handful of trusted MI-5 and MI-6 agents: the fear that the Princess of Wales would become pregnant and beget a bastard sibling to Prince William, the future king. But this scenario, on the paper Archie had just read, was the worst possible ending since the alleged father was a foreigner. More than that, he was a non-Christian.

"So what I'd like you to do is have your chaps cease their efforts in Paris immediately and return to London, now, this afternoon. We'll talk in the morning and we can set up a meeting to give this more thought. I'll collect The Committee, and I'd like you to join us in this process," Sir Warren said in somber tones.

"I'm flattered that you would want my observations and input presented to The Committee," Archie truly was. "But. . ."

Sir Warren cut in: "You can all be back in time for dinner if you hop to it and pack up now. I'll leave it to your wonderfully devious mind to fabricate some believable excuse."

"But, Sir Warren," Archie offered, "The decision to call off all activity here and recall the team to London is not mine to make. Dickie Crawford is senior man in Paris, and, as such, he runs the show."

"What?" Sir Warren was taken aback. Under certain circumstances, an old SIS order put London agents under the control of the resident agent when they were traveling on assignment outside the U.K. had been initiated shortly after Sir Warren retired, and never previously been an issue. He had forgotten about it. This Paris assignment fell into the 'certain circumstances' category.

Sir Warren had just been informed that the princess and Dodi were at this moment flying towards France from their Mediterranean holiday. His motive to get the regular SIS surveillance called off was to avoid the possibility of any of the regulars getting in the way or coming across Megan's foreign rogues this night. Based on his most recent update from Smythe-Pembrooke, Sir Warren felt certain

Megan's team would carry out their mission sometime today.

"Actually, I was working on the daily report when this document arrived. You realize that I'll have to include it in the report. But how do I say I got it?"

"The usual, a source you cultivated, an informer, someone who's name you need to keep confidential. That always works. No one will question it. . .Now about getting you and your fellows back here. . ."

"I'm sorry, sir," Archie interrupted. "That's just not going to be possible. The meeting will just have to wait till I return, perhaps later in the day tomorrow."

****

The hour had arrived for Diana and Dodi to end their Mediterranean cruise. On the *Jonikal* the couple had adjoining, but separate, cabins. Dressing for their departure to Paris, Diana choose a black blouse under a comfortable and casual beige suit.

As Princess Diana climbed into the *Jonikal's* tender for the short trip to shore, she had no idea her movements were being so widely noted. Within moments of the tender pushing off and getting underway, the ship's bridge radioed that information to the communication base at Fayed's St. Tropez villa Castel Ste-Thérèse. According to standard procedures, the villa forwarded the information to Harrods security operations base in London and simultaneously to the Ritz Hotel in Paris, to alert the latter of an impending arrival. Shortly after 2:30 PM, two vehicles left the Ritz to meet the Gulfstream when it arrived. Henri Paul, driving one of them, noticed that the Range Rover he was driving was being followed by photographers.

Fayed's intricate web of security called for precise and prompt information about the whereabouts of all family members when they were traveling.

But MI-6, and the resourceful media hounding Diana and Dodi, knew this as well and regularly monitored all such transmissions. Sir Warren, in turn, routinely monitored MI-5 and MI-6. Thus he was aware the couple would very shortly be flying to

Paris even before Archie and the regular surveillance team heard the news from their informer on the hotel's security staff. Finally, Megan and her K Team rogues would learn that Dodi and Diana were headed for Paris from the same informer, who secretly worked for both sides.

Once on land, the couple went to the Olbia-Costa Smerelda Airport, Italy, where they boarded the Harrods private Gulfstream IV jet near lunchtime.

The distinctive exterior of the plane is painted in the green and gold colors of Fayed's London department store. The sumptuous interior carpet, walls and seats display pleasant beige, rose and pale aqua Egyptian themes accented by a touch of brown marble trim.

The cabin is separated into two sections. The private front half, where Diana and Dodi were, offers a half dozen wide and luxurious armchairs separated by marble end tables. Both Dodi's bodyguard and butler, Trevor Rees-Jones, and Rene Delorm, at first occupied the rear portion of the cabin with regular size seats, traditionally for personal staff. However, the decorating theme from the front is nicely carried through. At some point, the butler was invited to join the couple in the forward compartment.

Even before the jet completed taxiing down the runway the paparazzi were hustling and frantically arranging for their own passage to Paris.

Moments after the Air Harrods Gulfstream was airborne a flight attendant, one of Harrods 8,000 employees, served refreshments and made the usual offering of magazines. The parent company has more than 20 separate locations within UK, which besides the main store, include other retail outlets, warehouses, distribution centers and administration offices, and a fleet of aircraft.

Contrary to widely held public opinion, the private jets Dodi and Diana seemed to be constantly flying around in this summer were not simply the ostentatious toys of the idle rich. They were part of the business.

Disillusioned by the service being provided for his own aircraft, in 1995 Mohamed Fayed's Harrods Holdings, Ltd. purchased Hunting Business Aviation along with facilities and services as part of his flagship business. Besides various private charter jets, Air Harrods also operates a fleet of helicopters available for corporate travel needs, celebrities and others who want and can afford private air transportation. All aircraft are recognizable by the green and gold colors associated with the Harrods name. British Prime Minister Tony Blair has traveled aboard Air Harrods.

Despite the enjoyable past week's activities, Diana had missed her sons and had spoken of them on the *Jonikal* several times. Her eldest, Prince William, had been christened William Arthur Philip Louis Windsor, with water from the River Jordan, on August 4, 1982, the Queen Mother's 82nd birthday. Now a bright and sensitive 14 year old, he and his mother shared a relationship much closer than the typical parent and teenager and more akin to siblings. She shared personal moments, private things and secrets with him much in the same way sisters growing up do. It was a bonding she had not had the luxury of with her older sisters, Sarah and Jane.

As soon as she felt the boy was at an age where he would understand and appreciate the complexity of life and their privileged position, Diana took William on visits to meet homeless people and to hospitals, exposing him to those who were dying. She wanted to make him aware of others' suffering. As her younger son Harry matured, he would be exposed to the same realities of life.

"I want William and Harry to experience what most people already know: that they are growing up in a multi-racial society in which everyone is not rich, or has four holidays a year, or speaks standard English and drives a Range Rover."

As the jet climbed into the afternoon sun Diana commented, "Oh, I'm so excited to see my two boys!" And while the jet winged its way to France, a relative of Dodi's told a London-based Arabic newspaper that "Dodi said that they were deeply in love and that the relationship was serious and they have decided to get married."

At 3:15 PM on Saturday, the private jet touched down at Le Bourget Airfield, some 10 miles north of Paris. And the press were there to greet it, just as the press and 150,000 wildly cheering people had been 70 years earlier when pilot Charles A. Lindbergh landed *The Spirit of St. Louis* there. But the non-media greeters for Diana and Dodi's arrival had come in just two vehicles.

Once the luggage was stowed in the dark green Range Rover, the car Dodi usually used in Paris and often described as black, the couple drove off in the larger Mercedes S-600 with Philippe Dourneau, Dodi's regular driver at the wheel. Henri Paul, assistant security director at the Ritz, fell in line driving the Range Rover. The two-car convoy grew larger as paparazzi in cars and motorcycles joined them heading for Paris.

Even though any efforts to snap photos of the couple on the road would be foiled by this Mercedes' dark tinted windows, the vehicle was nonetheless harrassed. Along the way, one of the press vehicles attempted to dangerously cut ahead of them to slow the Mercedes down.

As the ride from the airport was nearing its end, Dodi's butler Rene, riding in the Range Rover driven by Henri Paul, was dropped off at the Rue Arsene-Houssaye apartment with the luggage. Rene had called the Ritz from the *Jonikal* to request flowers and caviar and other items Dodi wanted there. The delivery from the hotel was waiting in the foyer. Paul drove the Range Rover back to the hotel.

According to Dodi's plan, the Mercedes continued on to the Villa Windsor in the Bois de Boulogne, west of Paris. The millionaire playboy proudly gave Diana a half-hour guided tour of the house and property before resuming their trip to the Ritz.

When driver Philippe Dourneau turned the Mercedes S-600 into Place Vendome and prepared to pull up in front of the hotel's main entrance, upwards of 20 paparazzi began rushing the car. He immediately accelerated and drove to the Rue Cambon entrance where he deposited his high profile passengers.

"That's an unexpected move," Megan said as she received the phone message from the paparazzi plant following the car on a motorcycle. Hardly a minute later the hotel's closed circuit video system her rogues had tapped into captured Diana, Dodi, and the bodyguard entering the Rue Cambon entrance.

"Call me if anything else unusual happens," she said to the agent monitoring the electronics in the hotel room. As she moved through the hotel Megan called Ali, the leader of the K Team.

"We need to bring all the drivers together now. There could be a hitch, something not considered, in the plan."

"Yes, I know. We watched the car come and go. They must have gone in the back way," he replied while his confederate continued peeking out of the 'closed for renovations' shop window.

Within a few minutes after Megan entered the shop, five of the eight drivers had assembled as instructed and Ali had the other three members of the team on a conference call setup so they could hear what changes would be incorporated into the previously rehearsed plan.

On Friday Ali had followed Megan's recommendation and put all of the chase car drivers through dry runs three times: the first run was in the morning, second was mid-day when the sun was brightest, and the third time was after dark. A final rehearsal run had even been done, this just before noon today. In all instances the two rogues who had strategically placed the mirror at the far end of the tunnel were in place. The entire event was done with open phone lines to Ali and Megan coordinating it all from the shop.

Now, Megan explained, it was possible that the principals could exit the hotel from the same Rue Cambon entrance they just arrived at. She recommended, and Ali agreed, that the three motorcycles had to be positioned near the back of the hotel. If the principals did what they were expected to do, and what the K Team had practiced for, and departed from the front via Place Vendome, the cyclists would have to play catch up with the five cars chasing the Mercedes from the hotel's front.

The only grumbling came from the two rogues in the truck at the other end of the tunnel. Ali told them they would remain in place from now through the conclusion of the mission sometime this evening. He asked Megan if she could bring some food and bottles of water to them. She agreed, since it wasn't likely the principals would be turning around and leaving the hotel immediately.

****

After seeing Archie at the Ritz, Bat and Jennifer continued their city tour of Paris with visits to the Eiffel Tower, where they had a brief lunch, Napoleon's tomb, Notre Dame Cathedral, and Sacre Coeur. It had been a full first day by the time they returned to their hotel.

Bat was casually perusing items in the Plaza Athénée's gift shop while Jennifer was taking a shower in their suite. His attention had been drawn to a child's single-seat pedal car painted in the hotel's signature 'Plaza red' and emblazoned with the Plaza Athénée logo across the hood. It resembled a Grand Priz Formula One racer from the 1950s with classic chrome wire wheels, narrow slick tires and spinner knock-off hub caps, grill and steering wheel. The interior was done in rich black leather. Almost too fine a 'toy' to let a child bump into things with, the pedal car had a price tag was $955.

For the hotel's guests, the gap was closing, Bat thought, between *'the difference between big boys and little boys is the price of their toys.'* This extravagant child's play thing cost more than the first <u>real</u> car Bat had out of high school.

"Excuse me. I knew I was right! I saw your wife at The Ritz and thought I recognized her, but wasn't one hundred present positive. Now I come across you. Small world."

Bat looks at the man but recognition fails him. "Do I know you?" Before the man could answer Bat adds, she's not my wife…yet. But I'm working on it."

"Well, it seems to be taking you long enough, all these years. I'm Mario LaRocca, remember?

Bat shrugs and gives the man a very confused look. "I'm sorry, I'm drawing a complete blank. Perhaps you have me confused with someone else? You look vaguely familiar but I don't recall ever meeting you."

"Sure you have. Tony LaRocca? The photographer who's head you damn near bit off on Nevis after your future wife saved that boy's life on the beach? Remember? I was in that pack chasing the royals with my camera?

"Oh, my goodness," Bat made the connection. He recalled the incident but couldn't picture what the photographer looked like, or his name. Nonetheless he replied affirmatively.

"Yes, I do remember you." He gave the man a quick up and down glance, "But several pounds thinner. You must be living the good life."

The man patted his stomach. "Yes, I've added a few. I was running around like a roach in heat back then but now I'm the magazine's photo editor and I have several minions doing the running around and leg work. I just direct the show."

Bat smiled and was about to make a graceful exit when he realized something the man said didn't add up. "You saw the woman who I was with on Nevis at the Ritz?"

"Yeah. Actually I was in front of the hotel and she was passing in a car. But she had to stop because a pair of limos was blocking the way. She's hard to forget, don't you think?

"When did you see her?"

"This morning, before Diana and Dodi breezed in, but she didn't see me. I was scouting the place with my photographers, looking for good vantage points to shoot from, inside and outside. Your lady was wearing a black wig, covering that beautiful red hair. But it was her, I'm sure." LaRocca changed the subject. "Are you two staying here, or there?"

"We're staying here. I mean me and the woman I'm *with*, which is not the one from Nevis." Bat furrowed his brow in mild confusion.

"But what you're saying is wrong. It's not possible. The woman I was with on Nevis is away on . . . a business trip in America," he lied.

A sly lecherous grin creased LaRocca's face. "C'mon, you don't have to play coy with me. You like living dangerously, don't you? Got one honey bunked out here and another one over at the Ritz. A pair of hotel bills like that should put a dent in your wallet."

Bat ignored the remark. "Are you certain you saw her, Megan, the one from Nevis, at the Ritz? Couldn't it just be somebody who looked a lot like her? After all, it's been. . ." Bat did some quick math, ". . .five years."

"Absolutely certain. It's my job to remember faces. I've seen her every day for the last few years."

"What???" Bat was taken aback.

"Oh, not in person. I got two shots of her on Nevis. The first, a full figured, and I *DO* mean full, as she was sprinting into the water like a gazelle, her hair aflame and blowing in the breeze behind her, and the second one on the blanket, ministering to that kid. That was her, no doubt in my mind. Great motion shot, that running one. Reminds me of a similar shot I took of Bo Derek when they were making the movie '10.' I have both your Megan and Bo tacked on the wall outside my dark room."

LaRocca continued talking but Bat wasn't listening. Megan Price here in Paris? What a coincidence. Bat nods at the photographer, pumps his hand with a *nice seeing you again* and heads for the elevator.

Jennifer was just getting out of the shower when he entered the room. He walked across the carpet and planted a tender kiss on her cheek.

"Hi, honey," she smiled.

"And a big *hi honey* back to you!" He paused, and she could tell something was distracting him.

"Something's up. . . you seem deep in thought, miles away. What's on your mind?"

"Oh, I just ran into a photographer I met briefly in the Caribbean a few years ago and he insists one of the British agents who was also there at the time is here, now, wearing a wig."

"So what's so strange about that?" Jennifer turned and moved over to the dressing table. She lifted a leg onto the overstuffed bench and began vigorously drying the limb.

"England is just across the Channel. The British and French visit each other's countries all the time. For them it's like a commute. And correct me if I'm wrong, but aren't wigs part of the disguises you and your former chums liked to play dress up in?"

"Of course, I understand that. But back then this agent, Megan Price, was eavesdropping on the Princess of Wales, whom she apparently didn't think much of. And here it is years later and Megan is in the same place as Diana again. And seen around the same hotel. Just seems funny, odd. All this time passes and British

Intelligence is still wasting a field agent on simple surveillance?"

"Perhaps *your lady friend* agent is providing security for the princess?"

Bat ignored the teasing 'lady friend' crack.

"Not likely. Since the divorce Diana isn't entitled to government protection any more. And besides, from what I've heard about Megan Price, she has a short fuse. If somebody with an Irish surname ticks her off, they could be very dead, very quick. Not the type you would want as a discreet bodyguard." Bat decided not to mention the wig would be to cover Megan's obvious red hair.

"Well, that settles it. The Princess of Wales is safe, she's not Irish." Jennifer half turned and faced him.

"But *YOU*, Bartholomew Lynch," she was shaking a finger at him mockingly, ". . .with a name like that, you'd better stay away from her. And for other reasons too!" She turned back facing the mirror.

Bat gave her a weak smile, dropped into a chair. In the mirror, she noticed he immediately began rubbing his leg.

"Are you in pain?"

"A little. Actually it's more of an uncomfortable tingling, itching sensation."

"Why don't you go out and walk around the neighborhood. Give your leg a good stretch? It's going to be at least another forty-five minutes before I'm ready for dinner."

Bat thought about it as he kept rubbing. "Only forty-five minutes? That'll be a first."

"Watch it, mister, I can hurl a hair brush pretty good from this distance."

"You know something? That's a good idea . . I mean, the walk to loosen up the leg, not the hair brush. Even a slow walk should get the circulation going and make this go away. I don't want to feel this way all through dinner."

"Then be gone already. Go, and do it. But, Mister, you can't leave this room without giving me a big hug and kiss. And later tonight maybe I can give you some tingle feelings in places other than your leg."

He glanced at the mirror and their eyes locked. He wondered if she could see all the love in his eyes that he saw in hers. They both puckered up at the same time and sent silent kisses across the room, then smiled broadly.

"That's fine, both of your ideas work for me, especially that last one about the tingles later," Bat said, as he lifted himself from the overstuffed chair. "But for now, I'm on my way."

While he waited in the corridor for the elevator, Bat's suspicious mind kept returning to the coincidence of Megan and Diana both being at The Ritz . . . and Megan wearing a wig. He recalled Archie Blair said she often wore a wig to cover her red hair on a mission. The elevator came and he got on. Once at lobby level, he exited the property and only paused when he was on the street. He continued to replay the things Archie said about Megan and how he had described her as *'Almost a sociopath. . . Positively deadly.'*

Bat had a funny feeling something was odd about the whole thing, that he was missing something. He shook his head as if to clear it. Just another coincidence, he thought.

'In our business, there are no coincidences.' It was like a flashbulb exploding in his head as he recalled Megan's off-hand quip in the Diana file at Langley.

No coincidences? Then what is she doing here when she is supposed to be somewhere else? The feeling that something was amuck was too strong to ignore.

"Taxi!" he yelled, followed by his best two-finger New York whistle. A somewhat startled cab driver sitting at the curb less than twenty feet away rolled the vehicle up to the curb in front of him.

"Take me to The Ritz," then added, "15 Place Vendome."

The cab driver rolled his eyes. *Americans: why do think they need to mention addresses of well-known places in Paris?* He wondered sarcastically.

During the trip, Bat changed his mind and instead told the driver to pull around the back to the hotel's Rue Cambon entrance.

As he hoped he would, he found Archie in the Hemingway Bar, propped up on a stool, looking bored and casually nursing a Perrier. The place was about half full, with people crowded at the establishment's small tables.

"Blair, do you ever drink *real* booze in saloons, or just that French pussy water?" Bat had come up behind him and uttered the remark in a low voice.

"Hello Bat, didn't expect to see you again so soon." Archie half-turned to face him and they shook hands. Bat got the feeling that the bubbly mood Archie had been in earlier had drained away. His British friend seemed somewhat sullen.

"I'd say pull up a stool, but as you can see they're all full. And the answer is 'no,' I never drink when working, not even during my break or on down time." Then leaning closer and in a conspiratorial voice added, "Furthermore, do you have any idea what they get for a drink in this place? Even a bottle of water costs a bloody fortune!"

"So why are you sitting here? Go somewhere else if you're on a break."

"Force of habit. I like to stay in the same building where I'm sleeping." Archie said dryly. "You want to go to a table? There's a few open, over there." He pointed to a corner across the small room.

"Hell, no. If we do that then for sure one of these eager beaver waiters will expect me to buy something. On my income that's out of the question. But if you feel like stretching your feet, let's walk a bit."

Archie shrugged, "Sure." He raised his glass and emptied it in two short gulps and lifted the bottle and perused its contents. "Hardly a mouth full left anyway. . . Let's go."

They left the bar and began slowly walking around in the public areas of the main floor.

"Archie, I came back to mention something I find odd, then I have to go or Jennifer will have my head."

"And what would that be?" Archie asked with a slight hint of surprise.

"Megan Price. I just bumped into a photographer at my hotel. We met during that Nevis trip about five years ago. This guy insists he saw Megan cruising past The Ritz, but her hair was dark.

Remember what you said about her and wig?. Also, you said she was off on some mission in the Middle East or something."

"And so she is. Your photographer friend is mistaken. If you must know, she's in Egypt to be precise. Something to do with the Jews and a Mossad mole, I believe. But that's hush-hush, you understand. I never told you that." The mention of Megan seemed to snap Archie a bit out of his melancholy.

"This guy was pretty certain. He has a photographs of her. He knows what she looks like."

"Photos? Taken today? Preposterous! I'd certainly like to see *those* photos"

"No, not today. I didn't mean today, on the beach in Nevis. The point is he knows what she looks like. Apparently he was smitten by her and hung one of the photos on his wall."

"Poor man. He's having a fantasy. Looking at a five year old picture and then believing he is seeing the woman of his dirty dreams here, in Paris."

"But Archie, it just struck me as odd that this is the hotel the princess is staying at, and you're here, and then I'm told Megan Price is here, too."

"I never said she was staying here. They'll probably stay at Dodi's apartment up near the Arc de Triomphe. But they're here already, arrived only minutes ago. They'll relax, stay for dinner, perhaps. He always, always does. He brings his lady friends here. After all, this is his daddy's hotel and, like his father, Dodi is an ostentatious show-off."

"That's neither here nor there," Bat said in mild frustration. "This is Paris, Archie. The princess is here, you're here, and so is Megan, the dangerous agent that you once told me was a 'loose cannon' no longer sent on overseas missions unless a subject is to be terminated."

"Bat, please believe me, I can absolutely, positively tell you without hesitation or reservation that Megan Price, wig or no wig, is not here. She is not part of my team. We have no orders or plans to harm or murder Fayed, or anybody. You have my word. The photographer is wrong. Megan is not here."

Bat looked deep into his eyes and was relieved to feel Archie was sincere and, indeed, telling the truth. He let out a sigh.

"I'm sorry. I guess I've spent too much time looking over my shoulder and reading various foreign personnel profiles over the last several years. Then going over the Diana file on this last trip in Langley. Everything. For some reason, tonight the pieces just seemed to be adding up to something sinister."

"Personnel profiles you say? What personnel?"

"Our people in the CIA, NSA and FBI who keep tabs on the royals as well as your MI-5 and MI-6 spies."

"Bartholomew Lynch, I'm offended. The Crown would be offended. All the people in my country would be offended to know the sister intelligence agencies of our American ally were spying on us!" The comment was facetious and lighthearted.

"Right," Bat chuckled. "As if you chums at SIS don't do the same thing to us."

Archie smiled. "Well, be a good boy, will you? Next time you have a chance to get into these files make sure the description of me includes references such as 'dashing, handsome, well bred, single and available. If not, then please make the appropriate editorial changes."

Bat nodded. Archie knew neither Bat, nor anyone else, could change a single word in any files without several layers of approval. They continued slowly walking through the corridors.

"I have to agree with Jennifer. This place is magnificent," Bat said appreciatively.

"It is. But the Plaza Athénée isn't exactly shabby or advertising Holiday Inn prices either," Archie reminded him.

"Oh, don't take me wrong. I like where we're staying. It's cozy and intimate. But this place is dripping with opulence. It's like a movie set. And, after all, it is The Ritz."

"Frankly, I've heard from people who know such things that it's dropped a peg since the Arab bought it. Just like our Dorchester in London. They'll never be the same. And, by the way, I think your hotel is owned by the same owners as Dorchester."

"Well, that's what happens when a few people living in the

right place become billionaires from the oil under their sand. They buy up things they like."

"Yes, but this Arab didn't just make his money in oil. He's Mohamed Al-Fayed a businessman with myriad interests. He also owns Harrods department store in London, an airline, and God knows what else. He's what you Yanks would call 'filthy rich.'"

"I don't want to split hairs, Archie, but Fayed is an Egyptian. They don't like being called Arabs. . ."

"Arabs, Egyptians, they're all the same to me. He's Third World *nouveau riche*," Archie paused and quickly added "Thick wallet, no class. And all the money in the world can't buy social acceptance. You are what you are."

"I'm surprised to hear such opinions from you, Archie. I never realized you were such a snob."

Archie stopped in his tracks and faced Bat. "Snob? Is that what you think? I've always considered myself a monarchist, the same as most right-minded people in my country. We're not snobs.

"Is it being a snob to be repulsed by the thought of a future king of England having Arab, or pardon me, Egyptian half brothers or sisters?" He turned and resumed walking again. Bat joined him. They were entering the Ritz' fabled Hallway of Temptation, an attractive long corridor lined with glass display cases holding various luxury goods and *objects d'art* for sale.

"What the hell are you talking about? What future king? What brothers and sisters?"

Archie stopped again and looked directly into Bat's eyes.

"You haven't a clue, do you? You have no idea what I'm talking about."

"No, I don't. You mentioned the engagement ring earlier. But Diana could just be going through the motions to piss off the Royal Family. To put a burr under their saddle and watch them squirm a bit. Do you know how many engagements are broken each year?" Bat paused, then added. "But enough of that. This conversation is way off track. I told you what I came back to say, and now I have to go back and get ready for dinner. . ."

"Before you leave, let me tell you why I was sitting in the

Hemingway Bar alone. I was thinking of how to finish writing up the report I have to file tonight without giving Her Majesty a royal heart attack."

"You're writing a report for the Queen?"

"Of course not. But don't think for a moment she isn't made aware of significant things SIS collects. And I'd say events I've become aware, suggest today is quickly becoming very significant."

"Doesn't she know about the engagement?"

"I suspect she, and the rest of The Firm, is aware of the rumors. The events of the last hour, however, seem to confirm what the tabloids have been saying. And, as you said, up till now they most likely figured Diana is just doing it to turn the screws to them. If that was the extent of it, the royal displeasure could be cured with a large glass of bicarbonate."

"So? I'm still lost. I don't understand the point." Now Bat stopped walking and turned to Archie.

Archie didn't look directly at him, instead he seemed to be looking off in the distance and his eyes had a glazed, far away look.

"After he gives her the ring they'll announce the engagement on the morrow." Archie now focused his eyes directly on Bat.

"So you seem to think." Bat challenged. But maybe she'll get cold feet and realize taking a step like that would really be going too far. The woman can always say 'no.' It's a feminine prerogative, you know."

Archie's face was emotionless and his speech was flat.

"Pregnant women rarely say no when the father of their expected child pops the question."

Bat was totally stunned and looked at his friend in disbelief.

"The princess is pregnant? How could you possibly know something *that* intimate?"

"Oh, please, Bat. You were in the business. Do I have to spell it out for you. We even know she farted near the Queen once and blamed it on the Corgi's. We've been keeping tabs on her since she tried to kill herself, well before that Nevis trip when we met. And, incidentally, we have people close to her whom she trusts fully."

"Did you just hear about this? You didn't seem this

400

distraught when we spoke earlier."

"Yes, as a matter of fact. I received a document some time after you left here this morning. If it's true, it is a catastrophe. Of course, it could just be some malicious propaganda to stir the pot, but I'm obliged to include it in my report. My superiors believe it is authentic. So you'll understand why I'm not quite myself at the moment. This is absolutely the worst case scenario. Absolute worst. Now she is going to marry that Muslim. Getting pregnant was something we've always known was possible, with all her sleeping around, but with. . .an Arab? God Almighty, what will this do to the Monarchy? To poor Prince William?"

"Well it sounds more like a perceived social crisis than a political one," Bat commented.

"Oh, Bat. Come, come. You're really missing the point . . ."

"Not from what you've just said," Bat interrupted, "Could Megan be here to take out Dodi Fayed before he pops the question to Diana?"

"Bat that's outrageous! You watch too many James Bond movies, really. There is no such thing as a 'license to kill,' anymore. We don't have 007 numbers in MI-6, and we really wouldn't consider the hop from London to Paris as an 'overseas mission.' "

Bat thought for a moment. "I guess I'm a victim of my own cloak and dagger life. I sometimes feel I live and breathe intrigue."

Both laughed. Bat felt Archie was now working overtime trying to seem nonchalant and casual despite the obvious shock he couldn't hide earlier over the news that Diana was pregnant. It was time to go.

He shook Archie's hand, saying "If I don't get back right now and take Jennifer to dinner she'll think I've met and run off with. . ." he caught himself before blurting out *Megan*, "...some French floozy."

They had circled around the hotel main floor and were now back where they had started near the Rue Cambon entrance and the Hemingway Bar.

"Any place in particular?" Archie called as Bat approached the door."

"No, we were just going to stroll the Champs Elysées and pick the first romantic looking restaurant or bistro that catches our eye." Bat paused, expecting a suggestion.

"This is Paris, Bat. They're all romantic! So why not just come back here? The food and service are superb. And dinner at the Ritz is an experience everyone should enjoy at least once in their life."

"Pricy, I would expect?" Bat asked.

"Not for a successful author and her consort. You really should do it."

"Actually, dinner tonight will be coming out of my wallet, for a very special reason," Bat winked. "But okay, I'll mention it to her. . . .Take care," he smiled and waved as he went out the door.

****

The engagement ring Diana and Dodi had selected in Monaco, and for which she had been fitted by the jeweler Repossi himself, was supposed to be delivered to the Ritz this evening. But Dodi couldn't contain his anticipation and he elected to pick it up personally while Diana was busy at the beauty salon in the Ritz.

Shortly before 6 PM, Dodi asked Claude Roulet, second in command at the Ritz, and bodyguard, Kes Wingfield, to walk over to Repossi's shop, a few hundred yards from the Ritz Place Vendome entrance.

By now Dodi had become obsessed with privacy and security and instead of also walking he was driven the short distance to Repossi's in the tinted glass Mercedes 600 that had picked up the couple at the airport. Bodyguard Trevor Rees-Jones accompanied him during the almost comical short drive and waited in the car while Dodi went inside.

The $200,000 ring was ready and waiting as expected and he took it. However, another ring caught his eye and He asked jeweler Alberto Repossi if he could take both rings and let the Princess decide which she preferred. The two rings were given to Roulet. Dodi told the jeweler he was pressed for time and asked if details about price and payment could be done later, once Diana had made a choice. Repossi agreed. The original ring that Diana had selected was a band of yellow and white gold, with triangles of diamond clusters surrounding a stunning emerald.

Dodi handed off both rings to Roulet for safe keeping for the return trip to the hotel.

Not long after Dodi got back to the Ritz's $8,500-a-night Imperial Suite, Diana returned freshly coiffed from the Hair Salon in the Ritz Health Club. The 2,195 sq ft. suite offered two bedrooms, three bathrooms and a sitting room and had a view overlooking Place Vendôme

Shortly afterward, Roulet knocked on the door and delivered the rings to Dodi, who took them and disappeared into the next room of the suite. Dodi returned the second ring to Roulet. Fayed intended to slip the original ring on Diana's finger that night and asked him to give it to Renee Delorm at the Rue Arsene-Houssaye apartment.

At 7 PM, the couple left the Ritz via the Rue Cambon back exit to head back to Dodi's apartment, the K Team was caught off guard. All planning and preparations had focused on their arrivals and departures using the front entrance on Place Vendome. Though the Rue Cambon exit was also being watched, a departure from there meant the K Team cars had the near impossible tasks of scrambling from their practiced routes and still be in position at their designated blocking points in the Place de la Concorde.

It was not to be. The Mercedes was driven by Dodi's usual driver, Philippe Dourneau, and he managed to make the right turn onto the Champs Elysées from the Place de la Concorde without the slightest difficulty before stopping for some impulse shopping at Sephero, a large perfume shop on the Champs Elysées, before going to Dodi's apartment. The press were in pursuit.

But the world famous boulevard was jammed with tourists this warm August evening. When the several paparazzi suddenly appeared around the car aiming their cameras, the naturally curious tourists gathered as well. Any attempt by Diana and Dodi to exit the vehicle would have been a mob scene. Consequently, they abandoned the idea and drove away without even attempting to get out.

Back at the rogue K Team base in the shop across from the Ritz, Ali called Megan in the hotel room and advised her that the plan had failed. In disgust she hurled her car keys across the room damaging a wall painting before falling behind the bed.

"Get all those jerks back to the shop. We've got to make some changes and see if we can salvage this mess."

Five minutes later she listened as Ali told her they were intent on keeping the mission alive. He pointed out that it was too early in the evening to think Dodi and Diana would stay at the apartment for the rest of the night. Ali was convinced they would return to the hotel, no matter how late. Megan didn't share his optimism but didn't let it show.

Ali sent the K Team drivers back to their assigned positions and told them to wait for further instructions. Megan returned to the hotel room where the German and one of her MI-6 rogues were monitoring the hotel's closed circuit television system.

****

Shortly after the failed perfume stop, Diana and Dodi made it to his Rue Arsene Houssaye apartment off the Champs Elysées with little difficulty, other than the annoyances of their paparazzi motorcycle escort. The pursuers had long ago worked out a system whereby the photographer rode on the back and concentrated on framing any potential shot while the driver's attention was totally on following the orders shouted in his ear and trying to drive the cycle accordingly.

The building is divided into five apartments. Dodi's has a balcony directly overlooking the Arc de Triomphe. It had been from there on Bastille Day that Dodi had embraced his American model girlfriend, Kelly Fisher, before flying off to board the *Jonikal* and be with Diana and her sons.

Once in the apartment, Diana told Dodi she wanted to take a long bath, despite just having her hair done. But first she did some unpacking and sorted out her toiletries, including a shower cap which she put on.

Dodi, in turn, decided to remove the salt air grime collected prior to leaving the *Jonikal* that morning and showered in the large master bathroom with its over-sized jacuzzi, spacious shower stall, and even a sauna.

His butler, Rene, took out the clothes Dodi wanted to wear for dinner that night: blue jeans, grey shirt, suede jacket and cowboy boots.

After his shower, and while Diana was still soaking in the tub, Dodi entered the kitchen and put a finger to his lips as he approached his butler, the former maitre'd he had hired away from Spago's restaurant in Holywood some years earlier.

"Rene, make sure there is champagne on ice when we come back from dinner. I'm going to propose to her tonight! We'll be back around midnight."

The heir to the Fayed fortune turned slightly to make sure the Princess wasn't approaching and removed a small, grey velvet box from his robe pocket. He opened it, proudly showing off the ring.

Some minutes later Diana appeared wearing a black top with matching jacket, white trousers and black shoes. Her freshly coiffed hair had survived the shower and accentuated her attractive slight suntan acquired on the *Jonikal*.

They talked softly while holding hands on the living room couch with romantic music playing in the background and enjoyed caviar Rene had sent over from the Ritz and found in the foyer when they returned to Paris only a few hours earlier. Diana sipped a glass of wine and Dodi nursed a vodka on the rocks. A few minutes before 9:30 PM, they left the apartment for dinner.

The Ritz concierge had made a reservation for them under a fictitious name at the bistro Chez Benoit, a fashionable restaurant near Pompidou Center in the Marais district, off the Rue de Rivoli. When they left the apartment Diana and Dodi were followed there by the ever-present disorganized convoy of photographers on motorcycles.

The restaurant's location, like so many in Paris, is in an area that is also popular and was busy with tourists this warm August evening. Many of them, noticing the tumult being caused around the car by the paparazzi, joined in the gawking. Realizing it would be difficult to leave the car, as it had been earlier when they tried to visit the perfume shop, the couple didn't even attempt it. Dodi and Diana spoke to each other softly for a few moments then he told their chauffeur to take them back to the Ritz. Since the reservation at Chez Benoit had not been made in their names, the manager would later deny the pair had been expected.

Megan, who was still in the hotel room, was casually watching the tap of the CCTV security video when she saw Diana, a security officer, and Dodi brush past some photographers and enter the hotel's Place Vendome entrance.

What the hell are they back here for? Megan wondered. *The loving couple should be having their last meal together in that restaurant.* Surprised at this apparent stroke of luck, Megan called the K Team assassins in the shop across from the hotel.

"Hello?" Ali answered.

"It's me." Megan said. She recognized the deep accented voice on the other end.

"We have an interesting development. The package has returned to sender!" she told him.

"Yes, we know. Our 'artist' called us. It seems they were scared off from the planned stop by too many other artists. Now they are back at Papa's Place. . ."

". . . You were right! It's a *gift*," Megan said. "We'll have a second chance to stamp the package cancelled tonight. Do you understand what I'm saying?" Megan hated talking in coded phrases. It usually took longer to say what needed to be said and, in the case of individuals to whom English wasn't a first language, it greatly raised the potential for misunderstanding.

But not this time. The K Team operative she was on the phone with fully understood that this change in plans gave them another opportunity to arrange the accident. It was indeed a gift.

Also surprised to see the couple back at the hotel, the Ritz night security manager called Henri Paul, who had gone home for the night, and asked him to please return. Driving his Austin Mini Cooper. Paul was back at the hotel 17 minutes later.

Paul wound up in the Vendome bar, where Dodi's two English

bodyguards also happened to be. The acting head of Ritz security drank what appeared to be pineapple juice or some similar yellow liquid beverage. The "yellow liquid" was in fact, a strong anisette-based aperitif called *pastis,* with an alcohol proof equal to whiskey.

****

Prince Charles spent that beautiful August Saturday on a fishing trip with his two sons at the more than 50,000 acres of mountain, forest and farmland that comprise Balmoral Castle estate. The royal country retreat is on the banks of the River Dee between Ballater and Braemar in Scotland. It was here some 15 years ago that the media observed the first public kiss between Charles and Diana.

Less than a week earlier photographer Mario Brenna had taken and sold photos of the first public kiss between Prince Charles' former wife and Dodi Fayed on board the *Jonikal.* Unbelievably, it was widely reported that the paparazzi earned £3 million (more than $5-million U.S.) for the photos he sold to the *Sunday Mirror*, the *Daily Mail* and *The Sun.*

As youngsters, Charles, his brothers and sister had enjoyed all of nature's discoveries at Balmoral, so absent from their very proper and formal city world at Buckingham Palace. Charles wanted very much to pass such joys to his own sons.

The wildlife at Balmoral ranges from the usual forest animals to red deer, wildcats, common grouse and the largest species of grouse: the *capercaillie.* At Balmoral, they are typically referred to by this Scottish-Gaelic name, which literally means 'horse of the woods.'

Balmoral has been a favorite country escape destination for the Royal Family for more than a century since Queen Victoria and Prince Albert bought the lease in 1848 without even seeing it. Victoria had written in her diary: *'It was so calm and so solitary, it did one good as one gazed around; and the pure mountain air was most refreshing. All seemed to breathe freedom and peace, and to make one forget the work and its sad turmoil.'*

Entering the main drive at Balmoral, one is at once surrounded by huge evergreen conifers that shade the route. Red squirrels are commonly seen feeding at the feet of the tree trunks.

The road goes directly up to the castle, with its grand turreted clock tower and stone carving of the Royal Arms of Scotland on the south face. The six crests of Saxe-Coburg are displayed in gilt on the window gables, below which on the west side is the rose garden. All gardens at Balmoral are designed to be in full bloom when the Royal Family is in residence between August and October, as they were now.

While on the estate during the day, Charles and his sons wore the Balmoral tartan, strictly reserved for members of the Royal Family and the Queen's Piper. In the evening, they changed into the specially designed Balmoral tweed, worn only by the Royal Family and the estate's staff.

Now, after an enjoyable day of outdoor activity, the Prince of Wales was relaxing in Balmoral chatting and bonding with William when the telephone rang. Younger Harry had dozed off, the result of a busy day.

It was Diana calling from Paris. Despite media stories to the contrary, the Princess and Prince maintained a civilized relationship since their divorce a year earlier and spoke to each other at least twice a week. Charles handed the phone to William. She told him she was in Paris and would be home the following day. She told her son how much she missed him and his brother. In turn, William told his mother about their day. They chatted a bit more about other things before the phone call ended. It was the last time the future king would ever hear his mother's voice.

****

Shortly after the Kevin Costner-Whitney Houston movie *The Bodyguard* came out in 1992, Londoners had been surprised to see The Princess of Wales crossing the street heading for a theater and chatting away with three longtime girlfriends as if she was just another young married woman without a serious care in the world. Obviously with the quartet, but not intruding on them, was a solitary detective. All of these young women enjoyed the romantic adventure immensely and thought Costner was a drop-dead gorgeous hunk "to die for." *The Bodyguard* instantly became one of Diana's all-time favorites.

Now, years later, in the United States, actor <u>Kevin Costner</u> had received what he hoped was the final draft of a movie sequel, of sorts, based on same theme of the original.

Sarah, the Duchess of York, had met Costner during a trip in China the previous year and happened to mention that *The Bodyguard* was one of her sister-in-law Diana's favorite flicks, Costner was flattered. But when Fergie continued and said the Princess of Wales bought the video and had watched it several times, the handsome, boyish-looking actor mentioned he was considering a sequel, which, of course, he'd be in, but he hadn't decided on the female lead.

"You and Diana would make wonderful lovers on screen. Why don't you ask her? I'll bet she'd do it."

Fate, chance, or opportunity often works in strange ways. If the studio's initial choices for the lead roles in *The Bodyguard* had taken the parts, the above conversation might never have happened. The script was written in the mid 1970's, supposedly with Steve McQueen in mind.

The Hollywood leading man who had begun his career in Westerns on television was offered a hefty payday to star in the film. However, by this point in his life McQueen's failing health restricted the number of movies he was making. The film project was picked up in 1979 by Ryan O'Neal, another television actor who made it in Hollywood. O'Neal planned to star in the movie and wanted singer-actress Diana Ross for the romantic female lead. But the project fell through, and McQueen died in 1980.

In the tradition of scores of 'what might have beens' in Hollywood, Costner and Whitney Houston got the roles. Costner would later say he based his *Bodyguard* character, including the haircut, on Steve McQueen's 1968's title character in *Bullit*, believed by many to be McQueen's best work.

In the updated 1992 version of the original 1970s Bodyguard script, Costner portrayed a former Secret Service officer, unhinged and full of guilt because he had been unable to prevent the attempted assassination of President Ronald Reagan. To regain his confidence, and make a living, he accepts a security job protecting a popular singer, played by Houston. Predictably the two have a romantic relationship. The long-delayed adventure-love-story was a box office hit.

When Fergie returned to London, she told Diana about the exchange with Costner. Diana wasted no time calling him in Los Angeles and the pair talked about the original film. The princess and boyish looking actor hit it off immediately. He toyed with the idea of asking the soon-to-be-free Princess of Wales if she would be interested in being in the movie. But first he approached Warner Bros. for their backing, which they gave.

On a pleasant summer evening in 1996, Costner called Kensington Palace and asked for Diana.

"It's Kevin Costner. He would like to speak with you," her butler Paul Burrell announced.

Like a star-struck teenager, the Princess of Wales let out a shriek. "Put him through, Paul, and come up." She wanted to share the experience with the man she often called "My rock."

Costner proffered the possibility of her accepting a starring role in *The Bodyguard* sequel.

"But I can't sing," she giggled. "What would I be expected to do?"

Costner told Diana that her character would display traits of dignity and sophistication, while still being somewhat similar to the style of the Whitney Houston role in the original, but Diana would play a princess.

With main location shooting in Hong Kong, Costner's script revolved around a princess who is kidnapped then falls in love with the bodyguard who rescues her. Costner told Diana he envisioned her playing 'Julia,' a woman working in Hong Kong for the release of political prisoners. Though the script was not ready yet, Costner did have a story outline. He told her his character would again be the professional bodyguard who protected the singer in the original film. Costner told the Princess his character would, in turn, eventually fall in love with her 'Julia' character. She laughed when he told her there would be a kissing scene.

Diana encouraged him to go ahead and work on the script, though neither put a time limit on the project.

"Go ahead and do this script and when it's ready I'll be in a really good spot." Diana told him that once the divorce decree came through she was going to be a free woman.

"When I come to you with the script," Costner told her, "I'm going to try to be hard to resist. I'll tell you truthfully this is going to be good or I wouldn't be doing it."

Diana laughed. She was so smitten by the idea of playing a role in a real movie, the thought of uprooting herself from her sons in London to work on a movie halfway around the world didn't occur to her at the moment.

They also discussed Costner's need to work on his projects without necessarily scheduling or devoting specific time for this one. The eventual script would be kept on the back burner until Diana was ready to do it.

"She wanted the right to reinvent herself", Costner would later tell British talk show host Michael Parkinson. "I had talked with Princess Di a couple of times. I explained to her that I was going to try to make this movie for her and she was genuinely interested," Costner told. The pair had discussed the possible film for more than a year.

"There was a very real thing between us in terms of doing this movie," he would later say. "She hadn't said yes to it, but she had indicated to me that she knew her life was going to change."

After reading the just-delivered script, Costner was very enthusiastic. He liked it and believed Diana would like it and sign off on it as well.

He looked at his watch. As eager as he was to share what he felt with Diana, he realized it was nearly the middle of the night in Europe.

Costner decided he'd call her the next day, Sunday, August 31.

CHAPTER TEN

Unknown to Ali or Megan, because the K Team driver hadn't bothered to mention it, one of their cars had nearly been involved in an accident. When the earlier effort to implement the plan this evening went amuck one of the rogue drivers who had not gotten to the Place de la Concorde in time to prevent the Mercedes turning onto the Champs Elysées had cut off a large truck. The driver breathed a sigh of relief as he saw the vehicle swerve onto the sidewalk to avoid hitting him. The rogue didn't stop, but instead continued following the much practiced route, as a personal dry run, before returning to his base unscathed.

The truck, however, had not faired so well. When it jumped the curb the truck hit a traffic signal junction box hard enough to move the four foot high metal casing several inches out of kilt. The Paris police ticketed the driver, ignoring his explanation about being cut off.

They were more concerned with the condition of the junction box which, as they watched, emitted occasional sparks. They dutifully called in the problem pointing out that perhaps a fire was possible if the box wasn't attended to fast. The report went along through channels until it eventually reached the desk of a night manager at the Paris Power & Light office. The man groaned when he read it. It was his job to make sure such issues were addressed. He knew that wouldn't be easily done on a summer Saturday night with only a skeleton crew on duty to service problems in the entire city.

But, as he read the codes and followed the system schematic, he realized this particular box controlled a majority of the traffic video cameras running along the Seine as well as the lights in the tunnel at Point de l'Alma.

****

By the time Bat returned to the Plaza Athénée after seeing Archie, Jennifer was ready for dinner. As he showered and freshened up he told her the essence of his conversation with Archie.

"That's incredible," she said as Bat exited the shower and began drying himself off. "That poor woman's life has been an open book for the spies on two continents to read."

"That's what caught your attention?" Bat asked while vigorously rubbing the towel on his head. "I thought the part about her being pregnant and Dodi preparing to ask her to marry him was pretty significant myself."

"Well, of course it is, but what's more alarming, and rather distasteful, I might add, is that so many people know about it," she said, stepping out of the now very humid bathroom.

Bat switched on the overhead exhaust fan in an effort to clear the steamed up mirror.

"I can't argue with that," he said while he finished drying himself. "Hand me that robe, will you?"

Jennifer leaned back into the room and removed the thick robe from the hook behind the door where Bat had hung it. "Thanks," he said as he slipped it on.

"You know, so many people, young women especially, envied Diana when she married Prince Charles. It was a fairy tale…that's what the newspapers and magazines called it, and it was. It really was, and we believed it."

Bat kissed her on the cheek as he walked past and went over to sit on the edge of the bed. He crossed his legs one at a time and used the towel to finish drying.

"It was every little girl's dream come true: to grow up and have a real prince fall in love with you, carrying you off and living happily ever after with people, servants, everybody adoring you and fawning over your every wish."

"Yup. A fairy tale. That's how it happens in the movies. This is what happens in real life." Now fully dry he quickly began dressing.

"And that's how it happens in my books as well. The stories always have a happy romantic ending, no matter how difficult the problems and obstacles are for the couple. That's how readers want love stories to be."

"Are all the men in your books princes?" Bat asked teasingly as he moved back into the bathroom to blow dry his hair.

"No, of course they aren't. A man doesn't have to be a real honest-to-goodness prince to be seen as one by the woman who loves him."

"Hey, then that's pretty good for me, isn't it?" He wisecracked and smiled as he paused before turning on the hair dryer.

"You? What gives you the idea I think of you as a prince?" she landed a soft punch on his shoulder as he turned the machine on.

"I'll be in the sitting room," she said as she again left the bathroom, but the high-pitched whirl of the blower overpowered her words.

Bat and Jennifer had enjoyed and felt so comfortable with the livery driver who had taken them around all day that she made a point of getting the man's phone number so they could hire his car to go to dinner and do a nighttime tour of Paris afterward. By the time she and Bat came out of the Plaza Athénée he was waiting there. They got into the car and the driver half turned to address them.

"I heard you say something earlier about the Negro piano player in the Hilton. But I'm afraid it's going to be impossible to get in there tonight. It seems every tourist in Paris wants to hear him play *As Time Goes By* tonight while gazing at that great view of the Eiffel Tower. Perhaps another night?"

"Oh, darn it. We only have tonight and tomorrow night, and I called and made a reservation for the Bateaux-Mouches dinner cruise on the Seine for tomorrow," Jennifer pouted.

"Hey, cheer up," Bat said warmly, touching a finger under her chin. "We'll do the piano thing on our next France trip, when we can stay longer and maybe visit the wine country and Normandy, the whole nine yards."

She turned to him and smiled.

"See? That's why you're *my* prince." They kissed softly.

"This would be an appropriate time for me to say something typically French about romance," the driver joked. "But there are two cars backing up double parked waiting for me to pull out of this space. If you want American food I can drop you off at the McDonalds on Champs Elysées," he joked again.

"No thank you," Jennifer laughed. "I have an idea!"

The driver moved the vehicle out of the spot and began driving down the street slowly.

"How about the Ritz?" she said.

"The Ritz, again? I've been there twice today already." Bat protested mildly.

"Yes, you have been, but if I recall correctly you didn't get to see a thing. It's a beautiful hotel. You spent all your time hanging around the bar with your war buddy."

"Not true. We walked around a bit."

"Tell me one thing you saw? Describe something." Jennifer challenged.

"Okay. . . that hall. The one with all the expensive stuff in the glass cases."

"Very good. That's the Hall of Temptation. But you could have read that in any guidebook, Mr. Guidebook editor!" Jennifer paused, then added, "I don't know how I could tell Kimberly we were in Paris and *didn't* have dinner at the Ritz."

Bat recalled Archie had made a similar recommendation '. . . dinner at the Ritz is an experience everyone should enjoy at least once in their life.'

"Then the Ritz it is. I wouldn't want you to tell your sister I opted for take-out Chinese in our hotel room."

"The restaurant at the Ritz is the L'Esparon. You won't regret it." The driver offered.

A short time later, Jennifer and Bat alighted from the vehicle in front of the Place Vendome entrance. They went through the revolving door past a smiling bellman in a green uniform with a matching cap and strolled through the baroque central corridor. The plush silver blue carpeting silenced the footfalls of guests passing through. Jennifer paused and took in the surroundings again.

To the right, a few steps above the entry level was the cashier's desk, attended by uniformed staff in tail coats. Golden candelabras illuminated the lobby and, although not visible from where she and Bat were standing, she knew from her previous visit that a large mural featuring Rubin-style cherubs hung at a landing on the wide, ornate staircase leading to the next level.

When Mohamed Fayed purchased the historic hotel in 1979, he hired decorators to refurbish it in the rich belle époque style that resembled its original décor.

"Honey, did you know that the bathrobes in the rooms are the same shade of apricot that Cesar Ritz believed to be so fetching for one's complexion? And ladies are always served a long-stemmed rose with their drinks?" Jennifer asked.

"The bathrobe at the Plaza Athene worked fine for me. And in the Caribbean I once had a drink with a paper umbrella stuck in it," he replied playfully.

"You're hopeless!" she replied. Then continued telling him what she knew about the hotel.

"Coco Chanel lived here for thirty years. Edward VII was one of its first guests. He became king when his mother, Queen Victoria, died." Jennifer went on. Bat realized she had done her advance reading and was genuinely thrilled to be in the historic hotel. *She has a marvelous knack for remembering details and trivia*, he thought.

"Here's something else that makes a hotel like this special: It's not uncommon for guests to request the same maid, special showerheads, temporary gyms, or even a separate room to keep *their flowers!* Once the hotel knows a repeat guest is partial to a particular room, it is photographed by the housekeeper, and arranged exactly that way when they next return."

"I've heard the Savoy in London, and a few other really top notch places do that as well," Bat commented.

"Yes, I'm sure there are others, but I think the Ritz was the first to do that. I've even read that the basement is full of personal belongings, favorite paintings, fur coats, even eyeglasses to be set on the bedside table for special guests."

"It just goes to prove, honey, if you have lots of money there is no limit to the luxuries one can enjoy. Did you ever hear what

Hemingway said about the Ritz?"

Jennifer, thought for a second. "Just all his remarks about the bar. I wasn't aware he ever spoke about *anything* else," Jennifer joked as they walked over to the desk to ask directions to the restaurant.

"Well, this wasn't about the bar. Hemingway wrote, or said: *the only reason for not staying at the Ritz is if you can't afford it.'* Methinks the man knew what he was talking about."

The liveried Ritz employee behind the desk had heard the comment and shot a disapproving stare at Bat, before turning to await Jennifer's question.

The gilded theme of the hotel's lobby is carried through in L'Esparon with its cloud sprinkled trompe l'oeil sky ceiling, long white, full-skirt tablecloths and gold trimmed beige arm chairs. Jennifer and Bat were seated at a table for two near a window overlooking a lush and richly planted garden. In the car she had asked the driver for menu suggestions, along with the correct French pronunciation.

Her advance investigative work was a wise move. Jennifer ordered filets of sole tempura and, because he didn't have a clue what anything else on the menu was, Bat did likewise. While they waited for their food they sipped wine and chatted softly, smiling a lot and frequently holding hands across the table as one would expect lovers in Paris to do. When their meals arrived Bat was pleasantly surprised. He had expected to see a child's portion plopped in the center of a large plate. As it turned out they both enjoyed the meal. They passed on having dessert and were finishing up with coffee.

"Well, let me tell you something," Bat said softly. "You did such a good job ordering that delicious meal that the next time, nay, make that *every time* I'm in Paris I'm going to let you order for me again."

She laughed. "Thank you, but you really should be thanking our driver."

When the check came Bat grabbed it, despite Jennifer's insistence that this was a business trip and it was a business expense for her. He would hear none of it. He glanced at it and put his credit card on the tray. The waiter vanished and returned hardly a minute later. Bat included a generous tip and before he could rise and go to pull back Jennifer's chair, she began getting up, but froze for an instant before fully standing.

"Oh, my God!" her comment was barely audible but Bat could see the stunned look on her face. Half turning to his right Bat locked eyed with the Princess of Wales as she and Dodi passed. Bat simply smiled and nodded, but Diana had looked away an instant before he did.

Once in the corridor Jennifer's excitement continued as they headed for the entrance. She was beside herself with glee.

"That was her, Bat! Princess Diana! She walked right by our table."

"Yup, that was her. Hardly changed a bit in four or five years. But she wouldn't remember me. I had a full beard, a real one, when we saw each other on Nevis."

"Are you telling me that you've actually met her???? You never said anything about that."

"No, no, no. Not a 'how-do-you-do' meeting, just a casual walk-by, just like this, on the beach. I told you about that trip where I ran into Archie. In the scheme of things she's probably walked past a million people since then and, beard or no beard, she wouldn't have remembered me."

"How was dinner?" their driver asked as they entered the car. "Was it what you expected?"

"Excellent, a night I won't soon forget," Jennifer said as she snuggled close to Bat.

"Yes, it was a good choice," Bat nodded. *But I could have fed a family of four for a month with what it cost!* He smiled to himself.

"I was thinking of just driving you around to some of the places we saw during the day so you could appreciate them all lit up at night. Is that agreeable?" the driver asked.

"Yes, but be sure to include the Opera House, we didn't stop there today but I'd like to tonight," Jennifer said.

Diana and Dodi were aware that various people in the

restaurant were trying not to be obvious looking at them. The couple had ordered their food and were waiting for their drinks. Yet four men at a nearby table made Diana feel uneasy. Unlike other people in the restaurant these four seemed not to care that their staring was very obvious. They had what looked like shopping bags on the floor under the table and this unnerved Diana. Suspecting photographers, Dodi called the captain over and whispered something to him.

The captain immediately went to the table and spoke to the four. The shopping bags actually contained various purchases, not cameras. They were foreign tourists, not paparazzi. The captain returned and told Dodi.

But the whole incident had been observed by others in the restaurant and suddenly Diana felt foolish and even more uncomfortable than before. She said something to Dodi, who nodded as they got up and left. On the way out Dodi asked that their food be sent to the Imperial Suite. The couple would dine in private in the $2,000 a night room.

While they waited for their meals both Diana and Dodi busied themselves making more phone calls. She spoke to *London Daily Mail* columnist Richard Kay, one of the small group of journalists she considered a trusted friend. He had virtually covered her 17 years of public life. Diana told the newsman she intended to 'radically' change her life by reducing her public appearances.

Dodi called his cousin and said he hoped he and Diana would marry by the end of the year. The engagement ring was at his apartment, Dodi had also taken an inscribed silver plaque he had given Diana on the *Jonikal* and slipped it under her pillow. It read:

> *As if . . .*
> *I have tried many things, music and cities,*
> *The stars in their constellations and the sea—*
> *When I am not with you I am alone,*
> *For there is no one else,*
> *And there is nothing that comforts me but you*

But as romantic as that story sounds, it comes with baggage. In the 1980s when Dodi was dating Tina Sinatra he had seen the plaque in her home and quickly became fond of the sentiment. So much so he asked if he could borrow it and have it copied. The plaque had been a wedding gift from Tina's former husband, Richard Cohen. Tina didn't have a problem lending it to Dodi.

Their romance ended without the plaque ever being returned to Tina. One wonders how many pillows Dodi had slipped it under before Diana's.

****

The driver was surprised to find himself marveling at the sights of Paris at night. He had often driven passengers through the streets, avenues and boulevards after dark, but this time he was seeing it through the eyes of the romantic couple in the back. The woman, he recalled hearing, was a writer, and she had a marvelous felicity for verbally describing things in colorful language most others wouldn't even think of.

"Here we are, the Paris Opera House!" he announced as he brought the vehicle to a side curb some distance away. "I park here so you can appreciate the building while walking toward it."

Bat got out of his side of the car and came around to help Jennifer out. The couple held hands and slowly walked toward the flood-light illuminated masonry and cut stone Neo-Baroque building considered to be one of the most beautiful buildings in the world. As they drew closer they could see the definition of the several columns and statues of the façade. Even at night the gold gilt of the two very large figures at both ends of the top reflected light. They continued walking until they were almost directly in front of the building.

"Oh, it's beautiful, honey. Isn't it?" she said, quickly adding before he could answer. "Do you remember that first night when we met on the *Windrush*, outside the showroom?"

"Of course I do. How could I forget? I think I began falling in love with you from that moment on."

She turned and slung her arms around his neck. They kissed long but softly for several seconds.

"Do you remember what the musical stage show was?" she asked coyly, without breaking the embrace.

Bat thought briefly, and silently thanked his guardian angel for helping him remember.

"Yes . . .a medley of scenes from *The Phantom of The Opera.*"

"Yes, you do remember!" they kissed again. A bit longer this time. And when they were finished they broke their clinch.

"I wish we had stopped during the day and gone inside, Bat. They say it's more beautiful and magnificent inside than outside."

"We will, we will. . .I'm sure we'll return. So the Opera will be high on our list of places to take the time to go inside."

"Bat? That's the third time you've alluded to us returning to Paris. Do you know something I don't know?" she asked.

He couldn't prevent the smile that was trying so hard to explode on his face.

"As a matter of fact I do. I had a call back from American Book Publishers just before we left. It was the day you and Kimberly took the boys to the movies."

"And? Go on, get to the point! I think I feel a surprise coming on. This sounds promising."

"More than promising. It's in the bag."

"I'll tell you all about it in a minute. But there's something I have to do first." Bat reached into his pocket and removed a small box as he went down on one knee.

Jennifer's jaw dropped open and she was speechless as he opened the box and removed a diamond engagement ring.

"Darling," he began, "I love you more than I ever thought possible . . ."

"YES! YES! YES! I will, I accept, I'll marry you." she practically used all her strength to pull him back up. "Oh my wonderful, wonderful darling. I love you so much." They kissed again. This time more vigorously and with greater passion, and kept kissing over and over again to the great delight of tourists nearby. A few car horns honked and more than a few passersby broke into applause. Their driver even got out of the car some fifty feet behind them and, clowning around, took exaggerated self-congratulatory bows while grinning from ear to ear. "I drove them here! I drove them here!" He exclaimed, stabbing a finger at himself.

Finally, the hugging and kissing ended.

"You're sure, Jen? Absolutely positive you want me as your husband for the rest of your life?"

"No. Not the rest of my life. For eternity." They kissed tenderly again, even longer than the previous time.

"Now to return to what I was saying. . ."

"Who can remember anything you said before kneeling and saying 'Darling'? . . ."

"You said I had mentioned returning to Paris three times. Here's why: I accepted a great job with American Book Publishers to head up the photography department for their new series of *Around The World* guidebooks. That's at least 20 books right now, and more will be added. Each country is a title by itself and it kicks off with the first five books about Western Europe. I'll put together a small staff, maybe use some freelancers, but I'll be coming over . . . no: *We'll* be coming over as often as you want . . . to two or three countries per trip. And you can bet Paris and the rest of France is one title I'll be doing myself."

"Where will you be located and when do you begin?" she asked.

"That's one of the great perks! The main office is in New York with a division in D.C., but mainly I'll be working from home. I'll be shooting everything with a new digital camera. I can email them the photos or discs. I told them I could start immediately. But I also said I would need time off for a honeymoon."

"Oh, darling that's wonderful. I'm so happy for you . . . for us, I mean," she said as they began walking back to the car. Jennifer couldn't remember ever being happier.

"So tell me, wonderful woman. Do you want to wait to be a traditional June bride or are you one of those who pray for snow on your wedding. Maybe December, just before or after Christmas?"

"How about maybe just before Halloween? Before I start showing much?"

"Okay, we can push it up to Octob . . .showing???? Showing what????"

"Bartholomew Lynch, you're going to be a daddy! If it's a boy, would you mind very much if we called him 'Little Bat, Jr.'?

CHAPTER ELEVEN

Archie was pensive. His hands were locked behind his back as he slowly walked around the lobby and corridors of The Ritz rehashing the events of the last few hours. Not only was Sir Warren's suggestion to shut down the operation and return to London this very night impossible, it struck Blair as very odd. Could the pregnancy report have unnerved the former deputy director so much that he was truly befuddled and didn't know what to do next?

He paused in front of the Vendome Bar and glanced inside. A pianist was playing soft mood music while a nearby harp was idle and unattended. Pulling the surveillance off Princess Diana so Archie could huddle with The Committee the following morning to discuss the situation didn't even *sound* logical, he thought, as he stepped into the richly wood paneled room.

He strolled through the room, past the pianist, and paused again when he came to the open double doors leading out to a garden terrace replete with statuary, lush plantings and cozy glass-topped wrought iron tables with matching chairs. The terrace was nearly empty with only three tables occupied out of ten times that many.

From several past experiences, Archie expected that Sir Warren already had a backup 'Plan B' or a contingency plan. He had beaten the drum so often and loudly about his fears of the consequences of a possible bastard pregnancy that for him *not* to have an alternative ready would have been totally out of character.

Archie shook his head and was about to turn and leave when his attention was drawn to a female figure wearing long black clothing hardly ten feet away facing in the opposite direction. At first he thought it might be a nun, but when she made a half turn and reached into a large satchel next to her chair he quickly realized it was a Muslim woman, replete with a face veil.

With all that garb on why would anyone choose to boil out there in the heat when they could be in the air-conditioned inside, he wondered. Archie had hardly finished the thought when he found

423

out why. The woman retrieved a large phone from the satchel and put it to her ear. Archie recognized the phone immediately. He was certain there was not another one like it in the world. He fought the impulse to rush over and confront Megan Price, but instead he went into the garden and quietly slipped into a chair at the table closest to and behind her.

Bat Lynch was right after all. The photographer really did see Megan. Archie's mind was racing. *Her secret overseas mission was Paris. . . and Diana!* He strained to hear what she was saying but couldn't. The pieces were starting to fit together, he thought, and he was filling with rage. Sir Warren did have a backup Plan B and Megan was part of it. Archie felt he had been played for a gullible fool, a pawn, in Sir Warren's private spy game.

He waited until she returned the phone to the satchel and rose from her chair to leave. He quickly caught up and purposely strode in step beside her, inching up just enough so she could recognize him, but he didn't say a word. They walked together side by side through the Vendome Bar and into the corridor. She never tried to drop back or forge ahead. Finally, she slowed down as they approached a door Archie knew was a housekeeping storage room. She looked from left to right before opening the door and going in. Megan closed the door once Archie was through it and flicked the wall light switch. She had obviously been in the room before.

She undid the button and the veil dropped revealing her face. Her look was somber.

"Was it the phone? My hair is covered." she said casually.

"Yes, that monster phone. Big mistake keeping it all these years, it's a dinosaur," he replied. Then added,

"How long have you been here, Megan?"

"That doesn't matter. We both have our jobs to do. . . but you and the rest of the MI-6 team are supposed to be on your way back to London this very moment, so we wouldn't trip over each other tonight."

"Is that what Sir Warren told you? That he was getting the regular surveillance team out of the way so you could go about your dirty business?"

"Well, to tell you the truth, the old man seems to be losing it. He didn't remember, or didn't know, that the agent in residence would be in charge of you and your London crew. Yes, that was just him letting me know that the regular MI-6 team would still be around Paris, and I should watch out so as not to bump into you."

"Who's here with you, Megan? I'd like to know who has been laughing behind my back all this time?"

"No one from the service. I'm working with foreigners . . . rogue agents. In truth, it's their show, I'm just an observer and adviser."

"What are you talking about? foreign 'rogues'? You couldn't make me believe that in a hundred years MI-6 would turn over the Diana problem to foreigners. Unless. . . you're not officially here for the service."

"Very good, Archie. That's correct. I am *not* here for the service. I'm on one of those nasty little 'Committee' missions Sir Warren and Smythe-Pembrooke come up with every so often. And nobody has been laughing at you. This is a special operation. Diana is not involved. . .or I should say she is not the target."

Megan moved from where they were standing to a low stack of wooden boxes she could sit on. She moved a 12-inch plumber's wrench from atop the boxes to give herself proper room. Archie casually leaned against the wall across from her.

"I'm missing something here," Archie said. "Diana and her boyfriend arrived in Paris today. Sir Warren tries to disband my team because he doesn't want us bumping into you or vice versa? And you're trying to tell me Diana isn't involved? Do I look like I was born yesterday?"

"No, I said she wasn't *the target*. She's involved. These rogues are from the Middle East and they have a score to settle with Mohamed Fayed. Diana has been the 'Judas Goat' leading Dodi here to slaughter."

"Why would Sir Warren and The Committee want to get involved in somebody else's war?"

"Oh, Archie, come, come. I know you received the pregnancy report today, Sir Warren told me. Now think about it. A staged car accident in which Diana's lover is killed and she is injured enough to terminate her pregnancy. And if that doesn't do it, there are sympathetic people at the hospital who will make sure she isn't pregnant when she leaves."

"I've thought about it, Megan, and I'm *not* convinced that pregnancy report is genuine. It's too convenient. I think it's bogus, and now I realize why: to justify your mission with these killers!"

"Bogus? That's ridiculous. But even if it is a fake, and just more of Sir Warren's zealous shenanigans, so what? After the accident and Diana's trip to the hospital, we'll never again have to worry about her getting pregnant. A friendly doctor will see to that."

"Do you hear yourself?" Archie asked in amazement. "You're saying the end justifies the means. What have we become judge, jury, and God Himself in making such decisions? MI-6, The Committee, Sir Warren, me, you, all of us . . .We're now deciding who will die and who will never be born because these lives do not fit into our neat, organized tradition and structure to preserve the monarchy?"

"Powerful thinking, quite moral. You should be applauded," Megan snapped. "But I don't recall you ever having such bouts of conscience when we worked in the field, and I snapped a few necks to save your ass. . ."

"How can you be sure Fayed will be killed but Diana will survive?" Archie interrupted.

"That's under control. She'll probably be cut up and bruised, maybe even get a broken arm or leg. Just enough to guarantee an ambulance ride to where everything will be taken care of. . ."

The strong vibration of her phone interrupted their conversation. Archie waited as she quickly reached into the satchel and retrieved it. She expected it to be Ali telling her Dodi and Diana were leaving the hotel. Instead it was the German watching the video monitor back in the room.

"Yes?" she said as she rose from where she was sitting.

"Hello," the German replied. "I just got some news that may or may not be of interest to you, but I thought I should pass it on." Megan silently shook her head, *"The man was still going out of his*

426

way to show his value for future missions," she thought.

"Go on, and please make it quick. I'm in the middle of something." She looked at Archie standing across from her, and shrugged. As she did she nonchalantly picked up the wrench and toyed with it.

"I just got off the phone with Rolf, he was drunk and told me both back seat belts had been filed down."

"What??? How can that be? I specifically told you only the driver's side rear, and when they were installed I doubled checked with you and *you* assured me only one belt had been worked on, and that's the one that had been installed in the seat behind the driver!"

"Hold on, hold on. Everything you say is true. That's what Rolf told me at the time. But tonight he mentioned the big Englishman had called him, before he worked on the belt, and said things had changed and they now wanted *both* belts filed down. But not to say anything to anyone, including you."

"Smythe-Pembrooke? The one who hired you?"

"Yes, if that's his name. The one who hired us."

"How did he know how to reach Rolf?"

"I have no idea. The only phone number that was exchanged when we met was the contact number for you."

"And Rolf filed down both belts? Why? Why would he do that and not tell you?"

"Because your Englishman gave him an extra $5,000. Now Rolf was feeling guilty and wants to share it with me. I think he realized I would find out eventually and just wanted to play it safe."

"You are absolutely sure about this? He couldn't just be drunk and lying to you?"

"Why would he lie? Would you offer to share that kind of money with someone if it was a lie?"

"Stay in the room. I have to do something. Don't leave there until I get back." She hung up and dropped the phone into her pocket. She tapped the wrench against the palm of her free hand as she was thinking.

"What's that all about?" Archie asked.

"There's been a new development." Her mind was racing. Sir

Warren and Smythe-Pembrooke had deceived her. It wasn't just the K Team trying to kill Dodi. That was just the convenient cover. All along this whole thing had actually been *a plot to murder Diana*!

"My God, Sir Warren always *intended* for Diana to be killed in the car as well!" She looked at Archie. "It appears I've been played for a bigger fool than you, Archie . . . But I can still stop it."

"Wait a minute," he grabbed her by the shoulders. "Stop what? The accident?"

"Yes. Get out of my way, I've got to get to the shop across the street." She tried to break free of his grip but he stepped sideways blocking her.

"If you're telling me the truth, then let me go with you. Trust me, Megan, I can help."

"Are you crazy? They'll kill you on sight! These bloody murderers won't ask questions."

"Then let me get some of my team. I'll call them. It'll only take a few minutes to group up."

"I'm sorry, Archie. That's not going to happen."

All he saw was a blur as Megan smashed the heavy wrench against his right temple. One well-placed shot from the heavy object was enough to make him crumble, unconscious, to the floor. Had she wanted to, Megan could have killed him with it. She dropped the wrench to the floor and picked up her satchel from against the stack of wooden boxes she had been sitting on.

Megan affixed the veil across her face as she rapidly moved through the Ritz. Just as she reached the revolving main door to the street her phone vibrated again. She went outside and slowly walked parallel to the hotel instead of immediately crossing Place Vendome as she removed the phone from her pocket.

"Yes?" she said.

"It's been done. They will be in the Mercedes 280S." The German rogue said.

"Go on. . ." she urged.

"Your paparazzi had a chatty conversation with the head of security and bemoaned the fact that the large Mercedes 600S has tinted windows and there was no chance of getting good photos of the couple kissing. He told the security man there was big money to be made from such a picture, several thousand dollars, maybe more, and offered to split it with the security man if he could make sure the couple drove off in the smaller Mercedes 280S, because the windows are not tinted."

"That's according to the script. What about the rest? Did the security man go for it?" Megan asked.

"Absolutely, it was then suggested using decoy cars to throw off the paparazzi. The plan is to let the big Mercedes and the Range Rover line up in front of the hotel door. The regular drivers and bodyguards will be in them. Since these two vehicles have been traveling in tandem most of the day it will suggest that the couple is getting ready to leave. Your agent on the motorcycle will create a diversion, wheelies or something in the street, and that will be the cue for the two cars to take off, as if the couple got in when everybody was looking at the motorcycle antics." He paused, expecting a comment from Megan, but she just continued listening.

"Anyway," he went on, "the couple will exit via Rue Cambon and depart from there. The security chief liked the idea so much that the fool will drive the 280S himself. Which makes the job easier for our drivers, since he isn't trained in defensive driving and believes all we want to do is take a photo. He has no idea how this will end."

"Now, we have to see how persuasive the security man is. Fayed still has to go along with the idea." Megan said. "Can you think of anything to delay their departure? Or even better, change things back so they use the larger Mercedes?"

"The security chief is on his way to Fayed's suite to suggest the plan now. What's going on? Why would you want to change anything? Considering all the problems the couple has had with the paparazzi today, Fayed will most likely agree to the plan. I'll bet they've probably had that conversation by now."

"Just considering all possible contingencies, keep me informed of any changes. And, most importantly, call me immediately when you know they are leaving."

The German found her answer confusing but before he could question her further, she added.

"You should be able to see them. The CCTV system captures anyone going through that Rue Cambon foyer." She ended the call abruptly and turned, crossing into the street.

Megan's rage at Sir Warren and Smythe-Pembrooke for deceiving her, using her as their tool, and setting her up as a patsy by employing rogue agents was so intense she would have killed both of them with her bare hands, had they been there.

She understood the scenario. If anything went wrong and the plot was discovered before or after the accident, she would be labeled as a rogue agent who was solely responsible for the whole thing. She also knew she would never be brought in alive to tell her version of events. Sir Warren would have someone in mind already to kill her to keep her silent. *"Damn, damn, damn! How could I have been such a willing fool?"* she wondered.

Ali and one other K Team rogue who would drive the Uno were in the shop observing the Ritz entrance and surroundings through small openings in long sheets of brown paper covering the windows. He opened the door a crack as Megan reached it. She slipped into the room. It was illuminated by a small low-wattage lamp in the far corner, causing the cluttered, long folding table, chairs, and people to cast long, eerie shadows. The table was the kind often used by decorators for unrolling and cutting wallpaper or wall covering.

"Why are you here?" Ali asked. He was obviously surprised to see her. "Shouldn't you be monitoring the audio in the suite and the videos from around the hotel? Has it been arranged that they will be in the proper car?"

"Yes, they'll be in the right car." She had to admit that, since the K Team motorcyclists and drivers would report as much when the couple actually left the hotel.

"But there's been an unexpected development. I've just been told the seat belts weren't filed down enough," Megan improvised. "My colleagues in London have run tests with similarly filed seat belts and they didn't open, even at extraordinary speeds. We're going to have to postpone the mission till we can . . ."

"We postpone nothing, you stupid fool! The accident happens

tonight. We get it over with, one way or another, tonight. If they are not killed in the accident our drivers will finish the job when they rush to the car."

Megan realized Ali meant his people would either shoot the car's occupants or pump poison into them. Either way their actions would leave an unmistakable trail saying murder, not accident!

"You can't do that! Anything other than this appearing as a genuine accident undermines all the work we've put in. Besides, if you do what you are thinking, we'll all be hunted down as murderers."

"You think we care about your accident cover story? No! We want to strike a blow at the Fayeds, and it's actually better if he *knows* it wasn't an accident and that we were involved. That way the fat pig will know all the security in the world can not prevent us from reaching him!"

Megan suddenly realized the K Team had also been playing her, probably with the knowledge of Sir Warren. She had been set up by everybody: Smythe-Pembrooke, double-dealing against her with the seat belts; these K Team bastards, who planned to kill Dodi any way they could; and Sir Warren, her mentor, protector, and in many ways a surrogate father, the person she followed and blindly obeyed. His was the cruelest cut of all because she knew that once Diana was dead Sir Warren would have her terminated as well.

He wouldn't have to send an MI-6 agent to kill her. These bastards would probably do the job! she thought.

As she stood there considering her limited options, the walkie-talkie on the table squeaked.

"Hello, this is the truck. Anything happening?"

Ali turned away from Megan and lifted the device up and spoke into it. All the drivers communicated via cell phones to the K Team base in the Place Vendome shop. The exception was the truck at the other end of the tunnel. It transmitted and received all messages through the direct, and private, walkie-talkie.

"Stay alert. Something should be happening in the next several minutes. Are you able to locate the 280S?"

"Yes," the answer came back. "The GPS tracking device is

showing that it's been moved from Place Vendome to around the corner. It's just sitting there. Parked for now."

"Good," Ali replied. "We will tell you when we are positive the son of the pig is in the car and it is moving toward you." He ended the exchange and turned to Megan:

"Now I think you should return to the CCTV monitor."

Then he ordered the other rogue, "It's time to get into position with the Uno. Go now. The keys are there." He pointed to them on the table.

As the man rose from the chair he had been seated in several feet away and moved toward the table, Megan knew she had to act now. Ali turned back, surprised to still see her standing there.

"What are you waiting for, English whore? I said go back to the hotel room and monit. . ."

She had stepped back as he was speaking and lifted a groin kick that rocked him but, surprisingly didn't double him up or send him to the floor. As he glared at her and reached for the gun tucked in his belt Megan pulled out her heavy phone and thrust the short stubby antenna into his eye as hard as she could. He let out a terrible scream as he fell backwards into the long table, toppling it over and spraying its contents onto the floor.

But the man who was supposed to drive the Uno was already upon her with his knife drawn. He rapidly stabbed Megan three times in the stomach before she locked her hands around his neck and with every ounce of strength in her body she snapped it. He went limp and dropped to the floor like a deflated balloon.

Megan could feel the hot, burning pain of her deep cuts and the sensation of blood quickly running over her fingers as she used her hands in a feeble effort to compress the most serious wound. She was bleeding badly, but her total rage, fueled by adrenalin, overpowered her personal concerns.

As she reached down to take the knife from the man she just killed Megan felt dizzy and wobbly. She took two steps toward Ali, still on the floor moaning, and dropped to her knees. She tried to slit his throat but with his defensive wiggling, and her rapidly sapping strength, she was unable. In frustration she held the knife like an ice pick and stabbed away at his neck several times till he stopped moving. In a final jab she left the knife sticking out of his throat.

She dropped both arms to the floor and, now on all fours, waited for an instant for the room to stop spinning. Megan reached and removed the gun from Ali's belt and stuck it in her pocket. As she did she pushed herself back up to a kneeling position and searched her pockets for her car keys. Soon she remembered that when the first attempt failed earlier this evening she had thrown the keys across the hotel room in disgust and had forgotten to retrieve them.

In the shop's dim light she could nonetheless see the various things that had fallen to the floor when Ali knocked over the table. The Uno keys were right next to the walkie-talkie. Megan held her stomach and inched forward toward them. She bent over with much pain and retrieved the car keys.

She considered wrapping part of her garment tightly around her stomach but considered that would just be a waste of time. And she knew she didn't have a lot of that. Megan had to get to the truck at the other side of the tunnel where the two K Team agents were and incapacitate the laser so it couldn't bounce the signal off the mirror to inflate the airbags, or the strobe in the Uno, which she would now be driving.

****

The three Paris workers sent to check and repair the traffic signal transfer box the truck had hit earlier in the day were not happy campers. It was almost midnight on a Saturday in the summer. Instead of partying with family and friends, or perhaps in bed sleeping, they had been called in to repair the junction box. They were told it had been sparking earlier in the day but now, as they patiently watched for several minutes, it seemed to be operating normally. They listened and observed the various clicks and nothing seemed out of the ordinary. Finally, not able to determine any problem, they decided to simply manhandle the large and heavy metal box the few inches back onto where it normally sat on the concrete foundation.

As they did, all police radio communications in the area from the Place de la Concorde to the Pont d 'Alma tunnel suddenly failed. So did the traffic CCTV cameras leading to and inside the tunnel.

Unaware of these developments, the trio got back in their vehicle and headed for their depot to sign out for the evening. It would be more than an hour before all systems were repaired and functioning properly.

****

It would have been easier for their driver to simply have taken Bat and Jennifer to the Opera when he picked them up at the Ritz. The two are in relative close proximity. But Jennifer insisted on first seeing the Champs Elysees lit up at night and still crowded by throngs of tourists. The driver didn't want to correct her by mentioning that the boulevard would still be full of pedestrians well after midnight. As things worked out, saving the Opera till later had been perfect. Now, they were crossing the Pont Neuf returning to the Right Bank after having driven around and past Notre Dame Cathedral and the Palace of Justice on the Isle de la Cite, the island in the middle of the Seine.

"I'm sorry, but I don't think I'll remember or appreciate anything else we've seen of Paris at night since we left the Opera," she told Bat. "Let's go back to the hotel." She whispered while cuddling closer to him.

"I heard that!" the driver joked. Once across the bridge he turned left, and they were traveling parallel to the river.

"You couldn't possibly have heard what I said," Jennifer replied in mock protest.

"Well, actually I should have said, '*I saw that.*' I read your lips. This is a rear view mirror, you know," he said, tapping it with an index finger.

"Then get to it, my good man. The lady beckons me to her boudoir! This is no time to dilly-dally. Step on it!" Bat answered in good humor. The happy mood continued for the few minutes it took as the vehicle traversed the distance from the turn, past the Louvre,

Tuileries and the Place de la Concorde until reaching the stretch of road leading to Place de l'Alma and the right turn they would take onto Avenue Montaigne and their hotel.

"Oh, don't turn!" Jennifer blurted out at the driver. "Let us out here at the river. We can walk up to our hotel. I just don't want this perfect night to end suddenly."

They made arrangements with the driver for a pick up to the airport on Monday. Tomorrow they just wanted to leisurely walk around and sightsee without a car. As the car pulled away, Jennifer took Bat's arm and they walked to the chest high stone and concrete barrier overlooking the river and the several Bateaux Mooches dinner boats moored there. The massive, illuminated, Eiffel Tower loomed in the near background and lit a portion of the night sky.

"I'm sorry, darling, that was inconsiderate of me," she said. "I should have asked you if your leg was bothering you. Will all this walking be too much?"

"No, really. It's fine. I just had that bout of itching earlier, but it's gone now. But I am getting strange tingling sensations in other parts of my anatomy." He quipped.

"Well, then, we won't linger here very long. I just thought spending a few moments together here, with the river, the boats, the Eiffel Tower, it's all a perfect way to begin ending a perfect night."

He didn't reply. Instead he turned her towards her and they kissed slowly and tenderly.

****

Only several hundred yards away from where Bat and Jennifer were, the two K Team rogues were poised in the back of the large truck with its special one foot square removable panel on the side of the vehicle for lining up and firing the tripod-mounted laser at the mirror which would bounce it into the tunnel.

Ali had told them earlier that the mission would absolutely be accomplished this night, and with every minute that passed their anticipation grew as they knew it would happen shortly. The accident scenario all depended upon precision driving and timing.

If Fayed was in the Mercedes, Ali would simply depress the walkie-talkie's 'transmit' key rapidly several times. That would be the signal that the plan was in play.

Besides the chasing motorcycles, there would be two vehicles entering the tunnel before the targeted Mercedes. The driver in a Peugeot had to slow down sufficiently so the Mercedes would swerve and change lanes to go around it. But the smaller Uno, less than a car length ahead, would also make a move to change lanes causing the Mercedes driver to impulsively initiate a sharp swerving turn the other way.

The timing was critical. At the precise moment that the Mercedes first swerved to avoid the Peugeot, an electronic signal from that driver would fire the laser in the truck outside the tunnel. Once the laser bounced off the mirror, it would drop the Uno's specially fabricated back panel and deploy the large strobe that had been fitted into the rear of the car. A hundredth of a second later, the computer chip would release the airbag. It was a bit redundant, they knew, but each was a fail-safe for the other.

The Mercedes would smash into one of the tunnel's concrete center pillars. Except for the computer chip to activate the airbags, the plan was almost identical to the MI-6 1992 attempt made against the Serbian leader, Slobodan Milosevic.

But Ali had included a little insurance he hadn't mentioned to Megan. The two motorcyclists with the syringes to inject Dodi and the driver were also armed with guns and would finish off Dodi Fayed if the vehicle failed to crash in the tunnel. If the crash took place as scripted, they would rush over to the car and kill Dodi and the driver with the previously noted injections. If not, the guns would do the job. One way or another, Dodi Fayed would not leave the tunnel alive.

Outside the tunnel, as soon as the laser was fired the two men with the truck would open the double doors and drop down the two metal ramps. The Uno would exit the tunnel seconds after the accident. Because of its special strobe package it had to be hidden immediately. The truck driver would start the vehicle while the other guided the Uno driver up the ramp. The doors would be shut and the truck would drive away.

According to the K Team escape plan, all vehicles involved in the incident would head out of Paris and make their way toward Mons, Belgium, hardly 150 miles distant. Along the way the vehicles would stop at an abandoned and flooded old quarry and sink the Uno, several of the motorcycles, and various electronic gear. None of it ever to be seen again. The team members would split up into three groups and make their ways home by different routes.

Ali was supposed to remain behind and remove anything tell-tale from the Place Vendome shop. In the days following he would go to the rental agent and, with a great display of feigned embarrassment, acknowledge that the business he had hoped to open in the shop had fallen through and, therefore, he was forfeiting his deposit and escrow money. But now, as Ali lay dying on the shop's floor, that part of the plan would never happen.

****

As their dinner in the suite was ending, Dodi called his father in London to say he and the Princess would be leaving the hotel soon and going to his apartment. The senior Fayed didn't like that idea at all.

"Don't go," Mohamed Fayed said to his son. "There's a lot of press out there, a lot of people. Why don't you just stay in the hotel?"

Nonetheless, Dodi wouldn't change his plan. He and Diana would return to the apartment so he could present the ring and formally propose marriage to her.

"We can't, Moo-Moo, we have all our things back at the apartment, and we have to leave from there in the morning." Dodi had replied with the affectionate nickname he called his father.

As instructed, his butler already had the champagne chilling on ice. The engagement ring Dodi and Diana had picked out together eight days earlier was in the apartment, as was the silver plaque Dodi purloined from Tina Sinatra and put under Diana's pillow.

"Just be careful. Don't step on it. There's no hurry" his father advised. "Wait until you see the atmosphere is perfect, get in your

437

car, and go away. Don't hide; it is unnecessary. You have security with you. If somebody wants to shoot you, fine, then at least we know they shot you. But go out the back, and change the driver..."

Dodi nodded and listened. He didn't go into detail explaining that Henri Paul had just recommended a very similar plan. And Dodi had agreed to it.

****

As Megan's German rogue watched the CCTV feed in the hotel room minutes before Dodi and Diana's departure, he noticed that, despite the oppressing hoard of media keeping pace with the couple's every move, the princess joked and laughed and appeared unconcerned. The couple seemed to be carefree waiting in the hotel's Rue Cambon foyer. To him it was as almost as if they were playing a game with the paparazzi, and enjoying it.

Three floors below the hotel room with its monitor Megan crossed from the shop to the Uno parked at the extreme end of Place Vendome. The clothes around her midsection were rapidly becoming soaking wet with her blood. Getting in and seating herself behind the wheel was excruciatingly painful, but she managed to do it and drive away.

Malcolm 'Big Mal' Fletcher, the agent whom Megan replaced on the Nevis trip more than four years earlier, spotted Archie Blair staggering in the corridor. He ran over and braced his friend from toppling over.

"What the hell happened to you, Archie?"

"Megan. She tried to kill me."

"Megan Price? She's not here. They got her on some Russian mission or something. You must have had a bad whack on the head," Big Mal laughed. "Did you fall against something?"

"Listen to me you thick shit! She *is* here, Sir Warren himself sent her. Megan sucker-punched me on the side of the head with a brick, or that friggin heavy metal phone of hers. The crazy bitch was sent here to assassinate Princess Diana!"

"Are you crazy? That's the most ridiculous thing . . ."

"There's no time to convince you or explain everything. Help me to the front door. I have to go outside. Hurry."

Megan ignored the several cars beeping at her as she tried her best to negotiate the traffic going around Place de la Concorde. Her slow and erratic driving made her the object of shouted curses and obscene finger gestures from a number passing vehicles. But she ignored it all. It took her total concentration not to be involved in, or cause, an accident. She was barely doing 20 mph as she exited the Place de la Concorde and headed onto the Cours Albert 1er riverfront expressway along the right bank, and parallel to, the Seine river.

Around 12:10 AM, Princess Diana and Dodi's bodyguard, Trevor Rees-Jones, were seen on the CCTV at the Rue Cambon rear entrance to the Ritz Hotel. Outside, and out of camera view, the hotel's acting security director, Henri Paul, parked the dark blue Mercedes 280S, often reported as black, and left the engine running. The car offered a 2.8 litre engine capable of a top speed of 130 mph in a straight run.

A few photographers, mostly on motorcycles, including the MI-6 informer, were waiting. When Diana first appeared on the monitored video, the German rogue tried to call Megan but she did not pick up the phone. He continues trying several more times during the next five minutes.

Finally, he feared something must have gone wrong. Megan always answered the phone. The German decided to start closing the hotel room operation down, just in case, by packing up everything except the monitor he continued to watch. What he saw next caused him to again frantically try to reach Megan.

Diana and the bodyguard left the foyer and went into the street. They were out of camera range. As she exited through the doorway, photographer Jacques Langevin of the Sygma agency managed to snap off five pictures before Diana covered her face. Seconds later, Dodi followed them through the same door. Rees-Jones escorted Diana to the rear passenger side and Dodi joined her on the rear driver's side.

At the Place Vendome entrance, the ruse that Dodi had agreed to worked, briefly. As the larger Mercedes with the tinted windows and Dodi's Range Rover remained parked with their engines running, the vehicles had attracted the bulk of the paparazzi as well as curious passersby and hotel guests who wanted to see what all the fuss was about. Word quickly flashed through the crowd that Princess Diana was expected to exit the hotel at any moment.

Instead it was Archie Blair, supported by Big Mal, who exited through the revolving door. In his still somewhat shaky state, Blair appeared intoxicated to several people in the crowd. Before they had reached the hotel's entrance Archie had told Big Mal that Megan had mentioned going to a shop in Place Vendome where the assassins were holed up. Fortunately Big Mal correctly figured it must be the place with the windows covered and the paper 'UNDER RENOVATION' notice taped on the door.

He used his cell phone and alerted the other four members of the MI-6 surveillance team that they had a situation at the front of the hotel. The quartet came through the door moments after Archie and Big Mal, who were already crossing the square and halfway to the shop. As the other agents went into a light trot to catch up, the informer who was supposed to create a diversion by doing wheelies so the Mercedes and Land Rover could pull away, had to break hard to avoid hitting them. He didn't get the chance to show off his riding skills.

But the two decoy vehicles suddenly drove off. Some of the paparazzi started to follow them but very quickly the signal came from those on Rue Cambon that Diana was in a Mercedes at the back of the hotel.

The instant Henri Paul received the signal that the decoy cars had left the front he sprinted off in the dark blue Mercedes surprisingly fast, catching the paparazzi off guard. But they adjusted instinctively and quickly and immediately gave chase several hundred yards behind the Mercedes 280S.

The thought of racing away from the back entrance of the hotel before the paparazzi got wise to what was going on was ill-conceived. With even just a few photographers watching the Rue Cambon entrance it wouldn't take long before teammates were on cell phones alerting their associates waiting at the Place Vendome entrance. In the built up and congested streets in the heart of urban Paris, even a fast car can quickly be caught up to or overtaken by determined pursuers on much more manageable motorcycles.

The exception, of course, would be a long, straight stretch of roadway where the 280S could use its greater speed to pull away. And such a straightaway in fact existed.

The Mercedes headed down Rue Cambon. By the time it reached the traffic light at the Place de la Concorde, no less than half a dozen paparazzi had caught up with it.

Anticipating the moment the light would change, Henri Paul sped off. But he was effectively blocked from turning onto the Champs Elysees. And, according to the K Team plan, had no choice but to drive through the counterclockwise traffic circle and head onto the Cours Albert 1er riverfront expressway on the right bank of the Seine, heading west. The 4,000-ft. straightaway leads to the Alma tunnel. But at the end of the expressway there's a dip followed by a hump in the road as it swings to the left and angles sharply down into the two lanes in each direction of the underpass at Place de l'Alma, commonly called the Pont de l'Alma bridge tunnel.

****

Diana's former sister in law Sarah Ferguson, the Duchess of York, was in Tuscany, Italy, vacationing with her young daughters, Beatrice and Eugenie. The other once former newcomer to the Royal Family, whom The Firm thought had also failed to comport herself in a proper way, had retired to bed that Saturday night.

Buckingham Palace's two 'loose cannons,' once so close, hadn't spoken in nearly a year. Diana had shut Fergie out of her circle of confidantes after reading that Prince Andrew's ex-wife claimed she had caught a bout of Plantar's warts from wearing Diana's shoes. The malady is a strain of HPV that makes skin cells grow rapidly and give the appearance of hard surfaces. It often feels like having a stone imbedded in the foot, making walking quite painful, and can cause infections such as vaginitis.

For some time, Fergie's phone calls to Kensington Palace were not returned, and letters to Diana came back unopened. Nonetheless, Sarah Margaret Ferguson, Duchess of York, believed her good friend from their salad days as royals would eventually come around and things would again be as they were in the past.

After all, there was so much for the two former sisters-in-law to catch up on and laugh about. The woman some chided as 'Rent-A-Royal,' had inked a million-dollar Weight Watchers contract and just finished taping TV commercials that were scheduled to air nationally in the U.S. very soon. Ironically, one of them included a smiling Fergie saying that losing weight was *"harder than outrunning the paparazzi!"*

U.S. President Bill Clinton and First Lady Hillary Clinton were at their tenth party in less than two weeks on Martha's Vineyard. It had been during a similar party on Martha's Vineyard three years earlier that Diana was observed as being quiet and moody after learning that her former lover had written a 'kiss-and-tell' book revealing intimate moments of their relationship. At this still relatively early hour in the evening several fellow partygoers on the island speculated and wondered if the Princess of Wales would turn up as a surprise guest. She would be surrounded by celebrities if she did. It seemed everyone who was anyone was there: The media world was represented by Katherine Graham, publisher of the Washington Post, television's Diane Sawyer, columnist Art Buchwald, and author William Styron. The entertainment field had director Mike Nichols actors Ted Danson and Mary Steenburgen and singer Carly Simon, a close friend of the late Jacqueline Kennedy Onassis, who was comfortable with either group because of her family's publishing ties.

****

In the truck, the two K team members watched the blip from the GPS device on the Mercedes 280S move through the map grid on their screen.

"Okay. The target car is moving," one said to the other. He slid the walkie-talkie closer to the GPS device on the small bench and waited.

"If the Fayed pig is in the car, we will know it any second now!" he declared. His smiling partner nodded in agreement.

Ali, prostrate on the floor of the Place Vendome shop, could see the walkie-talkie only inches from his outstretched arm. He used what little strength his dying body had to try to move himself closer to reach it. In a great push, he managed to half the distance between his fingers and the device. Then he had to pause to muster the strength for a final effort. He didn't have to say anything once he reached it, just depress the 'transmit' key a few times and his confederates in the truck would make things happen automatically.

****

Bat and Jennifer had been lazily leaning on the stone wall and looking down at the several Bateaux Mooches moored at the Port d'Alma quay, adjacent to the bridge. The bridge is among the several that provide access across the Seine between Paris's Right and Left Banks. The tunnel runs parallel to the river and crosses underneath the Right Bank's entryway to the bridge.

"Oh darling," she said, turning to face him and he did likewise. "This has been an absolutely magnificent day. I think I shall remember every moment of it for as long as we live." She outstretched and crossed her arms behind his neck as he gently pulled her toward him. Even before their bodies pressed together they were kissing tenderly.

"We should leave quickly and resume these feelings back in our suite." He whispered in her ear between several rapid kisses to her neck. "I know the French are quite tolerant about displays of *amour*, but even they would take pause at what is going through my mind to do right here, right now."

"Oh, my goodness, Mr. Lynch, whatever do you have in mind? I may not be that kind of woman!" she chided as they held hands and began walking to the curb to cross the road.

"Is that so, Miss Carson? Then would you please return that ring I gave you earlier?"

"Not on your life! I said 'yes' even before you popped the question. You're stuck with me now." Jennifer said squeezing his hand tightly.

"Look at this slow poke, will you?" Bat said as Megan rolled past them going less than the 35 mph speed limit. Bat had given the car a glance but hadn't taken a hard look at the driver. Even if he did he would have been hard pressed to recognize Megan, still disguised as a Muslim, sans the face veil, but with her facial features twisted and contorted in pain.

****

Archie, Big Mal, and the other four MI-6 agents reached the door of the shop and, upon seeing it was not fully closed, but ajar, cautiously approached and entered the room. Even in the low light they could see there were at least two bodies on the floor.

One of the other agents felt for a pulse on the man who's neck Megan had snapped while Big Mal bent over, straddling Ali at the waist to avoid stepping in the large pool of blood around his upper torso, and pressed his fingers against his neck to check for a pulse.

"This one's dead as a door nail," the agent said.

"So's mine," Big Mal added as he looked around the floor for a rag or paper towel to wipe the blood off his fingers.

The absence of any blood around the first man made Archie suspect he had been taken out by Megan, but he couldn't be sure.

Big Mal straightened himself out. One of the other agents handed him a handkerchief to wipe with.

"Any wounds, perhaps blood I can't see from here?" Archie asked.

"Nope. Nothing." The agent easily moved the man's head from left to right and up and down.

"Looks like a classic broken neck. Professionally done," he commented.

Archie nodded, "I thought as much." Then he again glanced at the very bloody and very dead Ali and wondered if Megan had done that sloppy job as well. If she did, she was probably badly injured herself. Megan was not one who would use a knife as a weapon of choice.

"Check them for identification, though I doubt anything we find will be truthful."

Archie's cell phone rang. It was the MI-6 resident agent who hadn't received Big Mal's call when he alerted the others. Archie brought him up to speed and asked for forensic people to get fingerprints to help identify the two victims. When he got off the phone. Big Mal was staring at him.

"What???" Archie asked.

"Where's Megan?" Big Mal queried.

****

Bat was shaking his head and still looking to the left as the white Uno began the decline into the tunnel and disappeared from view. They had stopped midway across the road with traffic exiting the tunnel moving behind them and traffic going into it passing in front of them.

"Some people's children," Bat commented as he stepped into the road. He never saw the dark blue Mercedes and, the several motorcycles trying desperately to catch it, racing toward him.

It was Jennifer's scream while impulsively yanking Bat back out of harm's way that saved him from being hit by two speeding motorcycles which were catching up, side by side along the left side of the car. They were so close that, had Jennifer not acted when she did, both motorcycles would have certainly hit him.

Jennifer threw her arms around Bat while quickly back stepping a few paces, and dragging Bat with her, yet mindful of the traffic moving behind them.

He snapped his head to the left and shouted.

"You crazy sons of bitches!" He was trembling both with rage and the knowledge of how, once again, he had escaped death.

"Oh, my God. My dear, dear Bat. I don't believe what almost just happened." She kept her tight hug around him and began rapidly kissing all over his face.

****

Megan felt faint as the car rose and dropped over the slight hump at the entrance to the tunnel. She had the sensation that her eyelids were becoming very heavy and she had to use all the muscle control she could to keep them from closing. She fought as hard as she could to control the Uno and had to remind herself to put pressure on the accelerator pedal. The momentum the car had gained coming down the tunnel's inclined entrance was sapping off.

She knew she wouldn't have the strength to physically fight with the two K Team members in the truck and destroy the laser. But in her dazed and confused state she had hatched a plan. When she left the tunnel Megan intended to accelerate as fast as she could and crash the Uno into the truck. She somehow thought that would not only disrupt the alignment between the laser and the mirror but probably knock the device off the tripod and send it crashing to the floor. It was the best she could do. All she had to do was make it through the tunnel.

Her driving was now more erratic than before, and after scraping against the tunnel's right wall she had to struggle to straighten the car in the lane. Megan suddenly felt a jolt against the Uno and instinctively slammed her foot to the floor and accelerated. A bright flash illuminated her rear view mirror and she heard two sounds, but didn't take her eyes off the road ahead. She realized she was slipping fast and needed to keep her attention on driving.

Hardly 20 seconds after the motorcycles that missed hitting Bat chased the Mercedes 280S, driver Henri Paul lost control of the car and the front, a little left of centre, smashed into the tunnel's 13th center pillar which separates the incoming and outgoing roadways of the tunnel. The dark blue German car spun 180 degrees and bounced into the north wall, where it came to rest facing in the opposite direction from which it had been traveling. Both front airbags had deployed at impact, but the front end of the car crumpled as the sudden impact had thrust the back of the car upwards, crushing the front part of the roof.

Megan continued through the tunnel unaware of the carnage behind her. But the rogue MI-6 agent, who had once served her queen and country, and SIS, with unquestioned loyalty and blind faith, took her last breath of life as the Uno rolled to a stop against bushes on a lawn hardly a few feet away from the truck she had intended to crash into.

Outside the tunnel Bat and Jennifer had ended their embrace and were again attempting to finish crossing the road when the explosively loud sound of the crash shot out of the tunnel. They stopped and booth looked to their left.

"Oh, my goodness! What was that?" Jennifer asked.

"It's not good," Bat replied. "One of those crazy motorcycle bastards probably caused an accident." They had to again back up to where they had been as oncoming vehicles approached. Very quickly they realized traffic ahead had stopped and had begun to back up, and there was no traffic moving from the other side either.

In the tunnel, traffic in the two lanes which had been following the Mercedes, and in the two opposing lanes on the other side of the center pillars, had all come to an abrupt halt.

Usually the moments after a terrible accident are filled with a sudden, unnatural silence. But that wasn't the case in the Pont de l'Alma tunnel. The weight of Henri Paul's body against the horn made it blare loudly through the covered road.

The two K team assassins had watched the GPS blip do a strange bounce then disappear from the screen. One continued watching the screen while the driver got out to investigate what, if anything, was happening at the tunnel. In a few seconds he rushed back to the truck.

"Come! Quickly drop the ramps. The Uno is here. I'll drive it into the truck. I don't know what happened. It doesn't look like it was in an accident but the English bitch looks very dead."

The driver pushed Megan's lifeless body into the passenger seat and himself was covered in her blood, which had pooled in the seat, by the time he got the vehicle safely into the truck. As the second man made unsuccessful efforts to raise Ali on both the walkie-talkie and then his cell phone, the driver began initiating the plan to exit Paris and France.

Within ten seconds of the crash, the first paparazzi arrived at the site and frantically began snapping pictures.

The first motorists who approached the car didn't immediately recognize Princess Diana. The driver, still pressed against the screaming horn, and the man sitting behind him appeared dead. The only woman in the car had been thrown off her seat and was crumpled in the gap between the front and rear seats. But she showed signs of life. The man sitting in the front next to the driver also seemed to be alive and appeared to be the only one wearing a seat belt.

The woman had blood on her forehead and rivulets of blood trickled from her nose, mouth and one ear. Despite that small amount of blood, she didn't appear to have any noticeable external lacerations. The badly twisted and multiply-fractured left leg of the man who had been seated next to her was draped across the blond woman's lap, while one of her arms lay on his cowboy boot.

Outside the tunnel, Bat and Jen noticed that people had gotten out of some of the forward cars and were moving rapidly into the underpass.

"We should go and see if we can help," Jennifer said with good intentions.

"What could we do? Do you have nurse training? Any medical training? I don't. We'd probably just be in the way," Bat replied. Actually he was trying to protect her from a possible bloody accident scene.

"I don't know. Maybe if there is a small child there crying I could try to calm it down."

"Let's finish crossing. That damn car horn is getting to me. And, if I recall, we were planning to go back to our hotel and do some serious cuddling up!" Traffic was now backed up several car lengths beyond where they stood.

"Cuddling up? *Serious* cuddling up? Is that what you former spies call it?" She smiled and kissed his cheek before they began walking.

For Bat and Jennifer, this had been a wonderful day in the City of Light. Their engagement in romantic Paris made it a day and evening they would never forget. But when they awoke the next morning they would learn of another reason to remember it.

For the couple in the crumpled Mercedes at rest in the tunnel, the engagement Dodi had planned would never be, and it was a day and evening millions of people around the world would never forget.

It had now been more than a minute since the accident and the horn was still filling the tunnel with its macabre clarion. Finally, someone from the quickly growing crowd of passing traffic that had stopped on both sides of the center island pillars to gawk, reached in and moved the apparently dead driver's body off the horn. Now the only sound in the tunnel was the rapid clicking of cameras as several photographers vied for space and best angles for their morbid photographs. A man who had been traveling in the other direction, and appeared to be a physician, had quickly determined that the woman and the man who had been seated in front of her were still alive. The two men on the driver's side of the car were dead.

"That's Princess Diana!" a woman called out.

"What?" another voice queried.

"That's her. It's Diana!" the first woman said, much louder this time.

"Yes it is," one of the photographers confirmed as he kept moving around and shooting. "The Princess of Wales herself. Probably the only survivor in this friggin, sensational, crash. And the bloke with her in the back is her playboy lover, Dodi Fayed. His father owns Harrods, and the Ritz Hotel. But all his daddy's money can't do a thing for him now. He's surely a goner."

The news rippled through the crowd and quickly to those outside the tunnel with great speed. By the time it did, Bat and Jennifer were already out of earshot some distance up Avenue Montaigne, holding hands and getting closer with each step to their suite in the Plaza Athénée.

The MI-6 informer, who had been posing as a paparazzi, had been one of the first on the scene. He phoned the MI-6 resident agent who, by this time, had joined Archie in the Place Vendome shop, and reported the accident.

Princess Diana was alive, he said. However, Dodi and the driver, appeared dead, and the bodyguard didn't look as if he had much of a chance. Even as the informer was reporting this information, other paparazzi, real paparazzi were calling it in to their respective services. Within a half hour of the Mercedes 280S impacting the 13th pillar in the tunnel, spinning and bouncing against the far wall, news reports were reaching CNN, the BBC and other major news outlets.

At about 9 PM, EST time, someone who wandered away from

the Martha's Vineyard party to catch the score of a Boston Red Sox game saw the running news flash about the accident at the bottom of the screen. The news spread through the party crowd in seconds. Though most continued to make chit-chat with the shakers and movers, a few quickly became ensconced in the study watching CNN's coverage. The network had preempted it's regularly scheduled program once it was confirmed that Dodi Fayed and the limousine driver had been killed.

In Tuscany, Italy, it was a phone call from London that awoke and advised Sarah Ferguson that "Dutch" and Dodi had been in a very bad car accident in Paris, and Dodi was dead. As with early reports from all news outlets, little was said of Diana's injuries, other than that they had not been fatal. Some media quoted people saying Diana was walking around and talking to emergency people. Later it would be learned such optimistic chatter had not been true.

As new details about the accident were being added and reported on television, the initial speculation was that the crash might have been the result of a chase by photographers on motorcycles and in cars. Fergie remembered her now terribly haunting line in the Weight Watchers commercial saying that losing weight was *"harder than outrunning the paparazzi!"*

The bubbly redheaded former wife of Prince Andrew immediately wanted to console and comfort her stubborn friend. She quickly dialed Diana's mobile phone, it rang, and rang, and rang. But there was no answer.

Finally she left another message, which this time, for a reason quite different than had been the case since Diana had cooled their relationship, would never be returned:

"Dutch, I'm here! How can I get to you? . . . Dutch?"

---end---

Two epilogues follow

FIRST EPILOGUE
the fictional characters

CIA agent Charlie Stone was best man, and Kimberly was matron of honor for Jennifer and Bat's wedding, before Halloween that same year. Kim's very proud five, "almost six," year old son, Blake, was ring bearer. Jennifer and Bat became the proud parents of a lovely baby girl the following April. "What's a preemie?" the inquisitive Blake asked repeatedly before being told.

In 2000 Jennifer and Bat welcomed a son, Bartholomew Lynch, Jr. to the family. Predictably, he is called 'Little Bat.' In 2003 they were blessed with twins, a boy and a girl. Neither of the births in the new millennium were 'preemies.'

Jennifer's romantic novel, *Love's Tender Rage,* about the Women's Air Service Pilots in World War II, hit best-seller lists the week it was published and was made into a movie. Bat's successful photography career has won him several awards and his work continues to be in great demand.

****

Archie Blair's team removed and disposed of the two K Team bodies from the Place Vendome shop. A special MI-6 'Clean Team' was brought in to make the place spotless and the rental lease Ali had on it was quietly broken.

****

In the Top Secret confidential report Archie Blair gave to the SIS director, he truthfully reported all the facts as he knew them, including the details suggesting Megan Price had been involved in the plot. And, as requested, gave his personal opinion that she had been acting on behalf of retired deputy director, Sir Warren Wormsley and Austin Smythe-Pembrooke of The Committee.

Within two months of the events in Paris, Sir Warren and Smythe-Pembrooke were killed in a plane crash in the Mediterranean while they were en route to an international philately convention in Israel. Neither man's wife shared their interest in stamps and chose not to attend. Neither the wreckage of their private aircraft, nor their bodies were ever found. Nonetheless, it was reported that an internal spark probably ignited fuel cells, causing the aircraft to explode in mid-air.

At the memorial service for the two men, not a single member of the Royal Family was in attendance. Archie Blair refused to sit with, or even talk to, his father, Miles. The two never spoke again.

The Committee, without the leadership of Sir Warren, lost its influence and died a natural death. It ceased to exist as anything more than a paper tiger thereafter.

****

Before celebrants rang in 1998, Archie Blair resigned from MI-6 and moved out of Britain altogether. Rumors persisted among his former SIS colleagues that he had taken up residence somewhere in the Caribbean, pining over the mysteriously missing, and presumed dead love of his life, Megan Price.

When Archie's father, Miles, died of natural causes in 2006, the private nurse told family members that he had been quite happy earlier in the day after reading an old West Indian newspaper that someone sent him. The paper, found on the floor next to his bed, was open to a page showing a classic 1964 Morgan being offloaded onto the pier in Charlestown, Nevis.

Megan Price's body was never found.

SECOND EPILOGUE: the factual story

Details about all non-fiction information in this book, can be found on the Internet.

There are more than 200 people and characters named in *The Diana Plot*. Only 29 are fictitious.

In the last 17 years of her life, Diana appeared on more magazine covers than any individual before or since. In the nearly ten years since her death that margin has continued to grow.

More than 450 books have been written about Diana.

Diana's life, marriage, and death are featured, or mentioned, in a staggering 10.3-million websites or web pages on the Internet.

Nearly one million online sites address various murder and conspiracy plot theories, to wit:

- 76% of respondents in a *CBS-TV* poll believe we will never know the whole truth;
- 50% of respondents in *The Sunday People* poll said Diana's death was suspicious;
- 82% in the above poll, said the Royal Family would *not* have supported a Dodi-Diana marriage;
- 33% of respondents in *The Mail on Sunday* said they believed Diana was victim of a murder plot;
- 27% of respondents to a *Sunday Express* pole said they believed Diana was murdered.

****

In November, 1998, the U.S. Central Intelligence Agency (CIA); the National Security Agency (NSA); and the U.S. State Department Defense Intelligence Agency (DIA) admitted they had spied on Princess Diana. The revelations were in response to a Freedom of Information Act request from *APBNews*, the widely read online media service that employed nearly 300 people until the company suddenly went out of business in June, 2002 after an *NBC* deal to purchase it failed.

****

On August 28, 1998, former MI-6 operative Richard Tomlinson, gave Judge Herve Stephan information for the French inquiry into the accident. The following May, he put it all in a sworn statement. Some highlights:

One of the "paparazzi" who routinely followed Diana was a part-time MI-6 agent; a security officer at the Ritz was an MI-6 paid informant; MI-6 officers met at the Ritz Hotel more than once; details of the plan to assassinate Serbian leader Milosevic in a tunnel by disorientating his chauffeur with a strobe flash gun; MI-6 officers are briefed in training about this tactic used by special forces against helicopter pilots; MI-6 was routinely asked by the Royal Household to provide intelligence on members of the Royal Family during overseas trips. Friendly services such as the CIA, cooperated; MI-6 had six agents in Paris the day of the crash.

Slobodan Milosevic, whom Britain's MI-6, and other Western powers tried to assassinate at least three times in 1992, was found dead in his prison cell on Saturday, March 11, 2006. The most celebrated attempt, using a strobe light to cause his car to crash in a tunnel, has often been mentioned by conspiracy theorists as what was actually done to Diana's Mercedes 280S in the Paris tunnel.

****

The fairytale was over. Cinderella was dead.

****

Prince Charles married Camilla Parker-Bowles, the love of his life, on April 9, 2005.

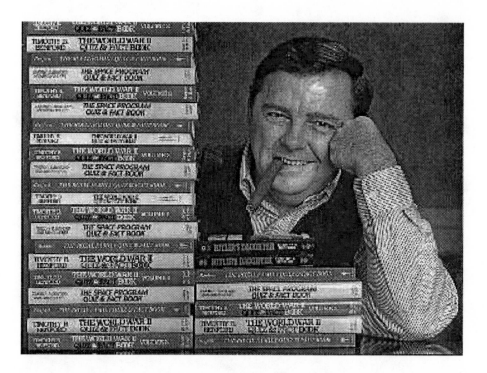

Award-winning author and best-selling novelist TIMOTHY B. BENFORD is president of Benford Associates, Inc., an international public relations agency specializing in the tourism industry. A former newspaper and magazine editor, several of his books have also been published in Spanish, French, and Polish. His first novel, *Hitler's Daughter,* won the West Coast Review of Books Porgie Award and was made into a USA TV Network Movie of The Week. Benford continues to write extensively about myriad subjects including history, numismatics, classic cars, World War II, and travel for publications in the U.S., Canada, and the U.K. He resides in Mountainside, N.J. with his wife Marilyn.

Most of Timothy B. Benford's books remain in print. For information and availability of signed copies, contact him c/o American Book Publishers at: **AmericanBP@aol.com**.

Printed in the United States
88077LV00004B/82/A